The
Magnolia
Palace

A
NOVEL

FIONA DAVIS

DUTTON

DUTTON
An imprint of Penguin Random House LLC
penguinrandomhouse.com

Previously published as a Dutton hardcover in January 2022
First Dutton trade paperback printing: January 2023
Copyright © 2022 by Fiona Davis
Excerpt from *The Spectacular* copyright © 2023 by Fiona Davis
Penguin Random House supports copyright. Copyright fuels creativity, encourages diverse voices,
promotes free speech, and creates a vibrant culture. Thank you for buying an authorized edition of this book
and for complying with copyright laws by not reproducing, scanning, or distributing any part of it in any
form without permission. You are supporting writers and allowing Penguin Random House to
continue to publish books for every reader.

DUTTON and the D colophon are registered trademarks of Penguin Random House LLC.

THE LIBRARY OF CONGRESS HAS CATALOGED THE HARDCOVER EDITION OF THIS BOOK AS FOLLOWS:

Names: Davis, Fiona, 1966– author.
Title: The magnolia palace: a novel / Fiona Davis.
Description: 1. | New York: Dutton, Penguin Random House, 2022. |
Identifiers: LCCN 2021031241 (print) | LCCN 2021031242 (ebook) |
ISBN 9780593184011 (hardcover) | ISBN 9780593184028 (ebook)
Classification: LCC PS3604.A95695 M34 2022 (print) |
LCC PS3604.A95695 (ebook) | DDC 813/.6—dc23
LC record available at https://lccn.loc.gov/2021031241
LC ebook record available at https://lccn.loc.gov/2021031242

Dutton trade paperback ISBN: 9780593184035

Printed in the United States of America
1st Printing

BOOK DESIGN BY LAURA K. CORLESS

More Praise for *The Magnolia Palace*

"Iconic buildings are larger-than-life characters in Fiona Davis's novels, and *The Magnolia Palace* is no exception." —*New York Post*

"Fascinating . . . Allows Davis to also explore the struggles of young women to be taken seriously while adding an unvarnished look at the wealthy. . . . Davis smoothly layers fact onto fiction. . . . Excellent." —*Sun Sentinel* (South Florida)

"Readers are transported back to 1919 New York in this richly captivating tale." —*Woman's World*

"There are many pleasures in Fiona Davis's novels . . . Davis imbues [Manhattan landmarks] with intimacy and familiarity through the deeply felt emotions of her characters. Equally intriguing are the points of intersection between generations of young women. . . . Quietly seeking the truth about themselves and the world, Davis's heroines overcome pain and loss to reach a resolution, in the past and present." —BookTrib

"A book that's as beautiful as it is mysterious. The dual POV keeps the reader on their toes until the entire story comes together." —*BuzzFeed*

"The pages breeze by as potential romances develop (maybe not the ones you'd expect) and a mystery involving the whereabouts of the Magnolia diamond unfolds. Deeper issues also undergird both narratives, which confront stereotypes about models and explore how a tragedy can warp family relationships years later. The two narratives dovetail in a satisfying way. Mystery- and art-lovers should relish this exciting escape into New York's past." —Historical Novel Society

"Bestselling author Fiona Davis builds upon the secrets of the Frick Collection in a delightful blend of emotion and adventure. . . . Davis knows exactly how to structure a story and how to switch between time lines. . . . A captivating story whose characters are richly drawn, *The Magnolia Palace* pays particular attention to those who might go unnoticed: the deaf private secretary, the museum intern, the organ player. We discover their private lives and public exposures, which reveal the daily messiness of human lives, the construction of the self, and the truths we try so hard to hide." —*BookPage*

"Combining a mansion turned museum, a missing diamond, a mystery, and the lives of two young women separated by half a century, Fiona Davis stirs up a beguiling story that unfolds like a clever game of Clue. Suspicions abound and an iconic New York City landmark stands poised to reveal a page-turning tale of wealth, family dynamics, and long-held secrets."

—Lisa Wingate, #1 *New York Times* bestselling
author of *Before We Were Yours*

"Fiona Davis is at the top of her game in this intriguing, high-stakes novel about an iconic New York City landmark, the Frick mansion, and two women, fifty years apart, whose stories intersect within it. A family saga and historical thriller in one, *The Magnolia Palace* is a fast-paced, immersive delight."

—Christina Baker Kline, #1 *New York Times* bestselling
author of *Orphan Train* and *The Exiles*

"Rich with family drama, tangled romance, cryptic clues, and long-buried secrets, *The Magnolia Palace* is sure to be loved by Fiona Davis's devoted and new readers alike. A can't-miss for anyone who has sauntered through an art museum and found themselves tempted to peek behind a painting or two."

—Sarah Penner, *New York Times* bestselling author of *The Lost Apothecary*

"I savor every glorious new Fiona Davis novel and *The Magnolia Palace* has it all—two intriguing heroines, two fabulous time periods to get swept up in, and a delicious mystery that keeps you on tenterhooks. I loved every minute of it!"

—Martha Hall Kelly, *New York Times* bestselling
author of *Lilac Girls* and *Sunflower Sisters*

"Once again, using her trademark brilliance, Fiona Davis transports her readers into a mysterious past lurking beneath the surface of our modern-day world. In *The Magnolia Palace*, two very different women from two eras enter the Gilded Age realm of famous industrialist and art collector Henry Clay Frick and his imperious daughter, Helen, and become part of a thrilling mystery centered on the Frick mansion that stretches through the decades. Readers will never look at a historic building quite the same way again."

—Marie Benedict, *New York Times* bestselling author of *The Mystery of Mrs. Christie*

"The magic of Fiona Davis is the tenderness with which she crafts her settings, so that they bloom into characters themselves. We come to know them. We come to love them. And they help us to understand our place in time. *The Magnolia Palace* is a love letter to art and history. An intriguing, beautiful read."

—Sarah Addison Allen, *New York Times* bestselling author

"No one brings New York City to life like Fiona Davis. With *The Magnolia Palace*, Davis turns her brilliant storytelling to the Frick mansion, focusing on the strong women who made the Frick a New York icon—some on canvas, others scions of the famous family. It's historical fiction at its best, marked by the complexity of female friendship, the glamour of the art world, and having the moxie to reinvent yourself."

—Karin Tanabe, author of *The Gilded Years*

"Another brilliant historical thriller from Davis, this time set in a Gilded Age mansion in New York City. You will fall in love with Lillian, the penniless young artist's model surviving the Spanish flu of 1919; Veronica, the young model of the 1960s; and Davis's deftly written and beautifully woven feminist storytelling."

—Tara Moss, #1 internationally bestselling author of *The War Widow*

"Fiona Davis has deployed an unmatched skill for unspooling compelling dramas amid some of New York's most glittering historical moments. . . . *The Magnolia Palace* tells the story of two different women whose lives are changed at the Frick mansion, giving readers the chance to soak in dual eras of history all while great love, epic loss, dazzling fortunes, and foul play are afoot."

—*Town & Country*

"Davis smoothly combines fact with fiction and offers beautiful descriptions of the family's art collection. The colliding narratives and comprehensive descriptions of the historic mansion make for Davis's best work to date."

—*Publishers Weekly* (starred review)

"Davis adeptly interweaves two compelling story lines to shine a light on another NYC landmark. . . . This is historical fiction at its best, with well-developed characters, detail, art history, and mystery."

—*Library Journal* (starred review)

"Davis embellishes the real lives of the Frick family and Audrey Munson, a sculptors' muse, in a tale that will thrill fans of Anna Pitoniak and Karen Harper. She also jumps skillfully between the roaring twenties and the swinging sixties as another model explores the Frick Collection decades later. Davis's insider's perspective on the esteemed Frick family gives equal weight to those who kept the family afloat." —*Booklist*

Praise for *The Lions of Fifth Avenue*

A *GOOD MORNING AMERICA* BOOK CLUB PICK!

"The magnificent Fiona Davis has written a page-turner for booklovers everywhere! I was on the edge of my seat. . . . This is a story of family ties, their lost dreams, and the redemption that comes from discovering truth."

—Adriana Trigiani, *New York Times* bestselling author of *The Good Left Undone*

"In a compelling novel that's part family saga, part high-stakes heist, and part love story, Fiona Davis creates an intricate and beautiful puzzle that kept me turning page after page as I tried to solve its central mystery along with her characters. A gripping and satisfying story for booklovers the world over."

—Jill Santopolo, *New York Times* bestselling author of *The Light We Lost*

"Davis delves into the history of the New York Public Library in this delightful mystery. . . . The characters and story are stellar but the real star of the show is the library, which Davis evokes beautifully."

—*Publishers Weekly* (starred review)

"*The Lions of Fifth Avenue* is a book written for booklovers."

—*O, The Oprah Magazine*

"Davis gives readers a mystery and a historical novel all in one absorbing tale."

—*Library Journal*

"Davis's latest NYC-set historical novel is grounded in researched detail, transporting readers between the 1910s and the 1990s. Bibliophiles and fans of Naomi Wood and Paula McLain will especially enjoy this glimpse inside the history of the institution and the tireless dedication of those who serve it."

—*Booklist*

Praise for *The Chelsea Girls*

"Davis tells a very good story and deserves all the praise she won for her other books set in famous New York landmarks. . . . What finally emerges from the mix of detailed research and solid writing is a tale that is intricate and subtle, unpredictable and exciting."

—*The Washington Post*

"Davis, who has given juicy supporting roles to New York landmarks in *The Masterpiece* and *The Address*, uses Chelsea as a metaphor for the grandeur that was within reach but spirals into a much darker place."

—Associated Press

"The glitz and glamour of the Chelsea Hotel provide a perfect backdrop for Davis's story of friendship, ambition, and behind-the-scenes theatrical intrigue. Hazel and Maxine are complex characters struggling with conflicting questions of loyalty, love, and professional success in a turbulent time. Their story is both a sharp-eyed commentary on female friendship and a vivid glimpse into the life of a New York City icon."

—*Shelf Awareness* (starred review)

"A fascinating and wholly immersive celebration of friendship, love, loyalty, and courage during a turbulent and often underrepresented period in American history, *The Chelsea Girls* will delight. Davis brings her setting to life as she whisks readers away to the iconic Chelsea Hotel and the theater world during the McCarthy era. Richly detailed and transporting, historical fiction fans will love this one!"

—Chanel Cleeton, *New York Times* bestselling author of *When We Left Cuba*

Praise for *The Masterpiece*

"Fiona Davis in *The Masterpiece* continues a winning formula that showcases the stories behind New York City landmarks. . . . A hard-to-resist and a timely reminder that for far too long the work done by women has been dismissed and disrespected."
—*USA Today*

"Fiona Davis has made a name for herself in writing about famous New York City locations, and in *The Masterpiece* she delivers another unputdownable gem."
—*PopSugar*

"A touch of glamour and a dose of captivating history fill Fiona Davis's latest novel."
—*Southern Living*

"An enthralling portrait of a woman artist in the Depression era juxtaposed with that of a newly divorced mom in the '70s. . . . Set against the backdrop of NYC Beaux Arts gem Grand Central Terminal, where they both find work, the two stories artfully converge for an unexpected but satisfactory ending."
—*Family Circle*

"Davis is extremely deft with historical fiction, making history nearly jump off the page. . . . [Her] stories are character-driven, and these characters are skillfully developed. They live life to the fullest, with challenges, joys, love, and loss. . . . Davis skillfully and beautifully merges their stories in a book I found very difficult to put down."
—*The Free Lance-Star* (Fredricksburg, VA)

"Fiona Davis is a master of making the past come roaring to life with rich and luxurious detail. *The Masterpiece* is her best yet. With formidable women, dazzling prose, and the glamorous backdrops of the New York art scene in the '20s and '70s, this is a must-read."
—Taylor Jenkins Reid, author of *The Seven Husbands of Evelyn Hugo*

"In a story as masterful as its title, Fiona Davis paints a captivating picture of the once famous art school in New York City's iconic Grand Central and its brilliant female artist, interweaving this little-known past with New York City of the 1970s where another woman works to preserve the legendary structure from potential destruction. As the women at the heart of *The Masterpiece* rescue Grand Central and its art, they rescue themselves in a compelling demonstration of the way in which history reverberates in the present."

—Marie Benedict, author of *The Other Einstein* and *Carnegie's Maid*

Praise for *The Address*

"A delicious tale of love, lies, and madness." —*People*

"*The Address* is compelling, historically minded fiction with unexpected—and entertaining—twists and turns. . . . The novel delights." —*Ms.*

"Historically rich and poignant on matters of gender, social, and economic inequality, *The Address* is old New York at its finest." —PureWow

"Lively and detail-rich—set against the backdrop of NYC's infamous Dakota building—with a thread of mystery that makes it easy to enjoy, hard to put down." —*Family Circle*

"Spanning over 100 years, Fiona Davis's mystery is packed with deceit." —*Us Weekly*

"Fiona Davis again proves she is the master of the unputdownable novel." —*Redbook*

Praise for *The Dollhouse*

"Rich both in twists and period detail, this tale of big-city ambition is impossible to put down." —*People*

"*The Dollhouse* is a thrilling peek through a window into another world—one that readers will savor for a long time." —Associated Press

"This suspenseful novel about a woman who took a decidedly different path—and the journalist who wants to uncover her secrets—will quicken your pulse." —*InStyle*

"An ode to old New York that will have you yelling for more seasons of *Mad Men*." —*New York Post*

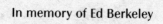In memory of Ed Berkeley

Chapter One

NEW YORK CITY, 1919

Lillian Carter stood half naked, one arm held up like a ballet dancer, the other hanging lightly down at her side, and calculated how long she could avoid paying rent while her landlord was in jail. If Mr. Watkins was released right away, she'd have to avoid him until she pulled together enough money to pay for the one-bedroom apartment she leased in the crumbling, five-story tenement building on Sixty-Fifth Street. Not an easy task when Mr. Watkins and his wife lived off the lobby on the first floor. On the bright side, the Watkins couple had shouted each other to pieces in a terrible fight earlier that morning, the screeching carrying on for a good forty-five minutes before silence finally reigned. Not long after, as she left for work, Lillian had passed the police as they tramped up the front steps. Maybe they'd keep the tiresome man for a few days this time, as a lesson. Not that she felt any sympathy for his bulldog of a wife. Mrs. Watkins had hated Lillian on sight, especially after she discovered what Lillian did for a living.

"Angelica, your drapery has fallen. Again."

Mr. Rossi waited, holding a boxwood shaper in one hand and a rag in the other. Even after six years of posing, Lillian had never quite gotten used to being called by her stage name, chosen by her mother, Kitty, to protect her family's reputation, which was a real laugh. As if they were the Astors or something. Lillian pulled the silk up over her shoulder so only one breast was exposed. The material was slippery and refused to stay in place.

Mr. Rossi was a quick worker, and the clay figure in front of him was nearly finished. This would probably be her last day on the job, and she'd only been posing for an hour. So far today, she'd made seventy-five cents. A little over one cent a minute. She kicked herself for not charging more. Kitty, before she died in February, had told her to demand no less than a dollar an hour, one of more than a dozen pieces of instruction she'd thrown out at Lillian between coughing fits, as if she were trying to fill up a lifetime of parental guidance before she went. Lillian should have written these things down, but she had been too busy making tea and fetching blankets, calling again and again for the doctor, who was too busy with other patients stricken by the Spanish flu to come.

"Angelica. Please."

The drapery had fallen. Again.

"It's cold in here, I'm afraid my shivering is making it fall. Could you light the fire?"

Mr. Rossi's bulging black eyes were punctuated by heavy brows, but any hint of menace was tempered by an unfortunately high-pitched voice. "I have nothing to light it with. It's the first of October, not cold at all."

"Well, you're wearing clothes."

"I'm sorry, Angelica. Do you need a break?"

He had been unrelentingly polite to her since she'd knocked on his studio door last week, asking if he needed a model. He'd let out a gasp, recognizing her instantly, and she'd pushed her way inside and talked nonstop until he agreed to let her pose. Since he'd only recently taken over a studio in the popular Lincoln Arcade building on the Upper West Side, he hadn't had time to learn from the other, long-term tenants that she was, at the ripe age of twenty-one, washed up.

"No, I don't need a break. It's fine." She was lucky to have this job, she reminded herself, only her second since February, a lifetime in the New York art world.

But instead of continuing, Mr. Rossi wiped his hands on his apron and approached the model stand. "Can you angle yourself a little more?" He pushed his right hip forward slightly, as an example. "And twist like this."

Her body responded automatically, clicking into the desired position.

"Yes, that's better." But his face didn't register approval. She knew why. Her hips and legs no longer resembled the earlier statues he'd seen of her. The clean lines once heralded as the classical idea of perfection were now more padded, to put it gently. Since Kitty's death, she'd felt a consistent, gnawing hunger in her gut that would only be satiated with butterscotch candies and lemon meringue pie. Her skirts had hidden the ripples of fat at that first meeting. "Maybe let the cloth down, all the way over the legs."

Her face burned with embarrassment. The irony that she was upset to have to cover her body, when most women would be filled with shame to have to reveal it, made her let out a nervous giggle.

Mr. Rossi regarded her. "Are you all right?"

"Yes, just a little tired. My landlords got into a rousing fight early this morning. I didn't get much sleep."

"I'm sorry to hear it." He blinked a couple of times, as if he wanted to say something more, before going back to the clay study. The silence of the studio, which usually lulled her into a kind of trance, instead haunted her today.

She put a hand to her head. The exhaustion of the past several months weighed down on her. "You know, I might take a break, if you don't mind."

Mr. Rossi dropped the tool on the table beside him with a loud clatter. "Very well." He lit a cigarette but didn't move from the spot, as if ready to begin again right away.

"Perhaps I could have a quick coffee?" she asked.

He didn't answer but retreated to the small kitchenette in the back. All of the studios in the Lincoln Arcade featured the latest modern conveniences, drawing Greenwich Village artists and sculptors uptown in recent years, and creating a new Bohemia hailed as the "Sixty-Seventh Street Studio District." Kitty had predicted the northward trend early and rented an apartment west of Broadway, which meant they were constantly running into potential employers, at the post office or the grocer's. Lillian would have preferred a duplex at the recently constructed Hotel des Artistes building, with its high ceilings and gothic splendor, but Kitty had dismissed it as too expensive. With the way Lillian's bank account had dropped precipitously over the past several months, she was grateful for the decision.

Then again, if they hadn't been living in Mr. Watkins's dumpy building, crowded in with all the other tenants, maybe her mother wouldn't have gotten sick.

Mr. Rossi came back carrying two cups of coffee and handed her one. She stepped down from the model stand and reclined in a practiced move on one of several sofas that were scattered at odd angles around the space. She recognized the shabby pink one.

"You got that from Lukeman, right?"

Mr. Rossi studied it, confused. "I suppose. When I first set up here,

I found a number of castoffs in the basement. Lukeman's studio is two floors up, so I wouldn't be surprised."

"I posed on that sofa for *Memory*." She waited for his reaction.

"Which is that one?"

For goodness' sake. "The *Titanic* memorial? In memory of Ida and Isidor Straus?"

Mr. Rossi gave a vigorous nod. "Of course. I've heard of it but never seen it. I haven't been here long, you see. There's a lot of the city that I haven't visited yet."

She'd enjoyed modeling for Lukeman, even though the position had been a challenge, lying across the couch sideways, one leg dangling over the edge. Before they'd started, the sculptor and Kitty had talked about how important the memorial was, commemorating the wealthy couple who had died together on the *Titanic* after the wife gave up her seat in the lifeboat to her maid, choosing instead to die with her husband. They'd been last seen sitting on deck chairs together as the ship sank into the icy waters. The completed statue, Lukeman explained, would stare down at a reflecting pool, and as she posed, Lillian lost herself in imagining the joy of the couple's love, the sadness of their terrible demise. The result was one of her finest portrayals, of which she was most proud.

And Mr. Rossi hadn't even seen it.

"It's beautiful," she said. "A true work of art."

"Whenever you're ready, I'd like to begin again."

She'd only taken a couple of sips. "Do you mind if I finish my coffee first?"

"Look, Angelica. We've already taken two breaks."

"What are you saying? That I'm stalling?" She had been, of course. Every fifteen minutes was another eighteen cents.

His mustache twitched as he crossed his arms.

He'd been warned. The other sculptors must have told him, after he'd already booked her for the job, that she was yesterday's news, no longer the darling of Bohemia.

Maybe if he saw *Memory*, he'd soften and truly appreciate all that she'd accomplished. "I suggest, Mr. Rossi, if you have the time, that you take one morning off and view it. It's not far uptown, on West End and 106th Street."

"I don't have time to take a morning off. I have to work, I have commissions to fulfill."

"Oh, now, I've been working steadily for years, and trust me, you can always ask for more time. Artists are often accommodated by their patrons that way."

"Right. I hear you're an old hand. How many years have you been at this?"

"I began when I was fifteen."

"Of course. I am in awe of all of your past likenesses. You were an inspiration to so many." His gaze drifted to her hips.

Past tense. *Were.*

He sighed. "Why don't we stop for today? You look tired."

"No, I'm fine. Really." She headed back to the stand, tripping on the drapery. She recovered quickly and climbed up, waiting for instruction. She couldn't lose this job. If she lost it, she wouldn't have enough for groceries, never mind rent.

"It's not right, I'm afraid. I can pay you for your time, of course, but I may need to step back and rethink this piece."

"Please, Mr. Rossi. I'm sorry." She was trying not to beg. If Kitty were here, they'd all be laughing together, her mother flattering him about his thick mustache and strong hands, teasing him as he blushed.

She wanted her mother so badly right now. In the weeks after Kitty's death, the job offers had come in one after another as the news had spread and the artists had reached out in support, making sure Lillian was all right. But in those cold, dark days, she'd been unable to leave the apartment other than to fetch the bare necessities. She'd lain on the lumpy sofa covered by a quilt, sometimes sleeping, sometimes staring up at the cracked ceiling, and ignored every entreaty. Without her mother to smooth out life's rough edges, Lillian had faltered, wallowing in her sadness in a way that Kitty would never have tolerated, which only made her sadder. After years of blaming her mother for being too controlling and protective, including the raging fight they'd had right before she'd fallen ill, Lillian's ceaseless, brittle ennui was proof that she was lost without her.

She wished more than anything to be able to once again witness the infinite ways her mother used to drive her batty: the tinny laugh, the way she hummed under her breath as she dried the dishes. To have one last look at those almond-colored eyes—a mirror of her own—but edged with a spiderweb of wrinkles. Together, they'd made a remarkable team. Watching her mother unravel over the course of her illness, from a force to be reckoned with to a frail, childlike creature, clutching at Lillian's wrist and whimpering in pain, had been her undoing.

Unable to force one more appointment from Mr. Rossi, Lillian headed to the luncheonette across the street from her building. She was starving, craving a bowl of potato soup and a slice of pie. Her mother would never have allowed such decadence.

But just this one time wouldn't hurt. She'd be more careful tomorrow, and eat only a tin of sardines. Today, after the way she'd been treated by Mr. Rossi, she deserved a little something special.

A gaggle of policemen stood across the street, arrayed on the steps of her building. Odd that they were still there. Perhaps Mr. Watkins had had another go at Mrs. Watkins. If so, Lillian could hold up her rent check for a good long time while he sat in jail. This might work out perfectly. Mother always said Lillian had marvelous luck, from being plucked from the chorus line to becoming muse to the greatest artists of this century.

And Mother was never wrong.

Her belly full but her change purse nearly empty, Lillian dawdled in the stairwell of her apartment building, trying to get a glimpse inside Mr. Watkins's apartment on the first floor. Lillian raised one eyebrow at Mrs. Brown—the building's unofficial gossipmonger, who lived next door to the Watkinses and was peering out of a crack in her door—but got nothing in return other than a quick shake of the head and pursed lips.

A police officer emerged from the Watkinses' apartment, leaving the door open behind him. At first, Lillian wondered when the Watkinses had gotten such a deep-red rug, almost scarlet, before realizing it was some kind of dried liquid, not a new runner.

Blood.

Another policeman stepped to the door to shut it, but not before Lillian caught sight of a woman's bloody hand, the fingers gently, almost daintily, curled in.

She backed away, bracing herself on the banister for support, and dashed up the two flights to her landing. Inside the apartment, the soup roiling in her gut, she filled a glass with water and sat down at the tiny table in the kitchen. For all his bluster, Mr. Watkins hadn't seemed like the sort to murder his wife. They'd argue, sure, but usually it was Mrs. Watkins who had the higher volume, drowning him out with a terrible squawk.

The last time Mr. Watkins had come to collect the rent, she'd invited him into the apartment in order to speak out of the earshot of the other tenants. He'd taken his time looking around, as if assessing how much he could raise the rent for a new tenant. Hers was one of the smaller apartments in the building, with only one bedroom, where she and her mother had slept. Two windows looked out on the dreary courtyard in the back, the black metal of the fire escape glinting in the late-summer sun. A galley kitchen served as the entryway, the table and chairs tucked in an alcove to one side, and the living area wasn't much larger. Mr. Watkins eventually turned his attention to Lillian, offering up a sympathetic sigh. "Your mother was a lively woman, now, wasn't she?"

A strange phrase, Lillian had thought. *A lively woman.*

Alive.

Not anymore. And she'd begun to cry.

Once the tears came, she didn't try to hold them back, half crying for her mother and half hoping that by doing so she might buy some time and goodwill. He'd put a hand on her upper back, then let it move to the nape of her neck, squeezing gently. "I'm sorry to upset you," he'd said. "But maybe there's a way I can help."

He'd asked her to meet him in his apartment in one month's time, when Mrs. Watkins would be away visiting her sister. The implications were clear. Horrified, Lillian fretted about what to do.

Days before, she'd finally come out of her stupor after receiving the first of two letters from a Hollywood producer that she hoped might change everything and had finally galvanized her into action. She'd accepted the first modeling job that she could—one that her mother would never have approved of—and soon after secured the session with Mr. Rossi. The two jobs combined gave her a modicum of hope that it was only a matter of time before she'd be able to pay off her back rent. So she'd written a note to Mr. Watkins that was mildly flirtatious yet postponed the "rendezvous" until her work schedule cleared up, hoping that would appease him without getting her tossed onto the streets.

But now, if Mrs. Watkins was dead and Mr. Watkins the murderer, she might be able to live here for free until the entire mess was sorted out. Kitty would have admonished her for thinking only of herself when a woman had been killed, but she would have silently made the same assessment. A knock on the door interrupted Lillian's thoughts. She rose to answer it.

"May I come in?" The police officer addressing her had ginger-colored hair and a matching mustache. A couple of curls slowly sprang back to life after he removed his hat and tucked it under his arm.

Once inside, the policeman cleared his throat. "The other tenants mentioned that you're Angelica." He glanced at Lillian's chest and blushed. "Sorry, Miss Carter, I mean."

A couple of years ago, a reporter had written an article about Lillian's Grecian attributes, coveted by sculptors and artists for their classical nature and symmetry, in particular her well-formed breasts and the dimples on the small of her lower back. Renown had quickly followed, and the policeman's reaction was typical of anyone who learned who she was, comparing the Angelica standing before them with the many creations around the city that were photographed for the article, from the barely clad *Three Graces* at the Hotel Astor (she portrayed all three, of course) to the golden-nippled, laurel-crowned *Civic Fame* at the apex of the Municipal Building.

She couldn't help but bask in his attention a little. Especially after Mr. Rossi's disappointed reaction earlier. "I am Angelica, yes," she answered.

He was about to speak when an older policeman showed up in the doorway.

"I'll take over." The older man barely glanced her way. "Miss Angelica Carter?" He consulted a small notebook and made a check mark on it before she'd even answered.

"Yes." She sat down at the kitchen table and placed her hands in her lap. During the course of her modeling career, having dealt with dozens of capricious artists, she'd learned to pick up small cues from the curtest of commands. This police officer wished to dominate both her and the younger man. If her mother were here (if only her mother were here), Kitty would have done all the talking, as Lillian placated the man with a single look. She knew exactly the one. Chin down, eyes up, projecting a demure naughtiness that always worked like a charm to quash the mercurial temperament of whatever artist she was posing for.

"Is there something wrong with your neck?" the older police officer asked.

It clearly wasn't working this time.

"I have some questions for you, Miss Carter. How well did you know Mrs. Watkins?"

They were probably asking questions of all the tenants. She would be as helpful as possible. "As well as any other tenant, I suppose. She was my landlord's wife. They fought, often. I'm so sorry it's come to this."

"To what?"

"That she's, you know, dead."

"We haven't released that information yet. How do you know that?"

"I saw, as I walked up the stairs," she stammered. "The door was open. There was a hand."

He scribbled something in his notebook.

She cocked her head, trying to see what he'd written. "Also, sir, you spoke of her in the past tense, just now. You said, 'How well did you know Mrs. Watkins?'"

"Well, aren't you a smart one?" He didn't mean it as a compliment. "How well do you know *Mr.* Watkins? You can assume by that question that he's alive. Maybe you'll be happy to hear that."

"Happy?" Now she was confused.

"Answer my question."

"He's my landlord."

"Nothing more than that?"

"No. What do you mean?"

"We found a note to Mr. Watkins from you in the pocket of Mrs. Watkins's dressing gown. I assume you're the only 'Angelica' in the building."

Lillian's stomach contracted, as if she'd been punched hard in the gut. She should have never written that note, should have put Mr. Watkins off in person. His wife must have found it and confronted him in a rage. Lillian tried to keep the panic out of her voice. "A note? My rent was due, so it was probably about that. Mr. Watkins was giving me time to raise it. You see, my mother died earlier this year, and ever since it's been difficult."

"I'm sorry to hear that." His face remained unchanged, cold. "So you've been living here alone since your mother died?"

"Yes."

He glanced over at the door to the bedroom. "It appears that you and Mr. Watkins were arranging a rendezvous in the coming weeks. Did the two of you enjoy an intimate relationship?"

He was twisting the contents of the note around—that was not what she'd meant at all.

"Intimate?" In her horror, she almost laughed at the image of tubby Mr. Watkins in bed but caught herself. "No. Never."

"Also, this was found in his desk." The policeman reached into his pocket and pulled out a magazine clipping of some kind.

She recognized the black-and-white photograph immediately. In it, she wore a bathing costume, black, and had her hands lifted behind her head, like she was sunbathing at Coney Island, even though it had been taken on the roof of the Lincoln Arcade building. Her arms were bare, her legs exposed from mid-thigh down. The ad, hawking the latest in bathing costumes, had run in the back of a magazine. Kitty had never permitted Lillian to do photography sessions for ads—she considered it unseemly—but when one of the lesser-known photographers had approached Lillian in the lobby of the Lincoln Arcade building that first day she'd gone out seeking work, the lure of a quick paycheck had been too tempting to pass up.

Mr. Watkins must have seen it in one of his wife's magazines and cut it out. The thought of him staring down at it, studying the lines of her shoulders and the curves of her knees, made her feel sick all over again.

"I don't know why he'd have that."

"If this is some kind of love triangle, and you had any knowledge that Mr. Watkins was going to murder his wife, it's better for you to tell me now."

A love triangle? How could she prove that something *didn't* exist? "There's nothing." Even to her own ears, the denial came across as feeble.

"We'll need to bring you in to ask you some more questions."

The earlier excitement of a few months rent-free evaporated. This man was headed in the entirely wrong direction. "I'm just a tenant, like all the other tenants. Mr. Watkins imagined things in his head, probably. I never gave any impression that I was interested in him."

He patted the pocket of his jacket. "The note tells me otherwise."

"I was just trying to put him off politely, it's simply a misunderstanding."

"The other tenants tell me you are an artists' model. I imagine you come upon a number of similar misunderstandings in your line of work."

She drew back. "There's nothing sordid about my line of work. I'm no different from you, earning a day's wage."

"I highly doubt that."

She had to figure out a way to reach him, to show that she wasn't a low-class pocket twister. "I'm going to be a film actress as well."

The police officer raised his eyebrows, impressed in spite of himself. Silent films were all the rage these days. "Hollywood?"

"Exactly. This time next year I'll probably be in pictures. I have letters here to prove it." She got up and rummaged through the pile of bills and papers on the sideboard. "Here. A producer wants to meet me, for an audition for his next film. So you see, I had no need to mess about with Mr. Watkins. I'm a career girl."

He studied the top letter, written on letterhead from the movie studio. Lillian knew the most important sentence by heart: *It would be my pleasure to speak with you about a role in my next venture, if you ever find yourself in sunny Southern California.*

"You wanna go to California and get famous?" He handed it back to her. "Well, in the meantime, you'll have to settle for *infamous*, caught up in a scandal like this. Your Hollywood letter doesn't prove anything, other than the fact that you've got a lot of pen pals. You'll have to come down to the station."

She needed time to think. "May I freshen up first?"

He gave a reluctant nod, and she turned and walked into the bedroom, shutting the door with a quiet click behind her.

The papers would go mad with the story of the murder. Throw "Angelica" into the mix, and the legitimate reputation that she was trying to rebuild would be ruined. Never mind it might scuttle any interest from the film producer.

There was no time to waste. She grabbed a change of clothes and stuffed them into a leather duffel bag. The producer's letters she tucked at the very bottom, taking care that they didn't wrinkle. As quietly as she could, she opened the window—the wood frame squeaked with age—and ducked out onto the fire escape. In a flash, she was gone.

Chapter Two

NEW YORK CITY, 1966

Veronica rose out of a foggy sleep in an unfamiliar room, awakened by a scream. She bolted upright, only to realize that wasn't a scream but a siren, just not the sort she was used to. In London, the police cars made a sound that reminded her of an off-key donkey, one that was slightly apologetic for disturbing the peace. In New York, the wails cut through the air like a mourner's keening.

She squinted at the clock on the hotel nightstand through sleepy eyes.

Nine o'clock.

Not good. That only gave her a half hour to get ready for what was possibly the most important photo shoot of her modeling career. To have come all this way and muck it up from the start—that simply couldn't happen. She scrambled out of her nightgown and pulled on black cigarette pants with a white tee shirt. In the bathroom, she washed off the mascara and eyeliner that she hadn't bothered about last night. Her skin was mottled, and a pimple threatened on her right cheek.

She was a mess, and it was all her own fault for not leaving the party sooner. When she'd heard that the photographer of this week's shoot had invited everyone involved to his penthouse apartment on the Upper East Side for a "get-to-know-you get-together," she'd been thrilled. Veronica was the least-experienced model in the group, and she might have downed a few too many glasses of wine to make up for it. Each one made her feel a little bolder, a little funnier, although for the most part she was happy to retreat to the terrace, where she stared out at the city, amazed that she was here. Inside, the party raged on, the photographer and his friends fawning over the other models in the carpeted sunken living room. A few of the men got up to dance to the Monkees' latest hit, their movements jerky and mechanical, as if powered by a circuit board that was not up to code.

It was only the first evening, she told herself. By the end of the week, she'd be part of the gang, and then she'd head back to London with a terrific job under her belt and the promise of a few smashing photos that she'd put at the very front of her portfolio. When a potential client turned to that page, she'd give an indifferent shrug and say, "Oh, right, that was shot by Barnaby Stone last winter in New York. For *Vogue*."

At forty American dollars an hour for two shoots, she'd also have almost four hundred pounds to deposit in her bank account. With everything she'd saved over the past several months from her modeling work, that would be enough to free her sister, Polly, from that dodgy Kent House and bring her home.

With dread, she took out the rollers that she'd haphazardly placed around her head before going to bed. It would have been better if she hadn't bothered, as only the right half of her head had set correctly. She stuck her head under the bathtub faucet to rewet it, then combed it straight. It was the best she could do, under the circumstances.

Her hair had certainly drawn attention at the party last night, as it couldn't have differed more from the long, straight tresses of the other girls. Veronica's thick bangs, cut in a straight line almost to her ears, were her "defining" feature, according to her agent back in London. The back was almost an afterthought, hitting midway on her neck.

It hadn't been the look that Veronica had been going for when she cut a photo out of *Rave* magazine and showed it to her mother. "What, you're going to pay someone two quid to do that?" her mother, Trish, had said. "Let me."

Veronica *had* felt guilty at the thought of spending that much money on herself, so she'd sat in the kitchen chair, let Trish put a tea towel around her neck to catch the bits, and closed her eyes, hoping for the best.

The model in the photo had thick bangs along her forehead with the rest long. But Trish cut the bangs too deeply at the sides, and then flubbed the trim at the back, so that by the time she was finished, Veronica looked like she had a mop on her head, the same cut she'd had back when she and Polly were five and their mother used an upside-down cereal bowl as a guide.

For all of her ranting and raving at Trish for destroying her hair, in the end, the cut had attracted a modeling agent in London, and later landed Veronica the *Vogue* job. While she looked quite mod in photos, the hairstyle tended to overwhelm her other features in person.

"She looks like she's a mushroom," one of the girls had said last night at the party.

Veronica had been around the corner, examining the contents of the bookshelves that lined a hallway. Heller, Capote, Pynchon. All men. Not even a little Flannery O'Connor, to break things up. She'd overheard the comment and known that it was meant for her.

"I like it." The voice was high and squeaky, and Veronica recognized it as belonging to the girl called Tangerine, who she'd briefly befriended on a shoot in London last year. Tangerine was shorter than the typical model, around five feet six, and skinny with huge eyes. "I wish I had the courage to chop all this off. Would be much easier to manage."

The other girl gasped. "Don't you dare touch it. Promise me!"

After a couple of giggly promises, they'd moved on, and Veronica had emerged, collected her coat, and left. Outside, snow flurries danced in the lamplight, like slivers of confetti.

If she was the first to leave, then hopefully she wouldn't be the last to arrive at the photo shoot location this morning. The others had more reason to be late, considering the amount of alcohol consumed.

She grabbed her two large suitcases—one filled with her modeling gear and the other with her street clothes—and checked out of the hotel. A porter helped her into a taxi, and she gave the driver the address that she'd scribbled down in her daily planner. The shoot encompassed two locations, shot over three days. They were to begin in New York at somewhere called the Frick Collection, a fancy museum that used to be a Gilded Age house, followed by a shoot at a mansion in Newport, Rhode Island, with a train ride connecting the two. Veronica wished she'd had more time in New York, or at least spent last night at a Broadway show or walking the streets instead of trapped inside Barnaby's smoke-filled flat. She'd thought it was important to get to know the crew, do a little bonding, but next time she'd skip it. If there was a next time.

Her agent, Sabrina, had told her that the New York City location was grand, but the one that the cab pulled up to wasn't particularly fancy, at least not by English standards. The building was low and white, protected by a wrought iron fence, and if she hadn't known better, she might have thought it was a bank, not a house. The snow had picked up overnight, leaving the sidewalks a slushy mess and collecting in small drifts in the corners of the six steps that led to double doors with the initials *HCF* etched in the archway. Above that, in the pediment, a naked woman carved in stone gazed down dreamily on all who entered.

She tried the doorknob, but it didn't budge. Was she supposed to enter through some other way?

After a moment, though, a young man in jeans and a yellow tee shirt opened the door. "Sorry, the Frick Collection is closed on Mondays," he said.

"I'm Veronica Weber, here for the photo shoot."

"Oh." He gave her a look, and she knew exactly what he was thinking. That she didn't belong. That she didn't resemble a model. Especially sans makeup and with her hair a floppy mess. "Huh. Okay then. I'm Steve, one of the PAs. We're just getting set up. The other girls are all upstairs, I can show you where you can get ready."

The reception area was dominated by a massive floral arrangement on a table in the very center of the hall, where delicate magnolia blossoms erupted from thick, dark stems. They walked on, past an organ tucked inside an arched setback at the base of a grand stairway. She wondered out loud if the instrument still worked and got a shrug in response.

On the second floor, Steve made a sharp right and a sharp left to a smaller set of stairs, which was probably only used by the servants back in the day. On the third floor, the chatter of the other models floated down a long hallway. He stopped and pointed to the women's bathroom, situated about midway. "In there."

She lugged her suitcases up a small set of stairs that led to the bathroom door and pushed it open. Inside, the tile floor was almost completely covered with all the accoutrements of the modern model, from shoes to rollers to makeup. The girls leaned over the porcelain sinks, staring into the mirrors, barely glancing in her direction.

"Hullo there," she said. "Room for one more?"

"Hi, Veronica," squealed Tangerine. "We missed you last night. Where did you go?"

"Tried to get some shut-eye. Jet lag, you know."

"I don't think we can squeeze you in," said the tallest one, a girl named Gigi who Veronica recognized from a recent cover of *Mademoiselle*. "It's tight already."

Veronica apologized—such an English habit, one that Americans mistook to mean that one was actually sorry—and kept walking down the hall.

She took the stairs down one floor and tried to locate another bathroom. Several of the rooms were locked, and the open ones led to administrative offices. The last door on the right was ajar, and Veronica stepped inside and let out a soft gasp. She was standing in an old-fashioned, perfectly preserved bedroom, featuring an upholstered bed with a fanciful silk bed crown that rivaled that of a theater proscenium. Above a drop-front secretary desk hung a portrait of a little girl with a strangely guarded expression, as if she didn't trust whoever was in the room with her. Veronica drew close and studied it. Neither the lacy pinafore nor the sweet curls could make up for the fact that this child came across as old beyond her years, as if the soul of a bedridden old woman lingered behind those eyes. Veronica shivered and tore herself away from it, looking about. Near the window sat a striped chaise longue almost the same size as the bed, the perfect spot for lying about and reading all day. The connecting bathroom had everything she desired, including a large mirror and decent lighting. This was much better than fighting for elbow room with the other models, and she'd be careful to leave it exactly as she found it. It was a museum, after all.

She opened up the suitcase with all her gear and began the lengthy process of unpacking. Models, even for the fanciest magazine shoots like this one, were required to bring along anything that might be called for during a session, including six or seven pairs of shoes, a bra that enhanced one's natural assets as well as one that compressed them, waist cinches, slips, stockings in both black and nude, scarves, gloves, and jewelry. The girls were in charge of doing their own hair and makeup, which entailed a heavy makeup case as well as rollers, brushes, combs, and bobby pins. The suitcase weighed a ton, and Veronica often had to remind herself to walk straight and not list to one side after carrying it around the streets of London for hours.

She dug out her makeup kit and got to work, layering on the foundation, drawing on liner so that it swooped out from the corner of her eye, applying a bright lip to contrast with her dark hair. This was New York, the most sophisticated city in the world apart from Paris, so she dusted her lids with an electric blue eye shadow as well. After running a brush through her hair, she put on a robe and, with one last look in the mirror, headed down to the main floor.

Because most of the house was quite dark and gloomy, she knew where to go by the light spilling out of one room near the front entrance hall. Inside, she stopped and stared, marveling at the enormous painted panels that covered the walls, depicting lushly romantic scenes of lovers. The Frick Collection was certainly full of surprises. To think a family had once gathered here daily, had lived their everyday lives surrounded by such beauty. Once again, the center of the room contained a vase crowded with magnolia branches, each blossom tapering from deep pink at its base to snow white at the tip.

Steve was now setting up tripods and lights with two other PAs, and she spotted Barnaby in the far corner whispering with the creative director from the magazine. The other girls had surrounded a clothes rack and were being handed outfits for the shoot by the stylist.

One by one, the occupants of the room turned and stared at her.

She waved a friendly hello and then caught sight of herself in a mirror hanging on the far wall.

The other models had gone for a natural approach, a soft lip, thin eyeliner with no shadow, and hair that hung flat and smooth. She, on the other hand, looked like a clown, with a garish smear of lipstick that competed unsuccessfully with her blue eyeshadow in the bright light. If she'd wrestled her way into the bathroom with them in the first place, she might have been able to correct her mistake before she got started.

So far Barnaby hadn't noticed her, and was still talking with the creative director. Veronica backed up, hoping to have time to escape and redo her face, when he turned and clapped for everyone's attention.

"Let's begin, ladies. Do we have everyone assembled?"

He looked at the gaggle of girls in the corner, and then his gaze fell on Veronica.

She braced herself for whatever he'd say next.

"Dear God." He grimaced, then laughed. "I love the hair."

She reflexively put a hand up to touch it. Maybe this wouldn't be so bad.

"But what on earth happened to your face?"

Veronica had been restocking the shelves of her uncle Donny's pawn-shop when she was "discovered." It was a couple of days after her terrible haircut, and she'd been thankful that Uncle Donny had let her get out from behind the till for a couple of hours, away from the customers' stares. He'd offered her the job of salesclerk a year earlier, soon after her father's sudden death, and on slow days she'd lose herself in the random objects in the display cases and shelves, wondering whose fingers had touched the dusty Imperial typewriter, or what kind of woman had worn the dangly Art Deco earrings. How had they ended up here, and what had it meant to have to give them up?

The clientele of Chelsea Pawnbrokers were a mixed bunch. Most were more likely to hock their grandmothers' smelly old furs than a Cartier watch, but every so often a toff with a posh accent came in and nervously thrust a gem-encrusted necklace across the counter. Veronica would sit back and watch as Uncle Donny examined it, sighed, then examined it some more, until the customer was just glad to have the sordid transaction done with and departed with less than half the item's value in wrinkled pound notes.

The day Veronica met Sabrina, she'd looked up to see a pleasant-faced, forty-something woman inquiring whether the ukulele in the shop window worked. Uncle Donny was over by the register, having a hushed conversation with a scrawny young man over a gold coin, so Veronica had answered honestly.

"It doesn't. I wouldn't bother."

"I appreciate that," the woman responded. "It's a birthday gift for my nephew, probably best to go to a proper music shop." She paused. "My goodness."

Veronica touched her hair automatically, waiting for a snide comment or, even worse, one of concern.

But the woman smiled even wider. "That is one smashing haircut. Who did it? Vidal?"

"Um, no. My mum."

"How old are you?"

"Eighteen."

"Have you ever modeled before?"

Veronica laughed, but then, realizing the woman was serious, took her card and promised to show up at her modeling agency on her next day off. There, she was inspected by the cadre of agents and sent out for photos to fill her "book." They insisted she quit her job at Uncle Donny's in order to be free for go-sees, which Sabrina explained were like auditions for models. Her mother was suspicious at first, but after she leafed through the portfolio, with shots of Veronica sporting long fake eyelashes and bright miniskirts, she squealed with delight.

"You're going to be on all the covers, I'm sure of it! That's my girl."

Veronica had dutifully shown up early to every go-see that she was given, and booked several jobs. They were mainly on the lower rung of modeling work, like catalogue shoots and print ads, and while she was making more than she had at the pawnshop, the cost of all of the paraphernalia she was required to buy ate into each paycheck, making Veronica wonder if it was worth it. Then, last week, Sabrina had called and told her that Veronica had a go-see for a big shoot, over in the States, where *Vogue* was looking for a British model to feature on the editorial pages. Veronica had shown up early, hoping to get in quickly so she'd have enough time afterward to visit Polly, but was told they were running behind. The other girls were gloriously, effortlessly beautiful, and all she could think of as she sat on the hard metal bench in the hallway was Polly waiting patiently for her in the shabby foyer of Kent House, staring down at the chipped linoleum floor, before being told to go back to her room.

By the second hour, Veronica was fuming at the fashion industry's notorious lack of consideration of models' time. When her name was finally called, she stomped into the room, tossed her portfolio on the table, then stepped back, arms crossed, scowling.

"So who do we have here?" asked one of the men seated behind the table.

"Veronica Weber."

"Great, great." He handed her book to the two others beside him. "Can we see you walk?"

She'd been told by Sabrina to imagine floating whenever she had to show off her walk: *Imagine a book on your head, keep it steady.*

Instead, Veronica imagined the disappointment in Polly's eyes. Her feet landed hard on the wood floor, and she kept her arms crossed.

"Wow." The man sat back in his chair. "That was something. I don't think we've met before, I'm Barnaby, Barnaby Stone." He introduced the two others at the table, but Veronica didn't catch their names. She was stunned they hadn't tossed her out yet.

"Hey," was all she said in return.

The three looked at each other without speaking, as if checking in on some psychic level to see if they all agreed that she was a joke, an absolute disaster. Veronica walked up to the table and grabbed her portfolio, then picked up her bag from where she'd dropped it on the floor. "Wait."

Barnaby tapped his finger on the table. "Are you free next week?"

After all that scowling and stomping, they were interested in her?

"I dunno." She didn't smile, didn't register anything other than disdain. "You'll have to check with my people."

Later that day, Sabrina called with the news. Veronica's flight to the States left that Sunday. She'd spend Monday in New York, Tuesday and Wednesday in Newport, and then head home Thursday. There was a chance, Sabrina said, that the New York arm of the agency might bring her back to the city after the Newport shoot and send her around to see more photographers and editors, so she should pack accordingly.

And just like that, she was on her way to a *Vogue* photo shoot with the hottest photographer of the decade.

And just like that, she'd blown it by lacquering on too much makeup. They'd hired her to project a cool aloofness, but she was jet-lagged and overwhelmed and simply couldn't think straight.

As she stood there, mortified, in the doorway of this beautiful room, she sensed someone behind her.

"Excuse me, you can't sit in those chairs."

A young man in jeans and a white button-down shirt made his way around her and pointed at a chair against the far wall that was currently occupied by Gigi, who sported a plucked magnolia blossom above one ear. She sat with a leg slung over the arm of the chair, and slid it off with a thump before rising to her feet, rolling her eyes as she did so.

"That chair's from the eighteenth century," said the man. He wore a pair of square-framed glasses that rested above sharp cheekbones. He waited, as if there was supposed to be a reaction to his statement. "Please, don't lean against the walls, either."

The girls lounging on the floor exchanged smirks as they shifted slightly forward.

"Right, thanks, man." Barnaby pointed to a white plastic bag filled with tape and film packaging. "Can you take out that trash for us, while you're here?"

"I'm sorry?" The man tilted his head slightly.

"You're the janitor, right?"

He didn't move from the doorway, only crossed his arms. With his height and those chiseled features, he could have been a model himself, although his frame was too skinny and the glasses he wore gave off a nerdy air. But Veronica was certain that Barnaby had only seen the color of his skin, which was black. When the man finally spoke, he did so slowly, as if he'd practiced these lines before, with every other Barnaby who'd walked through the Frick doors. "I'm an archivist for the Frick Collection. They asked me to keep an eye out today, since the museum is closed. You can put your trash in the basement." He looked at Barnaby disapprovingly, as if he were a child and not one of the most successful fashion photographers in the world.

Veronica cringed at the mistake, but Barnaby offered no hint of compunction. He strode forward and shook the man's hand, all smiles and warmth. "Thanks for letting us shoot here," he said. "Really love it. Fab location."

"Uh-huh."

"I promise we'll behave, Sonny Jim."

"The name's Joshua. Joshua Lawrence."

"Right." Barnaby snapped his fingers in the general direction of the nearest PA. "You. Get rid of that trash, now."

Veronica stepped out of the way as the PA shot by, plastic bag in hand.

Barnaby put his arm around Joshua. "Since you're the main man here, why don't you tell the girls a little about where we are right now?"

Joshua looked over at the clutch of models, who stared blankly back, not in the least bit interested in a history lesson. He cleared his throat. "The house was the residence of the Frick family starting in 1914. Henry Clay Frick was a steel magnate who loved art, and built the home with the express purpose of one day leaving the house and his extensive art collection to the city as a museum." Joshua twisted his hands in front of him, losing steam at the lack of response. Having just been the recipient of a roomful of derision herself, Veronica offered an encouraging nod when he glanced her way. He swallowed once and carried on, speaking slightly louder. "After Mr. Frick died, his wife and daughter Helen lived on here until Mrs. Frick passed away in 1931, at which point it underwent some renovations and became the Frick Collection, opening in 1935."

"I have a question," said Tangerine. "What's with all the magnolia flowers?"

"Magnolias have long been associated with the mansion. For a time, Mr. Frick was the owner of the famous Magnolia diamond, a flawless twelve-carat pink diamond. Today, the Frick Collection is well-known for the large magnolia trees on the main lawn."

"What happened to the diamond?" Veronica didn't want to draw more attention to herself, but her curiosity got the best of her.

"It disappeared in 1919. Rumor has it that the family thought it was stolen, but oddly enough, a police report was never filed. No one has seen it since."

"Too bad, that," said Barnaby, leading Joshua to the door, smacking him on the back a couple of times. "We could have used it in the shoot."

"There's more I can tell you about the family, if you like."

"That's all right, we'll take it from here."

After Joshua had gone—giving one last worried look over his shoulder—Barnaby pointed to Veronica. "Someone, give the girl a hand and clean up her face. Do I have to manage every little thing, or can you girls show some initiative?"

Embarrassed, Veronica turned and fled.

1919

As a young girl, Lillian would often rise out of bed on hot summer nights, sweaty and irritable, to find her mother standing nude in front of a window, staring out into the empty city street, her body silhouetted by lamplight. To Lillian, the female form was neither beautiful nor obscene. It was just skin and breasts and the moles that dotted her mother's arms, a constellation that Lillian would trace with her finger.

Her father had abandoned the family when she was a baby, and she and Kitty had moved to a boardinghouse in Providence, Rhode Island, where Kitty worked in a silverware factory. Kitty rarely spoke of her life before Lillian was born, but she knew that her mother had been raised in one of the smaller Newport mansions—"a glorified carriage house, really," she'd said once—before falling in love and eloping with a man who was not of her class. Despite being cut off from both her family and her inheritance, she'd insisted on raising her daughter with a soupçon of what was required in good society, from the correct utensils for the game course to the proper way to cross a room.

Desperate for culture, Kitty would bring Lillian to see whatever shows were playing at one of the five theaters in town, sitting her on her lap until the managers insisted that Lillian was old enough to have to pay for a separate ticket. Her mother's earnings went straight into Lillian's education at the local Catholic school, which was chosen not for the religious education but for its extensive arts offerings. The school provided its students music and singing lessons, which Lillian quickly took a shine to, performing for the other roomers at the boardinghouse every Friday night. She eagerly lapped up the attention, and it was her idea to move to New York City and try for a career on the stage. Kitty gave her notice at the factory within days, explaining to anyone who asked that Lillian was on her way to stardom as an actress.

They moved when Lillian was fourteen. A year later, Lillian landed a job in the chorus for a Broadway show at the New Amsterdam Theatre called *Pretty Girls*. The newspaper advertisements appalled Kitty, who threatened to pull Lillian out. *Pretty Girls*, the ads read. *Sixty of them. None of them Twenty. None of them Married.*

"It's disgraceful," said Kitty, giving the newspaper a sharp snap.

"It's Broadway," answered Lillian. "Besides, think of the weekly pay."

She was allowed to go on.

After each show, the stage door was mobbed by young men hoping to take one of the chorus girls home. Kitty made sure that never happened to *her* daughter, knitting in the dressing room during the performance before escorting Lillian through the gauntlet with a firm grip. Her presence also discouraged the other performers from becoming friends with Lillian, though, and she was never invited out after. Not that she would have been allowed to go.

One night, Lillian found a note stuck in her dressing room mirror. It was from an artist, or so the man purported, asking if she'd model for him, for money.

Lillian had begged her mother to consider the request, not ignore it.

She'd asked around and been told that the artist, a Mr. Isidore Konti, was the real deal. "We both know the show's not going to last long," she'd said to Kitty. "And consider Mabel Normand."

"The actress? What about her?"

"She was an artists' model for illustrators like James Montgomery Flagg, and now she's Charlie Chaplin's leading lady. This could be a lucrative stepping-stone, and better money in the meantime."

Lillian's chorus girl wages from *Pretty Girls* were going to the overdue bills that had accumulated in the year since they'd relocated to the city. They'd celebrated her first paycheck with a small cake from a bakery on Columbus Avenue, but other than that, they were still scrimping.

"Better money, maybe," conceded Kitty. "But what else will he be expecting?"

She finally relented after Lillian hounded her for a full week, provided Lillian stayed quiet and let her do all the talking. "He'll see soon enough what he's up against."

The man who showed them into his West Side studio didn't come across as lecherous in the least, and Lillian breathed a sigh of relief when he didn't balk at Kitty's presence beside her, and gently offered them tea. While he made it, Lillian looked around. The studio was a haphazard mess of clay-smeared workbenches and tool cabinets, the disarray softened slightly by the northern light spilling through the steel casement windows.

She didn't know then that the mess was the sign of a true working artist, versus the imposters who were trying to lure in stupid girls by appealing to their vanity. Eventually, Lillian and Kitty would turn around and leave if the artist's studio was too clean, if it featured a smattering of Persian rugs draped across the floors or candles glowing beside pristine velvet settees.

"More like a bordello than a workshop," Kitty would say loudly on their way out the door.

When he returned with the tea, Mr. Konti addressed Kitty, not Lillian. "I don't usually go to the theater." He was in his late fifties, and had a soft Bavarian accent and a graying beard. "I was brought by a friend, and struck by your daughter's expressive face."

"What is it exactly you're working on?" Kitty asked.

"A piece for the Hotel Astor, called *Three Graces*. Grace, Charm, and Beauty, with the same woman figure representing all three."

Kitty sat up a little straighter, and Lillian's hopes rose. The Hotel Astor was an elegant anchor of Times Square, with a thousand rooms. "Where in the hotel would it be located?"

"In the ballroom."

Even better.

"However, the muses will be lightly draped." Mr. Konti shrugged when Kitty gasped. It was a simple fact of the job. "She'll get paid forty-five cents an hour, and the work may take several months."

"Lightly draped?" Kitty gripped her purse tightly, like she was about to bat Mr. Konti about the head with it.

"I imagine two of the muses will be bare-breasted, one will be covered. You can see, looking around at my work, that there is nothing unsavory about my art."

Although Lillian wasn't entirely confident about posing in the nude, she had to admit that the studies around the room were beautiful, even to her untrained eye. His work had a languid elegance, and in the faces of his figures, she recognized glimpses of her own features, the long, straight nose and narrow jaw. She didn't know then that she had the ideal body for the times: slim shoulders, narrow waist, shapely hips that tapered down into long legs.

"You can decide, yes or no." Mr. Konti finished his tea. "We can start today. Or not at all."

"Not at all." Kitty rose, shushing Lillian's protestations. "My daughter is only fifteen, far too young for you."

"For *me*?" Mr. Konti wasn't angry, only amused. "What I do is not for my own gratification. It is to bring beauty forth in the world at large." He pointed a finger toward the door. "That sordid world, the city outside that's teeming with people whose lives are full of toil and trouble. If they walk by one of my statues and look up and see something beautiful, an idea or person who inspires them, then I have done my job. I do this not for me. It's for humanity."

"Grandiose, I must say." Kitty grabbed Lillian's arm. "We are leaving at once."

Outside, Broadway was indeed teeming with a rush of workers heading home after a long day. Kitty's face was red, and Lillian wasn't sure if it was from Konti's proposal or the afternoon heat that shimmered up from the concrete sidewalk.

"Mother, are you all right?"

Kitty leaned on Lillian, panting slightly. Lillian pulled her back into the shade of the building, out of the way of the pedestrians.

"I'm fine."

Lillian thought back. Her mother hadn't had breakfast with Lillian, saying she'd eaten before Lillian woke up. At lunch, she'd said she wasn't hungry as Lillian had finished up a generous helping of beans on toast.

Kitty began to step forward, but Lillian held her back. "You haven't eaten at all today, have you?" She didn't let her answer. "One hour with Mr. Konti equals a dozen eggs, some milk, and a loaf of bread. Think of it that way. I'll earn breakfast for both of us in one hour."

Her mother swallowed. She *was* hungry.

"I'm fifteen, that's not a baby anymore, and you'll be with me the entire time. Did you see his work? It's beautiful. Imagine, I'll be there inside the Hotel Astor ballroom. Fancy folks will look up and see me and think it's art. In fact, they'll see three of me!"

Her mother's tone was dry. "That's three pairs of breasts."

"Only two. He said one muse was clothed."

In spite of herself, her mother laughed. "You are a sly one, Lilly."

The unflappable Mr. Konti didn't appear surprised by their return. He didn't chide Kitty, or make her feel foolish about her change of mind. They came to an agreement, with Kitty speaking in soft, measured tones as if she were arranging the details for a garden party. Lillian would pose for four hours a day, six days a week, until the piece was finished.

Lillian had figured modeling over the course of an afternoon would be far less difficult than having to learn choreography and lyrics. The first session, he'd begun with the middle figure of the three, and told her to sit looking down and off to the left, everything from her chest down draped by a thin layer of silk. After thirty minutes, when he told her to take a break, it was all she could do not to collapse in a heap. Her neck cricked when she straightened it, and her arms were sore from being extended outward. Even her fingers ached.

She soon learned the best way to avoid the physical toll was to go deep into her thoughts while the sculptor worked. She'd lose herself in the details of the dress her mother had promised to buy her after the job was over: a sleeveless gown of Georgette crepe from Bonwit Teller. She imagined slipping it over her head, the feel of the material on her skin, the joy of twirling around and letting the layers of the skirt float up in the air.

After a few weeks, Mr. Konti asked her to pose for the second figure, whose drapery fell below her breasts. By then, Lillian was comfortable with his stare. He observed her musculature and tendons and bones: he was looking *inside* her, not *at* her. After five minutes she didn't feel odd at all being half naked in front of him. His age worked in his favor, as he came across as a gruff grandfather, not a potential lover. At that first exposure, Kitty, who was seated in a corner with her knitting, seemed to clack the needles together faster and louder, but slowly even she became used to her daughter sitting unclothed, collecting the payment at the end of each day with a businesslike nod.

As Lillian posed for the final muse, the drapery dipping dangerously below her hip bones, she learned the one unspoken rule of posing for a neoclassical work of art. After taking her place on the stool, she made the mistake of offering up a full smile. Konti admonished her, explaining that a nude model retained her dignity only if her lips remained closed. She might offer up the hint of a smile, but never a full one if she wanted to be successful. Lillian was not a commercial product, neither a Gibson girl nor a Ziegfeld girl. She was the vision of perfect woman, the embodiment of beauty. An angel.

"Angelica." Her mother came up with Lillian's model name that same session. "We'll call you Angelica."

Lillian knew Kitty had done so to avoid any detection by her family back in Newport of their rather unorthodox venture, and the moniker stuck. She didn't need a last name. More and more sculptors reached out requesting Angelica, and soon the only person who still called her Lilly or Lillian was Kitty, and only at home.

Instead, she became the belle of the Beaux Arts ball, the architectural and design movement sweeping the City of New York.

She became Angelica.

"No sleeping here. Move along."

Lillian startled into an upright position, rubbing her ankle where the policeman looming over her had given her a light thwack. The bright sun in her eyes was disorienting. Why was she outside and not in her bed? Where was her mother?

The harsh reality seeped back, like a thick mudslide. Yesterday, after fleeing her apartment down the fire escape, she'd made her way to Central Park, wandering through the Ramble, where few park-goers ventured and thick foliage provided some measure of protection. She needed to figure out what was next, but as the sun set and her stomach grumbled, she'd eventually settled on a park bench and fallen fast asleep.

"Sorry, Officer." She avoided looking at him directly, not wanting to be recognized, and scurried up the hill and behind a forsythia, where she checked her bag, the contents of which were intact.

She reopened the most recent letter from the producer, the one she'd shown the policeman, holding it firmly so the breeze wouldn't flutter it out of her hands. Mr. Broderick would be delighted to meet her. She just had to figure out how to get to him.

In the city, Lillian and Kitty had gone to the movies every weekend they could, just as they had regularly attended the theater in Providence. Silent films enchanted Lillian. In the hushed darkness, she became immersed in the story, choking up as the camera swooped in for a close-up of a heartbroken young maiden, or laughing out loud at a pratfall. Along with Mabel Normand, she adored the acting of Mary Pickford and Lillian Gish, and figured if they could make it in Hollywood, so could she. It was only a matter of time.

An ailing Kitty had excitedly shared an article in the newspaper about a film producer named Mr. Broderick who was searching for an actress with the "beauty and malleable expression of Angelica, the greatest model of our day" to cast in his next film. Lillian had immediately mailed off a letter saying she was Angelica and enclosing a photo. Months later, after Kitty had died, Lillian had received a warm response from Mr. Broderick, saying that while many women had written to him claiming to be Angelica, he could certainly see a resemblance. Lillian wrote back that very day, swearing that she was, and including a detailed list of some of the statues and artists she'd posed for as proof. His next letter, the one she'd shown the policeman, had included the invitation to see him.

The sooner she could get in front of Mr. Broderick, the better, as being associated with a big Hollywood studio might provide some protection from her current troubles. Even now, it didn't feel real that Mr. Watkins had killed his wife, that Lillian was any part of this sordid mess.

But that hand, Mrs. Watkins's hand. It had reminded Lillian of the work of a sculptor, lifelike yet entirely devoid of life. The artists always said that hands and feet were the most difficult parts of the human anatomy to reproduce, no matter with ink or paint, clay or marble. She glanced down at her own hand. There was dirt under the nails, and her fingertips were grubby.

She went into the public bathroom and washed up as best she could, tossing some cold water on her face and giving her hands a good scrub. A woman at the sink next to her—an obvious denizen of the park—gave her a toothless smile. Lillian didn't respond, leaving as quickly as she could, heading east.

If only she had a friend to confide in. Kitty's strictness had ruined any chances of becoming friends with her fellow chorus girls, and once she began modeling, she had few opportunities to meet other girls her age.

Still, it would have been lovely to have someone to run to right now, the safety of a confidante. Mr. Watkins had taken advantage after her mother was no longer present, saying kind things and rubbing her neck as Lillian cried. She put her hand on her neck now, remembering that day. Maybe she had arched slightly against the pressure. But not because she liked him in that way. Because at first she thought it was a paternal gesture, the way a father might reassure a child. She'd never known that kind of touch, so had no capacity to judge it.

Lillian stopped at the edge of the park and stared down the expanse of Fifth Avenue. Over the past twenty years, the wealthy families had relocated their homes from the more commercial lower Fifth Avenue to the tree-lined stretch across from Central Park. Mrs. Astor had been the first, in the 1890s, trading her Thirty-Fourth Street residence with its famous ballroom that fit four hundred guests for a French Renaissance–inspired château in the East Sixties. One after the other, New York's elite—the Carnegies, the Goulds, the Clarks, the Vanderbilts—had all followed. The craze had even coined a new word, *Vanderbuilding*, where each family vied to outshine the others with their fantastical mansions. Lillian had followed the stories in the newspapers, caught up in the gossip of a world she had no part in, but couldn't help being mesmerized by.

"Angelica!"

Her heart dropped at the sound of her name. Lillian turned around to see a newsboy hawking copies of *The World*.

"The star witness in the West Side murder has disappeared! Angelica, the most beautiful woman in the world! Read about it here."

Star witness? Lillian looked around. Luckily, the sidewalks were fairly empty this time of day. She approached, keeping her chin down, her hat pulled low. "Can I see the front page?"

"No, miss. You gotta buy it. Two cents."

She found the coins in her purse, then snatched the paper and walked away quickly, back to the safety of the park, where she sat on a bench and read through the article. It hinted at a nefarious relationship between Mr. Watkins and one of his tenants, the bohemian artists' model known as Angelica, who the police wanted for questioning regarding the death of Mrs. Watkins. Even worse, it included an illustration of a work she'd posed for a few years ago, where most of her body was on full display. It didn't matter that the statue had won esteemed prizes for its artistry. In newsprint, it came across as utterly indecent.

Just as the policeman had predicted, she'd become infamous. She was ruined. A bohemian, the paper said. The innuendo—that she was a loose woman, immoral—was more than implied. She'd already been tried in the press and found guilty.

But she had one thing in her favor. Angelica wasn't her legal name, and her last name, Carter, was fairly common. Thank goodness Kitty had insisted on keeping "Lillian" under wraps.

She had to get to the film producer in Los Angeles, and as far away from New York as possible. In California, she could start a new life, a new career. Once the studio was behind her, she'd have some power to fight these silly charges. She just had to cobble enough money together to buy a train ticket out of Grand Central.

A few years ago, she'd done some work in a studio nearby, a former carriage house on East Seventieth Street, off of Madison. The sculptor had tipped her generously. She'd go by and ask him for a loan, explain that her grandmother was sick and she needed to get to her immediately. That she'd pay him back right off.

She located the carriage house easily, but was dismayed to see that the name on the doorbell wasn't the same as the sculptor's. He must have relocated. Still, she hit the button and waited. No one answered.

The day was warming up, and she wished more than anything she could have a glass of water, something to drink. There was a water fountain in the park, back where she'd come from, but just before she reached Fifth Avenue, a figure carved above the entrance to a three-story mansion stopped her in her tracks. It was a reclining nude, leaning on one elbow, chin and gaze pointed down, as if assessing the respectability of anyone who dared pass beneath. Lillian had had to don a ridiculous headdress with two long braids as she'd posed for the artist, Sherry Fry. The figure's stomach rippled with muscles that did not exist in real life, and the shoulders and arms were meaty. Kitty hadn't liked the final outcome at all. "If he'd wanted a man, he should have had one pose for him," she'd declared, before allowing that the breasts were quite well done.

"What are you doing, just standing there?"

A woman appeared beneath the archway to the mansion's porte-cochère. She wore a plain, dark day dress and had one of those faces that made her exact age difficult to guess, with a thick brow and loose jowls.

Lillian braced herself, expecting to be shooed away, but instead, the woman drew close, lifting one hand. It shook slightly, as if affected by some kind of nerves.

"You're early," she said with obvious disapproval. "Go in through the servants' entrance, there." She pointed to the right, where a passageway between an iron fence and the front of the residence descended into a stairway. "Through the basement. The cook will give you a cup of tea while you wait. She's not ready for you yet."

A cup of tea had never sounded so appealing.

Before Lillian could say anything, the woman turned and disappeared into the shadows of the arch.

Lillian's stone likeness smiled calmly down at her, as if curious as to what she was about to do next.

The woman thought she was someone else. A messenger picking something up, perhaps. Or a scullery maid. Lillian could at least get a cup of tea out of it, until they figured out their mistake. She'd apologize and leave, but until then, why not? These big houses were filled with servants; probably no one would pay her any mind. Luckily, she was very rarely recognized from the statues themselves. Each artist she'd worked with had put his own spin on her visage, playing up whatever features he admired most, making her unlikely to attract attention from strangers when she was out and about in the world.

She'd drink her tea. And then disappear back into the streets.

Chapter Four

The steps the jowly woman had directed Lillian to led to a basement door, which opened up into an anteroom. To the left was an enormous kitchen, where she counted seven maids bent over their work, peeling potatoes or stirring pots, under the watchful eye of a man who had to be the chef, barking out orders in a French accent. The tantalizing smell of caramelized onions almost made her swoon. She hadn't realized how hungry she was.

The woman reappeared and told one of the kitchen maids to fetch Lillian a cup of tea. "You may wait in there," she said, pointing through a door to the staff dining room. The kitchen maid brought the tea in a few minutes later, barely looking at Lillian before rushing back to work.

The tea soothed Lillian's dry throat. It was nice being below street level, in the cool of a basement. No one cared who she was, and she felt deliciously invisible. But she couldn't stay long. She drained the cup quickly and was standing to leave, eyeing some scones cooling on a sideboard, daring herself to slip one into her pocket, when the woman's silhouette filled the doorway.

"Follow me. Upstairs." She turned and started out the door.

Lillian froze, trapped. How to make an excuse and get out of whatever was waiting for her upstairs?

If someone *did* recognize her as Angelica—and if anyone would, it would be the family who had purchased her visage to look at every time they passed under the porte-cochère—then they might call the police and she'd be done for.

"I'm afraid I must go," she said.

The woman kept walking away, one finger up in the air. "This way. Come on."

Lillian followed, but only so she could make excuses and leave. "I'm not well, you see. I should go. I'll make another appointment when I'm better."

Her words echoed up the staircase. Again, the woman didn't appear to have heard her, tromping solidly upward.

"Hello?"

No response. Lillian was about to pull on her elbow to get her to stop, but by then they'd reached the landing, and it was all Lillian could do not to gape. After the functional trappings of the lower level, the floor above was an absolute shock. The delicately veined marble walls blended seamlessly into the marble floors like a shiny stone waterfall. Through the lacy black iron balustrade of a grand staircase, she spied some kind of grand pipe organ with a gilded console and four rows of keys, like gleaming white teeth.

Lillian had seen photos of the interiors of the Fifth Avenue mansions in the newspapers, but they were very different, the parlors stuffy and dark, the mantels jammed with vases and delicate, useless knickknacks. This place was airy in comparison, lit by giant windows. She spotted a Renoir hanging across from the organ, which she recognized from leafing through one of the many oversized art books scattered about Isidore Konti's studio. She would have liked to stop and admire it, but the woman pulled her along, making a sharp turn into a room that, once again, left Lillian gaping like a fool.

As if she expected that reaction, the woman paused a moment, looking about with a dour expression on her face.

Silk drapes cascaded from just under the crown molding, held back by thick ties with tasseled ends. The floor was of parquet wood in a complicated pattern, and the sheen of gold gleamed everywhere, from the painted wainscot to the fireplace irons to the intricate bronze candelabras on the mantel.

But that was the least of the grandeur. The room's wall panels depicted a cavorting couple, the woman dressed in the loveliest of gowns from the eighteenth century, lined with ribbons and flowers, the sleeves puffy, the skirts filled out with dozens of petticoats. It was a dreamscape far from the world Lillian knew, and made her want to weep with pity at her own dishabille.

The woman gave an audible tsk of disapproval as she walked over to the far window and adjusted a curtain that didn't need adjusting. "Do your best to ignore the provocative decor."

"I think it's divine."

Again, her comment got no reaction from the woman, who still had her back to her.

She must be partly deaf, Lillian finally realized. "You're absolutely mad if you don't agree."

Nothing. No response. She was right.

The woman turned around and pointed to a chair. "You may have a seat here and wait. Miss Helen will be with you shortly."

Who was Miss Helen?

An older woman, this one dressed in lustrous black silk with a bosom so pronounced Lillian was surprised she didn't pitch forward, looked in from the doorway on the far side of the room. "Miss Winnie? Oh, there you are." She stamped her foot once, and Miss Winnie turned, sensing the vibration.

Lillian rose from where she'd been sitting, but the woman in black gave her a disinterested glance, as if she were as inanimate as one of the porcelain vases that dotted the side tables.

"Yes, Mrs. Frick?" answered Miss Winnie.

"I need you."

Miss Winnie followed her, Lillian all but forgotten.

Frick. That's whose house she was in. The Fricks, Lillian knew from the gossip columns, made their fortune in steel, and had two grown children. The newspapers had made a grateful fuss out of the fact that Mr. Frick had designated that his house eventually be left to the city and turned into a museum.

In any event, having Miss Winnie pulled away gave Lillian a chance to escape. She needed to get out, now. But as she was exiting, yet another woman lurched in. She was shorter than Lillian, perhaps a few years older, and had a spaniel with doleful eyes tucked under one arm. Her dress was plain but well-made, her frizzy ginger hair messily arranged in a puffy pompadour several years out of style. She stuck out a hand and shook Lillian's like a lumberjack might. Her complexion was dotted with freckles that grew darker right under her eyes, like copper tears.

"I'm Helen Clay Frick. You may call me Miss Helen." She placed the dog on the floor. "This is Fudgie. Do you like these paintings?"

The question threw Lillian off-balance. She answered truthfully. "Very much."

"*The Progress of Love*, by Jean-Honoré Fragonard. The poor man created them as a commission to the twenty-eight-year-old mistress to Louis XV, to be placed in her pleasure pavilion near Versailles. Mother hates it when I use that term—*pleasure pavilion*." She paused, as if imagining the discomfort it caused with relish. "In the end, the mistress rejected them, and eventually they made their way to J. P. Morgan, from whose estate my father purchased them."

The purchase had made the news. Lillian remembered her mother clucking over the sum: over a million dollars.

Miss Helen continued on with her lecture. "They are arranged in order: The man goes after the woman, they meet in secret, they marry, and then happily read through the letters of their courtship. It's the progress from early passion to long-term friendship." Her tone was dry, flat, as if she'd given this speech many times before. She probably had, as every visitor to this room must wonder about the artwork. It demanded attention. "The key in studying them is to notice the sculptures that are drawn in the background of each one."

Sculptures. Lillian rose and walked from one to the other, no longer distracted by the frippery of the main figures. One depicted a nude female looming on a pedestal in the very center of the composition, shown in the act of turning her back to Cupid.

"Venus," Lillian said under her breath.

"Yes. The goddess of love. You'll see that she's keeping the arrows away from Cupid, the god of love. Cupid is impatient, while Venus is holding things back. Why do you want this job?"

The sudden change in topic threw Lillian. She didn't know what the job was, but she wanted to stay in this room as long as she possibly could, surrounded by wealth and beautiful objects. "Because I think it suits my nature."

"And what is your nature, Miss—?" She sniffed. "I forgot my notes upstairs in my study. Remind me of your name again?"

"Lillian Carter."

She regretted saying her real name as soon as it escaped her lips. At least, in her stunned state, she hadn't answered *Angelica*.

"I don't like *Lillian*. I'll call you Miss Lilly. And I'll tell you right off that you're the eighth applicant I've interviewed this week and we have three more to go. I don't say this to discourage you, but to let you know that you have stiff competition for the position of private secretary."

A private secretary. Lillian had no idea what one did, or how. She rose to go. "Thank you for seeing me, then. I'll be on my way."

"Wait. You're leaving?" Miss Helen's mouth fell open.

"I think I ought to."

"But you haven't asked anything about it." She seemed disappointed.

Lillian imagined the other applicants had rushed to impress, not to leave. "I know when my services are not wanted."

"The pay is one hundred and forty dollars a month."

Lillian tried not to react, knowing that Miss Helen was expecting that. One hundred and forty dollars. Thirty-five bucks a week. She'd never made that much as a model. One month's pay would easily cover a train ticket to California, with enough left over for her to get settled.

"Do you type?" asked Miss Helen.

"No."

"Good. I prefer handwritten notes. Is your penmanship readable?"

"Barely."

"Even better. I like to make things difficult for other people. You should know that right off: I'm known to be difficult."

"I see."

There was something raw about Miss Helen that Lillian found strangely refreshing. Few women she'd met spoke with such candor.

Miss Helen rattled on. "Miss Winnie is my mother's private secretary, but she won't be of much help to you, keep that in mind. She's a sweetheart, but she can't hear a thing unless you're standing right in front of her. She's more of a companion, basically sits there while my mother drones on, but she's been part of the household for years—came on as a nursemaid—and Mother adores her. I do everything in this household, I might as well be called the mistress of the place."

"That must be very difficult."

"You have no idea. We've been in this house for five years, and it feels like five decades. I don't like New York City much at all. I proudly consider myself something of a social outcast." She sniffed. "But my father is the exact opposite. Today, for example, Papsie is giving a luncheon for his business colleagues, and it was up to me to figure out the menu, send out the invitations. I'm exhausted. And utterly bored."

Probably not as exhausted as the staff in the basement, cooking and arranging centerpieces and setting the tables for the luncheon, but Lillian held her tongue. "Perhaps a private secretary might be able to lift some of the responsibility from your shoulders."

Miss Helen studied her closely. Lillian did her best to keep her expression neutral, not to flinch under the scrutiny. Miss Helen shook her head. "You're too pretty. I don't want you running off with the footman after two weeks."

The woman was like a changeable two-year-old. Lillian wouldn't last a day working for her. "Well, thank you, then. I'll be off." But as she turned to go, a bust in the corner caught her eye. She drew close; it was as if a magnet was pulling her.

For the second time that day, she was staring at her own likeness. The sculptor Daniel Farthington had carved it a few years ago. He'd opened the large windows of his studio and told her to let down her hair so that it flew around her face as she posed, making her nose itch and leaving her irritable. She'd never seen the final product. Here it was. Curls danced around her head in frothy waves; her head was turned slightly to one side, lips curved in a smile. The wildness of the hair hid her features, so Lillian wasn't worried about being identified. Besides, she'd caught sight of herself in a mirror in the hallway, and she looked worn and wan after a night of sleeping in the park. Nothing at all like this sparkling nymph.

"Do you like that one?" asked Miss Helen. "It's—"

Lillian interrupted. "By Daniel Farthington. Done a few years ago, an homage to Houdon's *Comtesse du Cayla*. This is about flight and wind, movement and light. It's perfect for this room."

Miss Helen walked over and stood beside her. "You're right. I'm impressed."

Miss Winnie entered. "The next candidate is here, Miss Helen."

"Send her away. Send the rest of them away when they come."

She scrutinized Lillian until Lillian looked away. "This one will do."

"The Fricks are generous, kind employers, if you behave decently."

Lillian followed Miss Winnie's retreating backside along a hallway that ran the length of the building with a view to the driveway to the right. They passed through a living hall where a green velvet couch sat opposite a grand fireplace. The next open door offered a peek into what looked like a library, with low bookshelves running around the perimeter and grandly framed paintings above.

The rush of what had happened blew through her like a cold wind. What had she done? She'd gotten a job doing something that she had absolutely no experience for, for a woman who seemed this side of barmy.

If you behave decently, Miss Winnie had warned. Somehow, Lillian didn't think being associated with a murder investigation would be considered decent, and then there was the matter of her past employment. While the Fricks obviously took great pride in their statues of nubile young women, having a living, breathing one on the household payroll might raise some eyebrows. They entered a small anteroom and went up a back staircase. On the second floor, another long hallway ran north to south. The floor plan of the Frick mansion was rather simple, an off-kilter I shape, as if Mr. Frick preferred to showcase his artwork instead of how many square feet he could squeeze in between the property lines.

"The family's sleeping quarters are on this floor, along with Miss

Helen's sitting room, which is the third door on the left," Miss Winnie boomed. "That's where you'll be working." They didn't go down the hallway, but continued up the stairs to the third floor. "The female servants are up here, the men are down in the basement. You'll see a bathroom on the left. You're in here."

She opened a door and stood back, a small smile on her face, letting Lillian enter first.

The room was larger than the bedroom in Lillian's apartment, and furnished simply, with a brown-painted iron bed with a bedside table, a small chiffonier topped by a mirror, and a hooked rug on the floor. A chair with a rush seat sat in one corner. The sensible objects were even more so, after the extraordinary display on the two floors below.

But the view! A small square window looked out across Fifth Avenue, across Central Park, all the way over to the west side of the city. She recognized the ochre husk of the Dakota over on Seventy-Second Street, rising over the sea of green treetops. She imagined herself leaning on the windowsill and staring out as the clouds skidded by, like a princess at the top of a castle.

The job came with room and board. She beamed with delight, unable to suppress her joy. She'd make money here, and not have to return to her apartment. Before long, she'd have enough money to afford a ticket to California, as well as spending money to get her back on her feet, and her troubles would be behind her.

Miss Winnie was studying her, a strange look on her face. "Are you all right?"

"Yes. I'm fine. This is lovely."

"Well, you can settle in. I'm glad Miss Helen finally found a girl, as this has been quite a trial for Mrs. Frick and me. She's not easy, I'll warn you."

"You're Mrs. Frick's private secretary, is that right?"

"I am."

"Do you mind telling me what your duties are?"

"The usual duties."

"Of course." She had to find out more, even if Miss Helen had warned that Miss Winnie wasn't exactly up to the task. "I'm afraid my former employer didn't enjoy the same level of prosperity as the Fricks. I don't want to make any silly mistakes."

Years of modeling had made it possible for Lillian to hover outside herself in a way that regular people didn't. She knew exactly what position of the shoulders indicated strength, what indicated maternal softness. If she raised her chin a smidgen, a royal haughtiness would manifest; if she lowered it, a romantic invitation. No doubt part of the success in the interview with Miss Helen was due to her ability to remain still and straight, to not let a single, fleeting sign of insecurity or anxiety cross her face. Lillian looked down, exactly as she'd done for the *Titanic* memorial, letting a touch of sorrow and unease pass over her features.

Miss Winnie drew close and touched her arm reassuringly. "For Mrs. Frick, my job is fairly simple. She prefers to remain in her sitting room most of the day, and rarely receives visitors."

Lillian wondered why not, what was wrong.

Miss Winnie continued. "Miss Helen is in charge of the household, although I'll be honest, her heart's not in it. She worked with the Red Cross in the Great War, and the adjustment back to civilian life has been hard. So it's up to you to run the household, which will be similar to what you did before, I'm sure, but on a larger scale."

"Run the whole household?" said Lillian, bewildered. All that had been her mother's job, figuring out the weekly budget, rousing Lillian out of bed so they showed up to her appointments on time.

"You'll order whatever supplies are needed: tea, Virginia hams, the special soaps that the Frick ladies prefer, that sort of thing. The information will be on the prior invoices, of course. You'll keep the employment records, coordinate payroll. Oh, and they have two other houses, one in Pittsburgh, one on the coast of Massachusetts, and you'll be in charge of maintaining those as well."

By now, Lillian's head was swimming. There was no way she could manage all this.

"Miss Helen, as I mentioned, can be difficult. When she pitches a tantrum, it's best to wait it out, she comes around eventually. She's known to throw things, so I hope you have quick reflexes. She clocked a parlor maid in the head with a diary last week. Apologized after, of course. She never means it."

Lillian put her duffel down on the bed, her earlier enthusiasm fading away. She'd have to enjoy these amenities while she could, as she had no doubt she'd be back out on the street in a few days, once Miss Helen realized she was a fraud.

"May I make another suggestion?" asked Miss Winnie. Her tone was soft and good-hearted, as if she knew Lillian was panicking inside.

"Of course."

"No face paint. And your hair, it's better pulled back, out of the way. They don't like the newfangled styles. Unpack your things, and then come downstairs for the staff meal."

As soon as Miss Winnie left, Lillian stood in front of one of the sinks in the communal bathroom and scrubbed her face clean. Without the vestiges of blush on her cheeks and the remaining traces of kohl around her eyes, she looked younger, more fragile. She pulled her hair back into a tight bun at the nape of her neck. Hopefully what had made her successful as a model—the fact that she could take on multiple personas—would work here and keep her from being recognized. It helped that no one in this grand house, from the kitchen maid to Mr. Frick himself, would imagine that Angelica could be living and moving among them. Angelica, with her flowing cascade of dark hair, painted lips, and defined eyebrows, no longer existed, other than in the plazas and fountains of the city. She was Miss Lilly now, the demure private secretary to Miss Helen. She'd make this work, somehow. She had to.

After she'd hung her clothes in the small armoire, she tucked the duffel with the letters in it beneath her bed. Starving, she took the back stairs down all the way to the basement, and followed the sound of silverware and the aroma of stew to the kitchen, although with all the twists and turns of the hallways on that lower level, she wasn't sure she'd be able to find her way back.

The staff were well into their midday meal when she appeared at the door of the dining hall, and Miss Winnie waved at her to take a seat at the long mission oak table in the center of the room. The butler, an Englishman called Kearns, introduced himself, and then quickly ran through the twenty-some employees so fast that she could barely catch their positions, never mind their names. In addition to a butler, there was an underbutler, three footmen, a valet, and a flock of parlor maids, chambermaids, and laundresses. The Fricks also employed an engineer, two watchmen, and a car steward. In the kitchen alone, she counted the chef and three cooks, including one whose sole focus was preparing vegetables. Of course a grand household like this would require an army of people to run it, but she'd have to know who they were and what they did if she was going to do payroll. Whatever that entailed. The whole idea terrified her.

If only they'd been in the process of hiring a vegetable cook. That she could handle, peeling carrots and chopping onions. She'd work in the basement all day, hidden away from the general public and any acquaintances she might accidentally run into, and then retreat to her bedroom upstairs under the eaves at night.

Still, as Helen Frick's private secretary, she would make far more money than a vegetable cook might. She had to keep her eye on her long-term plan of getting out of the city, and this would be a useful platform from which to do it. With the salary, she could afford to buy a couple more dresses to replace the ones she'd left behind at the apartment.

She'd make herself presentable and then abscond as soon as she could for Hollywood. Only once she was in the hands of Mr. Broderick and had dazzled him with her abilities would she'd be truly safe. But for now, she'd have to figure out how to fit into this strange household.

A blast of sound made her drop her spoon into her stew, splattering gravy over the lace inset of her dress. The kitchen maid sitting next to her laughed and offered up her napkin. "That's our dreamy Mr. Graham on the organ. He plays every day for Mr. Frick. After a while you won't even notice the music anymore."

What rolled through the room was not music, to Lillian. It was a wall of sound, as heavy as a giant tsunami, emanating from that massive organ in the front hall. How could anyone bear it? The music stopped all conversation, and one by one the employees rose and went back to their duties.

Miss Winnie had told her that Miss Helen would not expect her in her sitting room until the next morning, and to take the day to settle in. Lillian hid in the safety of her bedroom, staring out the window of the room, wondering what her mother would think of her now. She was respectable, a working girl. Would Kitty be disappointed that she was no longer the shining Angelica? Or would she be thrilled that Lillian was putting all of Kitty's lessons in the method and madness of the upper classes to use, especially if it ultimately led to a shot at a film career?

It was a means to an end.

She skipped the staff supper, her appetite diminished by her nerves, but around midnight her stomach rumbled and she decided to see if she could find a piece of bread and cheese to tide her over until morning. The house was quiet and dark, but in the basement a dim light from the kitchen shone like a beacon. The night watchman sat at the staff table, a newspaper spread out in front of him. He stood and greeted her, saying that he was finishing up his break.

She pulled her wrap tightly around her. She hadn't expected anyone to be up at this hour. But of course, with the treasures inside the house, a night watchman was required. After he was gone, she picked up the newspaper he'd left behind.

The murder wasn't mentioned on the first page. Nor the second. Not until page eleven, along with the Broadway play listings, did she spot a headline: *Seeking Watkins Witness*. The article only contained two paragraphs, but it still sent chills through her. *The artist model known as Angelica is being sought by the District Attorney to give information regarding the murder of Mrs. Eileen Watkins by her husband, Mr. Walter Watkins. Angelica lived at the New York home of Mr. and Mrs. Watkins on West Sixty-Fifth Street, according to investigators.*

The way they worded it, it sounded as if she lived *with* them. She was a tenant in the building, for goodness' sake. Still, page eleven was better than the front page, and the fact that there was no photograph or illustration was even better. The nonsense was dying down, would die down.

As long as she could hide out in the Frick mansion, she'd be safe.

Chapter Five

1966

Upstairs in her makeshift dressing room, Veronica dumped the contents of her purse out on the bureau, grabbed some tissues, and wiped at her face, the eyeliner leaving behind bruise-like smudges. She was out of her element in this grand house, with models and a crew who were experienced and savvy, and hoped she wouldn't be fired before they gave her a chance to try again and show that she could pose and preen like the others. Prove that she wasn't a freak, which was exactly what she looked like right now. An overly lacquered freak with a mushroom on her head.

Sabrina had warned her that the fashion industry was a fickle one. One day you were considered a hot commodity; the next, you were worse than nobody. Barnaby had probably forgotten all about how she'd impressed him at her go-see, why she was hired in the first place. But she had to move beyond her fears and worries about what everyone was thinking or saying about her. It was her job to fold herself into whatever the shoot required, and she'd do so. As soon as she fixed her face.

"Are you all right?"

Tangerine peeked her head in the door.

Veronica nodded, moved by the sympathetic look on Tangerine's face. She had one friend here, at least.

Tangerine led Veronica into the bathroom and stood next to her in front of the mirror. "Don't let Barnaby push you around. He's all bark, I promise."

"I'm embarrassed," admitted Veronica. "This is my first really big shoot. I mean, it's *Vogue*."

"Good for you, then. It took me three years to make it to this level. Don't beat yourself up."

"Thanks." Veronica picked up a thick makeup brush then paused, nervous that she'd do something wrong again.

Tangerine took it from her. "Let me."

With a quiet assurance, Tangerine sat Veronica on the edge of the claw-footed bathtub and began putting Veronica's face back together. Her hair smelled like lavender, and Veronica relaxed, relieved that someone else was in charge. She glanced in the mirror every so often, noting the techniques Tangerine used for future shoots.

"Look down at the floor," instructed Tangerine, as she drew on a thin line of black eyeliner.

"Your shoes are smashing," said Veronica. In sharp contrast to her own cheap black pumps, Tangerine wore bright pink heels with a delicate pearl accent on the toe.

"Dior. Nice, right?" She stepped back and studied her work, tapping one toe. "Can I tell you a secret?"

"Sure."

"I stole them after a photo shoot for the House of Dior's 1965 line."

"What?"

"Everyone does it. I mean, look at all of the clothes and things they're tossing around during the shoots. They never keep track, and it's a way to earn a little pocket money on the side. Either you keep it for yourself, or sell it at a consignment shop. Super easy. We only have a limited shelf life as models, so we might as well make the best of it. Especially with the beastly way they treat us half the time."

Veronica didn't think she'd have the nerve to take anything. But after being on the receiving end of Barnaby's snark, she understood the impulse.

She looked at herself in the mirror. While she still wore eyeliner and false eyelashes, her mouth and cheeks were more subdued. "It's perfect."

"The focus is where it should be, on your eyes," said Tangerine. "God, I love your hair so much. Did Vidal do it?"

Veronica put a hand to her hair. Why admit it was all a mistake? "Yes."

She was learning.

"You're so good at this, Tangerine." Veronica wasn't ready to relinquish the thin thread of kindness that had come her way just yet. "How did you figure it all out?"

"My older sister. She's way prettier than I am, but went off and got married instead of working. She taught me the tricks of a perfect cat-eye from an early age. You just needed a sister."

"I have a sister. A twin."

"How fabulous. They should do a shoot with the two of you! Now, that would make waves."

Veronica nodded as Tangerine took a can of hair spray and molded her hair into a shellacked helmet. Polly would never be in a photo shoot. They might be twins, but no one had ever viewed them as a matched set, even when they were both young children. While Veronica had emerged into the world unscathed, Polly had been deprived of oxygen for too long. Although she understood what was said and communicated with a series of gestures and sounds, she didn't speak. Only Veronica and their parents understood her. To the outside world, she was something to be stared at, a girl with an odd, twitchy walk and a mouth that hung open. Big brown eyes that avoided one's gaze.

The four of them had lived quite happily in a row house in the London district of Notting Hill. When Veronica's father decided to step away from the pawnshop he'd founded with his brother and become a driver of a black cab instead, nine-year-old Veronica had been his study partner for the Knowledge, the training course required to earn a license. Famous for its difficulty, passing the Knowledge involved memorizing 320 routes through London, including places of interest along the way. A cabbie had to know the shortest route between any two points, as well as side streets, cross junctions, and traffic signals passed. Veronica loved poring over the map of London together, a sprawl of roads bisected by the snakelike River Thames. She would shout out the pickup spot and destination, gleefully point out his mistakes, and after he'd finally passed the last of the twelve exams that comprised the Knowledge, the family had gone out to dinner in a fancy restaurant with cloth napkins to celebrate. He'd made a toast to Veronica, praising her innate ability to remember the names of the smallest London alleyways, adding that he couldn't have done it without her by his side.

Seven years later, Veronica had come out of the front door on her way to school to find her father's taxicab idling in the driveway. He'd worked the night shift, and at first she thought he'd fallen asleep. She knocked on the window, and when he didn't respond, she yanked open the door with a hearty hello. He remained still and silent, his lifeless hands clasped in his lap, as if lost in prayer.

The rest of the morning was a blur of images: an ambulance slicing down their street; the sickly lack of color in her mum's face; Polly standing behind her, one fist pressed to her mouth. A heart attack, the doctor said.

Without him, Veronica's mum lost both her husband and his steady income. She took a job working for a solicitor on Portobello Road and made it clear to Veronica that her dream of studying history at university was no longer an option, even if Trish didn't say so out loud. Veronica passed her O levels and left school, putting in long hours at her uncle Donny's shop. Unfortunately, Veronica's and Trish's measly wages combined were not enough to pay for someone to watch over Polly while they were both working and still cover the household expenses. While Polly had achieved some degree of independence, she was prone to seizures and simply couldn't be left unattended.

Polly's things were packed up, and the three of them drove to Kent House, a Victorian mansion that had been converted into a group home. It had been a dull, wet day, and the series of gables that spiked out from the slate rooftop lent the place an ominous air. Veronica was barely able to hide her panic that this was where her sister would be living from now on. "She'll make all kinds of friends here," Trish said, patting her on the arm.

They unpacked Polly's trunk, arranging family photos along the windowsill, and kissed her goodbye. Polly stood in the doorway of her new room, one hand clutching the doorframe, and offered up a brave smile when Veronica turned around one last time to wave. Her heart had ripped apart in that instant. She'd heard the phrase before, but now understood it viscerally: her chest ached as if the membranes and chambers of that delicate organ had been cleaved open. While the loss of her father had been sudden and wretched, it was ultimately a matter of coming to terms with something that couldn't be undone. The loss of Polly was worse, in some ways. If Veronica had a decent job, they could bring her home, yet she was utterly unqualified for anything that paid well. She even considered getting a taxicab license and following in her father's footsteps, but dropped the idea after learning that only men were allowed to sit for the exams.

Veronica visited Kent House once a week, and watched helplessly as her sister declined. When they worked on a puzzle together in the rec-reation room, Polly's mischievous glee at finding the piece they'd both been searching for was replaced with an unsteady shrug. Meanwhile, at home, Trish burbled over dinner about the idiosyncrasies of her new boss, of how demanding he was known to be and how pleased he was with her work ethic. Once, Veronica made a snide comment about how Trish had simply replaced one caretaking job with another, but this one for a stranger, and Trish erupted. "Your hourly wage at the pawnshop is nothing to brag about. It won't do any good having Polly home if we're all hungry, now will it?"

The hurt behind Trish's eyes had revealed the true cost of sending her daughter away. A decision that she'd tried to paint as rosily as possible in order to execute it. Right then, Veronica had vowed to do everything she could to get Polly out, and at her next visit, she promised her sister that she'd find a way to bring her home. Then Sabrina had "discovered" Veronica at the pawnshop, and now here she was in New York City with the chance at hand, as long as she didn't make a mess of it.

Back downstairs at the Frick Collection, the stylist approved Veronica's revarnished face with a nod and put her in a crepe Yves Saint Laurent jumpsuit with flared trousers. Barnaby had the girls mimic some of the poses in the wall panels before deciding the room wouldn't work at all, so they all tromped over to the library, where a book titled *The Lives of the Queens of Scotland*, bound in handsome maroon leather, was handed to Veronica. She was tempted to leaf through it, but instead took up a position next to the fireplace and tucked it under one arm, as directed. This seemed to please Barnaby, although Veronica caught the Frick ar-chivist hovering in the doorway to the hallway looking concerned, only disappearing after she placed the book back into the bookshelf and everyone broke for lunch.

Down in the basement, the models were directed to a large room with several tables. A long buffet along one wall was set with sandwiches, fruit, and sodas. Starving, Veronica headed right to the food, but as she was reaching for one of the sandwiches, Tangerine grabbed her arm.

"In America, the photographer goes first."

"Barnaby gets to eat first?" Veronica asked.

Tangerine nodded. "Not sure why, that's just the way it is."

Indeed, everyone waited at the tables—a hierarchy in itself, with the stylist and editorial director at one, models at another, and crew at what was left, the rest having to stand or go sit on the stairs—until Barnaby finally waltzed in, plopped a sandwich on a plate, and joined the editorial director's table. Only then did the rest descend.

Back at the table, Tangerine nibbled at some grapes.

"Is that all you're having?" asked Veronica.

She shrugged. "I have to lose a few pounds. My agent says I look like a truck."

"That's crazy. You're skinny as can be."

"You're so sweet."

Even though she was starving, Veronica left half of her sandwich on her plate, not wanting to appear greedy.

After lunch, they returned to the room with the panels and changed into silk Givenchy evening gowns. Veronica's was jet black, and it picked up the radiance in her hair, making her skin look even paler than normal, but in an arty way that she hoped would please Barnaby. She made a note to wear more black when she went out on go-sees.

They gathered in the big living room in the center of the house, which had French doors that led out to what in summer must be a large lawn, but today was covered in snowdrifts that were getting larger by the hour.

"All right," said Barnaby, rubbing his hands together. "Everyone outside."

"What?" asked Tangerine.

"I want you girls leaping in snow. I'll shoot from the doorway."

The models all wore their own high-heeled shoes, which would be ruined by the snow. Veronica had paid twenty-four pounds for hers. What a waste. Not to mention their expensive clothes. "What about the outfits?" she asked.

"I don't care about the outfits."

Veronica noted a grim expression on the editorial director's face. *She* certainly did, although she didn't seem eager to share that fact.

One by one, the models gingerly made their way down the stone steps. The snowflakes acted as a gauzy filter for the weighty stone wall and gray trees rising above Fifth Avenue, the perfect winter tableau. Maybe Barnaby knew what he was doing, after all. They wouldn't be out here long, certainly.

Within minutes, Veronica's ankles turned to ice, the snowflakes bit into her bare cheeks and arms, and the wind, which had picked up, almost swept her off her feet.

They posed as directed, shivering together in a huddle while the PAs replaced the film in the camera, then posed again. Veronica couldn't feel her fingers or her toes, and her silk shoes were sopping wet.

"I have a brilliant idea," said Barnaby, pointing up with his free hand. "I'm going to go to the floor above and shoot down at you. I want you all on your backs making snow angels when I give the order."

"What?" asked Tangerine. "In the snow?"

"Of course."

"Can we come in and warm up a little while you set up?" Veronica ventured.

"No, won't be long. Stay put."

It would take him at least ten minutes to reset on the floor above.

And then they were supposed to roll around on the ground? Veronica and Tangerine exchanged glances.

"But it's freezing," said Tangerine, her lips blue.

"Tangerine." Barnaby pointed a finger at her. "I wouldn't think you would be so cold, with that extra layer of fat you carry around."

To Veronica's astonishment, not one of the other models said a word in protest, even though they all had chattering teeth. She remembered the go-see where, fed up by the lack of consideration for the models' time, she'd channeled her frustrations and discovered a power she didn't even know she had. She drew on that now. He had no right to be so cruel.

"This is inhumane," she said. "We're all going to get terribly sick. And that's an awful thing to say to Tangerine. You should apologize."

"Stop it," hissed Tangerine. "Shut up."

Veronica turned to her. "We don't have to be treated like this."

Barnaby spoke up. "Are you going to hold up the shoot even further than it already is? Let me remind you, we all have a train to catch, and right now you're the one keeping these girls stuck out in the cold."

"Yeah, shut the hell up." Gigi practically spit out the words.

Barnaby spoke with crisp displeasure. "I will make the next few days hell for you if you don't obey me. You got that, Veronica? If you're so cold, go inside. We'll do this without you."

She thought of Polly, of all the money she was earning, and grudgingly allowed her courage to dissipate. "I'm fine," she muttered.

Ten minutes later she was flat on her back in a foot of snow, waving her arms and legs back and forth while Barnaby yelled out orders from the upper floor of the Frick Collection. The evening gown stuck to her body, the wet cutting into her skin like acid.

"Veronica, you're not trying," brayed Barnaby. "More arms, please."

A strong gust of wind swept a coating of powdery snow over them, causing the girls to shriek. They'd be buried alive if this continued. Veronica sat up. "I can't anymore. It's too cold."

Barnaby lowered his camera. "That's it. Get out of my sight. Now."
He didn't have to say it twice.

Veronica ran past the crew and disappeared deep into the house.

Upstairs, Veronica stripped off the soaked, utterly wretched gown, and used her scarf to dry herself off. Shivering still, she pulled on her street clothes, thankful that she'd packed a thick turtleneck and jeans. Outside the window, the snow was coming down even harder. She watched it, mesmerized, miserable at herself for not being able to cope, frustrated at having stood up for Tangerine, only to make matters worse. She packed up her suitcases and sat for a moment, unsure of what to do next. Go down and wait? Leave and catch the next plane back to London?

She glanced out the window again. As much as she'd like to return home, she couldn't imagine flights were taking off in this weather. In fact, she wondered if the train would make it out to Newport. Storms like this occurred so infrequently in Britain, she was unsure of how it all worked here. Americans most likely soldiered through regardless of the weather, as the models had earlier. That stupid, snowy caper had been ridiculous.

But was Veronica willing to put her plan for Polly in jeopardy over one lousy photographer? Sabrina would be terribly disappointed as well. Veronica let out a long breath. No, instead, she'd go down and talk to Barnaby, try to reason with him, and get him to agree to a fresh start in Newport. It was the grown-up thing to do.

She gave one last look at that unnerving portrait of the little girl on the wall and walked out.

As she rounded the corner, the high-pitched squeals of the other models rang up the stairwell. They were on their way back upstairs. For all of Veronica's earlier swagger, she wasn't ready to see the other girls yet, to have them regard her as if she were some kind of madwoman. Instead, she ducked through the nearest open door and closed it softly behind her.

She was standing in a small vestibule that opened off to the left into a larger room that was filled with strange shiny tubes. She put down her suitcases and walked farther inside.

The tubes must be the pipes for the organ in the stairwell. During her family's few pilgrimages to the local parish, Veronica had stared up at the pipes that rose behind the church organ and wondered how the sound traveled from the keyboard, if there wasn't someone back there blowing into them to make them work.

A narrow walkway cut through the maze of tubes, and she wandered through as carefully as she could toward a small window on the far side of the room, which looked to the north but didn't have much of a view.

The girls' voices had dissipated. They would need some time to change out of their clothes and pack up, so for now the coast was clear. Veronica was heading back to the vestibule to collect her suitcases when her right heel unexpectedly skidded along the floor and she lost her balance, stumbling backward. She fell hard on her bottom, breaking some of the impact with her palms. How pathetic. She had no right being a model if she couldn't even put one foot in front of the other without ending up in a heap.

She sat for a moment, legs out in front of her, and rubbed her stinging palms together. As she braced herself to stand back up, a flash of white caught her eye. Deep within the forest of organ pipes lay what looked to be a small pile of papers. They were slightly curled at the edges, and reminded her of the love letters her mother had stashed in a box at the back of a hall closet after her father's death. She reached in, sliding her fingers between the cold metal until she could grasp them, and slowly pulled them out.

The pages were covered in dust, and she sneezed twice. Sitting cross-legged, she gently fanned them to one side to shake off the residue. What a strange place for old papers. Maybe it was the instruction manual for the organ.

But it wasn't. Each page contained some kind of odd poem, written with a fountain pen in an old-fashioned calligraphy. They were numbered, and filled with strange references to pillars of salt, marriage caskets, seascapes. *You're halfway to the end of the course of clues*, read one.

A series of clues. The very first one had a date on it: *November 1919*.

When she and Polly were young, they'd entertain themselves with scavenger hunts on rainy days when they couldn't go out in the garden. Or rather, Veronica entertained Polly. She'd rummage through their toy chest and pick out the smaller items, like a penny whistle, or a tiny doll, and make drawings of what they were and where they were—a doll holding a biscuit to indicate the biscuit jar, for example. Then she'd hide them about the house and watch with glee as Polly tried to locate each one. Whenever her sister found one, she'd throw her head back and make her happy sound, which always made Veronica burst into laughter as well.

She couldn't remember the last time they'd done the treasure hunt—it must have been years ago. As they'd grown older, the toys were donated to the Salvation Army, and the silly games died out.

Veronica read through the clues, one by one, until the sound of a grandfather clock chiming deep in the house broke her out of her spell. How long had she been sitting there? She had to get downstairs, join the group, and try to make it up to Barnaby on the long train ride north.

The archivist from earlier might find these papers interesting; she'd hand them over before they left. She tucked the clues into the big pocket at the front of her sweater to free up her hands and stood carefully, wary of falling a second time. Her suitcases and small suede purse sat in the vestibule to the organ room where she'd left them, and before she headed down to the main floor, she opened up the purse to check for her train ticket.

It wasn't there. Dread coursed through her like venom from a snakebite, making her feel shaky and faint. In her mind's eye, she could picture it sitting on the bureau in the upstairs bedroom, after she'd dumped out the contents of her purse in a frenzy to find tissues. Clearly, the ticket hadn't made it back inside.

Lugging her suitcases, she rushed down the hall and took a wrong turn, unsure which direction she was facing. Through trial and error, she finally found the room tucked off the back hallway. The ticket lay on the rug, where it had fallen.

She scooped it up and was turning to leave when the lights suddenly went out.

Darkness and an eerie silence, both inside and outside of the mansion, enveloped her. She froze, listening for voices but hearing none.

She flicked on the light switch, but it didn't work. In the inky gloom, she made her way to the window. Outside, the streetlamps were unlit as well. As were all of the other buildings within sight.

It was as if the storm had erased the rest of the world, whipped it up into nothingness.

A blackout.

Her mother had talked about London's nightly blackouts that prevented German bombers from finding their targets during the war, how terrifying it was not knowing what was lurking in the night sky. Veronica closed her eyes for a moment, reminding herself to breathe, that she was perfectly fine and just had to find the others.

She groped her way through the hallway to the stairwell. Cursing the kitten heels she'd put on that morning, she clunked her way down to the reception area on the ground floor, where she'd first come in.

"Hello?" she called out.

Someone still had to be here, surely. She headed past the reception desk toward two pairs of glass French doors that led out to the street.

The inside ones were locked, and there was no bolt or button to unlock them, only a keyhole. She cupped her hands and stared out through the front door's glass windows, onto the street. A carpet of white covered the road and sidewalks. No people, no cars. And even if someone did come by, she wasn't close enough to the outer doors that her shouts or banging would be heard. Not that many people would be out on a night like this.

She turned around and yelled, not caring that she sounded like a maniac. "Is anyone here? Help!"

And was met with silence.

1919

"Miss Helen will see you at nine o'clock, Miss Lilly." Miss Winnie's voice rang out across the staff dining room.

Lillian twisted around from her seat at the table where she'd been finishing up her oatmeal so that Miss Winnie could see her lips. "Where shall I present myself?" she asked.

"Her sitting room on the second floor. Take the front stairs. East side of the house, second door on the right."

"Thank you."

She had thirty minutes to spare, so she decided to explore the house more fully. The south wing, where the entrance off the porte-cochère was, included a ladies' dressing room, a butler's pantry, and a dining room with windows that looked out to the park. The living areas of the house extended off at a right angle: the Fragonard Room, where she'd had her interview with Miss Helen, the living hall, and then the library. The door at the end of the hallway was slightly ajar, and she stepped close to peer in.

"No!"

She whirled around to find a maid standing behind her, an apologetic smile on her face. "Sorry, I didn't mean to scare you. You don't want to go in there unannounced, I promise. You'll have your fanny spanked right off."

She had a wide face and a toothy grin, and Lillian couldn't help but smile back. "Thank you, I was trying to get my bearings. Today is my first day."

"Ah, the latest human sacrifice for Miss Helen, is that right?"

The idea unsettled Lillian, but then the maid laughed again. "Oh, your face! You are right terrified, aren't you? Well, don't be. My name is Bertha, I'm her lady's maid, and have been for the past four years, so if you need any help you come to me. They put you in the room next to mine upstairs. I hope you couldn't hear my snoring through the walls."

Before Lillian could answer to the negative, Bertha took her arm and guided her up the stairs. "Let me take you around, show you the place. Back there, where you were about to go, is the art gallery and Mr. Frick's study, where the master of the house can be found most hours. So keep out, all right? He's a tetchy one. Tetchier than Miss Helen. Is that a word? *Tetchier?* Maybe, maybe not."

She barreled on, seemingly unconcerned with the answer. "You already know the third floor. Bedrooms for the women staff are up there, along with the bathroom and a small break room. The south wing has a trunk room tucked into the southwest corner of the house, but be careful because the sloping eaves will leave you with a big bump on your head. And there's also a linen room and the fur vault, which is kept locked." She gave a wink. "I tried the door, that's how I know."

They made it to the landing of the second floor. "There are two elevators on the other side of the house. One is for servants and the other for the family. Along the south wing here is a breakfast room, a service pantry, and a small office for Mrs. Frick. Shhh, follow me. You have to see where she sleeps." They both crept inside the most beautiful bedchamber

Lillian had ever seen, every surface covered with silks of the most delicate rose and gray. If she slept in a room like that, she might never get out of bed. A portrait of a young girl hung above a narrow secretary desk. She looked to be around four or five and had the same reddish hair as Miss Helen, but instead of brash, bright eyes, the girl had a haunting sadness about her. The boudoir, on the other side of the foyer, was decorated with fanciful panels that reminded Lillian of those in the Fragonard Room.

Back in the hallway, she discovered she'd lost all sense of direction. "Is Miss Helen's sitting room in here?" she asked, pointing to a door.

"No." Bertha opened the door anyway. Inside was what had to be the master bedroom, finished in dark wood, which connected to a sitting room with a mahogany grand piano. "This is for Mr. Frick. Did you know he made his first million by the age of thirty? That means it's too late for me. I'm thirty-four. Too bad, right?"

"What does he do?" Lillian knew it had to do with steel, but was unsure of the details. These were things she should know if she'd be working here.

"He made coke, which is used to make steel. He's lauded here in New York as one of the richest men in America, but back in Pennsylvania, where I'm from, it's a different story."

Now Lillian was intrigued. "Why's that?"

Bertha lowered her voice. "He was known to be brutal to any workers who dared to go on strike. And get this, someone even tried to kill him. A mad Russian anarchist broke into his office, and he barely survived. He was shot and stabbed"—at this Bertha made the appropriate gestures and accompanying ghastly noises—"and yet he lived. They said it was a miracle. But that was decades ago. These days he's better known as an art collector than a union buster."

"What are you girls doing?"

Helen Frick stood at the end of the hallway, hands on hips, a pink flush quickly consuming her freckles.

"Sorry, Miss Helen," said Bertha, going pale.

She'd been so friendly to Lillian, the first person to do so in some time, that Lillian hated the thought of her getting into trouble. "It's my fault," she said as Miss Helen approached. "I opened the door thinking it was your sitting room. Bertha was just guiding me out."

"My sitting room is on the east side of the house. Over here."

Bertha shot Lillian a look of thanks before scuttling past her employer. Lillian followed Miss Helen into the proper room, unnerved at how much she might have heard. The sitting room had several glass-doored bookcases and a desk angled in one corner, with a view out a window that ran almost from floor to ceiling. The morning sun poured in.

The bookcases were stuffed with the collected works of Jane Austen, Victor Hugo, George Eliot, Edgar Allan Poe, and more, the handsome leather bindings gleaming in the sunlight. Above the fireplace hung another portrait of the young girl with a ruddy complexion and strawberry-blonde hair—similar to the one in Mrs. Frick's bedroom—which Lillian was now certain had to be Miss Helen as a child.

On the far wall was a massive portrait of an intimidating older man: Mr. Henry Clay Frick, the man who built this mansion, and Helen's father. In fact, his visage was scattered throughout the entire room. A posed photograph was propped up on a bookcase shelf; another showed him golfing. On the desk sat a smaller portrait, drawn at a slightly different angle from the larger one, framed in silver. His likeness overwhelmed the room, like a Frick-faced hall of mirrors. In the paintings, his white whiskers and thick mustache were as bright as snow, his blue eyes pale and guarded; in the sepia photographs, they turned a ghostly gray.

"Now, Miss Lilly, I have to see Mother downstairs, so I've left you an article on the desk about the house and my family to familiarize yourself with."

"Yes, Miss Helen."

She took a seat at the desk. The article had been written in 1915, a year after the house was completed. It mentioned that the Frick mansion was built on the former site of the Lenox Library, before it had been folded into the Public Library on Forty-Second Street in 1911, and how Mr. Frick had hired the architect Thomas Hastings to build a simple, conservative home for his family and artworks. Mr. Frick, it said, had strong opinions on the matter of his new mansion, and wasn't interested in competing with his neighbors in terms of size or ostentation. *Mr. Frick desired a comfortable, well-arranged house, simple, in good taste*, it read. *The result was a long, bungalow-like residence with a fine picture gallery, with plenty of light and air.*

If this palatial manse was a bungalow, Lillian was Marie Antoinette. She stared up at the figure looming over her from the gilt-framed painting and stuck out her tongue. Mr. Frick might be worth millions and millions of dollars, but she wasn't about to let him—or his daughter—intimidate her.

"What are you doing?"

Miss Helen had silently reappeared.

"Nothing, miss." She pointed to the article. "Very interesting."

"You have a funny look on your face, Miss Lilly. Is there something you'd like to share with me?"

"Not at all, Miss Helen. I'm eager to get started."

"So am I. If I could bother you so much as to come sit at my own desk, that would be very much appreciated."

Lillian jumped up, hating that she was allowing Miss Helen to boss her around so. She rarely had to tolerate this kind of snippy self-importance from the artists she worked for. But it was only temporary. She'd get the first month's pay and be out of there before anyone could blink. That would show Miss Helen what it meant to abuse her employees so. Not that the woman would notice. She'd simply hire another one to take Lillian's place.

Only a month.

Miss Helen began with the day's correspondence. "You shall open all of my mail for me before I arrive, and lay it neatly in the center of the blotter, in order of agreeable to disagreeable. If it's marked *Personal* or *Confidential*, open it anyway. It's usually some salesman or social climber putting on airs to try to get my attention. Go ahead." She handed Lillian the stack of mail and a heavy silver letter opener, which probably cost more than Lillian's monthly rent. "Begin."

She had just lifted the opener to the corner of the first envelope when Miss Helen gave out a loud yelp. "No! You can't do it that way." She snatched the envelopes back to demonstrate. "First, gather the letters, unopened, in a pile with edges even and all the addresses facing toward you. Then pound them on the desk on their left narrow sides. This means the letters have less chance of getting cut when the envelope is open. Papsie taught me that."

It was all Lillian could do not to take the letter opener and jab it into Miss Helen's neck. Could she last a month under this fussy tutelage?

Over the next three hours, subjects ran from the elaborate filing system for said letters, the preferred method for adding appointments into the daily calendar, and the inner workings of the accounting ledger. Miss Helen had just opened up the checkbook to show Lillian how to prepare a check for her father's signature when a slight knock at the door interrupted them.

Mrs. Frick opened the door and stood in the entryway, one hand to her forehead. In a soft voice, she told her daughter that she couldn't possibly make it to lunch today. "I have a terrible headache."

"But you promised, Mother. Papsie wants us all to be together, including Miss Lilly. We can discuss his birthday dinner."

"That's ages away." She nodded at Lillian and brightened. "Besides, now you have a helper, you don't need me."

"I have a private secretary, Mother. Not a *helper*." She turned to Lillian. "This is Miss Lilly, Mother."

Mrs. Frick gave a wincing, brief smile, as if lifting the corners of her mouth caused her pain. "Nice to see you again, Miss Lilly."

Before Lillian could respond in kind, Miss Helen jabbered on. "The birthday dinner, Miss Lilly, is an important one with important people. We don't entertain often, which means when we do, it's written about in all the gossip columns. You'll be in charge of menus, seating, all that kind of thing. I assume you've done that before, in your previous employment?"

Lillian gulped. "Of course. Many times. When is the dinner scheduled for?"

"The nineteenth of December."

She would be long gone, and mentally filed it under *Ignore*.

As Miss Helen and her mother conversed further about the intricacies of whether Mrs. Frick ought to attend today's lunch, Lillian studied the checkbook. On the left-hand side of each check was a drawing of a young girl in a white ruffled shirt. Miss Helen's features were unmistakable. Even though the woman in front of Lillian had to be nearing thirty, her infantilized portrait was everywhere. No wonder she'd grown up to be such a spoiled creature.

Lillian looked at Miss Helen, studying her, then back down at the drawing.

"What?" Miss Helen's tone was sharp.

"Sorry. I was noticing your likeness to the girl on the checkbook. Such a beautiful child." A little false flattery couldn't hurt. "Your father must enjoy seeing your image very much."

Mrs. Frick gripped the frame of the door. "I must go." She looked slightly yellow, like she might be sick, and glided away.

Miss Helen grabbed the checkbook and closed it. "Now look what you've done."

"What have I done?"

"It's time for luncheon. Papsie wants to meet you, and insisted you join us. But thanks to you, we probably won't see Mother for a couple of days."

"Why is that? What did I say that was wrong?" She truly didn't understand.

But Miss Helen had moved on, and Lillian knew better than to inquire any further.

A surprisingly small mahogany table sat dead center of the generously dimensioned Frick dining hall. A dozen couples could waltz around the empty space if they wanted. Supposedly the table could be elongated for a dinner party, but right now, with only four places set, the airiness of the room felt cold and off-putting. Miss Helen had warned Lillian that her dining with the family was a rarity not to be taken for granted. "Since it's your first day, though, Papsie insisted."

Mrs. Frick, to Lillian's surprise and relief, joined them as well, and was greeted heartily by her daughter. Mr. Frick entered just as the footmen brought out a creamy bisque soup for the first course.

The paintings and photographs scattered about the residence didn't do the man justice. At nearly seventy, he was both imposing and magnetic, with fierce blue eyes, a neatly trimmed beard, and a massive torso. He walked with the energy of a much younger man, his eyes darting around the room, taking in a footman's jacket that was improperly buttoned and resting briefly on Lillian when Miss Helen made introductions.

"I hear you've lasted a half a day under my daughter's employ," he said. "Congratulations are in order."

Lillian had no idea how to answer him, but luckily didn't have to, as he'd already turned his attention to his wife and daughter. "Where's Childs?" he demanded.

"He stayed in Long Island, with Dixie." Miss Helen turned to Lillian. "That's my elder brother and his wife. She has three children and is expecting the fourth next month. They don't tend to visit often, as my brother's interests are very different from those of me and Papsie."

"Fossils," said Mr. Frick. "My boy likes fossils." He gestured about the room with his spoon. "Here we are surrounded by the most beautiful works of art from the past, and he prefers grubby old bones."

"He's quite brilliant in the sciences," offered Mrs. Frick, so quietly Lillian barely heard her. No one else seemed to, so Lillian gave her a quiet nod of acknowledgment.

"Are the grandchildren girls or boys?" Lillian asked.

"Three girls, so far," Mr. Frick answered. "Let's hope this next one is a boy. If so, they've promised to name him after me."

"Now, Papsie, you don't need a grandson to carry on the family name," said Miss Helen with a petulant pout. "Haven't I been happily in charge? Don't I step in whenever Mother is feeling low? I really don't see why Childs and his possible son get to be the chosen ones."

Mr. Frick dabbed the corners of his mouth with a linen napkin. "You know you're the chosen one. I do appreciate all you do for me, Rosebud."

Lillian glanced over at Mrs. Frick, who stayed focused on her soup as Miss Helen blushed red as a cardinal. "Oh, Papsie."

As if on cue, the two of them laughed with a forced hilarity, and Mrs. Frick joined in as best she could at the very end. Lillian got the distinct impression they were all performing some kind of peculiar family pantomime due to the presence of a stranger in their midst. If she weren't here, she was fairly certain Mrs. Frick would've taken her meal upstairs, and Miss Helen would do most of the talking as her father sat in a somber silence.

"Miss Lilly, are you enjoying yourself so far?" Mr. Frick's blue eyes drilled into her.

"Certainly, sir. I'm pleased to be here."

Quite the understatement. Two nights ago, her bed had been a slatted park bench. Last night, she'd slept under the roof of one of the richest men in America.

"Whom did you work for, prior to joining our household?"

Lillian's spoon slipped out of her grasp and clattered down on the rim of the soup bowl. Miss Helen had been so self-involved during the interview, she'd never managed to ask the most rudimentary of questions, and Lillian figured she'd avoided any further inquiry. Apparently not. "I worked for the Joneses of Albany," she ventured, choosing the most generic name she could think of.

Mr. Frick frowned. "I'm not familiar with them."

"They wouldn't be part of your circle, I'm sure," said Lillian. "Although they taught me a great deal."

"Miss Lilly knows a thing or two about art as well, Father," said Miss Helen.

"Is that so? Well, in that case, my love, your new hire appears to be a capable choice. You checked the references of Miss Lilly, didn't you?" He had a twinkle in his eye, but Lillian wasn't sure if he was teasing his daughter or not.

Miss Helen hesitated. "References?"

Mr. Frick was about to respond when a loud, musical crash sounded. The organist was back at it, and Lillian gave a silent thanks for the timing, as for the rest of the meal they ate in silence as the solemn strains of choral music reverberated around them.

The music and the meal ended, and Lillian braced herself for further discussion of her unseen, nonexistent references. But the conversation was forgotten as a young man bounded through the door to the dining room, a sheaf of papers tucked under his arm. He was in his early twenties, she guessed, with a boyishly beautiful face topped by a thick mop of unruly curls. He wore round spectacles under eyebrows that curved into imperious arches.

Lillian marveled at the gall of such an entrance, and expected Mr. Frick to roar at the impertinence, but instead, a huge smile crossed his face, transforming his gruffness into sheer delight.

"Archer, you fill our home with the sounds of the angels." Mr. Frick took the man's hand in his, giving it a good shake.

"I thought you might like Handel's 'Largo' today."

"I certainly did. And your 'Ave Maria,' simply spectacular." The man beamed in response before glancing over at Lillian. "Excuse my manners," said Mr. Frick. "I must introduce you to the newest member of our household: Miss Helen's new private secretary, Miss Lilly. Miss Lilly, this is Mr. Graham, our music maker."

Mr. Graham gave Lillian a wink, and all the blood rushed to Lillian's head, leaving her swaying slightly. The physical response to his attention was like nothing she'd ever felt before, and explained Mr. Frick's enchantment. With his long, tapered fingers and that untamed head of hair, Mr. Graham exuded a seductive mix of elegance and abandon. A musician with that much charm should be on the stage, she couldn't help thinking, not tucked away in Mr. Frick's organ niche.

"Do you have any requests, Miss Lilly?" Mr. Frick asked.

The only tunes Lillian knew were Broadway fare, which she was pretty certain would be met with utter disdain in this household. But as she scrambled for a suitable response, a flash of a memory came to her, of the sheet music sitting on Mr. Frick's piano in his sitting room, when she and Bertha had popped their heads into his private rooms. "'The Rosary' is lovely," she said in an offhand way, hoping that she'd remembered correctly.

Mr. Frick bellowed his approval. "One of my favorites! That's it, good man, can you play that for me next time?"

Mr. Graham lifted his eyebrows at Lillian, sending another electric shock through her, before answering, "It would be my pleasure."

After Mr. Graham retreated, Mr. Frick called for his automobile to be brought to the entrance.

"But we haven't discussed your birthday dinner!" said Miss Helen.

"There's plenty of time for that." Mr. Frick rose as a footman glided over to help pull out his chair. "I'm off to the club."

"It's going to rain, Papsie," said Miss Helen. "Bring your coat. You've had that silly cough for weeks now."

"I'm fine." He walked by Mrs. Frick without an acknowledgment, ignoring the weak wave of her hand.

Miss Helen turned to Lillian. "Quick, ask the butler for his coat. Bring it to the front entry at once."

At Lillian's urging, the butler, Kearns, was waiting by the front door with a black wool jacket slung over his arm by the time Mr. Frick was ready to go, with Miss Helen hovering right behind him.

"I don't need that. It's a hundred degrees out," said Mr. Frick.

Miss Helen took it from Kearns and held it out, speaking to her father as if he were a recalcitrant child. "Now then, you must listen to me. I can't have you falling ill, can I?"

Mr. Frick's earlier indulgence of his daughter at the dining room table was gone. "Enough. Keep it. I don't want to wear it."

Outside, the chauffeur held open the door to a sleek Pierce-Arrow motorcar. Mr. Frick stepped inside the vehicle without giving Miss Helen a second look.

Lillian retreated a few steps, not wanting to get caught up in whatever strangeness was going on between the two.

As the chauffeur took to the driver's seat, Miss Helen suddenly dashed forward and tossed the jacket through the open window of the back seat. "At least keep it in the automobile, you might want it later."

"For God's sake, woman. Leave me the hell alone."

As the car pulled out, Miss Helen looked over at Lillian with a triumphant smile on her face. "There. That's taken care of." But as the car turned into Seventy-First Street, Mr. Frick's arm shot out and tossed the coat out the window, where it landed in the gutter.

Miss Helen's cheeks puffed out in anger; she looked like she was about to explode. "Get the coat," she demanded of Lillian, pointing. "Go get it at once."

Lillian half walked, half ran to the street and gathered it up. It had landed in a puddle, and she held it away from her as she turned back to the house so as not to muddy her dress. A beautiful coat, tossed like it was a piece of newspaper. She thought of the laundresses downstairs who would now be tasked with cleaning it, knowing that they'd be reprimanded if the master found it dirty the next time he called for it.

By the time she got to the front entry and handed the coat over to the doleful Kearns, Miss Helen was nowhere to be found.

Late that afternoon, Miss Helen was in a desultory mood, snapping at Lillian for not paying proper attention to whatever inane protocol she was teaching her, or suddenly collapsing on her chaise longue like a fainting maiden, complete with breathy sighs. Lillian didn't mention the incident with the coat, and Miss Helen didn't bring it up.

"God, this is so boring," said Miss Helen from the chaise longue.

Lillian couldn't have agreed more. While the residence no doubt appeared magical from the outside, the actual running of it was as mundane as that of any household: ordering toilet paper and laundry soap, making sure everyone was fed. Luckily, Miss Helen received very few invitations, and those she did receive, she preferred to decline, which meant Lillian wouldn't have to deal with mountains of correspondence.

"Is this what you do every day?" asked Lillian as the clock neared the time for supper. Part of her hoped there was some other aspect of the job of private secretary that she might enjoy. Something, anything, to make the paperwork even slightly interesting.

"It is. Why? Is it not to your liking?"

She'd spoken out of turn. "It is to my liking, Miss Helen."

"No, it's a complete bore. The only thing that gets me through the day now is a secret project I've been working on."

Lillian perked up. "Secret project? What's that?"

In spite of it being "secret," Miss Helen didn't need any urging. She rose and led Lillian down the back stairs, past the closed door to Mr. Frick's office. They'd both heard the automobile pulling into the driveway a little over an hour ago. Miss Helen had run to the window as if her beau were returning from the war, then sat back down at the desk with an inscrutable expression on her face.

Now, though, she was brimming with excitement. They kept on down to the basement, where a door led to a game room with a handsome billiard table. Beyond that was a long hallway of some sort. Lillian laughed with excitement when Miss Helen turned on a light switch and she realized what it was.

"You have a bowling alley?"

"We do." Miss Helen gestured around. "Hardly anyone uses it."

With its red-tiled floors, paneled walls, and vaulted ceilings, this was like no bowling alley Lillian had ever encountered.

"Would you like to see how it works?" said Miss Helen. "The balls are terribly heavy."

Using two hands, she lifted a ball from a curved stand at the top of the lane, readied herself like a cat about to pounce, and then stepped forward, the bowling ball clunking clumsily onto the lane of gleaming maple and pine. Three pins fell in a loud clatter. Lillian clapped appreciatively.

"Usually there's a boy down the end to send it back. You'll have to do so. Go on."

Lillian walked alongside the lane, then carefully lifted the ball from where it lay in a shallow groove. She started to walk back, holding it close to her belly, when Miss Helen stopped her.

"There's a gravity-driven return system. See that ramp? Place it on that and watch."

Lillian laid the ball carefully upon a narrow wooden rail at hip height and let go. It began rolling, picking up speed, traveling the whole length of the alley as if an invisible engine were propelling it. The effect was quite magical, and Lillian gave a little hop of delight once it reached its destination, right where Miss Helen had first picked it up.

Maybe if she showed enough enthusiasm, she could convince her employer to play a few games with her each day, to break up the monotony. "What fun! So you enjoy bowling?"

"Goodness, no," sniffed Miss Helen. "That's not why we're here."

Or not. "Then why are we here?"

"That."

To the left of the bowling alley, under a series of archways, was a narrow passageway. Several trunks and crates were lined up along the far wall, next to a wooden table and chair. On top of the table, amid piles of documents and photographs, was a handsome leather-bound book.

"This is my secret project." Miss Helen walked over to the table and opened the tome with great care, like it was a sacred text. "The boxes contain research materials that tell the history of several of my father's very favorite artworks. I've been compiling them into this book, so that he has the provenance behind the acquisitions at his fingertips. Isn't that marvelous?"

Lillian peered over Miss Helen's shoulder as she leafed through it. The top of each page contained the name and artist and the date created, followed by a list of who had owned it previously, and then a paragraph explaining the worthiness or story of each piece.

Someday, maybe someone would compile a similar book of all of the statues that Lillian had posed for. Simply thinking about it made Lillian stand up a little straighter, even after what had been one of the longest days of her life. They'd mention how she got started, working for the famous sculptor Konti on the *Three Graces*, how she'd disappeared for a time, only to reappear as a star of motion pictures.

"Miss Lilly, you're not listening to me." Miss Helen threw up her hands in exasperation.

"Sorry. You're creating a book about your father's artwork."

Miss Helen nodded. "It's a gift for his birthday in December."

"It's remarkable. He'll love it."

"Do you think so?" Miss Helen gave a childlike smile. In many ways, she was quite witchy, but then, all of a sudden, the perpetual frown on her face would disappear and Lillian could imagine what she'd been like as a little girl, trying to cajole her mother out of her melancholy, or please her father with her intelligence and wit. What a lot of pressure for one girl. Her brother appeared to have taken the opposite route, finding an interest that had nothing to do with the family and then creating a family of his own. How easy that must have been for him, being a man, while Miss Helen was still living at home, unmarried, her life a prism of others' needs.

"He'll treasure it, I'm sure."

Miss Helen looked so pleased with herself, happier than Lillian had seen her since they'd met.

"You ought to do this for all of his artwork," said Lillian. "The home is to be a museum after his death, isn't that right? That sort of compilation would be an asset for any museum."

Miss Helen clapped her hands together. "I could do that. Why, I have all of the background material."

"It would be like a library for his art."

"Wait a minute, I have a very good idea." Miss Helen was now pacing the room, hands on her hips. "What if I created a library for art history?"

"That's what I just—"

Miss Helen spoke over her. "There's a similar library in England, which I visited during my travels. I can base it on that. A library filled with books about art, a project of my very own, one that will live on after my father's death, or even mine. I'm sure I wrote something about that London library in my diary. It's upstairs. I'm going to go find that now. A library for art history. Brilliant, right?"

"Brilliant, Miss Helen."

Miss Helen pointed at the table. "You stay here. Papsie's book should be finished up right away so I can put all of my energy into the library idea. There are three paintings left—they're listed at the top of the last three pages. Go through the trunks and crates and find any mention of them, and then fill it out in the book as I've done in the previous entries. And do try to match the handwriting best you can. No mistakes. I'm going upstairs."

All of Lillian's pity for Miss Helen vanished. The woman had a very short attention span, and now was on to the next thing, like a dog going after a squirrel.

Wearily, Lillian sat down and spoke through gritted teeth. The thought of being stuck in the basement for the rest of the evening, with no supper, rankled.

"Of course, Miss Helen. Whatever you need."

Chapter Seven

Practically every night, Lillian woke in the witching hours and wandered the Frick mansion. If she didn't get up, she'd toss and turn, thinking of her mother's last heaving breath as she tried to pull air into her lungs, her eyes wide with feverish delirium. That image would then bleed into the one of Mrs. Watkins's lifeless hand. The upcoming trial was still in the news regularly, but there had been no more drawings of Lillian in the papers, thank goodness.

Her lack of sleep hadn't helped matters. In the two weeks since she'd begun working for Miss Helen, Lillian had had to be reprimanded daily for some mistake or miscue. Miss Helen's patience was wearing thin as Lillian was always a step behind, either forgetting to update the daily expenses or misfiling a letter from the florist under *Agreeable* instead of *Disagreeable*. She had a headache at the end of every workday, and that same headache woke her up at three in the morning, full of facts and figures to remember that were soon overridden by images of death.

As she passed down the main stairwell, where the organ's pipes gleamed in the moonlight, like the bars of some gilded jail, Lillian reminded herself that she only had two more weeks to go until she would receive her monthly wages and have enough money for a train ticket. Heartened, she ran her fingertip along the banister as she descended, pretending to be the mistress of the house checking for dust, and walked along the main passageway. If it *were* her house, she'd switch the paintings around, placing the oversized Turner seascape in the living hall, where it could be viewed from a distance. Yes, that would work much better. The Vermeer of the laughing girl wearing a gold-and-black bodice she'd take into her own bedchamber, and position so it was the first thing she saw in the morning and the last before falling asleep. She loved passing by her favorites every day, noticing how they looked different in the morning light versus the afternoon sun, catching the surprising details that emerged with each viewing. To think that her mother had been raised in a house like this where art adorned the walls. How much had Kitty given up for love?

Lillian had wondered about her father often, most recently right before her mother had become ill. They'd passed the New York Public Library on Fifth Avenue, where Angelica appeared as Beauty in a statue south of the main entrance. She'd stopped, admiring herself. Her figure sat sidesaddle on a horse that wasn't quite to scale, but that didn't matter. What mattered were the smooth lines of her one exposed leg, the serene expression on her face.

"I always wanted to learn how to ride," she'd said to Kitty. "Did my father love horses?"

Kitty stiffened. "Not that I remember. It was a long time ago."

"Do you think he would recognize me? I mean, I must appear in a dozen spots around the city by now. Maybe, if he visits, he notices them."

"Who knows where that man is by now? Whatever you do, don't

make the same mistake I did, don't marry for love. Find someone who will give you a leg up, not cripple you with useless drivel. Or better yet, don't marry at all."

Lillian knew she shouldn't push, but she couldn't help herself. It was like an itch that rose every so often, a scratch that had to be addressed or she'd go mad. "Do I look like him?"

Kitty's lip lifted in a sneer. "Not at all. You take after me. And that kind of thinking won't do you any favors. In fact, you should be ashamed of yourself."

"Why?"

"Look at you up there. The only thing covered is one leg, and barely that. That's not how a father wants to see his daughter. It's a good thing he's gone, otherwise you'd never be allowed to do what you do. To have become 'Angelica.'"

"But then I would've had a father."

Kitty stopped in her tracks. "What are you saying?"

"Nothing."

But it was too late. "Oh, I see. You would prefer not to be the most famous artists' muse in New York City, in the country? What, would you rather be working in a silverware factory in Providence, the two of us side by side, day after day, packing spoons for rich people? You haven't worked a day in your life, not really."

How dare she? "What I do is hard work, and don't you ever say otherwise."

"I'll say what I like. You stand there, staring into space, doing absolutely nothing. That's not work."

"What about you, sitting in a corner, knitting? You haven't had to lift a finger since I started working, don't forget that."

All of Kitty's bluster disappeared. "You think I'm taking advantage of you? I thought we were a team all this time. Perhaps I was mistaken." Tears brimmed in her eyes. Kitty was the one who should have been an actress, not Lillian. She could cry on cue—Lillian had seen her do so when an artist tried to lowball them on their fee—and her emotions tended to the mercurial. When pushed, she pushed back, harder.

Lillian should have never brought up her father. "Sorry, Mother. Of course we're a team."

Kitty had smiled and flung her arm around Lillian's waist, and then bought some caramel candies for the walk home.

That fight had been in January, right before her mother began coughing and took to her bed. Right before the end.

By now, Lillian had come to the doorway to the art gallery and Mr. Frick's study, where Bertha had first come upon her and warned her to steer clear. Bertha had begun to sit next to Lillian at the servants' meals, and her bright cheer helped make life at the Frick household a little more bearable. At night, she'd knock twice on the shared wall in between their rooms, a signal to say "Good night," and Lillian would knock back. Lillian thought it was as close as she might ever get to having a friend.

Lillian was drawn to the partly open doorway, unable to walk past without peeking in. She knew from the street view that the space was enormous, like a giant ballroom. It seemed a shame to not know what was inside when she'd become so familiar with the rest of the house. She inched closer, and stood where she could peer in without moving the door.

At least thirty paintings hung in intricately carved frames along the long, velvet-covered walls. The furniture was minimal, some sofas and a few tables with sculptures on top, but the focus was on the artwork. Light from the full moon seeped in from the large skylights and gently illuminated the room.

There was no movement, no sign of life. She stepped inside, lured by so much beauty.

"Miss Lilly."

She jumped, turning in the direction of the unmistakable baritone of Mr. Frick.

He sat on one of the sofas against the near wall, dressed in a dark suit, legs wide to accommodate his belly. "You can't sleep, either?"

"Sorry, sir. No, sir."

"I prefer to visit my beauties late at night, when there are no other people about to bother me."

She stepped back. "I'll leave you alone."

"No, no." He indicated the cushion next to him. "Why don't you join me?"

Only then did she notice what was on his lap: Miss Helen's art book. Her heart sank.

It was supposed to be his December birthday gift, after Lillian had left.

"Turn on the lights before you do. It wouldn't be proper to sit in the dark with a pretty young lady now, would it?"

She flicked on the switch. Individual spotlights gently illuminated each painting so that the landscapes seemed like windows to the outside and the portraits breathed with life. Lillian took a seat on the sofa, a respectable distance away from Mr. Frick. He touched the book on his lap with his hand, and her eye was drawn to a dotted white scar, like tiny teeth marks, that curved along the webbing between the index finger and thumb.

"My daughter gave me my birthday gift early this year. I accused her of thinking that I wouldn't last that long—jokingly, of course—and that set her off crying, poor girl. She said she'd done it because she simply couldn't wait to share it with me."

But Lillian knew the real reason. Mr. Childs's wife had given birth to a boy a few days earlier, and Miss Helen wanted to prove her own worth to the family, offer up her own contribution. "She's a kind woman," she offered.

He laughed. "I don't know how many people would say that. My Helen is like me, temperamental, at times. When we have to be." Another long look. "What do you think of that painting?" He pointed to the right, to the one hanging near the doorway.

She swallowed hard. "It's quite grand."

"Let's walk over and study it, shall we?"

He got up with a loud exhalation, carrying the book with him. She and Mr. Frick were about the same height, although he must have weighed twice as much.

"Do you know what it's called?"

Of course she did. It was one of the paintings that Miss Helen had asked her to write about in the bowling alley that long night. The last one in the book. "*The Choice Between Virtue and Vice*," she said.

"Exactly right. By Veronese, painted in 1565. So long ago. My daughter wrote about it in her gift, would you like me to read it out loud?"

"You don't have to, sir. It's very late, I should go to bed."

"No, I'd like you to listen."

The painting was large, around five feet wide by seven feet tall, and featured a medley of bright colors and bold movement. In it, a man was twisting away from a woman in blue silk, and toward another in green, who clutched at him with both hands. Lillian squirmed beside Mr. Frick as he read out loud, his voice echoing around the room, a man who was used to being listened to and obeyed.

"*A young man on his wedding day is lured into the arms of a woman in green, signifying envy, and away from the beautiful bride, whose hair is decorated with white flowers, signifying purity. The bride holds a piece of wedding cake in her left hand, and is about to toss it at him.*"

What was she to say? It had been a very long night in the bowling alley after Miss Helen had left. Lillian had just wanted to go to bed, so instead of finding the correct description for the last entry, she'd quickly made something up, confident she wouldn't be around for its unveiling.

"I noticed something interesting about this page, and the two before it," said Mr. Frick.

"Is that right?" Her shoulders rose, like she was about to be tackled.

"The handwriting is different from the prior entries, which I know to be my daughter's hand."

"Right." Better to be honest. "She'd asked me to help out, and I'm afraid I—"

He cut her off. "You made it up. This beautiful gift, ruined by a jokester."

She'd been close, and then gone and ruined everything by her laziness. First thing in the morning, he'd point out her pathetic description to Miss Helen and she'd be back out on the streets.

Mr. Frick stood waiting for her response.

"I'm so sorry, Mr. Frick. By the time I got to this entry, it was midnight, and I had a full day of work ahead of me. I know art means so much to you and your daughter, and it does to me, too, more than I can say. But I was simply so tired, I couldn't think straight."

She expected him to bellow at her. Instead, he stared at her kindly, gently even, his blue eyes a little watery. "My Helen is a taskmaster, like her father. But there is much more to her than that."

Lillian stayed quiet.

"Did you know my daughter was at the front lines in France during the war?"

A vague memory of Miss Winnie mentioning Miss Helen and the Great War during Lillian's first evening at the Frick house floated back. To be honest, the idea of Miss Helen with her poufy hair meandering around war-torn France seemed ridiculous, an impossibility.

"She went as part of the Red Cross for seven months, helping women and children refugees," said Mr. Frick. "After returning home, she created a thrift shop, with proceeds going to the veterans, raising over fifty thousand dollars. I don't tell her enough, but she's a remarkable girl." He coughed a couple of times. "What she saw in Europe affected her, and I often wonder if it was a wise decision. She's delicate, prone to fainting. In Grand Central, she can only walk around the perimeter of the concourse now. Otherwise, she suffers a spell."

That explained why Miss Helen rarely went out on calls or appointments, even though she was often invited. "I had no idea."

"Before the war, she was an unusual child, but she had friends and interests, would go on sleigh rides with girls from school, took dance lessons, that sort of thing. The first month after she came back from Europe, she would wake up at three A.M., screaming, night after night. I would set my alarm for two thirty and wait in a chair by her bed so I could calm her and get her back to sleep. Then I'd creep back to my bedchamber." He sighed. "I'm a much better businessman than I am a father. Neither of my children like me, not really."

His abject honesty touched her, but she had to disagree, at least on one count. "Miss Helen is quite devoted to you."

"My employees are devoted to me as well. It doesn't mean they like me."

They stood for a moment, without speaking.

"Do you mind if I illuminate you with the correct story behind the art?" Mr. Frick's low baritone made it clear that declining was not an option. "You see, I find the history of the paintings as valuable as the paintings themselves. And the paintings, as you know, are quite valuable."

"Of course, Mr. Frick."

"You had it backwards. The woman in green is Virtue, and is guiding Hercules away from Vice, whose dress is partly undone. Her fingertips end in sharp talons, which have ripped his stockings, drawing blood. The work depicts the lure of pleasure versus the difficult ascent to true happiness."

"Oh. That's quite good." She hadn't even noticed the blood on the man's calf in the small reproduction she'd had to study in the bowling alley. Nor Vice's talons, which on the actual painting looked quite savage.

"I do not find your interpretation amusing."

Would she get what they owed her—two weeks' pay—if she was fired right now? There was no one to complain to if they refused. No one to stand up for her.

He paused. "Well, slightly amusing. You have quite an imagination. Particularly the bit about the wedding cake."

She jumped at the opening. "We'd worked so hard all day and then she wanted me to finish the book because she decided to create an entire library instead."

"Right, the library idea. She said you gave it to her."

Lillian was stunned that Miss Helen had sought to give her any credit at all. That wasn't in her nature. "She enjoyed doing the research for your book so much, you see. It made her happy."

Mr. Frick frowned. "I don't want her creating a library, it's too much for her. We must keep her safe. I forgive you for the made-up entry in my book. I understand that it was not what you were hired to do, it was out of your bailiwick. My Helen is not your typical woman, and I want to see her happy."

"I think creating the library would make her very happy."

"It would tax her considerably. Like my wife, you see, who has a delicate disposition. What would make us both happy is to see our daughter married, like her brother."

This was an unexpected turn of conversation. "May I ask how old she is?" Lillian hadn't dared to ask the question of Helen.

"Thirty-one."

Most girls were married off by twenty, at the latest. Lillian's face must have shown her surprise.

"My daughter hasn't had many offers, it's true, but it didn't help that we uprooted her and moved to New York. She's never been happy here.

Perhaps a husband will help settle her, find a new social circle. I won't mention your lapse, your invention, to my daughter if I get something from you in return."

"What's that, sir?"

"I need your assistance. My daughter has edges that require softening. I've spoiled her and relied on her too much over the years, and she does not have any innate ability to attract a mate. We will be introducing her to someone shortly, and I'd like you to guide her through the process."

How odd, that Miss Helen ruled her territory within the house with an iron hand, but yielded to a delicate disposition out in the larger world. Lillian didn't pity her, not exactly, but this conversation had made her understand Miss Helen slightly better. "I'll do what I can, but your daughter is determined, in many cases, to go her own route."

"I'm a businessman, and I think like a businessman, so I'd like to make you an offer, an incentive, if you will."

An incentive. Now this was getting interesting. "What's that?"

"If my daughter is engaged by Christmas, I'll give you a bonus of, say, a thousand dollars."

One thousand dollars. An enormous sum, on top of her salary. But getting Miss Helen engaged to be hitched would take time.

Lying low in the Frick mansion had worked this far, so maybe it would be worth the risk to stay on. Worth the extra money, for sure. She'd be able to afford a first-class train ticket, and as many new clothes as she pleased. That way, she'd show up at the producer's offices looking like a starlet in the making, not a boring private secretary.

As a model, Lillian had learned to be patient, and she'd have to tap into that skill in the coming weeks if she was going to pull this off. It was important that she carefully bide her time and wait for the right circumstances to align to make her escape, not pull the plug either too soon or too late.

"I promise I'll do my best. Thank you, Mr. Frick."

She would get Miss Helen engaged, collect the money, and be on her way.

"Oh, no, I can't possibly wear that!"

Miss Helen grabbed the dress Bertha was holding in front of her like a shield and tossed it onto the floor. From the mass of frocks on the floor, they'd been at it for some time.

"Miss Helen." Lillian assumed her disappointed schoolteacher countenance as she stepped around the sea of silks and lace. The tone sometimes snapped her employer out of an impending tantrum. "Why won't that one do? It's beautiful."

"It's the wrong color. I can't wear mauve or pink." She grabbed a thick chunk of her hair. "I'm a strawberry blonde, this will make me look like a giant tomato."

Miss Helen often wore mauve and pink, but Lillian didn't bother pointing that out. "What about the lilac one? It shows off your figure."

Normally, Miss Helen wouldn't think twice about her clothes. It was one of the aspects of her character that Lillian secretly admired, the fact that she put all of her energy outward, and couldn't be bothered to cover up her freckles, which most women would do, or that her hairstyle made her look like a frump. How many hours had Lillian spent bathing in milk or smoothing olive oil on her skin? Sure, it was part of the job of being an artists' model, but the obsession with whether or not she was showing herself off to her best advantage always weighed heavily. Miss Helen didn't bother with all that. Sure, it meant she was a spinster at the age of thirty-one, but with Lillian and her father's help, that could change, and fast.

The past week, Lillian had thrown herself into the preparations for tonight's dinner party, a supposedly "impromptu" gathering of the Fricks' friends and business acquaintances, but in truth an excuse for Miss Helen to be thrown together with the beau her father had chosen for her, a man named Richard Danforth. To be honest, the work had helped take Lillian's mind off the Watkins murder. News of the case had been on an uptick lately, as Mr. Watkins's lawyer had begun granting interviews to reporters in an effort to sway public opinion before the trial. "Angelica" came up repeatedly in the press, and Lillian gave another silent prayer of thanks for Miss Helen's reclusiveness. She rarely had to leave the house. In fact, Miss Helen preferred to have her by her side most of the working day, as she corresponded with the art librarian in England for her project. This morning, for the first time in ages, Lillian had not woken up wondering what would become of her, whether or not the police would knock on the door that day and summon her off to jail. Instead, she found herself thinking of the roses she'd picked up for the centerpieces that were expected to arrive that morning, and making a mental note to check with the chef downstairs about the presentation of the caramel cake for dessert.

At first, organizing a dinner party for thirty-two guests felt similar to what a general might go through in planning an attack during wartime. The final menu, which the chef concocted and then defended madly against any of Miss Helen's suggested changes, began with melons, followed by potage petite marmite, filet of sole, jambon de Virginie, and asparagus with hollandaise butter. He allowed the caramel cake for dessert only because Lillian spent a good hour smoothing over his ruffled feathers after Miss Helen bluntly rejected an upside-down pineapple cake, calling it "gauche and tropical."

The invitation list was drawn up and sent around for approval from all three Fricks, and then changed three times over. Same for the seating arrangement, where almost every guest was moved about repeatedly on the large chart that Lillian had drawn up, other than two chairs, the ones belonging to Miss Helen Frick and Mr. Richard Danforth.

But now, watching Miss Helen fall apart in her bedroom before the event had even begun, after all of Lillian's toil, vexed her to no end. Lillian needed the match to work. She'd already begun imagining a luxurious California lifestyle appropriate for a movie star, financed by Mr. Frick's generous offer. Her reveries involved renting a bungalow with a swimming pool where she'd lounge after long days on set, acting alongside Douglas Fairbanks or Lillian Gish. While many girls might dream of such a thing, it was very much within Lillian's grasp. Once she put her mind to something—acting on Broadway, or becoming Angelica—she'd always attained it. So far.

Downstairs, the guests were already assembling from the sounds of chatter rising up to the second floor from the main gallery. Cocktails and a viewing of the art began the festivities, before continuing down the hall to the dining room, where four tables of eight burst with roses and lilies set in heavy crystal vases. According to the schedule, which Lillian had tucked into the clipboard she'd carried with her all day—to the point that it had become almost another appendage—after dinner the men would retreat to the library and the women to the Fragonard Room, both of which had been dusted and swept, then inspected by Lillian before the tasks were checked off her master list.

There was something quite satisfying about checking something off a list, about creating a plan that was broken down into its parts. Once she'd stopped feeling like it was beneath her, Lillian had embraced this part of her job wholeheartedly, and not only because of the potential payout. It made her feel competent, and she found she rather liked being in charge. The same skills she'd used as a model—patience, the ability to bide her time and then strike with a suggestion when her employer wouldn't get defensive—had, until now, transferred quite beautifully to the role of private secretary.

"Hell's bells and buckets of blood," cried Miss Helen. "I look like a dowdy matron. What's to be done?"

The histrionics were getting out of hand. Lillian dismissed Bertha and closed the door to the hallway. "If you like, I can help. Do you want my help?"

"I should be downstairs already, but I'm not even dressed."

"Let's try the lilac."

She and Miss Helen stared at the reflection in the looking glass once Lillian had done up all the tiny pearl buttons at the back. The color softened Miss Helen's edges and, with its dropped waist, could almost be considered fashionable, offsetting the lacy collar that worked better on a young girl than a woman. Miss Helen nervously tugged at the sleeves, on the verge of tears.

What to say? The answer came in a flash. "Last time you wore this, your father remarked quite favorably on it," said Lillian.

That was enough to calm Miss Helen's fussiness. "He did, didn't he?" She did a half turn, admiring herself in the mirror, finally.

"Now how about I fix your hair? Perhaps we can try something new?"

"No. Papsie likes it like this."

At least the woman was dressed. Lillian knew better than to push her luck. "Well then, shall we go down?"

Miss Helen's chin wobbled. "I don't want to. I don't want this." She walked over and sat with a thud at her dressing table, biting her lip.

"It's a dinner party, you've been to many before, I bet."

"But not like this, where everyone will be looking at me and looking at him and wondering why on earth a man like Richard Danforth would waste his time."

"Because you are a catch, Miss Helen. You are smart as a whip and a good daughter, and let's not forget that you were on the front lines in France during the war. Talk about courageous."

"How do you know about that?"

"Your father told me."

Miss Helen grew quiet. "It was the first time I felt a part of something. That I was a useful member of society."

"What kind of work did you do?"

She managed a sad smile. "The Frick unit was in charge of refugees in more than seventy French towns. For each family, we'd take their histories, give them coal cards, explain how to find their lost relatives, help get them established. The face of one young woman was marred by dog bites. She said that when she and four others were rounded up to be sent to Germany for committing subversive acts, the French villagers came out to offer up a silent tribute. Angered, the Germans set their dogs on the five of them and laughed as they were mauled. She had been a beautiful woman—she showed me a photograph—and they'd butchered her. It still haunts me."

Lillian's regard for Miss Helen rose tenfold. She'd displayed a colossal courage in joining the war effort in Europe during that terrible time. Even the voyage across the Atlantic would have been dangerous, never knowing if a German submarine was headed your way.

"I did everything in my power to help everyone I could, but it took a toll," said Miss Helen. "I became prone to fainting spells after days and nights of unending bombing. And the sirens, I'll never forget that sound, like a pickaxe into one's brain. After six months, I had to come home. But I assure you, the savagery committed by the Germans will not be forgotten, not by me in any case. I can't walk these halls filled with portraits of countesses and duchesses who have not a blemish among them without remembering what was left of that poor girl."

"That must be very difficult. But your father is quite proud of what you accomplished overseas."

The invocation of Mr. Frick only increased Miss Helen's agitation this time around. "If I let him down, I'll feel terrible. Every time something like this happens, where I'm the focus of attention, I can't help but feel how much better my older sister would have been in the same situation, if she'd lived."

"Older sister?" echoed Lillian.

"Martha. By now, she'd be married and have children and I wouldn't have to do this silly dance. It doesn't come naturally to me, you know." She placed a hand protectively on her jewelry box. "If I show you something, will you keep it a secret?"

"Of course."

Miss Helen lifted the burl wood lid and pressed on something inside, which caused a hidden compartment near the base to slide open. A cameo lay on the red velvet interior. "This is Martha's likeness. I was three when Martha died, just before her sixth birthday."

Lillian leaned over her shoulder. The image of Martha on the cameo was the same as the girl on the checks and in the many portraits around the house. Miss Helen looked quite similar, but her forehead was squarer. So that was Martha dominating Mrs. Frick's rooms and Mr. Frick's checkbook, not Miss Helen. How horrible, to have the ghost of your dead sibling staring back at you wherever you turned. "She was lovely."

"Martha was Father's favorite," said Miss Helen with an air of melancholy. "I will never measure up."

"I'm sure that's not true."

"It is, and I can prove it." Miss Helen turned Martha's cameo over and clicked it open. Inside sat a pink diamond the size of a large pebble, glittering in the lamplight with the most remarkable of colors, from the softest pastel to a shimmering rouge. "My father bought it for Martha to celebrate her birth. It's known as the Magnolia diamond, and quite rare. When I was born, they didn't bother with such extravagance." She tucked the jewel back into the cameo, then laid it gently in the drawer of the jewelry box and closed it all up. "I'm not feeling well, can you tell my father I won't be able to join?"

Sympathy and frustration warred within Lillian in equal measure. She knew what it was like to feel like you couldn't please a parent, but Lillian needed Helen to not only attend but dazzle if Lillian was to meet her end of the bargain with Mr. Frick. Yet if she let her irritation show, Miss Helen would only feed off it. She took a deep breath.

"Can I tell you a secret?"

Miss Helen looked up at her, surprised at the sudden turn in conversation. "A secret?"

"Yes. I'm not one for crowds of people, either. Whenever I have a difficult time of it, I imagine that all the people around me are wearing absolutely nothing at all."

"What!" Miss Helen put a hand over her mouth. "Without any clothes on?"

It was a trick that Lillian put to use whenever she posed in the nude for an unfamiliar artist. She'd imagine what he looked like under his smock, all those dangly parts that she'd only seen on statues, which made her less self-conscious and helped her focus on remaining still, although every so often she found herself prone to giggles.

But Miss Helen didn't need to know the details. "Yes. They're the ones who are ridiculous, not you."

Miss Helen burst into peals of laughter. "How risqué! My mother would be mortified at such an idea. You say it works?"

"I promise."

"Very well. I want to go downstairs now, to try your technique out. But I'm coming back up if it doesn't work."

After she was gone, Lillian let in Bertha to clean the mess. She was tempted to ask her about the story of Martha—certainly Bertha would know what had happened; she knew all the gossip—but there was no time, so instead, she rushed downstairs, her heart beating fast. The guests still had fifteen minutes left before dinner. In the butler's pantry at the far end of the hall, Lillian spied the three footmen assembling slices of melon on silver trays. She turned back and peered in through a crack in the door into the main gallery.

Inside, New York City's finest citizens were engaging in self-consciously sophisticated conversation with each other in between sips of champagne. The evening gowns on the younger women in attendance ventured to the modern, shimmering with delicate beads, the waistlines barely existent, or lightly draped with a loose tie. A woman in turquoise and black whispered to another wearing a daring clementine-colored chemise dress, while above their heads a framed Van Dyck noblewoman in a bulky neck ruff smiled demurely down, as if listening in.

She'd done it. She'd organized and pulled off a high-class soiree in the Frick residence. If only Kitty were still alive to see what her daughter had accomplished.

"Excuse me."

Lillian turned to see a woman with a long, pale face punctuated with dark eyebrows and topped with a jet-black head of hair. She recognized her instantly: Mrs. Gertrude Vanderbilt Whitney, the well-known patron of the arts and a skilled artist in her own right. They'd met a few times before, when Mrs. Whitney had stopped by the studio of the sculptor Karl Bitter as he developed a figure based on Lillian, one that now stood in front of the Plaza Hotel. Mrs. Whitney had expressed interest in Lillian posing for her, but nothing had ever come to fruition.

Mrs. Whitney narrowed her eyes and held up a shiny gold lorgnette.

"Angelica? Is that you?"

Chapter Eight

1966

Veronica checked her watch. She'd wasted more time than she'd thought up in that room with the organ pipes, reading through the pages of clues, and the train carrying Barnaby and the models had already pulled out of Penn Station. Surely, this blackout was only temporary. If she could just get downtown, she could catch the next train before the storm worsened.

She tried the French doors throughout the ground floor—in the reception area, the living hall—but all were locked.

What were they thinking, leaving her behind? Then again, everyone had probably assumed that she'd left already, walked out on the whole shoot. Which she would never do. She imagined the irate phone call to Sabrina from *Vogue*, with the vow to never work with Veronica again. Her career would be over. She'd spent a good deal of her wages from the past few months on shoes and scarves and girdles, and she'd been counting on this paycheck to start a savings account for Polly. She had a return ticket home, but nothing else to show for all her trouble. What if the agency made her reimburse the magazine for the hotel room? Or the plane ticket? She'd be in a bigger hole than when she'd started.

The shadows were lengthening, and soon it would be hard to see. Veronica remembered seeing a couple of candles in the room where she got dressed, and took the stairs up one flight. Back in the fancy bedroom, she grabbed a book of matches from the fireplace mantel and lit a tapered candle on a brass holder. It cast a golden, unsteady glow around the room. Above her, sparkling reflections from the crystal chandelier danced across the ceiling.

The administrative offices she'd stumbled into earlier would have phones, she realized. Unfortunately, only a couple were unlocked, and neither phone had a dial tone. She hit *0* for the operator several times before finally slamming down the handset. There was no way of contacting anyone for help, not until the lines were restored.

Someone else must be here, a security guard, maybe. She walked out into the hallway. "Hello!" she yelled. "Is anyone here? I'm up on the second floor. Hello?"

Her voice echoed down the corridor, but there was no response.

The silence was unnerving. Since she'd first arrived in New York City, she'd been overwhelmed by the unceasing cacophony of horns, sirens, and people shouting. Now, between the power outage and the snowfall, everything was muffled, as if the grand Frick residence had been picked up and dropped into a thick woolen sock.

But any moment the lights would come on, the phones would be restored. They *had* to be. Then she'd call the police, have them come and rescue her. For now, she retreated to the bedroom, finding comfort in the familiar room.

She placed the candle on the small table next to the chaise longue and sat, hugging her knees. The clues in her pocket gave a crinkle, and she carefully drew them out and studied them in the flickering light. She might as well examine them while she waited, a way to keep from dwelling on the fact that she was trapped and all alone.

Each had a series of numbers at the top right corner, 1/20, 2/20, up to 11/20. She placed them in order on the side table and read the first line of the first clue: *Get set for a quest to find the magnificent magnolia treasure.*

The magnolia treasure.

The archivist had mentioned that a valuable pink diamond had gone missing way back when, but that a police report had never been filed. The Magnolia diamond, he'd called it.

What if the person who'd written the clues had hidden the diamond somewhere in the house, and then forgotten all about it, or died, and no one had been able to find it? If there were twenty clues in total, and only eleven here, it meant that the "magnificent magnolia treasure" had never been found. The clues obviously hadn't been moved in some time, gathering dust all these years.

No, her imagination was getting ahead of her, visions of pink diamonds dancing in her head.

Still, she picked up the last clue of the series, number eleven:

> *A natural beauty came from naught*
> *Yet this blushing lady was quite sought*
> *Out. A lover of Horatio*
> *Holding a hound*
> *Off you go*
> *Take a good look around.*

A ghastly poem, but something in it triggered a memory of a painting of a girl holding a dog. Veronica was sure she'd seen something like that during the day's shoot. She tucked the clues back in her sweater pocket and gathered her courage, curious to see if her memory was correct. She poked her head out of the doorway; the hallway was still and quiet.

She studied the paintings on the walls, using her candle to illuminate them, then headed downstairs to the room with the romantic panels. In one, a pretty spaniel sat at the feet of two lovers, staring back out at the viewer. The woman in the painting wasn't holding the dog, so it couldn't be that one. Veronica made her way from room to room along the first floor. No paintings with dogs.

The wind howled outside, but she found that staying focused on the task at hand kept her claustrophobia at bay. For the moment.

In the library, she stood in the center of the room, looking slowly around. There was a portrait of a flushed George Washington looking like he'd downed a few too many, an oil of a sailboat on rocky seas, and a series of ravishingly beautiful women wearing puffy wigs. Above the fireplace was one of a gruff-looking man with thinning gray hair looking off to the side as if he were about to bark out an order to an unseen underling. Mr. Henry Clay Frick himself, according to the nameplate.

But there, in the corner, was the painting she remembered. It was of a young woman in a simple red dress, her cheeks a maidenly pink, holding a spaniel.

This had to be it.

But then where was the next clue? When she'd constructed a scavenger hunt for Polly, the clue was always nearby, easy to spot. The Frick house had been perfectly preserved, so maybe it was still around.

Even though she knew she shouldn't touch anything—this was a museum after all—she very carefully lifted one corner of the frame away from the wall and peered behind it, in case a clue had been tucked back there. Nothing.

The painting hung just above a small bookcase with a vase on top. There was no note inside the vase nor underneath it. She sat cross-legged on the floor, pulled out a book from the shelf, and carefully leafed through it. Nothing. Same with the volume next to it. She was about to give up until she spotted a familiar square of white tucked in the binding of the fifth book.

She'd been right.

Her thoughts raced ahead with the possibilities. Her father had always said she had a mind like a steel trap, that her memory was excellent. What if she was able to follow the rest of the clues and find the treasure? *The magnificent magnolia treasure.* The lost Magnolia diamond.

If she found it, there might be a reward.

Or, on the other hand, the people who ran the Frick Collection might be angry at her for nosing about where she shouldn't. The American laws might be harsh about that sort of thing, and she'd end up in jail.

The missing diamond was never reported to the police, and no one knew for sure what had happened to it. Say she found it—who would know? A prick of mischievous delight surged through her at the possibilities, as far-fetched as they were. No one would miss it. It was the perfect crime, really. Veronica had all the right connections if, in fact, a pricey gem did one day fall into her lap. Uncle Donny ran a discreet side business handling items with dodgy provenances—it was one of the reasons her father had quit to drive a cab, as he didn't approve. Uncle Donny would know not to ask questions, as long as he got his cut. A pink diamond, worth who knew how much, would most definitely spring Polly from Kent House.

Veronica shivered. For God's sake, the cold and dark were getting to her, affecting her judgment. She was astonished at herself for even entertaining such a thought. She was no crook.

"What the hell are you doing?"

Veronica let out a squawk, slamming the book shut and banging into the bookshelf as she straightened up. The vase on top teetered but didn't fall over, thank God.

Shaken, she looked up to see the figure of a man filling the doorway. It was the archivist who Barnaby had insulted. Joshua.

Her relief at having been found was replaced by horror at the fact that she'd nearly knocked over what was probably a very expensive vase.

"Joshua? Oh, my goodness, what a fright you gave me!"

"You were at the shoot earlier, right?" he asked, coming closer.

"Yes. I'm Veronica, one of the models." She slid the book back into the bookshelf and rose to her feet. "I'm so glad to see you, you have no idea."

"What are you still doing here?"

"They all left without me. I got locked inside." All was not lost. Once Joshua let her out of here, she could hop on the next train and catch up with Barnaby in Newport by the morning. "Look, I need to dash, my suitcases are still upstairs. I'll grab them and meet you by the front door."

He walked over to a corner table where an old-fashioned gas lamp sat, struck a match, and lit the lamp, taking an inordinate amount of time to adjust the flame, showing no sign of urgency. After studying her for a moment, his gaze drifted around the room. He was checking to see if she'd damaged or stolen anything, for certain.

"What time is it?" he asked.

She checked her watch. "A little past eight."

"No luck, then."

"What do you mean, no luck?"

"I don't have a set of keys."

"But you work here."

"I'm a part-timer. Part-timers don't get keys."

"You said you were an archivist."

"I'm a part-time archivist. Well, officially, I'm an intern."

This quibbling rankled. "I have to get out. Can I climb out a window?"

He shook his head. "If you do that, the alarm system will go off.

Tommy the security guard sets it before he leaves for the night, and there's no way you can get out without triggering the intrusion sensors."

"Then how were you planning on leaving?"

"I was just wondering that myself."

The man made no sense, and meanwhile the clock was ticking. "I'm sorry, what?"

He gave an embarrassed shrug. "I was trying to catch up on all the work I missed while the photo shoot was going on, and I fell asleep at my desk." Indeed, his shirt was wrinkled, his eyes red. "I'm as stuck as you are."

"Fine. Then we trigger the alarm. I'll explain to the police what happened. I can't stay here all night, it'll be too late."

He took a deep breath. "I have three things to say to that proposal."

The urgency of her situation seemed to elude him. "Go ahead."

"First of all, if we open a window, the cold, wet air will rush in and damage the artwork. Second, if the city is in a blizzard-induced blackout, which it appears to be, you won't be able to get to the train station anyway, especially wearing those on your feet."

She looked down at the kitten heels. He had a point. Two points.

"And thirdly?" She had the distinct impression that this was a man who enjoyed hearing himself talk.

"Thirdly, if I am here when the police show up, I may as well cancel all of my plans for the next three days, until my parents can get me out of jail."

"What?" But it slowly dawned on her what he was saying. A Black man standing beside an open window of a Fifth Avenue museum, the alarm blaring—the situation would not end well.

While she'd only read about the protests in America in the papers, she'd witnessed firsthand the effects of the clashes between Blacks and whites in the UK. Several years ago in Notting Hill, a group of white teenagers had attacked a mixed-race couple, resulting in a week of violence. She and Polly had watched tearfully from their bedroom window as hundreds of whites gathered out in the street after dark, targeting Black men and sometimes even Black women, beating them bloody as the police stood by and egged the hooligans on. The situation in the United States was equally charged, if not more so.

A new idea hit her. "But if the power is out, won't the alarm be turned off?"

"The system has its own backup generator. State-of-the-art security here at the Frick. Just installed last month. We wouldn't want any strangers coming in and ransacking the place." He eyed the vase and bookcase once more. "What were you just doing?"

"Trying to pass the time." It wasn't a lie.

"I see. Please don't touch anything else. I was headed to the kitchen to see if there's anything left over to eat. We should probably stick together. You coming?"

With that, all hope of escape deflated. She was stuck in a cold, dark house with this kid who was of no use whatsoever, who wasn't even a proper employee. With no way of getting out.

She gave one last glance at the bookshelf and followed Joshua out of the room.

Two tired-looking sandwiches sat on a plastic tray in the basement kitchen; everything else had been piled up in the trash can. Joshua went to a cabinet and took down two plates, setting a sandwich on each one. "This looks like roast beef, and this one, ham. Do you have a preference?"

She pointed to the ham. "That one, I guess."

"Would you like some water to go with it?"

"God, what I wouldn't do for a cup of tea."

He looked about, hands on his hips. "They have a catering kitchen down here, let me see what I can find. Stay here."

He was gone before she could say anything further. A few minutes later, after she'd devoured half her sandwich, unable to wait any longer, he walked into the room with two steaming cups of tea on a tray.

"The catering kitchen is full of the basics, so we won't starve."

"That's good to know, thank you." The tea was warm and comforting, and made her forget for a quick moment what a mess she'd gotten herself into. On the table was an oversized book, and she pulled it toward her. The cover showed the same garden off the side of the house where she and the other models had squirmed in the snow, but in the spring. The snowdrifts were replaced by a wide expanse of green lawn, and the trio of French doors that led into the living hall were bracketed by two enormous magnolia trees in full bloom.

"It's a history of the Frick Collection," said Joshua. "I left one on each table for the photo shoot, in case anyone was interested."

Veronica felt bad that she hadn't even glanced at it during her lunch with Tangerine, nor had any of the others, she was sure. "Those trees are splendid."

"They're some of the largest magnolia trees in the New York area. Planted in 1939 by the board, and chosen because they represent transience, as the blossoms emerge and then drop away every spring." This bloke was a walking advert for the place.

"Like the way this was a house and then a museum. The way the family was here and now they're not."

"Exactly."

Same with the diamond: a family heirloom and then an unsolved mystery. But she didn't say that out loud. Instead, they ate their sandwiches in an awkward silence.

Once Joshua was finished, he sat back and placed his hands on his thighs. "While we may not be able to get out, one thing I know we can do, because they did it during a holiday party in December, is light the fireplace in the living hall. I don't know how much wood there is, but at least that way we won't freeze to death before dawn."

Up in the living hall, Joshua arranged some kindling and logs from the rack beside the fireplace while Veronica stood watching.

He placed a log on the fire and turned halfway around to look at her. "Do you want to take a seat or something?"

"I wasn't sure if I should. If it was allowed."

"As long as you don't break it, I think we'll be okay. Your girlfriends didn't seem to have any awareness of how to sit in a chair this morning."

He was thinking of Gigi, with her leg slung over the arm. "They're not my friends." She carefully settled on the sofa, the cushions overly soft from years of use. "To think this was all the rage, once. Green velvet with a fringe."

"Not your style?"

"Not really." The fire soon sprang to life, warming her toes. She settled back and studied the three portraits on the wall in front of them. "Not that I have a style. I mean, I still live at home. But I don't think I'd want those three old men hanging in my living room, if I had a living room."

Joshua pointed out each one, from left to right. "Sir Thomas More, St. Jerome, and Thomas Cromwell."

"Funny how they're positioned so it appears as if More and Cromwell are giving each other the evil eye. Makes sense, considering they were enemies in real life. Your Mr. Frick must have had a wicked sense of humor."

"I like to think he did. I particularly love the one of More, with those rich velvet sleeves and the five-o'clock shadow on his face."

Veronica had to admit that it grew on her, especially once he'd pointed out the technical artistry. "How did you end up working here?"

"My mother's an artist, and we used to visit the Frick regularly when

I was a kid. She was the one who suggested I apply for an internship, insisting it would be a good use of my art history major, not to mention a stepping-stone to a career in the arts."

"Where do you go to university?"

"I'm a senior at Brooklyn College, where my father is a history professor. My mom and dad like to joke that this internship is the perfect mix of their two professions."

"Huh."

"Huh what?"

"That would make me a taxicab driver who takes steno."

"I'd hate to be a passenger in your cab, then."

"True. Might make for a bumpy ride."

When Veronica next opened her eyes, she was stretched out on the couch, covered by a thick quilt that she recognized from the bedroom upstairs. Between the jet lag and the long day, she'd completely zonked out in the living hall of the Frick.

She sat up and looked about. It was no longer night, but instead of a bright sun streaming through the windows, a wretched wind shook the panes while sleet battered the glass like hundreds of fingernails tapping away. The storm was worse than when it had started. Her watch read nine o'clock in the morning.

Joshua entered, holding two mugs of coffee, and handed one to Veronica. "I was listening to the radio in the kitchen, and the mayor's declared a state of emergency due to the snowstorm. The city's shut down through tomorrow morning,"

"You mean we're stuck here until Wednesday?"

"I'm afraid so."

Her modeling career was lost for good, then. She had no way of reaching anyone to tell them where she was, or what had happened. Veronica had been given one opportunity to turn things around for her family, and gone and mucked it all up. It would be back to her uncle's pawnshop, back to her old life of worry and loss. Poor Polly, she deserved so much better than that. While some of the other residents of Kent House had no idea where they were, or why, Polly knew exactly what was going on, that she'd been put away because they couldn't afford to keep her anymore, like some child's pony bought on a whim.

Something had to be done.

The treasure was still out there. Whereas last night the idea of taking something that was not hers seemed more theoretical than real to Veronica, today something had shifted. She could not return to England with nothing to show for all this. Polly was counting on her.

Maybe this extra day was a sign, a gift of sorts. She wouldn't let these next twenty-four hours go to waste.

"You said you'd fallen asleep last night, before we found each other," she said. "Where do you work?"

"I'm down in the basement, in the old bowling alley. There are no windows, no light, so sometimes I lose track of time."

"There's a bowling alley in here?"

"The Fricks had it installed with the very latest in 1914 bowling alley technology. Works like a charm, still. If we get bored enough, I'll take you down and you can try it out." He seemed less suspicious of her than he'd been last night, or maybe the fact that they were stuck for longer than expected had tempered his distrust.

"Entertainment. I like that. Why did they put you in the bowling alley?"

"When they were putting in the alarm system, the workers discovered several boxes of files and letters down there. They'd been tucked away in a closet and forgotten all these years, so I'm going through and cataloguing them, finding connections."

His eyes danced as he spoke; this was a man who enjoyed his work. She felt flashes of that sometimes at the pawnshop, like the day she was unpacking boxes from an estate sale and came upon a pile of old letters. Uncle Donny said to just toss them in the bin, but she'd saved them for when the shop was slow and read through each one, imagining what the letter writers might have looked like, where they might have lived, who they had loved.

"Intriguing," she said. "What have you found so far?"

"Lots of things, including a series of correspondence between Henry Clay Frick's children, Childs and Helen."

"How do they feel about the discovery?"

"Childs died last year. I'm not sure if Helen Frick, or 'Miss Helen,' as she's referred to by the staff, knows. I'm guessing that's why they have me down in the basement, working in secret. She's difficult, you see."

"How old is she?"

"Almost eighty, I believe."

"It would be hard, I suppose, to have your home ripped away from you and opened up to the public as a museum. Tossed out into the streets."

"She moved to a six-hundred-acre farm upstate, so I wouldn't say she was tossed into the streets. As for being difficult, well, she has strong feelings against certain types of people."

Veronica paused, trying to figure out what he meant. "You mean she's racist?"

He laughed. "Not quite. She hates Germans. For years, she wouldn't let anyone with a German surname work for her in any capacity, or even enter the art reference library she runs next door. Refused to have German-made equipment on her farm. Something to do with World War I, apparently."

"She sounds beastly."

"I don't think she cares what people think."

"What's your last name?" Veronica asked.

"Lawrence. So I'm safe from her wrath. And yours?"

She swallowed. "Weber."

"Dear God, girl. That won't do at all. I have to say, the reversal is refreshing." In the firelight, his face looked almost smug. "This must be what it's like to be white."

She suppressed her laughter, not sure if it was appropriate or not.

"That was meant to be funny."

"Sorry. I thought it was. But then I thought I oughtn't think that."

"*Oughtn't?* Now, that's a ridiculous contraction. Very British."

He was taking the piss. "Why is it ridiculous?"

"I don't know. Very fancy, upper-crust."

That was rich, coming from a man with university education and a posh internship. "Not what a model would say?"

"No, I didn't mean that."

The fire emitted a large snap, a welcome interruption. Joshua got up and used one of the irons to maneuver the logs around.

Veronica hadn't meant to sound so harsh. The conversation had gotten away from her, and she reminded herself of why she'd brought up his work in the first place. "If you like, you can catch up on whatever you need to do today. Why waste the time if you're here anyway, right?"

He looked over at her, wary. "Are you sure?"

"Sure. I'll be fine. Off you go."

She waited five minutes after he left before heading to the adjacent library and opening up the book with the clue inside. It lay exactly where she'd left it.

I'm fifty-two
Feeling quite blue

Although I look like a king
I've got absolutely no-thing
to my name.

Whereas the previous clue had triggered a memory of the painting it referred to, this one drew a blank. The trail was going to be much harder to follow than Veronica had expected, she realized with a thud of disappointment.

Just then, she heard Joshua coming up the back stairs. That was fast. She slammed the book shut with the clue still inside, shoved it back on the shelf, and raced to the couch in front of the living hall fireplace just as Joshua entered carrying two Danishes. "I came upon these in the back of the fridge. It's not much, but it'll keep us going."

There was no way Veronica was going to be able to solve the mystery of the magnolia treasure, even with the extra day of searching. Not with Joshua checking in on her every five minutes, and also because she simply didn't know where else to look. The house was enormous. If she was going to figure this out, she'd need his help.

If there was a reward, it would certainly be worth the risk. And by working with Joshua, she couldn't be accused of theft or meddling.

She took a deep breath. "The reason I missed everyone leaving yesterday was that I found something in that strange room with the pipes behind the main stairway. I got lost in examining it, and then they left without me."

"You were in the organ chamber? What on earth were you doing back there?"

"Hiding. The shoot didn't go as well as I'd hoped, and I needed a break from them all." She didn't want to admit what a disaster the day had been, and luckily, he didn't follow that line of questioning further.

He wiped each of his fingers with his napkin, not taking his eyes off her. "What was it you found? Music or something?"

"No." She extracted the notes from the wide pocket in the front of her sweater and handed them over. "Do you know what they're talking about?"

He moved closer to the window to study them. "I think they describe the works of art here. You found these in the organ room?"

"I meant to mention them last night, but then I fell asleep. Sorry about that."

He waited a beat before turning back to the notes. He clearly wasn't sure whether to believe her.

"I think it's a scavenger hunt," she volunteered. "I used to do the same for my sister, when we were young."

"And these were just sitting in the organ chamber?"

She shrugged. "They were on the floor, deep amongst the pipes, as if they'd fallen."

Joshua held them carefully by the edges and ran through them one more time. "These are incredible. Just incredible."

His voice rose with excitement. "And I think I know who wrote them."

Chapter Nine

1919

A ngelica," Mrs. Whitney repeated, "isn't that you?"

Lillian clutched her clipboard to her chest and stared at Mrs. Whitney, who stepped even closer. Inside the gallery, a bell rang, signaling that the Fricks' dinner party guests were to make their way to the dining hall. They moved as a herd, and Lillian stepped into the back entryway to let them through.

To her dismay, Mrs. Whitney joined her in the small space. "You look exactly like an artists' model I've met several times downtown. Her name's Angelica."

"You must be mistaken. I work for Miss Helen." Lillian looked down at her clipboard and checked something off. "Please, if you'll walk this way, dinner is being served."

But the woman wouldn't be put off. "It's remarkable, really. You could be twins."

Only then did Lillian notice a man standing close by, having just come down the back stairwell. It was the organist, Mr. Graham. She was trapped.

"I'm afraid I've never heard of her." Lillian was perspiring in her dress. This couldn't be happening.

Mr. Graham stepped forward and touched her lightly on the elbow. "Miss Lilly, can I see you upstairs, please?"

He retreated into the stairwell, and Lillian, relieved, hastily excused herself from Mrs. Whitney and followed him. On the second floor, he headed south at a decent clip, a thick stack of music tucked under his arm. Had he heard Mrs. Whitney call her Angelica? She couldn't tell.

"That woman was awfully rude, I thought." Mr. Graham looked briefly in Lillian's direction but kept walking. "I didn't like the way she was looking at you, as if you were one of Mr. Frick's enamels."

"Thank you for that. I suppose my face rang a bell. It tends to do that." By now he'd turned left, toward the front stairwell. They descended together, side by side. He wore a tweed suit with a matching striped blue tie and pocket square, the trim cut of his jacket the latest in fashion. At the bottom of the landing, he placed the papers on the organ's music stand.

She should be checking in on the dining room, ensuring that the first course was ready, but first she needed to get a better sense of how much he'd overheard. "How long have you worked here, Mr. Graham?"

"It's been four years. Now tell me the truth."

The room blurred around her and then came back into focus. "The truth?"

"Yes. How did you like it?"

She blinked in confusion. "Like what?"

"'The Rosary.' I played it the other day and Mr. Frick was quite pleased. I was hoping you were as well."

He was smiling, flirting with her, and something about the set of his face and the crinkle of his eyes made her smile back. "Right, yes, it was lovely." Not that she had any idea of how the melody went, of course. She hoped her response sounded convincing.

"I'm thrilled to hear it. I don't get much feedback, tucked away under the staircase."

She looked down at the organ, unnerved at his attention. "It's quite an instrument."

"You don't see many like these in a private residence," he said with a touch of pride, like a jockey bragging about his fastest racehorse. "She's a beauty."

Lillian gestured to the brass pipes that rose up above the stair landing. "They're a work of art in themselves."

"Believe it or not, that's just a pretty facade."

"A facade? Then where are the real pipes?"

He pointed to a door one floor up. "Behind the false ones, through that door. All four thousand seven hundred of them."

He settled in, but Lillian remained standing, shifting uneasily from foot to foot. If he'd heard any mention of Angelica, he'd hidden it well. She prayed that he'd missed that part of the conversation, or, if not, that the significance hadn't registered.

He sat down, fiddled with some of the stops, then took a deep breath before letting loose a chord that was so loud she almost fell down the last two steps of the landing.

"Mr. Graham!"

He smiled at her. "Just kidding." He adjusted the stops, looked back at the sheet of music, and eased gently into a Bach sonata.

She frowned and headed to the dining hall, hoping that no one had spilled anything when that silly man blasted their ears off. Peering inside, she first located Mrs. Whitney, who was deep in conversation with Mr. Frick, her back to the door. At the table near the fireplace, Miss Helen sat looking miserable, an empty chair beside her.

Where was the man of the hour?

As if on cue, a blast of cold air swept through the hallway from the opening of the front door. A gentleman in formal attire handed his coat and hat to the butler. He walked the first few steps with an uncertain gait, as if the marble beneath might turn to quicksand, but when he saw Lillian staring at him, he quickened his step and offered a broad smile. "I apologize for my lateness." He gestured to the clipboard. "Mr. Richard Danforth, present and accounted for."

The final piece of the puzzle.

"Thank you, Mr. Danforth." She crossed his name off her list with an exaggerated swipe. "We are delighted to have you."

"May I ask who is expressing this delight?"

"I'm Miss Helen's private secretary, Miss Lilly." It gave her a zing of pride, saying the words *private secretary* out loud. She stood straighter, eager to get him over to Miss Helen's side. He was a nice-looking man, with a cleft chin and mild blue eyes. Would he find Miss Helen frumpy? Or would he be able to see the vulnerable, accomplished woman beneath her veneer of haughtiness?

She passed Mr. Danforth off to a footman, not wanting to attract Mrs. Whitney's attention again by entering the room herself, but peeked through a crack in the door as he was brought around to his setting and graciously took Miss Helen's hand. Miss Helen said something and they both laughed, and then Miss Helen looked over and spied Lillian staring. She winked and turned back to her guest, ever the gracious hostess, as if she did this kind of thing twice a week.

Lillian spent the entire dinner sitting in the main hallway, listening to the strains of the organ. Across from her hung a large Turner oil of the Rhine as it flowed through Cologne, Germany. On the left side of the canvas, a tourist-filled ferry boat floated serenely on calm waters, but her eye was drawn to a scraggy-looking dog drinking river water near a black drainage pipe in the bottom right-hand corner, as workers toiled on the sandy banks. New York had that same mix of beauty and ugliness, the mansions of Fifth Avenue and the slums of the Lower East Side.

The sharp sound of Miss Helen's laughter brought her to her feet. The pitch veered toward hysterical, which Miss Helen fell into whenever she was overstimulated or overtired. Lillian edged to the doorway and looked in. Miss Helen was giggling helplessly by now at something that Mr. Danforth had said, and while he smiled at her mirth, he had turned slightly away, perhaps embarrassed at her unsightly display. Mr. Frick frowned from across the room, staring hard at his daughter.

Lillian ran to the butler's pantry. "Go in there and let Mr. Frick know that it's time for the men to move to the drawing room," she said to Kearns.

"That's not the way it's done," Kearns said. "Mrs. Frick or Miss Helen are to rise first, and encourage the ladies to join them in the Fragonard Room."

Mrs. Frick was too timid to do anything so bold, and it appeared that Miss Helen had lost all sense of time and comportment. "You must. I will explain to Mr. Frick if he complains."

Reluctantly, Kearns entered the room, and she watched as he whispered to Mr. Frick, then pointed right at Lillian.

She locked eyes with him and he nodded, understanding, and rose to his feet.

Miss Helen wasn't going to make this easy.

The next day, Miss Helen was in a good mood, humming to herself as she sat on the chaise longue in her sitting room, leafing through an oversized book on early Renaissance art while Lillian sifted through the thank-you letters from the guests. By all accounts, the dinner party had been a success, and Mr. and Mrs. Frick had even come down to the staff dining room during breakfast and thanked them all for their service. Mrs. Frick had pulled Lillian aside and clasped Lillian's hand in hers. "You've been taking such good care of my daughter," she'd said, as Miss Winnie beamed from behind her.

Miss Helen hadn't brought up their intimate conversation from the night before, and Lillian knew better than to make reference to it. She sliced through another envelope, recognizing the name immediately. "This one's from Mr. Danforth, would you like me to read it out loud?"

Miss Helen slammed the book shut. "No. Hand it over. I'll read it myself."

As she did so, Lillian stacked the others in a neat pile, as she'd been trained to do that first day. By now, it came naturally, and Miss Helen rarely corrected or admonished her.

"Oh my." Miss Helen had one hand to her mouth, so Lillian couldn't tell if she was smiling or frowning.

"What is it? What does his note say?"

"It says that he'd like to call on me." She looked up, her eyebrows knitted with concern. "What shall I write back?"

"You should encourage him. In fact, why not ask him to tea tomorrow?"

"I can't, that would be improper." She let the note fall into her lap. "Perhaps in a week."

"Perhaps in a week you'll have him for tea?"

"Perhaps in a week I'll respond."

That wouldn't do at all. If it were up to Miss Helen, the courtship would go on for years. "But you had such a nice time together."

"I don't know what I'd talk about at tea."

"What did you speak of during dinner?"

"He asked about my dogs, and so I described each one that I've owned over the years, starting with Charlie and ending with Fudgie, and how each had a completely different personality. He said he loves dogs, you see."

Lillian managed a weak smile. "How many dogs have you had over the years?"

"A dozen."

Dear God. "I'm sure he was entranced."

"I couldn't tell, really."

"Well, if you had him to tea, perhaps you could ask him if he's owned any dogs, and listen to what he says?"

Miss Helen considered the idea. "I suppose I could. Here, take a look at what he wrote."

The letter was more than a thank-you note, certainly. Mr. Danforth spoke of Miss Helen's graciousness for the invitation to dine at the residence, but also noted her winning smile and quick wit.

"Oh, Miss Helen, he's interested in you. I can tell."

"Is that right?" Miss Helen looked at her art history book longingly, as if she'd much prefer to dive back into its pages rather than deal with the vagaries of courtship. "Will you write back for me? You'll know what to say better than me."

Lillian jumped at the opportunity. She'd be able to make Miss Helen appear less nutty than she was, and create a foundation that might stick. If it was left up to Miss Helen, goodness knew what she'd say. Something about Fudgie's beefy dog breath, probably.

She sat for a moment, gathering her thoughts, before penning the return note. As Miss Helen, she thanked him for his kind words, which no doubt revealed a doubly kind heart, and asked him to visit tomorrow, when she hoped she could learn more about his interests and desires. The word *desires* was a strong one, but time was of the essence, and she signed it and sealed it before Miss Helen could ask to see it.

"I'll have the footman deliver it this afternoon," Lillian said, "along with the rest of your correspondence."

"No." Miss Helen smoothed her dress. "Take it to him now, yourself. That way I can tell Papsie at luncheon of his response."

Lillian checked the address. He lived in the East Fifties, an easy walk, and she wouldn't mind getting some fresh air. She'd pull the veil of her cloche down over her eyes in case she passed an acquaintance. Or Mrs. Whitney.

"Your advice last night helped me immensely, Miss Lilly," said Miss Helen. "At first, when I walked into the gallery and all of those people turned to stare at me, I wanted to run away, back to my room. But then I imagined them all in the altogether, and it made me smile and then they all smiled back."

"Well done!"

"However, I didn't do so with Mr. Danforth. First of all, it wouldn't be proper, and second of all, I didn't need to. By then, I was feeling ever so confident."

Good girl, Lillian almost said, before correcting herself: "I'm sure you were, Miss Helen."

Lillian collected her hat and handbag and headed out. It was unseasonably warm, and the October sun brightened the facades of the shops along Madison Avenue. At a florist, she stopped to admire some rust-colored chrysanthemums, and vowed to buy a bouquet for her room on the way back. She'd been saving every penny of her paycheck, and deserved a little pleasure for all of her hard work.

Mr. Danforth's residence was in the city's Turtle Bay neighborhood, one of a long line of brownstones. Lillian let herself through the wrought iron gate to ring the bell.

A manservant, stooped with age, answered. She explained her errand and asked if she might wait for a response to take back to her mistress. He paused a moment before ushering her into a parlor of dark wood walls and overstuffed chairs. After he left, she slowly turned around, taking in the room. It was as different from the Fricks' mansion as could be, a throwback to the Victorian era, with almost every space filled with vases, framed photographs, and lace doilies. There was barely room to maneuver without knocking over a table topped by a bulbous glass lamp, or tripping over an embroidered footstool that had seen better days.

Mr. Danforth rushed into the room holding the note in his hand. He saw Lillian, and a look of relief washed over his face. "Hello, Miss Lilly. The private secretary, is that right?"

"It is."

"For a moment, when my man told me we had a female visitor, I thought Miss Helen might have come to deliver her invitation in person."

She wasn't sure if his relief was due to not wanting Miss Helen to see the state of his residence, or not wanting to see Miss Helen. "My mistress is otherwise occupied this morning."

"Of course, she must be a busy woman, no doubt."

"Her social calendar is quite full," Lillian lied.

"Well, thank you. I see she sent along an invitation to tea."

"She asked that I wait for a reply, if that doesn't inconvenience you."

"I suppose not." He gestured around the room. "I hope the surroundings don't cause you too much distress. I can only imagine what it's like coming from the Frick mansion to my humble abode. A study in contrasts."

He had been worried about the decor, then, not Miss Helen's presence.

"This is my family's home," he continued, "where I grew up, and where my parents lived until they passed away earlier this year, from the Spanish flu."

He was most likely still mourning the loss, then. Unable to throw anything out. She understood the inclination to keep things as they were. After Kitty died, Lillian didn't get rid of any of her clothes or shoes. Whenever she opened the armoire, a wave of sadness would wash over her. But then, as she glanced at the individual items, the memories would bring her a muted joy. Like that of her mother dancing around the flat in her alligator-trimmed, Louis-heeled shoes, which Lillian had bought as a surprise after a particularly lucrative session.

By now, all of their belongings had probably been left out on the street to be picked over by scavengers. The thought of her mother's slips and stockings, dumped into the trash to clear out the apartment for the next tenant, made her want to weep.

"Miss Lilly, are you all right?" He gestured to the sofa. "Would you like to sit down? It's warm out there, I know."

She sat as he poured her some water from a pitcher. She took several sips, letting the cool liquid revive her, bring her back to the present.

"Thank you, this helps." She placed the glass on a side table, next to a photograph of a handsome-looking couple. The man had the same sharp chin as Mr. Danforth. "Are these your parents?"

"Yes. Taken several years ago." He avoided looking at the photograph as he answered her.

"My mother died in February of the flu," Lillian volunteered. "She was getting better, I thought, and then she declined so rapidly."

"I'm sorry to hear that. So you understand."

She nodded.

"In any event, I assure you I am planning on updating the decor, as soon as I have time. I don't plan on living in an homage to the last century forever."

"One can't rush mourning."

He studied her in the dim light. "You're very wise. How long have you been Miss Helen's secretary?"

"It's a month today."

"You did a bang-up job organizing last night's festivities."

"Thank you. Really, Miss Helen is the one in charge, I simply carry out her instructions."

"She seems to enjoy her hounds greatly."

His face remained neutral. She couldn't tell if he was making fun of Miss Helen or not. His actual response to the invitation hadn't been forthcoming, not yet, and this might be Lillian's only opportunity to convince Mr. Danforth to accept it, especially if the conversation last night hadn't been quite as successful as Miss Helen believed. "She does love her dogs. But she's also well traveled, well versed in the arts. Miss Helen has a more forceful personality than other society ladies, but I find it refreshing. Did you know she went to France during the war?"

"Miss Helen?"

"Yes. She volunteered with the Red Cross, and was practically on the front lines with the soldiers." Lillian couldn't believe she had to be the one supplying this vital information. Miss Helen should have brought it up herself; it would have been easy enough to do.

"Well, that makes me admire her even more. What a terrible time, for all of us."

"I do believe that you and Miss Helen might find you have a great deal in common, if you give her a chance. Will you give her a chance?"

"You're quite a fierce advocate of your mistress."

A thousand dollars bought quite a deal of advocacy. Probably better not to share that tidbit with him. "Will you come?"

He studied Lillian for a moment before heading to the writing desk near the front window. "I shall. I'll compose a note for you to take back to her now. If you like, I can have some coffee sent up while you wait."

"That would be most kind."

She watched him as he took a pen out of a drawer along with a page of stationery paper. He was quite handsome, in a boyish way, but his movements were tentative, reminding her of the way he'd entered the Frick house, the uncertainty of his gait. It was as if he were trying to maintain control of himself, to become neither too excited nor too sad, fighting for a middle ground that didn't upset the equilibrium of the moment.

She sipped the coffee the butler brought and studied the room more closely, noticing that the wallpaper curled down from the crown molding in sections, and the rugs were quite worn. Miss Helen's fortune would certainly help matters, if the household's disarray was an indication of the state of his finances. The grandfather clock chimed eleven, yet Mr. Danforth had only scribbled a few words, and was now staring out the window, lost in some other place or time.

"Mr. Danforth." When she spoke, he jumped as if she'd broken the silence with a loud cry.

"Yes, sorry?"

"I didn't mean to startle you. I really should be heading back."

"Right." He ran a hand through his hair. "May I admit something?"

"Of course."

"Miss Helen's letter was quite charming. I feel my response will be rather dull in comparison." He stared down at the note. "What do you think I ought to say? I want to convey my interest, but not appear unseemly."

Lillian rose and stood behind him, looking down at the note. All that was written on it was Miss Helen's name and the date. Did she have to do everything? For goodness' sake, she was a Cyrano de Bergerac squared, writing love letters to herself. "I'd be happy to help."

She rattled off a couple of sweet sentences, followed by a request that he use the occasion to meet Fudgie the hound. "That should do it."

He signed it and sealed it in an envelope, his relief palpable. "That's that, then. Are you walking back or taking a car?"

"It's a lovely day, I was planning on walking."

"Do you mind if I join you part of the way? I have a luncheon at the Plaza, which is on your way. I'd be happy to escort you."

"Of course."

❧

The fresh air and sunshine revived Mr. Danforth, and he spoke freely, giving Lillian a behind-the-scenes account of some of the guests at the dinner. He also described his upbringing, having attended a posh boys' school in Manhattan, followed by four years at Harvard. His mother had come from the South, and her family owned a number of cotton mills. Mr. Danforth's father had run the business until his death.

"Have you taken over the family business, then?"

"For now. It's been sadly declining in production and revenue, even before my father died. I was supposed to go into the office today, but I simply couldn't bear it. I'm glad I stayed home, though, as your appearance has certainly brightened it."

"What would you prefer to do, if not the family business?"

He hesitated before speaking, as if trying to decide whether it was safe to confide in her. "I believe this century is going to be an exciting one when it comes to medicine. I'd like to be a doctor. Help people who are ill."

"Is it too late to switch careers?"

"It appears to be."

Meaning, if the match came through, he'd be swept up into the Frick family business. Then again, Miss Helen was attempting to fashion her own life with the library idea, independent from her family, in spite of her father's opposition. She might enjoy having a husband who worked in medicine. Lillian made a note to herself to mention it as a topic of conversation for tomorrow.

By now, they had reached the fountain in front of the Plaza. It always

reminded Lillian of an aquatic wedding cake, with tiers of water splash-
ing down, one over the other, and at the very top, the bronze statue of
the goddess Pomona.

Mr. Danforth stared up at it. "I'm always curious why they chose the
goddess of fruit trees for this particular location."

"I'm impressed that you know that," she said.

"I mean, she is holding a basket of fruit."

Lillian laughed. She recalled the weight of it, of having to hold it off
to the side and slightly bent over, which had sent her back into spasm.
How lovely it was to see it out here, in the fresh air, where anyone who
wanted could walk right up and study it. That was what she'd loved most
about being reproduced in marble to adorn the city's buildings and
bridges, that the works of art weren't hidden away in private houses or
fancy museums; they were for anyone to enjoy. "The fountain was designed by Thomas Hastings, the same architect who designed the Frick
house. The statue was by Karl Bitter. Pomona, the goddess, represents
abundance."

Mr. Danforth turned to her. "Now *I'm* impressed. I see why you're a
good fit for the Frick household." He looked back up at the statue. "Pomona." He looked at Lillian. "I'll say, that's incredible."

She shouldn't have drawn attention to it. What had she been thinking? "I really should go."

"No, hold on." He put a hand on her arm and pointed upwards. "You
have the same profile as our goddess there. Do you see it?"

On one hand, it sent a surge of pride through Lillian that he'd recognized her. It was like when she was at the height of her modeling
career, feted and heralded as a great artists' muse, almost as well-known
as the artists themselves. She'd imagined traveling to Europe to pose for
Degas and Picasso, using her fame as a springboard to film acting. The
possibilities had been endless.

But Mr. Danforth was heading into dangerous territory. Lillian didn't answer, but instead made herself blush. It wasn't difficult. After all, he was comparing Miss Helen's private secretary to a naked woman. In public.

"Oh my. I'm sorry. That's very forward of me. But I wasn't talking about, well, the rest of her. I meant the shape of the face. Oh, God. I'm making it worse, aren't I?"

She should respond like a blushing maiden and leave quickly, but she couldn't stand the idea of the poor man twisting in the wind. He didn't deserve that. So she looked at him straight in the eye, a reassuring smile on her face. "It's fine, Mr. Danforth. Miss Helen will see you tomorrow, yes?"

"I'll be there, I promise."

At that, she headed uptown, eager to escape further scrutiny.

Chapter Ten

"Miss Lilly, Mrs. Frick would like you to join her in the breakfast room."

The other servants gathered around the basement dining table looked up at Miss Winnie in the doorway, then over at Lillian. "Fancy stuff," said Bertha, who sat next to Lillian. "You'll probably get the good coffee up there."

She rose and followed Miss Winnie down the back hall, her swaying hips bringing to mind the Clydesdale horses that transported barrel-stacked carts around the city.

According to Miss Helen's breathless report yesterday, the tea with Mr. Danforth had been a success—she'd remembered to ask two questions for every one he asked of her—and they had plans to walk in Central Park with Mrs. Frick later that day. Miss Helen had been brimming with happiness as she recounted the visit, and Lillian figured it wouldn't be long before they'd announce the engagement, and she'd collect her money and head to California.

In the breakfast room, a buttery sun streamed through the windows. Above the sideboard hung a Millet painting of a peasant woman sewing by lamplight. The simplicity of her dress and the gloominess of the setting were an odd fit for this room, which boasted a fireplace of two different types of Italian marble, silk patterned wall hangings, and an elaborate folding screen in one corner.

Mrs. Frick noticed Lillian's stare. "Mr. Frick insisted the Millet be placed in the breakfast room, as a daily reminder that he came from nothing. Please, sit down."

Lillian and Miss Winnie took their places at the table. Mrs. Frick had stayed mainly out of sight these past weeks, only appearing when she was absolutely required to. Now that Lillian had gotten to know how the house was run, part of her couldn't help but resent the woman's lack of participation. Everything fell on Miss Helen's shoulders—and thereby Lillian's—when it really should have been Mrs. Frick's responsibility.

"Mr. Frick has certainly accomplished a lot." Lillian unfolded her napkin. "I didn't know that he came from nothing."

"He only went to school in the winter months, yet owned his first company by the age of twenty-two. I think that's why sometimes he gets frustrated with the children, with their silly squabbles." A maid poured coffee into cups and saucers patterned with magnolias. "My daughter says you have an eye for art."

"Not really. Her expertise is far beyond mine."

"Well, I must say that you appear to be working magic with her, in more ways than one. We hear the tea with Mr. Danforth went well, yesterday." Mrs. Frick looked over at Miss Winnie, who nodded sagely.

"I believe so." Lillian suppressed the temptation to knock wood.

"My husband will be pleased to hear it."

Lillian took a sip of the coffee; it was indeed much better than the kind they served downstairs. Or maybe the fine china only made it seem so.

"I'm curious, Miss Lilly, what you think of Mr. Danforth," Mrs. Frick asked once the maid had left.

"He appears to be a quite suitable suitor," said Lillian.

Miss Winnie chuckled but stopped when Mrs. Frick didn't crack a smile.

"A suitable suitor," echoed Mrs. Frick. "You're making a joke. Do you *not* find him a suitable suitor?"

"Not at all," said Lillian quickly, backtracking. Mrs. Frick was difficult to read. "I believe they might make a good match. Of course I haven't been employed here long, but Miss Helen seems to be as excited about Mr. Danforth as she is about the library."

"The library." Mrs. Frick put down her cup and grimaced. "Mr. Frick and I both say better to leave such an undertaking to the scholars and universities, not our silly Helen. Especially once she's married. We can't have that."

Lillian hoped she could make her see otherwise. "These days, things are different. Women are encouraged to have outside passions, just as men are. After all, we have the right to vote. Why stop there?"

"A woman's passion should be her husband and children."

Funny for her to say that, considering that Mrs. Frick rarely left her rooms and didn't show much of a passion for anything, leaving it to her daughter to act as her husband's companion.

Mrs. Frick sat back in her chair, hands in her lap. "I know what you're thinking, that I'm not a good example of what I preach. But I'm ill, you see."

As far as Lillian could tell, Mrs. Frick's color was a healthy pink, her build sturdy and strong.

"When the children were very young, I was different." She looked at Miss Winnie. "You remember? How light and gay I was."

"Such a gay young thing," Miss Winnie repeated.

"When Helen was a child, she took on the impossible burden of trying to make me and her father happy after a grueling time. She succeeded with one of us." The words trembled on her tongue.

"Now, now, Mrs. Frick," Miss Winnie said. "Let's not dwell on the past."

But Lillian wanted to know more. Something awful had rocked this family to its core, and her curiosity was piqued. She'd asked Bertha the other night about the long-dead sister, but Bertha had only offered up what Lillian already knew, that there had been some lingering illness.

"I'm so sorry, Mrs. Frick," Lillian said. "Miss Helen speaks very fondly of Martha."

Mrs. Frick's eyes turned red. She grabbed her handkerchief from under her sleeve and covered her mouth. "I can't." She shoved her chair back from the table and trundled to the door, her skirts swishing beneath her. Miss Winnie tried to follow, but Mrs. Frick waved one hand behind her, the other still pressed to her mouth. "Leave me alone for now," she mumbled into her fist. She paused at the doorway. "But in a half hour bring me my rose water."

Lillian remained seated at the table, stunned. "I'm sorry, I didn't mean to upset Mrs. Frick."

Miss Winnie poured herself more coffee. "She gets this way, sometimes. It always passes."

The tragedy had occurred decades ago, yet the child's name still couldn't be raised without sending Mrs. Frick running from the room. Lillian had known other families who'd lost children, from accidents, scarlet fever, mumps—there were so many ways for vulnerable young children to succumb—but the surviving relatives eventually soldiered on. Then again, maybe Lillian couldn't understand, not having had children, or even siblings, herself. She'd never really had an itch to get married and settle down, as there was so much else out there to experience, and Kitty's sour outlook on the subject undoubtedly influenced her own.

Miss Winnie waited a moment before speaking. "Before she became ill, Martha was a joy of a child, with pink lips, curls, a delightful disposition. To think I was barely a girl myself when I joined the household back then. All of thirteen years old, imagine that? Unfortunately, the first three years of Miss Helen's life were the last three of her sister's, which meant Miss Helen was surrounded, every day, with pain and illness. You may have seen Martha's image scattered about the house."

That was an understatement. "She was a pretty child. May I ask what happened to her?"

Miss Winnie glanced toward the door, as if checking that Mrs. Frick was truly gone. "When the family was on tour in Europe together, they hired a foreign nursemaid. For two years after that fateful trip, our Martha was in terrible pain, and no one knew why. Her symptoms came and went, so they'd think she was fine one day, before falling ill the next. The Fricks brought in doctor after doctor, who told them she was teething, or it was acute indigestion, but no cure ever worked. One morning, a strange bump appeared on her hip. It was filled with pus, and, to the doctor's astonishment, a dressmaker's pin emerged from the wound. Without proper supervision in Europe, Martha had picked up and swallowed this tiny, deadly piece of metal, which had slowly wound its way through her body and worked itself back out. But it was too late by then. She had two more years of lingering sepsis, and passed away in terrible agony. On the anniversary of Martha's death every year, Mr. Frick calls me into his study, takes out a lock of hair that belonged to her, and pours us both a drink. Then we toast to her memory." A dark shadow crossed her face. She lowered her voice, even though no one else was around. "Don't tell Mrs. Frick about that, she wouldn't approve."

How interminable it must have been for Mr. and Mrs. Frick, when Martha was in pain but no one could figure out why, and then the grisly discovery of the pin? There were no words. Lillian understood now why

Miss Helen was always fighting her way up from feeling second best. She was the daughter who'd lived, and whose close resemblance to Martha only reminded them of their loss. "I'm so sorry."

Miss Winnie let out a loud exhale. "Many, many years ago, that all was. You'd never know it, though."

Lillian thought of the cameo and the checkbook, all those portraits spread about the house. Her heart went out to Miss Helen, for the futility of her role in the family. It wasn't her fault that Martha had died. She ought to go off and build her library, just as Mr. Danforth ought to pursue a medical career—who cared what the rest of them thought?

Even though Lillian's future was financially dependent on the success of Mr. Danforth and Miss Helen's engagement, and she liked Mr. Danforth and held a tenuous respect for Miss Helen, she hated to think that her misrepresentations to them both might result in a disastrous match. Miss Winnie had been with the family forever; she knew each member inside and out. Lillian couldn't help but ask, "Do you think this marriage is a good idea?"

Miss Winnie answered without missing a beat. "Probably not. Then again, Mrs. Frick and Mr. Frick have managed."

Lillian hoped that Mr. Danforth and Miss Helen would do better than those two.

"Don't let Mr. Frick and Mrs. Frick fool you, there's still a spark between them, in spite of all the years." Miss Winnie pointed to a pink magnolia blossom that lay at Mrs. Frick's place setting. "Every morning, without fail, Mr. Frick selects a flower from the arrangement in the front hallway, then brings it down to the kitchen so they can deliver it up to Mrs. Frick with her breakfast."

In spite of herself, Lillian was touched at the thought of Mr. Frick dawdling over a vase of flowers, searching for the exact right one. She could imagine Mr. Danforth doing something similar. But still, would they really work as a couple? "Mr. Danforth is not wealthy, you know." Lillian hoped she came across as concerned, not as a gossip.

"They know all about that. There's nothing to be hidden from New York high society. I don't think they care. Miss Helen's over thirty, after all."

"Then why bother? She's rather set in her ways."

"Mr. Frick insists. I suppose he's feeling his age lately. He wants to be sure she's taken care of." Miss Winnie paused and studied Lillian. "Why all the questions? Do you think they're a bad match?"

If she wasn't careful, she'd sabotage all of her hard work. She needed this marriage to happen, there was no question about that, and as Miss Winnie implied, Miss Helen and Mr. Danforth were as good a pair as any.

Now that she was embedded with the Frick family, it was easy for Lillian to forget how vulnerable she was out there in the world. She must keep in mind what was at stake: a web of scandal and possibly jail, or an escape far away with Mr. Frick's betrothal bonus. "I'm more than happy for her." Lillian finished her coffee and rose. "Like you said, they'll get used to each other and figure it out. Eventually."

Later, in Miss Helen's sitting room, Lillian was finishing up the day's love note from Miss Helen to Mr. Danforth when Mr. Frick entered the room.

"Is my daughter here?"

She knew better than to divulge that Miss Helen was working in the basement that morning. "She went out for an errand, I believe. Can I help you?" As she spoke, she slid the note closer to her body, but doing so only attracted Mr. Frick's attention.

"What are you writing there?" he asked, stepping forward and looking over her shoulder. Up close, he smelled of peppermint and a woody aftershave. He let out a sharp exhale of breath and maneuvered around the desk, lowering his massive frame into the wooden chair across from her. She hoped it would hold his bulk. "You're writing a love letter from my daughter, aren't you?"

How to explain? "Miss Helen has directed me to do so."

"Even better, I bet it was your idea in the first place." He pointed his finger at her. "I'm right, aren't I?"

Today appeared to be the day she was going to upset both elder Fricks in the span of a few hours. So be it. "As her secretary, I'm hired to put her thoughts onto the page."

"Her thoughts? Or yours?"

She waited him out without answering.

"Oh, I don't mind," he said with a wave of his hand. "That's what our agreement was about, after all. I rather like your initiative. You remind me of myself, we both know how to pull strings, to get others to do our bidding. You're a chameleon, which is what I was when I started out, working as a desk clerk, pleasing whoever was in charge, but making sure that I pleased *his* boss even more. I like the fact that neither of us is afraid to take a creative approach in carving out a path to success."

One of the richest men in America had just admired Lillian's skills, had said they were alike, and a small smile escaped her lips at the thought. Yet she didn't want to be too much like Mr. Frick. She heartily disapproved of the way he pitted his family members against each other. Besides, her reasoning for manipulating Miss Helen and Mr. Danforth was driven by her dire circumstances, while Mr. Frick's was more malicious, more darkly gleeful.

"Do you like living here, Miss Lilly?" he asked.

The change of subject was a relief. "I certainly do. To be able to view a Gainsborough portrait or an ethereal Hoppner day after day is one of the most heavenly experiences of my life."

"I do like being surrounded by beautiful women." His smile grew even wider. "Even if some of them are only two-dimensional."

No doubt Mr. Frick preferred the mystery of the portraits to the real-life complications of his wife and daughter. "Maybe that's the reason for their allure." She couldn't believe she was being so forward. But he didn't disagree. He stared out the window, and when he finally spoke, his voice wavered.

"As I said, you are astute. I seem to have failed with the women in my life; to them I'm a disagreeable old coot. I do love them, though." He rose stiffly to his feet and pulled out a handkerchief. "I must go. Enough of this wasting the day. Tell Helen I was looking for her."

He was gone before she could answer.

Lillian was overseeing the packing of Miss Helen's trunk by Bertha when Miss Helen dashed into the room with a stack of books.

"You must find room for these, Bertha."

Bertha stared at the pile of books, then back at the trunk, which was already bursting with underclothes and dresses. "There's none."

"Then go to the trunk room and bring another one in."

Bertha left, but not before giving Lillian an eye roll behind Miss Helen's back. Lillian took the books from Miss Helen's arms and gently placed them on the bed. "More research for the library?"

"Of course. I can't afford to lose an entire week."

Mr. Frick had been feeling unwell and his doctor recommended sea air as a cure, so the family was headed to Eagle Rock, their estate on the Massachusetts shoreline. Lillian was to stay behind, and she looked forward to seven days of relative freedom. It would give her time to catch up on the bookkeeping and file invoices, among other duties. To do so without interruption gave her a strange thrill of excitement. Making the monthly books balance or firmly declining an invitation with a sweet note of regret was her forte, it turned out. For now.

Even better, she planned to put on her veiled hat and head to Times Square to see Mary Pickford in the motion picture *Daddy-Long-Legs*, in order to study her technique. It would be good preparation for California, and she deserved a break, after all the hard work of the past six weeks.

"How did it go last night?" Lillian asked without looking at Miss Helen.

"Wonderful. We heard Rachmaninoff, and after, Mr. Danforth walked me all the way home."

Things were going beautifully, and Lillian's earlier worries about the match were unfounded, thank goodness. "Imagine, soon enough you'll be walking down the aisle." She was laying it on a little thick, but there was no time to waste. "Did you invite Mr. Danforth to Eagle Rock?"

"He can't come along, some phooey business nonsense. Probably better he not get to know Mother and Papsie too well right off, as there will be plenty of time for that when he moves in after the wedding."

"Moves in. Here?" Lillian couldn't think of a worse way to begin a marriage than living in the Frick house, under the intense scrutiny of Miss Helen's father.

"Of course he'll move in here. This is where all of my research is. And Papsie, of course. Anyway, I asked Mr. Danforth if he'd miss me, and he said he certainly would. Then he kissed my hand." She paused. "Then I told him I had a surprise for him."

"What's that?"

Her cheeks burned with excitement. She went to her nightstand and picked up an envelope with Mr. Danforth's name written on it. "I've put together a scavenger hunt for him to do while I'm gone."

"A scavenger hunt? Where?"

"Here, of course, all around the house. There are twenty clues hidden about, and in here is the very first one. When he comes, you can give him the envelope and then let him wander about. It will get him acquainted with the items that are most dear to Papsie and me. If he's going to join the family, we must make sure he's fluent in the collection. That's requisite number one."

Lillian put a smile on her face, not letting on how little she wished to have to babysit Mr. Danforth this week. "How nice of you. Do you know when he's going to visit?"

"No. But he promised he'd find the time. You'll be here to receive him, of course. And you have Thanksgiving dinner to plan. I've left some notes with my ideas for the menu." She pointed to a messy pile of papers. "Somewhere in there. You can straighten out my desk while you're at it."

So much for her free time. Lillian swallowed a sigh and continued packing.

The day after the family left, the house quieted down, as if it were going into hibernation without its owners around. There was no organ music, no food service, and the staff were allowed to take mornings or afternoons off, as long as the basic needs of the mansion were met. Lillian did manage to get out one afternoon, merrily shirking her duties and spending the hours in a dark picture palace. She adored everything about *Daddy-Long-Legs*—the costumes, the shining eyes of Mary Pickford, the elaborate sets. She could see herself right there in the middle of it all. Angelica, no longer a frozen creature of stone but a live woman, thinking and feeling and saying lines out loud, even if the audience wouldn't be able to hear her voice. She could do this; she was certain of it.

When she'd posed as Angelica, the artists would often ask her to step down from the raised platform during a session and ask her opinion of their work, listening carefully to what she said. She'd relished being part of the artistic process. In fact, the more she considered it, the more she realized that her command of the art world had given her a leg up not only as an aspiring starlet, but also as an employee of the Frick household. She instinctively knew what role she should play at any given time: confidante when speaking with Mr. Frick, older sister when talking about courtship with Miss Helen, trusted secretary when handling Miss Helen's affairs. She was already an actress, in many ways.

After the film, she walked to Grand Central and asked one of the clerks in the information booth the best way to get from New York to Los Angeles. He handed over the schedule for the 20th Century Limited, which headed to Chicago, where she would transfer to the Los Angeles Limited. She imagined the landscape of America rolling by from the train window, leaving the entire Frick family farther behind with every passing mile.

She bought a newspaper on her way home, and leafed through it before chucking it in the trash can. There was only one mention of Angelica in connection with the Watkins murder, and at the very bottom of the article. The trial was scheduled for January, but she'd be long gone by then.

The next day, Mr. Danforth arrived promptly at four o'clock, looking wary. Lillian met him in the library, where she handed over the sealed envelope and gave him Miss Helen's instructions, including the fact that Lillian was not to assist Mr. Danforth in any way.

"I'm sorry, I-I'm supposed to do what?" he stammered.

"It's a scavenger hunt. I'm not sure, exactly, what she had in mind. She didn't let me in on the planning. You're to read whatever's in this and follow it, and then you'll be directed to the next clue. And so on."

"How many clues are there?"

"Twenty."

He laughed. "Leave it to Miss Helen to keep me occupied while she's away. I assured her that a week was not an imposition in the least, that she should go and take care of her father and enjoy herself at the sea."

"I don't think she means to keep you occupied. She wants to share the treasures of the house with you, so you understand the passion that she and her father have for their art collection."

"Right. Hand it over. I shall begin."

She did so and watched as he opened it. "Best of luck to you."

Within a half hour, one of the parlor maids knocked on the door to Miss Helen's sitting room, where Lillian was working. "Mr. Danforth is asking for you," she said. "He's in the art gallery."

"That didn't take long," she joked as she entered.

"This is some kind of a test and I am sure to fail it," Mr. Danforth said, a note of panic behind his words. "I don't know much about art, and I haven't even found the first clue. I worry about disappointing Miss Helen. I know you've been given strict rules, but will you help?"

The note was dated *November 1919* at the top, with 1/20 written in the top right corner.

> *You're about to set out on a quest for the magnificent magnolia treasure*
> *To offer you this puzzle gives me great pleasure*
> *A tiny box holds the first clue*
> *To find it, search for the putti*
> *Where my father used to fulfill his duty.*

Lillian didn't know much about poetry, but she knew it was a terrible rhyme.

"A *tiny box*? This house is enormous," said Mr. Danforth. "If all the clues are like this, I'll still be looking when they return."

"Let me think." Lillian looked around. "Mr. Frick's office is there at the far end of the gallery, where I assume he fulfills his duty. I remember

Miss Helen telling me that it used to be on the opposite side, before they acquired J. P. Morgan's collection of Limoges enamels."

They walked over to the enamels room, which Lillian had never liked. It was heavily paneled and cave-like, the opposite of the simplicity and clean lines of the other rooms on the first floor, as if the architect had focused all of his fussiest inclinations on one of the smallest spaces.

"Could that be it?" He pointed to a tiny jewel-colored box. Lillian recognized it immediately from Miss Helen's cataloguing.

"I think you're right. As far as I know, it's a marriage casket, decorated with putti, or cherubs."

"*Marriage casket*—what an odd combination of words."

"I agree. It's enamel, from the mid-sixteenth century." She was amazed at what she'd retained.

Mr. Danforth drew close and let out a whistle. "They appear to be playing instruments, or flirting."

"I don't know what the inscriptions say. How's your French?"

"Quite good, but this is Old French. *Loves give joy. Defeated by love.* Do you think the next clue's inside?"

Carefully, Lillian lifted the lid to reveal a piece of paper, which she handed to Mr. Danforth.

He refused to take it. "You can't leave this only to me. I promise not to tell Miss Helen you assisted, but you simply must."

"I'm not sure I should."

"Please." He paused. "And before you say yes or no, please accept my apologies for what happened at our last parting. At the fountain. I did not mean to imply anything untoward."

If he only knew. She allowed herself a maidenly blush and bit her lip the same way Mary Pickford had in *Daddy-Long-Legs*. "Of course, Mr. Danforth. No offense taken, I assure you."

"Thank you." He read the next clue, labeled 2/20, out loud: "*Stay where you are / Halt / And look for the pillar of salt.* Hmm, is there a salt-shaker here?" Mr. Danforth looked about.

"She's referring to the biblical story of Lot and his wife." Lillian turned and spotted her prey: a wide copper cup. "Over here."

They stood side by side, staring down at a wide cup of brilliant blue enamel. Lillian pointed out the details. "There's Lot, with his wife as a pillar of salt off in the distance." Her Catholic school upbringing had finally paid off.

"Right. She looked back at Sodom when the angels warned her not to. Never a good idea."

The scene was full of movement. Flames licked a city in one corner, trees with roots like fingers appeared in another, yet the eye immediately went to the exposed breast of one of the daughters, the flesh tone like a beacon in a colorscape of greens and blues. At the end of the story, Lillian remembered, Lot's two daughters get their father drunk and seduce him.

Good Lord. Only Miss Helen would find this sordid scene appropriate for inclusion. But Lillian knew why. Miss Helen only saw the beauty of the object, not the awkward seduction scene depicted, never mind how it might put off a potential suitor.

Mr. Danforth cleared his throat. "Um, right."

Before he could run screaming from the room, Lillian lifted the cup's base, where another clue lay, which led them to an eighteenth-century bronze bust in the library. From there, they were directed to a Degas oil painting of ballet dancers in the north hall. It was no easy task, and figuring out which work Miss Helen was referring to required multiple sweeps through each room. Soon enough, the sun was setting.

Mr. Danforth looked rather ragged. "I might as well move in and spend the week here instead of working."

Lillian had to do something if she wanted the engagement to come off successfully. "Why don't you come back each day, and I'll assist you until it's completed? We'll take a bit at a time."

"Would you do that?"

"Of course. And you should know that Miss Helen is planning on creating a library for art, which is another good reason for you to become familiar with the collection."

"A woman running a library? Would her father allow such a thing? I'm surprised."

She disapproved of his reaction, but didn't want to put him off. "If you want to win her over, I suggest you not denigrate the idea."

"Of course, you're absolutely right. Because I do want to please her. If you don't mind my taking you into my confidence, I'm planning on asking her to marry me on Thanksgiving."

Two weeks away.

Not long at all.

Once Mr. Frick paid up, Lillian would make some excuse about a sick aunt in California and be on the next train out. The nuptial arrangements would have to be taken care of by the next private secretary they hired. Lillian hoped whoever it was would be able to guide Miss Helen to an appropriate bridal dress, as Miss Helen might very well show up in a bustle-backed monstrosity if left to her own devices.

"That's wonderful," she said. "Have you asked for Miss Helen's hand from Mr. Frick yet?"

"I did, right before they departed for Eagle Rock. All is on course. That reminds me, Mr. Frick sent me this letter, to give to you." He reached into his coat pocket and pulled out a piece of paper. "Here."

The letter asked that Miss Lillian give Mr. Danforth the check that sat on the desk in his sitting room, the sum of which was to be used to purchase Miss Helen's engagement ring.

"It's rather embarrassing, to be honest." Mr. Danforth didn't meet her eyes. "I would have used my mother's ring, but it's not nearly as elegant as someone like Miss Helen should wear. Mr. Frick is aware of my reduced financial circumstances, which I'm sure you noticed during your visit. I know things are not typically done this way, and I hope that you, as a private secretary who probably knows the rules of courtship inside and out, aren't too shocked."

She placed a reassuring hand on his arm. "What is most important is that Miss Helen is happy, and I'm sure whatever you choose will give her great pleasure. I'll retrieve your check now."

As Lillian passed Miss Helen's bedchamber on the second floor, she remembered the Magnolia diamond tucked inside Martha's cameo in the jewel box. That would make a perfect engagement ring, but of course doing so would probably be considered a desecration to the girl's memory by Mr. and Mrs. Frick. How terribly unfair it all was to Miss Helen.

The check sat in the center of Mr. Frick's desk, the image of Martha looming up at Lillian. Back downstairs, she presented it to Mr. Danforth, who was waiting outside under the porte-cochère.

"You are a treasure, Miss Lilly, for your understanding and kindness. I will not forget it, I promise."

She watched, smiling, as he walked away. Only two weeks to go.

Three days into the scavenger hunt, Lillian and Mr. Danforth had culled through only ten of the twenty clues. Miss Helen's missives were hidden on the backs of frames, under bronzes, and in table drawers. One was discovered tucked under a corner of the rug in the living hall, where they stood staring at the dour Holbein portrait of Thomas Cromwell. When she and Mr. Danforth both knelt down at the same time to retrieve it, they bonked heads, hard. Each fell back on the floor, sitting on their rumps, Lillian not caring that she looked as unladylike as she'd ever done, with clothes on, of course.

"How's your head?" Mr. Danforth asked.

"Now it hurts as much on the outside as it does on the inside, from figuring out these absurd clues."

Mr. Danforth froze, his mouth open, before he burst out in laughter. "You are not what I expected from Miss Helen's private secretary."

"No, I suppose not. But then, Miss Helen is a rather unique individual herself."

He stood and held out both hands to help Lillian up. Once she was standing, he remained holding on to her hands. "I want to thank you, sincerely. I don't have the same appreciation of art that the Frick family has, and you've given me the opportunity to not seem such a dolt as I truly am."

For all her early bluster at having to manage Mr. Danforth, over the past few days she'd begun to look forward to their afternoon appointments. She found herself eager to see what they'd discover next, and relished the satisfaction of figuring out the answer. Especially enjoyable were his baffled reactions to each awful poem, which were usually followed by a grandiose reading of it in some vaguely European accent. His utter commitment to such ridiculousness made her laugh every time.

She took a seat on the sofa, still rubbing her head. "First of all, the Fricks don't *appreciate* art, they are *ravenous* about it, in a way that is not usual in the least. Mr. Frick and his daughter treat all of these masterworks like a pictorial stamp collection. They buy paintings worth thousands of dollars on a whim. No, not thousands, millions. The Fragonard panels were one and a quarter million dollars. Can you imagine?" She worried she'd gone too far, rattling on like that about the family's personal finances. "I'm so sorry, that was not very kind," she said.

He joined her on the sofa. "Another reason why you're a breath of fresh air. No need to apologize to me. Those Fragonards would take care of the renovations my townhouse is in dire need of. Along with modern furnishings."

"I understand that you'll move into the house after the wedding."

"Yes. That's the plan." He grew silent.

"Are you worried about that? I assure you, the staff are lovely and it's a divine place to live."

"Oh, no, of course, you're right. I guess it's a matter of parting with my parents' objects, having to disburse them. It's like letting go of a piece of them. If I'd seen them before they died, I might not be so maudlin about it. But the last time we spoke was before I left for Europe, two years earlier. I always assumed they'd be here when I returned. It's hard to move on."

She thought of her mother's clothes. "I know. I had to leave everything of my mother's behind when I fled."

"You what?"

"When I left."

He didn't seem alarmed by her misstatement. "Well, I look forward to working with you once I'm here for good. Miss Helen and I may need an interpreter, at times. I have to confess, she's a funny one. Then again, I'm a little off myself. Maybe we'll make a good match."

A prickle of guilt washed over her, knowing that she wouldn't be here when he moved in. He'd have to find his own way around his new wife and in-laws. Still, she wanted to help. "Mrs. Frick doesn't say much, and rarely leaves her rooms, but Miss Helen more than makes up for it. When she's chatting, it's best to let her run out of steam at her own time. If she's interrupted, she can get quite short. You can never tell what Mr. Frick is thinking, so don't assume because he's quiet and listening that he's not about to erupt in anger, usually about a delinquent payment or an unexpected bill. If he thinks he's being taken advantage of, watch out for the fireworks."

Mr. Danforth had gone pale. She'd said too much.

"This is from my perspective, of course, as an employee. As a son-in-law, you'll be treated quite differently."

When he looked at her, his eyes were slightly glazed. "I don't think I'm up to this."

"Well, we can take a break, come back first thing tomorrow. They're returning on the afternoon train."

"No. I mean any of it."

Was he implying he wasn't up to the marriage? Lillian was causing damage, speaking so openly. At this rate, Mr. Danforth would be running for the hills and the engagement would never happen. And she was so close. "Please don't say that."

He took out a handkerchief and wiped his face. "It's stifling hot in here, don't you think?"

"Look, let's take a quick walk in Central Park. The air will do us both good."

To her relief, Mr. Danforth accepted the offer.

His color returned in the brisk autumn air, and his spirits rose the farther they got from the mansion. "I have an idea," he said. "This way."

They followed the pathway along the East Drive, and as they walked along the southern edge of Turtle Pond she guessed where they were headed. "The castle?"

"Exactly."

Belvedere Castle loomed ahead of them. The first time Lillian and her mother had wandered by it during one of their few walks in the park—Kitty had never been one for meandering constitutionals—Lillian had been entranced. The castle had been constructed upon one of the highest points in the park, a giant cropping of schist that rose out of Turtle Pond, surrounded by elm and plane trees, a fairy-tale fortress in the dead center of a busy American city.

"I've always wondered what it was built for," she said as they climbed the steps that led to one of its terraces. "I imagined that they figured the mayor of New York could live here, like a king reigning over his fiefdom."

"In fact, it was built in the 1870s as a folly, a decorative structure with no real use. Something pretty to look at." Mr. Danforth gently guided her by the elbow to the edge of a terrace facing north, where the great rectangular reservoir of water just beyond Turtle Pond sparkled in the sunlight. "Although now the castle serves as a weather station."

"I'm glad it has a purpose," said Lillian. "Everything ought to have a purpose."

"Including people?"

"Most definitely."

"Miss Helen says that you're quite good at your job, so you can count yourself among the purposeful."

The thought that Miss Helen had complimented Lillian to Mr. Danforth came as something of a shock. "She did?"

"She did. And said that you were quite knowledgeable about art, as I've discovered during our scavenging sessions. Where did you learn so much?"

"Reading books," she answered crisply. "I suppose that means the Frick mansion is the opposite of a folly since Mr. Frick has already designated it as a museum for the city. He built it with a purpose in mind."

Mr. Danforth didn't reply right off. "*To gild refined gold, to paint the lily / To throw a perfume on the violet / Is wasteful and ridiculous excess,*" he recited.

"What's that from?" she asked.

"Shakespeare. *King John.*"

The words were beautiful but the sentiment unnerving, coming out of the mouth of the man designated to marry Miss Helen. "So you're saying that Mr. Frick's collection is one of ridiculous excess?"

"One of his paintings could feed an entire Lower East Side tenement block for years and years. I would add that there's some question whether or not the decision to leave his paintings and mansion to the city springs from guilt."

"Guilt about what?"

"Something that happened ages ago, probably thirty years or so. Long forgotten except by a few, probably."

She waited, and eventually he continued. "Mr. Frick and his rich friends had a private lake for their fishing club upriver from a town called Johnstown in Pennsylvania. There was a dam, which needed repairs, and it burst and pretty much wiped out the entire town. Over two thousand people died."

"How awful. And it was Mr. Frick's fault?"

"His and the other club members', for their negligence in not making the repairs. Afterwards, the members formed a relief committee to help the survivors, but it's rumored that they used their influence to pressure the investigators. No charges were ever made."

Over two thousand people dead. An utter catastrophe. Mr. Frick's reputation had been whitewashed in the ensuing years as he solidified his power, and his increasing wealth made him untouchable.

"So you see, Miss Lilly, the Fricks are the gilded ones of this great city. How lucky for them."

She gave him a look.

"Right, it probably comes across as ludicrous, me saying such a thing. But we Danforths are upper class only in name. My family's business has been in trouble for a long time, preceding my father's death. I have only my butler on hand these days, having had to let go of the valet, the cook, the whole lot of them." He laughed. "In many ways I'm a folly myself, with no purpose other than saving my family's name and fortunes by marrying up. Although, don't get me wrong, I am quite grateful that Miss Helen has found me worthy. She will keep me on my toes, of that I have no doubt."

That Mr. Danforth would feel comfortable enough with Lillian to confide such intimacies gave her a tiny jolt of pleasure, but she was saddened to hear his low consideration of himself.

"You'd mentioned the other day that you wanted to pursue medicine," she asked. "What drew you to that?"

"It's not a pleasant story, I'm afraid."

"That's all right."

"During the war, we were told to be on guard for the smell of garlic, to put on our gas masks at the first whiff. One of my fellow soldiers didn't have a sense of smell, it turns out, and while we were suiting up, he was shuffling a deck of cards, ready for another round of gin rummy in the trenches. Two hours later, he was in blinding pain, throwing up, screaming, and we got him to the medics, where all they could do was pour water over his face to try to flush it out. I'm sure there is more we could have done, instead of watching as he bled out of his nose and mouth, gasping for air as his lungs became ravaged with ulcers. I don't want to stand idly by ever again."

"This is your chance then, Mr. Danforth. Think of what power you'll have to change the world once you're a member of the Frick family. Miss Helen showed as much, during the war, helping refugees by the hundreds. I think you'll make a smashing couple."

He smiled wanly. "I suppose so. Can I confide a secret to you?"

She nodded.

"Before all this started to happen, this business with Miss Helen, I had applied to medical school. A few days ago, I learned that I was accepted."

"That's splendid. Then you must go."

"Well, that may not be so easy, now. The medical school's up in Boston."

A sudden gust of wind blew the scarf off her neck. They both reached for it and missed. Instead, it fluttered down to the rocks below, a slash of crimson amid the gray stone.

"Here, take mine." Mr. Danforth wouldn't accept Lillian's refusal, and before she knew it, his scarf, still warm from his own neck, was wrapped around her own as they headed toward the Frick mansion.

They spoke easily on subjects less fraught than war and gilded lilies during the walk back, the spell of their quiet exchange on the Belvedere terrace broken by the rambunctious presence of other park-goers.

Standing once again in the living room, Mr. Danforth nodded at the drinks trolley. "Do you think I might help myself to some brandy? My nerves."

"Of course."

He rose and poured himself a drink. "I insist you join me," he said.

That wouldn't be prudent. She didn't want the housekeeper or Kearns reporting back that she'd been imbibing the Fricks' good alcohol. Also, it would be scandalous for her to share a drink with Miss Helen's soon-to-be husband with no one else about.

Yet, she reminded herself, she was only *playing* at being a proper private secretary, a fact she really ought to remember if she was going to make a clean break after the engagement announcement. Back when she modeled, her mother would often join the artist in a quick drink after the session, and as she grew older, she was allowed one as well. Even if she'd been freezing cold for three hours straight, the first sip always fired her right back up. She could use that bolt of courage right now. "I accept."

Mr. Danforth took a couple of sips and let out a peaceful sigh. "This is nice. Thank you."

"No thanks are necessary."

He stared out the window at the lawn. "What is it you like about this house?"

She waited a moment before she answered. There was so much to say. The artwork, the carved floral garlands that climbed up the chimney in the library, the park view from her room, and the way the sun made everything turn to gold as it set. "The sense of possibility. That Mr. Frick came from very little and now lives like a king. That anything can happen. For example, if you really wanted, you could be a doctor. There's nothing stopping you."

"What about you? What would you do, Miss Lilly, if you weren't a private secretary?"

She didn't hesitate. "I'd be a silent film star."

She expected him to laugh, to spill his drink from the foolishness of her statement. But he didn't. "You are lovely enough for the stage and screen."

His words hung there, the only sound the ticking of the ebony barometer clock on the table behind them. Neither looked away from the other for a moment, and Lillian's pulse beat double time.

He finished his brandy. "Between our walk and the drink, I'm newly invigorated. Let's get one more clue in. Then I'll head home."

He pulled out the pile of clues from his dress coat pocket. "We're on number ten. *The sound of music is a devious feat / Here at One East Seventieth Street / Find the true source / And you're halfway to the end of the course / Of clues.*"

Lillian made a face. "Please, no Slavic recitations of that one. I couldn't bear it."

"I'll try not to be offended."

"Luckily, I think I know what she's referring to. Follow me."

She led him up the front stairway to the first landing and pointed to the organ's pipes, which were divided by four marble colonnettes. "I have it from a trusted source that these pipes are fakes." Up on the second floor, she turned left past the elevators and pushed open the wide mahogany door at the end of the hall. "This room is called the organ chamber, although I admit I've never been in here before."

To the left was a narrow aisle lined on either side with layers of pipes, thousands of them. They were of various heights and diameters, some no bigger than a drinking straw, others as wide as a man's leg, rising right to the ceiling. Unlike the fancy facade on the other side of the wall, these were utilitarian, but to Lillian, they were beautiful, even dizzying. It was like walking inside a three-dimensional work of art.

They ventured carefully. A misstep would be disastrous, to both the organ and the person who fell. "Our organist, Mr. Graham, says that there are four thousand seven hundred pipes in here," she said.

While she'd tried to avoid Mr. Graham after the encounter with Mrs. Whitney, a couple of weeks ago he'd stopped her in the hall and asked for a suggestion to freshen his repertoire. She'd jokingly suggested a popular song called "I'm Forever Blowing Bubbles." Soon after, he'd played a superb classical-style variation of that very tune, one that Mr. Frick had made a point of requesting regularly ever since, unaware that it was a modern hit. Whenever Mr. Graham played it, Lillian couldn't help but smile.

"The clue could be anywhere," said Mr. Danforth. "This is a nightmare."

They worked their way along opposite ends of the narrow pathway, and ended up facing each other in the very middle. There was very little room to maneuver.

He smiled down at her, his breath sweet with brandy. "If we don't find it, may I join you and run off to Hollywood?"

"Of course. We wouldn't want to face Miss Helen's wrath."

Lillian was light-headed from the brandy, and she wobbled slightly. Mr. Danforth lifted his hands to her elbows to steady her, and the intimate gesture caught her off guard. Her mother used to brush Lillian's hair each evening, but since Kitty had died, no one had physically reached out to her, other than Mr. Danforth helping her up from the floor when they bumped heads earlier. And now.

"Look, here it is." He let go of her and half turned, extricating a piece of paper that was sticking out of one of the pipes.

Right. The next clue.

But he didn't even glance at it, instead tucked it beneath the other clues before folding them all in half. "I'm tired of all this." He placed them on a small wooden bracket that ran between the pipes, a precarious spot, to be sure, and turned back to Lillian.

They stared at each other, unmoving, for what felt like hours. When he leaned in close, she didn't flinch or back up or do anything to stop him. Partly because she didn't want to trip and fall, but mainly because she was curious to know what his mouth felt like on hers. After all, she rationalized, she'd have to kiss on-screen, and should know how to do it properly. She would be gone soon, and it could be their secret. They shared a common grief, and it simply felt right, here in such tight confines, to do this. To kiss.

Their lips touched and everything else fell away: the Frick mansion, the paintings, the scavenger hunt. The only thing left was the marvelous sensation of Mr. Danforth's hands on the small of Lillian's back, of how he opened his mouth ever so slightly and she responded in kind.

Somewhere far away, the muffled grumbles of Kearns sounded. Probably a delivery had arrived at the wrong door. The servants' entrance via the basement often made it confusing.

When a shrill voice called out, "I'm home," Lillian quickly came to her senses.

Miss Helen was back, a day early. And from the sound of it, she was coming up the stairs.

Where the door to the organ room was wide open.

Chapter Eleven

1966

"These were written by someone in love."

Joshua laid out the notes on a French baroque table in the living hall and stepped back so Veronica could lean in and study them. The logs in the fireplace snapped and hissed quietly in the background.

Veronica agreed. "They're all quite flirty."

"'The magnificent magnolia treasure.' Huh."

She had to ask. "Do you think it's referring to that diamond you mentioned before the shoot?"

"The Fricks collected all kinds of objects with magnolias on them—place settings, prints—it could be referring to just about anything."

"Oh."

He seemed to register her disappointment. "I mean maybe, but I doubt it. So, we have numbers one through eleven out of twenty, and the first one has a date on it, 1919."

"Who from the Frick family might have been flirting in 1919?"

"The son, Childs Frick, was married and living on Long Island then.

The only family members in the house were Henry and Adelaide Frick, and Helen. I'd have to check, but I think this might be Helen Frick's handwriting."

"How old would Helen have been?"

Joshua thought for a moment. "Thirty-one. I remember seeing something in the Fricks' letters about an engagement around that time, but I'm not sure who the lucky guy was."

"Maybe we found her version of love letters. But why were they stashed away in the organ chamber room?"

"The tenth clue sent them there." He pointed to the text. "See, here, about finding the source of the sound of music. That would be the organ chamber room, of course."

She had been right to reveal her find to Joshua, as he knew every inch of the house, probably better than the Fricks had.

He began gathering the clues into a careful pile. "I'll bring these to my boss as soon as the building reopens, see what he says."

It was all she could do to not snatch them back. "Why wait?"

"I'm sorry?"

"We have nothing better to do. Let's see if we can follow them now."

He took off his glasses and rubbed his eyes. "Because it's dark and cold in here with no electricity."

"We have a lamp. That'll give us enough light, I would think. Especially during the day, even if it's rather gray."

"I'm really not sure if that's a good idea. I should check with my supervisor first."

His tentativeness irritated her. They had a long day ahead of them with nothing to do but stare into the fire, which would mean missing a perfect opportunity to snoop around. She reached down and chose one at random. "*Find the rabbit and you'll be doing your part / The warmth of this painting will cheer my sweetheart.* Rabbits? Is there a painting with rabbits?"

"Right in this room." He pointed to the wall opposite the fireplace, where a large landscape hung. "*St. Francis in the Desert*, by Bellini. Considered the greatest Renaissance painting in America. It's so popular, they have to regularly replace the carpet in front of it."

Veronica walked over, and indeed, the carpet a few feet from the wall was threadbare. The painting showed a man emerging from a cave, with a city looming in the distance. "Where's the rabbit?" She leaned in close. The head of a furry animal peered out of a hole in a stone wall, just below the main figure's right hand. "Found him! It's like he's hiding. He's cute, though. What's it all about?"

Joshua hovered right behind her, as if he was afraid she'd fall head-first into the canvas. "St. Francis received the stigmata in 1224, and the painting depicts that moment—you can see the holes in his hands there. He's looking up at the light coming from the sky in the upper left corner. It's all about revelation and warmth."

"Which matches the poem. Hey, you're really good at this, Joshua."

"Well, thanks." He beamed at her compliment. This was too easy, really.

"Let's follow the trail, starting with the very last one we have," she said. "For the scavenger hunts I did for my sister, I'd leave candy at the very end."

"You're hoping we might find some century-old licorice lying around?"

Or even a precious gem. She still held out hope. "What else is there to do?"

"Well, I suppose we could try." He studied the eleventh clue and recited it out loud. "*A natural beauty came from naught / Yet this lady was quite sought / Out. A lover of Horatio / Holding a hound / Off you go / Take a good look around.* Huh. That's a terrible poem. But the answer's easy, it's right next door."

In the library, he led her to the painting of the lady and the dog she'd come upon the day before. "*Lady Hamilton as 'Nature,'* painted by George Romney."

Veronica studied the woman's face, with its coy smile and tilted chin, as if she had only just noticed it. "Who was Lady Hamilton?"

"She was born Amy Lyon, the daughter of a blacksmith, and became the mistress to a series of wealthy English aristocrats, eventually catching Lord Nelson's eye. She was incredibly famous and widely celebrated, but after Nelson died, she lost everything and died in poverty."

The story aggravated Veronica. When she'd first studied the portrait, she'd assumed this was a woman whose life was light and airy, without a care in the world other than the happiness of her pooch. But of course Veronica was looking at the artist's depiction of the woman, not the actual woman. She grunted in response.

"What?" said Joshua. "Don't you like it?"

"The painting's lovely, but I'm annoyed that Lady Hamilton's only means of success depended on being attractive to powerful men." She pointed to the painting above the fireplace. "Mr. Frick wasn't handsome, but that didn't matter one whit because he was a man. It's not fair."

"I suppose it's not."

"So I guess now we look for the clue." She glanced down at the bookcase.

Joshua froze. "Wait a minute. When I first found you, you were sitting on the floor, looking at a book. You read this clue and figured it out and were looking for the next one."

She knew better than to deny it. "Yes, you're right. I was curious if I could find it."

"So why all the pretending?" A coldness had crept into his voice.

"I'm so sorry," she offered. "That was wrong of me. You see, yesterday, I tried to follow the clues to distract myself from freaking out at the thought of being trapped in the dark, and then you showed up. I knew the models and the film shoot had disrupted things here, and I thought you'd be mad that I'd nosed about. I'm sorry if I overstepped."

He frowned, but then something in him seemed to relent. "Did you find it?"

"The fifth volume from the left." She waited as he opened the book and drew out the clue.

He read it silently, and then, almost in spite of himself, looked up in triumph. He knew the answer. "This one's in the art gallery, right next door."

The twelfth clue referred to a solemn self-portrait by Rembrandt that indeed hung in the art gallery. The gold-and-red costume the painter wore belied his bankrupt state, Joshua explained as they studied it. *"The head of an old lion at bay, worn and melancholy."*

"That describes it exactly. Did you make that up?"

"Nope. That's how the Met described it in an exhibit in 1909, three years after Frick purchased it. Helen Frick's clue referenced a 'red-sashed lion.'"

"Well done. What do you think, shall we continue?" she asked.

"I suppose we should."

The tension between Veronica and Joshua melted away as they worked together. The clues tended to be found within close proximity to the painting or object described, tucked under the edge of a rug or taped to the underside of nearby furniture, and the next several hours were surprisingly enjoyable, if at times frustrating, as not all of the clues were as obvious as the ones for Lady Hamilton or the Rembrandt. Joshua was an able guide, and whenever he figured out the answer to a riddle, his eyes grew wide with excitement. Studying the paintings and sculptures in the soft glow of the lamplight made them even more intriguing, as if the figures were moving slightly in their frames, as if they were alive. They took a quick break to eat when they were hungry before eagerly carrying on.

The nineteenth clue directed them back to the art gallery, to a work by Goya called *The Forge*. The painting depicted three blacksmiths arranged around a sheet of red-hot steel, and stood out from the others around it—which tended toward passive-looking aristocrats or pretty landscapes—with its rawness. Muscular arms, a sledgehammer caught in mid-raise: it spoke of man's power.

"This one is so different from the others," she said.

"How do you mean?"

"It's not as pretty, I guess."

"Henry Frick was a steel magnate, that's how he got his riches," said Joshua. "Maybe this reminded him of those early days."

Veronica looked closer. One of the smiths—the one holding the sheet of metal—had gray hair and was stooped almost all the way over, his face precariously close to the fire. "I wonder if he identified with the young men or that older one."

"It might have changed as he aged. Paintings tend to do that."

"Like books."

"That's right." He glanced over at her with a look of surprise.

"Models can read, you know." She threw him a crooked grin. "Hey, you could write a paper on these clues and how they connect to the artwork here. I bet you'd get high marks."

"You know, that's a great idea."

After his early disapproval of her, it was nice to hear praise. A pleasant silence hung between them as they regarded the painting. "Do you like working here?" she asked.

"I like the research part of the job. Although at times I feel like I'm out of my element, surrounded by all these paintings of rich white folks, purchased by rich white folks. My father says it's a good place to start, and he's right. He's always right."

"You mentioned your mother is an artist. What does she think?"

"She understands my irritability—I guess that's the word I'd use, though it's not quite right. *Impatience* is better. But I've always been destined to work in the arts, I suppose. When I was born, she insisted I be named after the first documented Black artist in America, Joshua Johnson."

"What's his story?"

"He lived in Baltimore around the late 1700s and early 1800s. Made his living by painting portraits of affluent whites. He was most likely self-taught."

"I've never heard of him."

"That's it exactly." His nose wrinkled as he waved his hands in the air. "Why not? I mean, other than the fact that you're from England. But still, that's no excuse."

"I don't know if I could recognize many other artworks, to be honest. It's not like I go to museums often. I like Van Gogh."

From the curve to Joshua's lips, that was not something to brag about. Veronica didn't know this world, and had no idea how to talk about it, other than listing the things she liked (the Renoir in the hallway, of the little girls in fur) and the ones that she didn't (Goya's *Forge*). For the second time in two days, she was made to feel like a fool, and she resented it. "I take it from your silence you don't like Van Gogh. Too mainstream for you?"

"No. I love him, I consider him one of the top Postimpressionists. It's just the way you say it, makes me laugh. Van *Goff*." He stressed the last word. "In America, we say Van *Go*."

She grinned with relief that he wasn't making fun of her. At least he didn't think she was an idiot. "Right, sorry."

"Why are you apologizing?"

"That's just what we do."

"Who?"

"The British. We apologize. But usually we don't mean it, it's more of a way to keep the conversation going."

"I'm sorry you feel the need to do that." He flashed a quick smile.

She laughed in spite of herself. "I've been trying to kick the habit. Tell me, what was Joshua Johnson's artwork like?"

"The portraits are odd, slightly stiff. But with kind eyes. And he had an attention to detail that's extraordinary. Like a piece of lace that looks like it might flutter off the canvas."

"I'd love to see his work."

"You won't find it in this building, for sure."

"I suppose not." She waited a moment, but he didn't continue. "So, let's move on to the final clue, shall we?"

Joshua turned over the seat cushion of a wooden chair stationed beneath the painting. "There's something here," he said, peeling off a piece of paper. "Number twenty of twenty." They both leaned in close; she could feel his breath on her neck as she read aloud. "*Your prize is in the room where all this began / Find the right panel and voilà, thank me / You can.*"

Joshua shuffled through the clues, back to the very first one. "I'm pretty sure I know where to go. The first clue refers to what's now the enamels room, where Mr. Frick used to have his study. Right over here." He pointed to a doorway at the end of the room closest to Fifth Avenue.

Inside, glazed earthenware and brilliantly colored ceramics were on display. Joshua circled the perimeter, ignoring the art objects and instead staring intently at the dark wood walls, which were broken up into square panels. "It would make sense that there might be some storage space behind the panels, back when Mr. Frick worked in here."

They each took a wall, tapping and closely examining each panel. Veronica ran her fingers over the wood, not trusting her eyes in the faint light. They both ended up near the northeast corner of the room. Just as Veronica's fingers ran over a tiny imperfection on the side of a panel, Joshua gave a shout.

"There's a hole in this one, like there might have once been a knob or something in it." He inserted a pen from his shirt pocket into the hole and, with some effort, gently pulled it open.

Inside was a deep pocket of darkness.

He reached in and very slowly lifted out a short, narrow ribbon of silk, about five inches long, with a delicate chain attached to the top. The bottom was cut into an inverted V, and in the middle hung a gold-plated charm.

"What is it?" Veronica asked. Whatever it was, it was not a pink diamond.

"An old-fashioned watch fob, I believe." He held it closer to the light. "They made it easier to pull a watch out of a waistcoat pocket. The initials on the charm are *RJD*."

"Who could that be?"

He ran his thumb over the engraving. "Not sure. It's embroidered with a flower. A magnolia."

"Let me see." He was right. A delicate pale pink magnolia bloom had been sewn into the silk.

Veronica was overcome by a wave of dismay. All of their poring through books and lifting up chairs and peering behind paintings had come to naught. The magnolia treasure referred to a silk watch fob, not a shiny gem.

"Is it worth a lot?" asked Veronica, still hopeful.

"I sort of doubt it. But it will be a great addition to the family's archives. My boss is going to be over the moon."

Veronica leaned in and ran her hand inside the opening, checking just in case. The space was empty. The watch fob was the only treasure inside, and not even a treasure at that.

She stepped back and eyed the panel she'd been examining before Joshua had cried out. It would make sense that there might be more than one storage space, if this had been an office. As she ran her index finger along the grain of wood, she came upon another hole.

"I think we have another secret panel here, Joshua."

She scooted out of the way while he did his trick with the pen again, carefully guiding it open. This time, though, she was the one who reached inside, unable to wait a moment longer. Her fingers touched something hard and cold.

She pulled out the object. It was an old-fashioned cameo brooch with an ivory profile of a little girl with delicate features and curls. Veronica's mother had a cameo, similar to this, that had been left to her by her grandmother. Trish had brought it to Uncle Donny after her husband's death, hoping for a decent return, but it wasn't worth very much, even after Uncle Donny's overly generous valuation.

"Is this the same girl as the one in the portrait upstairs in the bedroom?" she asked.

"It could be." He squinted down at it. "Martha."

"Who's Martha?"

"The Fricks' other daughter. I need to go through the papers in the basement, see if there's any connection to what we've discovered. I have a vague recollection of one, I just can't put my finger on it."

"What should we do with the cameo and fob?"

He considered the question. "Put them back into their respective compartments, for now. Better not to move things around too much; we should treat them like we're like archeologists on a dig. The notes, though, definitely bring along, we'll need those for reference."

After the fob and cameo were secured, Joshua motioned to Veronica.

"Follow me."

"You weren't kidding. It's a real bowling alley."

Veronica stared at two long, gleaming lanes.

"The wood is pine and maple, and the gravity-fed ball return really works," said Joshua. "Do you want to try it?"

She looked at him. "Is that allowed?"

"Hold on a minute."

He placed the lamp near the center of the room and turned the flame all the way up so that almost the entire alley was lit. "Go for it."

She picked a ball off the feeder and kicked off her shoes. Now that the treasure hunt had fallen short of her expectations, just as Joshua had predicted, she wouldn't mind throwing something heavy around. "I've only watched this in movies. Are you sure it's all right?"

"As long as the ball lands in the lane, you're good."

She lifted the ball under her chin, then let her arm drop back and swing forward, letting go at the apex. The ball landed with a thud and she cringed, then watched as it slowly made its way down the entire lane and, to her surprise, knocked into the very center pin, which knocked all of the ones around it, like dominoes.

"Strike!" called out Joshua. "Well done!"

"Now I know what my next career move will be."

"Pro bowler slash model. Love it."

For the past couple of hours, she hadn't thought once about yesterday's debacle, but his comment brought it all back. Her modeling career was probably over, and her deep dread for what the future held made her stomach ache like it was full of jagged stones. Polly would be stuck in Kent House forever, with Veronica and her mum toiling away at jobs that hardly paid the bills. God, how she'd bungled it all. In contrast, Joshua appeared so accomplished and smart. She was pathetic, really.

Joshua was looking at her oddly. She fixed her face into a neutral expression. "How does the ball return work?" she asked.

He walked to the very end, where the pins had fallen, and picked the ball up. "Typically, there would be a servant boy here to do this."

"Typically. Of course."

He placed it on a narrow runner that ran the length of the lane, and let go. It gently rolled all the way toward her, stopping by her knees, ready to be hefted up and tossed once more.

"Do you want a go as well?" she asked. "We have all night."

"Maybe after we take a look at those letters, try to figure this out. I'll let you enjoy your brief moment of victory."

He led the way to a line of tables set up in the corridor that ran parallel to the bowling alley, separated by grand arched columns.

Boxes stood on one of the tables; the other was cleared as a work space, with a chair pulled up to it. She imagined Joshua asleep on the table, how sweet he must've looked with his head lying on his arms, glasses off. Down here, deep underground, it wasn't surprising he'd crashed and not heard her earlier cries for help. No noise penetrated this far.

"This is what you've been working on?" she asked.

"It is. The alarm installers found all these boxes in a cupboard at the very end of this corridor. When Helen Frick started planning her library, she worked out of this space, so it's not surprising."

"You said she hasn't been told of the find yet?"

He gave a quick shake of his head. "She's very private. But these aren't just about her, they're about the entire family, and so the archives department wants the opportunity to study them first."

"Do you think she'll be angry? I'd be quite upset if someone found my letters and didn't tell me."

"Most likely, yes, which is why I'm stuck down here until they're ready to approach her."

"Like a secret mission."

"Only if you care about sickeningly polite thank-you letters and six-course dinner party menus. I haven't seen anything of all that much interest." He gently leafed through a file of delicate, tea-colored paper.

"But I remember a letter from Miss Helen to her private secretary about some kind of game. It was sent from their home in Massachusetts back in November 1919." He pulled it out with a flourish. "Here."

Veronica read it aloud: "*Miss Lilly, I hope all is going well in my absence. I leave it in your capable hands to pull off the Frick House Folly I've arranged for Mr. Danforth. Please make sure he understands how vital the success is to our future union.*"

"Frick House Folly." Joshua repeated, rolling the words around on his tongue. "I wonder if she's referring to the scavenger hunt."

"Who was Mr. Danforth?"

"I don't know for sure, but maybe it's no coincidence that his last name begins with a *D*. I have a pile of correspondence here. Do you want to split it up, see if anything jumps out at us?"

"You'd like me to help?" she asked.

"Or would you rather bowl?" he answered with a smirk.

"Hand them over."

He pulled up one of the chairs from the billiard room, and they sat side by side at the table. Veronica wasn't certain as to what exactly she was looking for, but after a short while her worrying fell away as she became lost in the work. Marvelous details emerged about life in the house, from the polite notes to Mr. Frick from the organ player, a Mr. Archer Graham, writing to confirm another "pleasant season making music for you and your family," to a six-page dispatch written in 1914 from a fired cook who had been wrongfully accused of breaking the family's good china, lamenting that the Fricks' "orders are so unreasonable that it is impossible for anyone to carry them out."

Reading through the recently discovered documents brought the silent, empty house above Veronica's head to life, and almost made up for the fact that the quest for the Magnolia diamond had been a bust. She could almost hear the sound of the cook swearing after breaking another plate, or the droning of the organ while Mr. Frick read his newspapers in the library. If only she'd had the chance to study history at university, maybe she could have gotten a job like Joshua's, going through old letters and solving puzzles. It would have made her father so proud.

Dinner Party Preparations, October 29th, 1919, Eight o'clock, read one document. It included a six-course menu, followed by a guest list. She let out a soft cry.

"What is it?" asked Joshua, leaning over to see.

"A guest list for a dinner party in late October 1919. Including a Mr. Richard J. Danforth." She pointed to his name.

"RJD. That has to be him. Well done."

She flushed with pride. "I wonder why he never found his watch fob?"

"That scavenger hunt was fairly difficult, so maybe he never made it that far."

They continued back at their work, and this time it was Joshua's turn to call out. "Here's something curious." The page he held still bore the indentations from having been folded in thirds. "It's a letter from Helen Frick to her brother, Childs, a couple of months later: *For all I know, you and Dixie stole our dear Martha right out of his cold hands. How could you? You knew what the brooch meant to me, what it was worth. Your jealousy is an evil thing, brother.*"

"That's ominous," said Veronica. "Do you think 'the brooch' refers to our cameo?" Maybe they had found something valuable after all. Valuable enough to be worthy of a reward.

The lamp gave a final sputter and blew out, plunging the basement into darkness. Veronica reached out and touched Joshua's sleeve, and in response, he put his hand over hers. "Don't worry. It's all right. The lamp oil must be all used up. Hold on to me and I'll guide you up the stairs."

Joshua and Veronica took one careful step at a time in the inky darkness, like an ancient couple maneuvering along a cobblestone street.

Once they reached the stairs, he guided her hand to the metal railing, and she emerged onto the main floor, surprised to find that it was long past dusk. The day had gone much faster than she'd expected.

"I'll look around for another lamp," Joshua said. "Why don't you wait in the gallery? The skylights will make it less scary."

She straightened up, mock-defiant. "I'm not scared."

"Sure. That's why you had a death grip on me up the stairs."

"Just wanted to make sure you didn't trip, that's all."

The gallery was even more cavernous in the darkness. Instead of waiting for Joshua, she headed right back into the enamels room, Mr. Frick's former study.

She ran her hand down the edge of the panel door where the cameo was stored. It hadn't quite shut all the way, and she used her fingernail to carefully pull it open and lift out the brooch, moving closer to the window where the light was slightly better. Down in the basement, Joshua had shown Veronica a black-and-white photograph of Mrs. Frick from the last century, wearing a pearl pendant the size of an eyeball, her dark hair held back by a jeweled barrette. As her daughter, Helen Frick must have owned enough rubies and emeralds to fill a treasure chest, far more expensive than the cameo, yet the way she'd worded her letter to her brother was strange. *You knew what it was worth*, Miss Helen had written.

Maybe she was referring to its sentimental value. But what if she wasn't?

Without warning, the back of the cameo came loose. Veronica cried out in dismay as part of it rolled along the floor at her feet. Now she was done for. The brooch was an ancient, delicate thing, and in her excitement she'd handled it too roughly.

Miss Helen would be furious, as would Joshua. But as Veronica examined the cameo closely, with shaking hands, she realized that, no, it wasn't broken. A tiny button on the side had popped it open, revealing a space inside for a keepsake.

A keepsake that had fallen out. She got down on her knees and felt along the floor with her fingertips. It couldn't have gone far, whatever it was; the sound of the rolling hadn't lasted long. She touched something hard and picked it up.

Rising back to her feet, she held it up to the window.

A large blush-colored stone gleamed brightly in spite of the darkness, as if it were a source of light itself. The brilliance was undeniable. *This* was the item of value that Miss Helen had referred to, not the cameo itself. A pink diamond, a very large one.

The Magnolia diamond.

She'd found it.

The diamond had lain inside the cameo, tucked away in a secret compartment, for almost fifty years.

Veronica heard Joshua's tread. The doorway to the gallery filled with a dim glow—he'd been successful in his hunt for another lamp. She imagined showing the diamond to him, the joyful expression on his face when he realized what they'd stumbled upon.

But after that, what?

Veronica thought of Polly, waiting for her return to London, waiting for her to fulfill her promise to break her out of Kent House. This diamond could solve all of Veronica's problems: she could bring Polly home and hire an aide to care for her, Veronica could go to university instead of going back to work at the pawnshop, her mother could stop having to worry about every small expense. Uncle Donny would know how to handle this sort of transaction, how to discreetly arrange for it to be broken down so the stones could be recut and sold without raising suspicion. She could tell her mother that the money came from her photo shoot.

It would be easy enough to hide.

She clicked the cameo closed and placed it back in its secret compartment. As Joshua grew nearer, she rolled the stone between her thumb and index finger, unsure. In the pawnshop, Uncle Donny would sometimes touch his tongue to a diamond to test it. "It'll feel cold," he'd said. Veronica lifted the stone to the tip of her tongue. It was like tasting an ice cube. Then again, it *was* freezing inside the Frick mansion, so no surprise there. Maybe it was a fake. Maybe the last laugh would be on her.

But right before Joshua entered the room, she tucked it deep into the front pocket of her jeans.

Chapter Twelve

1919

W hat's going on in here?"

Lillian and Mr. Danforth pulled apart, the stolen kiss hanging between them like an invisible, intricate spiderweb, just as Miss Helen poked her head around the doorway into the organ room. "I thought I might find you in here! You've been scavenging, I see."

Mr. Danforth carefully turned around in the cramped space. "Miss Helen. You're back. A day early."

"And you've been cheating on me."

Lillian swallowed hard, grateful Mr. Danforth blocked her employer's view. Her body was still warm from Mr. Danforth's kiss, her knees shaking.

"Cheating?" His voice cracked, but Miss Helen didn't seem to notice. From downstairs came the sounds of the servants milling about. Mr. and Mrs. Frick must be right below them, handing over hats and coats, trailed by trunks and luggage. And here she was, caught kissing Miss Helen's suitor.

"Yes. I told you that you had to do the hunt on your own, but you've clearly enlisted Miss Lilly. You're a bad boy."

"Sorry?"

"Not you, this little love." She reached down and picked up a spaniel puppy with big brown eyes who had been mouthing at her skirts. "We have a new addition to the family. Meet Wrigley."

Mr. Danforth stepped forward and gave the dog a pet on the head, before Miss Helen twirled around, calling out, "Follow me!"

Outside in the hallway, Lillian closed the door to the organ chamber behind her and leaned on it a moment. She was certain her legs might give way any minute.

"Well? What do you have to say?" Miss Helen demanded of her.

She had to pull herself together or everything would be lost. "About what?"

"About the dog, of course."

Miss Helen's excitement for her new acquisition had left her oblivious to Mr. Danforth and Lillian's discomfort and nervousness. Then again, Miss Helen was never one for examining the vagaries of human behavior, apart from those of her beloved father.

Lillian spent a good minute oohing and aahing over the puppy before Miss Helen was satisfied. All the while, Mr. Danforth stood uncomfortably off to one side.

"We came home a day early because Papsie wasn't feeling better," Miss Helen said. "The sea air only made him congested."

"Miss Helen," said Mr. Danforth, "I must confess, I'm afraid I didn't make it through the entire scavenger hunt."

"I should be quite cross with you, but you've caught me on a good day. Maybe once you're living here I'll force you to finish it. In the meantime, we must get this boy settled."

After all of their hard work following clue after clue, Miss Helen had already moved on to the next thing.

Lillian hadn't realized until then just how wrapped up in the hunt she'd become, partly because of Mr. Danforth's company, and partly because it had brought the house alive for her. She had enjoyed conquering each new riddle, no matter how badly composed. The clues remained where Mr. Danforth had left them, balanced on a wooden bracket between the organ pipes. She should go back and retrieve them, but before she could do so, Miss Helen dumped the dog in her arms. "Take him to my sitting room and call down for some water. Then oversee Bertha as she unpacks my trunk, make sure everything is put away properly. She has an annoying tendency to arrange my shoes backwards, with the left one on the right side and vice versa." She threw Mr. Danforth a coquettish smile. "I swear she does so on purpose, just to goad me." Her smile vanished as she turned back to Lillian. "Once that's settled, I'd like to go over the week's correspondence with you. I hope you managed to categorize things correctly in my absence."

Lillian stood there dumbly for a moment. Mr. Danforth avoided her gaze. "Of course, Miss Helen."

Upstairs, Lillian's thoughts swirled as Bertha absentmindedly unpacked Miss Helen's trunk and chattered on about the fun she'd had gallivanting about town with a Park Avenue chauffeur during her afternoons off. "I think I've met my man," she said, wrenching a lid off a hatbox as Lillian lifted out art books from a trunk and placed them in a corner, to be brought back down later to the bowling alley. "Roddy's smart as a whip, and he can dance like no one's business. Perfect, right?"

"Right." Lillian was still recovering from Miss Helen's interruption of her first kiss and couldn't quite follow the thread of Bertha's story.

"What's the matter with you, Lilly?"

"Sorry, nothing. I'm happy to hear it." And she was. Bertha worked so hard for the Frick family, she deserved some fun in her life. A chance to have a family.

"How about you? I've noticed our dashing organist giving you longing looks whenever you pass by. Might be fun to be with someone with some musical chops."

"I'm sorry, what?"

"Mr. Graham. Boy, that hair. I'd love to run my fingers through his mane."

In spite of herself, Lillian laughed. "You are utterly ridiculous. You know that, don't you?"

"Go on, tell me you don't think he's a looker."

He was certainly the most dashing man she'd ever seen, but she'd never admit that to anyone, even Bertha. Her mother's advice rang in Lillian's ears as if Kitty were hovering over her even now: *Steer clear of sentimental crushes; do not rely on a man.*

But Mr. Danforth, if he went to medical school and became a doctor, might offer her a different kind of life. She shook off the thought. Lillian was not "Miss Lilly," not really. She was Angelica, and she would always drag the weight of that legacy behind her. For the first time, she wondered what it would be like to be a normal girl like Bertha and find a nice boy, settle down. But that wasn't in the cards. Even before the scandal with her landlord, Lillian's unorthodox past gave her two choices: she could make the move from muse to film actress, be in charge of her own life, or become mistress to a wealthy man who wanted to possess Angelica as a plaything until he tired of her. Even if she'd been interested in family life, no upstanding suitor would tolerate her past. Not even the kindhearted Mr. Danforth.

Three days later, Mr. Frick summoned Lillian to the library, where the family was gathered in front of a roaring fire. He sat in a wingback chair, his stout belly protruding between widely spread legs, while Mrs. Frick perched stiffly on the edge of the couch, her corset preventing any sort of similar relaxation. Helen took up the other armchair.

"Miss Lilly, my daughter says that she has not received a note or telephone call from Mr. Danforth since we returned from Eagle Rock," said Mr. Frick. "Is that correct?"

He looked over at Miss Helen, who shrank miserably into the velvet upholstery. Miss Helen hadn't had any correspondence; that was true.

But Lillian had. Three letters a day, all delivered to the servants' entrance, each one more passionate than the next, the romantic words like dynamite. He'd written that the moment together among the organ pipes had been an unexpected, utter delight, and that their ease of conversation was unlike anything he'd ever experienced before. Miss Winnie had caught the footman handing one to Lillian that very morning, and when asked about it, Lillian had quickly explained that she was advising Mr. Danforth on the setting for the engagement ring. Miss Winnie had nodded and gone about her business.

Lillian hadn't responded to his entreaties. He thought she was a proper young lady, and he wouldn't understand her past. He probably thought that her wish to become a movie starlet was a silly girl's dream, not a true goal close to being realized. They couldn't be more different. Not to mention that if Mr. Frick found out she'd diverted Mr. Danforth's attention from Miss Helen, she'd be subject to his wrath and retribution. No one crossed Mr. Frick. No one.

She fully intended to burn the letters—it was stupid to leave them lying about—but each night before bed, the very sight of them set the blood rushing in her veins, as she relived the kiss and the way Mr. Danforth had looked at her, like she meant everything in the world to him. So far she hadn't gotten up the courage to light the match.

Mr. Frick was staring at her, waiting for an answer.

"That is true, yes. Mr. Danforth has not reached out to Miss Helen, as far as I know."

"We had planned for the engagement to be announced over Thanksgiving. I worry that my daughter has said or done something foolish to dash our hopes. Can you enlighten us?"

How could he talk like that in front of his own daughter? An unexpected surge of pity took Lillian by surprise. She wanted to kneel down before her and explain that she didn't deserve her father's harsh words. That she was deserving of love, and Mr. Danforth's retreat wasn't her fault. "Miss Helen, I am sure, has done nothing untoward."

"Then what's the matter?"

The stupidity of Lillian's actions during the scavenger hunt hit her full force. She'd gotten caught up in the moment, in the lush surroundings, in the grand isolation of the week, acting as if the mansion and its artifacts were hers, acting as if Miss Helen's beau was hers as well. She must make this right.

"I've been privy to some questions from Mr. Danforth, regarding the ring setting, the proposal, and so forth." She looked over at Miss Helen, who had brightened considerably. "I'm sorry to have kept this from you, but he wants it to be a surprise. I assure you, all is well."

Mrs. Frick clapped her tiny hands together, and relief flooded Miss Helen's features. Mr. Frick, however, didn't change his visage at all, his blue eyes never leaving Lillian's. "Well then, I suppose that's good news."

"Father, why don't we send Miss Lilly to him tomorrow? That way she can answer his questions and report back. But, Miss Lilly, you won't tell him we're in on the secret, will you?"

Even if it would be painful for Lillian, it was the best course of action. "I won't let him know that you know. Don't worry."

The next day, she found herself standing again in front of Mr. Danforth's townhouse, holding a note from Miss Helen in her hand—one that Miss Helen had insisted Lillian write, of course. It was time for

Lillian to put a stop to Mr. Danforth's wrongheaded idea that they were a match. It simply couldn't happen. She'd placed all of her hard work from the last two months at great risk.

How cruel she'd been, to clumsily destroy Miss Helen's prospects. Sure, the woman was difficult and sometimes unnecessarily biting, but it wasn't all her fault. The war, as well as her family's manipulations, had damaged her, stunted her development. She deserved a happy home, out from under the thumb of her father and the ghost of her older sister. Mr. Danforth was the answer, and Lillian needed to get out of the way.

The butler led her into the front parlor. Before Mr. Danforth entered, she heard him give the butler an errand, something about a trip to the grocer, and the front door opened and closed. Through the window, she spied the butler heading for Third Avenue.

The door to the parlor opened and Mr. Danforth appeared. A cloud passed over his features as he took in her stony stare.

"Miss Lilly." He took her gloved hand, briefly.

Lillian held out the note. "From Miss Helen, to you."

He didn't open it right away. "She's wondering where I've disappeared to."

"It's been three days, so yes, she and Mr. Frick are worried that your intentions have changed."

"Have they?" He looked up at her, hopeful.

"I can't answer that."

He tore open the note and read it, and then, as if in spite of himself, he broke into a smile. "You wrote this, didn't you? Not her."

There was no point in lying. "How can you tell?"

"Having spent those days with you at the mansion, I understand your cadence. In fact, you wrote the other notes as well, didn't you, from the very beginning?"

Lillian looked out the window, hoping the butler would be returning soon. Being alone with Mr. Danforth felt more daring than when she'd stood naked in the middle of a studio. Like anything might happen. "I did."

He burst out into laughter. "So early on, then, you were in fact writing to yourself, back and forth. A proxy for the supposed lovers."

She couldn't help smile. "Ridiculous, I admit. Although, when it comes to society matches, probably not uncommon."

"Society matches." He sighed. "That about sums it up. I provide Helen the respectability of marriage and an escape from the confines of her father's will, while she gives me access to the Frick family fortune, an easy life ahead of me."

"As long as you both are decent to each other, there's no reason why that shouldn't work. I've known poverty, and I'd trade it in for a life of luxury in a heartbeat."

He gestured around the room. "So if I were wealthy, you'd be my wife?"

That wasn't what she'd meant at all. "Is that your proposal? If so, I'd work on the one for Miss Helen, if you want her to say 'yes.'"

"Maybe I don't." He moved closer. "I think you know what I want."

"I want Miss Helen to be happy."

"Do you, really? Miss Lilly, you are the most beautiful woman I've ever seen."

If he only knew how often she'd heard that exact phrase. The words were overused, worthless.

"I'm sorry," he said, picking up on the disappointment in her eyes. "I realize that's trite. I'm inexperienced at wooing, and don't know how to express myself very well."

"Sir, I'm back. I forgot the list of groceries."

The butler called out as he slammed the front door. The sound reverberated inside Lillian's skull, reminding her why she'd come. "Write a note to her today."

"What shall I say?"

"Tell her you'll see her Thanksgiving Day."

His face fell. "But what of us?"

"I came here today to insist that our friendship remain exactly that. I am not interested in your advances, and suggest that you turn your focus back on course. The Fricks are depending on you. I am not."

"I don't think you mean that."

"I expect a note from you to Miss Helen to arrive by three o'clock."

With that, she fled the parlor, practically tumbling down the brown-stone steps to the safety of the street.

Mr. Danforth did as Lillian had charged, and the relieved look on Miss Helen's face when his note arrived on a silver tray reinforced Lillian's decision. She'd done the right thing. In it, he stated that he had to visit his aunts in New Jersey first, but would join the family for dessert on Thanksgiving Day.

Lillian had set things right and now her plan was back on target. Once Miss Helen and Mr. Danforth were engaged, she'd get her payment from Mr. Frick and be off to California, putting this whole sordid mess behind her. She'd almost muddled up everything by falling for Mr. Danforth, but today she was clear in her desires: a career, not a messy love affair.

The table in the Frick dining room had been expanded so it could accommodate all the Thanksgiving guests: Mr. and Mrs. Frick, Miss Helen, Childs Frick, and, at the last minute, Lillian. Childs Frick's wife had been unable to attend, as one of the children was ill, and she didn't want to travel far from their Long Island estate. Miss Helen had insisted Lillian take the empty place. Dessert would be served later in the Frago-nard Room, after Mr. Danforth arrived, and Lillian figured she could make an excuse and avoid that particular course.

Miss Helen looked sweet, in a soft white dress and a long strand of black pearls around her neck, an ensemble suggested by Lillian to make her look a little more modern, a little more bride-like. Unfortunately, she punctuated her comments at dinner with a strange, high-pitched laugh that made her sound a little unhinged. Lillian hoped she'd not respond to Mr. Danforth's proposal with the same, or he'd go running for the hills.

After the first course was served, Mr. Frick lifted his glass. "I'd like to make a toast."

Lillian noticed that Helen's glass was almost empty. That explained the giggling. She tried to catch her eye, but Miss Helen was already calling the footman to refill everyone's glasses.

"It's grand to have the family together, again," intoned Mr. Frick. "Nothing makes a man happier than to see his children content. Even if they sometimes disappoint." His delivery was dusted with sarcasm. The rest of the family stiffened in their silk damask chairs, sensing that Mr. Frick was in one of his moods.

He turned to his son. "Childs, I'm proud that you'll be carrying on the family name, long after I'm gone."

"That's right, Father." Mr. Childs gave Miss Helen a smirk. "You have your grandson. Dixie and I couldn't be more thrilled."

"Now, Father," interrupted Helen, "I can carry on the family name equally as well." She looked over at Lillian. "Two years ago I changed my name from Helen Childs Frick to Helen Clay Frick. Remember, Father, how happy that made you? And now I'm to be married, which means I may give you a grandson as well."

Mr. Childs guffawed, but Mr. Frick shushed him with a look.

"Weddings make me sentimental," Mr. Frick said. "Perhaps because they remind me of things, people, who were lost. But life moves on, and now I know the Frick name will not be forgotten. I have my collection and my offspring, both of which will carry on after I'm gone."

"Please don't be sad, Father," cried Miss Helen. "I can't bear it."

Mr. Childs put down his glass without drinking. "How interesting that the collection comes first," he murmured.

Miss Helen spoke up. "Childs, don't be beastly to Father today, he's not been well. Which you'd know if you ever ventured to visit us."

"Quit it, sis."

The tension in the room made Lillian want to stand and upturn the entire table. Mr. Frick's maudlin drivel seemed solely aimed at driving his children against each other, as if he were King Lear.

"You're a bully, Childs. You always have been." Miss Helen turned to Lillian. "You know what he used to do when I was a child? He'd hide under my bed and grab my feet when I went to climb in. Or he'd make me stare into a mirror and tell me I was ugly until I cried."

"Both of you, the teasing needs to stop," said Mrs. Frick. Lillian looked over, shocked that she'd made a stand instead of fading into the wallpaper.

"Now, now, there's nothing wrong with a little teasing, Adelaide," answered Mr. Frick. "What else do these children have to make them resilient, having lived in grandeur with thirty servants their whole lives?"

"Twenty-seven," corrected Mrs. Frick.

The pause before Mr. Frick spoke was as thick as a summer storm.

"You like your numbers, don't you?" said Mr. Frick, finally. "Then how about this one: sixty. Not quite an old woman, but close."

Mrs. Frick looked miserably out the window, as if she wished she were anywhere else than this dining room.

Miss Helen rose from her chair, reaching for something in her pocket. "Father, look what I've had made for you."

She took out a small miniature and gave it to him as Lillian cringed. She'd done everything she could to dissuade Miss Helen from this idea. And to present it now, in front of the entire family?

"Let me see." Mr. Frick pushed his glasses up on his nose and peered down at the object, which in his big paw of a hand looked like a piece of sea glass.

Lillian already knew what he held: a picture of Martha that had been painted when she was around four or five, red-haired and pink-cheeked, wearing a white lace top and looking serenely out from a thin gold frame. Miss Helen, in a moment of what she considered inspiration, had commissioned an artist to add the figure of herself as a young girl next to that of her sister. They looked almost like twins, except Miss Helen's likeness had blonder hair and a larger forehead.

"I thought you'd like a portrait of your two favorite daughters," said Miss Helen.

Mr. Frick closed his palm over the image briefly, then held it up for the entire table to see.

Mrs. Frick looked as if she were about to be sick.

"You are so incredibly thoughtless," said Mr. Childs. "Why on earth would you desecrate that with your ugly mug?"

Miss Helen spoke through gritted teeth. "See, Father? That's what I've had to put up with my whole life. You understand why I did it, right? To please you."

Mr. Childs didn't back down. "You're only concerned with the will. Don't pretend it's anything else."

"Childs!" Mrs. Frick had found her voice again. "That's a terrible thing to say."

Mr. Frick sat back in his chair, watching with what Lillian was sure was amusement the disruption unfolding around him. His beastly mistreatment of his children this afternoon didn't square up with the softhearted man she'd met in the art gallery that late night, who was so tearfully proud and protective of Miss Helen. Late at night, among his treasures, was probably the only place he allowed himself to show any hint of compassion.

"Now we see what lies behind all of your flattery," intoned Mr. Frick.

"Both of you"—he pointed at Miss Helen and then at Mr. Childs—"ought to be ashamed. Martha would never have behaved so abominably. You'll just have to wait, won't you? Then again, patience was never your strength, either of you."

He rose, but then sat down again, hard, one hand to his belly.

"What is it, Father, another attack?" Miss Helen placed a hand on his shoulder.

"Help me to my sitting room, Helen, would you?"

Mr. Childs rose to assist, but his sister called to Lillian. "Take his other arm, Miss Lilly."

They brought him to the elevator and up to the second floor. By the time he reached the doorway to the sitting room he was looking a little less pale. He sat on the sofa, staring up at the coffered ceiling with a vacant expression on his face while Miss Helen fetched him a glass of water.

"Thank you, my love," he said when she returned and knelt down at his feet, watching him drink and then holding the glass out for Lillian to take.

"Of course, Papsie. I'm sorry if I upset you."

He put his hand on her cheek. "It's a beautiful miniature. I will treasure it always. I do wish you could have grown up with Martha as your big sister. She had such a gentle nature. She might have tempered yours."

The man knew exactly where to place the knife and turn it.

"I admonished Martha for two years, stop crying, stop complaining." Even though Mr. Frick's eyes stayed on Miss Helen, she was no longer his focus; he'd disappeared into the memory of another daughter. "We didn't know what she'd done. I thought she was being obstinate. It was my fault."

"No, it wasn't. You didn't know," Miss Helen assured him.

"I told them not to operate, to practice homeopathy, which I had great faith in. But what if I'd let them fix her properly? She might have improved, and those four terrible years of suffering would not have happened. In the end, she couldn't eat, couldn't drink, she wasted away. She could barely speak or breathe, she was so overcome with pain, her body riddled with sepsis. I gave her my hand to bite." He held out the hand with the scar Lillian had noticed that night in the art gallery. "You see?"

"I know, Papsie," said Miss Helen. "You did what you could. It was a different time, we didn't have X-ray machines, or proper medicine."

"That was when your mother became ill with her neuralgia. I shouldn't be so cruel. You'll tell her I'm sorry, won't you?"

"You can tell her yourself. She's fine, we're all fine."

"You're a good girl."

Miss Helen smiled like she'd been blessed by the pope.

Even with all their money, the family had been afflicted by tragedy that reverberated down the generations. Martha's death had made them all their worst selves: Mrs. Frick fragile and ill, Mr. Frick cruel, their son desperate to cause trouble, and Miss Helen far too eager to please.

Downstairs, the doorbell chimed.

"It must be Mr. Danforth," said Miss Helen. "See to him, Lilly. Have him return tomorrow."

In all the fuss, Lillian had forgotten he was expected. She found him walking down the main hallway, looking confused.

"Mr. Danforth," she said, "I'm afraid there's been a change of plans."

"Miss Lilly." He spoke loudly, as if playacting. "Is everything all right?"

"There's been some trouble. Please, come with me."

She took him through the library and out onto the loggia, which extended lengthwise along the south side of the art gallery. Four sets of coupled columns divided the walkway from the expanse of lawn. In the moonless night, they were practically invisible out here, and she needed some fresh air after the stuffiness of Mr. Frick's sitting room.

"There was an issue with Mr. Frick, I'm afraid. Miss Helen is up tending to her father."

"I'm sorry to hear he's still ill."

"Yes." She spoke quickly. "We'll have to reschedule the proposal. I'll check her calendar first thing in the morning and send you some alternate dates."

"I didn't come here to propose, Lilly. I came to explain that I won't be marrying Miss Helen."

Lillian felt something in her crumble. The money. Her money. Her dreams. And yet, was Mr. Danforth turning down a fortune because of Lillian? Could she have had such a dramatic effect on him? "No, that won't do," she said. But the words sounded feeble, and seemed to heighten Mr. Danforth's zeal.

"I'm not in love with her, and I don't think we'd make a good match. You, of all people, must understand that." He touched her arm.

A flash of light fell onto the grass, from a window in the living hall. Someone had moved the curtain, looked out. Mr. Danforth retreated farther into the shadows, pulling Lillian with him.

"I know I don't have a lot to offer, just a small yearly income," he said. "But I've thought about what we discussed. I want to study medicine up in Boston, and lead a simple life. All this"—he motioned back at the house, which loomed in the darkness like a tomb—"is not my cup of tea. I don't think it's yours, either, Lilly. We could lead a good, happy life together."

He was offering her a chance at a different life than she'd imagined. One of stability and companionship. She knew enough of his sorrow and kindness, along with the fact that he wasn't impressed by the Fricks' wealth, to understand that he was a good man. A good man who was in love with her.

The daily bustle of the Frick house had only served as a diversion from the fact that she was utterly alone as well, and as much as she wanted to believe her services indispensable to Miss Helen, she was replaceable, in a heartbeat. For so long she'd served others, standing patiently, fully exposed, for artists. Making sure Kitty was taken care of. Kowtowing to the whims and tantrums of Miss Helen. She'd molded herself into whatever shape was called for, and was good at it. How caught up she'd been, to miss this.

Accepting his offer would mean giving up her dreams of a film career. But was she really resting all of her hopes and dreams on a couple of dashed-off letters from a producer? Mr. Broderick probably sent out a hundred a week. Was she naive to consider herself special?

But Mr. Broderick was looking for an Angelica-type actress. He was looking for *her*. She'd worked so hard, come so close, and she'd never know if she could be successful in California if she didn't try. Never mind the fact that running off with Mr. Danforth would invite the wrath of the Fricks.

And finally, if they married, Mr. Danforth would have to be told the truth about Lillian. About Angelica.

"I'm not sure," she said. Did she have the courage to expose herself, inside and out? To stop hiding? But this was what love was all about, according to the songs and poems and books that had been written through the ages. It was about giving yourself to another person and trusting them with your secrets. She'd never imagined she'd have the opportunity, but Mr. Danforth's kiss had changed all that. He loved her, in spite of the danger circling around them.

"You may not be certain yet, but I am," he answered. "Meet me Monday in the park, on the terrace of Belvedere Castle. Eleven o'clock. We'll run off and get married and start a new life, together. Will you do that, Lilly?"

He paused, waiting. "Will you?"

The next morning, Lillian was told that Mr. Frick still wasn't feeling well and the doctor had been called for. She waited with Miss Helen outside the door to his sitting room while he was examined, and they walked the doctor to the foyer when he was finished.

The man had a somber look on his face. "It's pleurisy. That's what's causing his shortness of breath."

"I hope you didn't tell him that," said Miss Helen.

"No. As you requested, I didn't let on the seriousness of his condition. I told him the congestion was due to the lousy weather. Keep him on a liquid diet for now, and make sure he rests. I'll check back tomorrow."

Upstairs, Mr. Frick lay on the sofa clutching a royal blue comforter. He would be a shoo-in for St. Nick, with the white beard and large gut. But Mr. Frick was far from jolly, even on days he was in good health.

His valet stood nearby, writing something down.

"For lunch, I'll have sweetbreads and au gratin potatoes," dictated Mr. Frick. "Have a cigar ready for me after, with a hot Scotch."

"No, Papsie, that won't do at all." Miss Helen turned to his valet. "He'll have a thin consommé and tea."

"No," Mr. Frick thundered. "My last meal will not be soup."

"No one has said anything about a last meal. Please, Papsie."

The valet left, throwing Miss Helen a sympathetic look.

She sat in the chair next to her father. "You won't listen to me, will you?"

"Why should I? Why would you know better than me what I want to eat for lunch?"

"It's what's healthier for you."

"Bah. Let's play checkers."

"You play with Miss Lilly. There's something I must attend to." She rose and pointed to a polished marquetry checkerboard displayed on a small side table. "Miss Lilly, move that over near him and play. You know how to play checkers, don't you?"

"I do."

Mr. Frick bellowed as best he could as Miss Helen left the room, "Do not go changing my menu," but before he could finish the threat, he began to cough.

Lillian poured a glass of water from a crystal pitcher and handed it to him. He drank it down and the wheezing lessened.

He gave one final clearing of his throat. "Sit. Play with me."

Lillian's value, like that of the rest of the servants, fluctuated depending on the level of stress that ran through the mansion like an electric current. This morning, here with Mr. Frick, she felt on par with Wrigley the dog, commanded about and expected to obey.

She sat opposite Mr. Frick and adjusted the pieces that had slipped out of place. He moved first.

They played in silence for a while, the only sound that of his breathing, like a coal-choked train engine. While he pondered his next move, Lillian took the opportunity to study the artwork on the walls and mentally compare each one to the entries destined for Miss Helen's library cataloguing system. Doing so soothed her, got her mind off the fact that Mr. Danforth was expecting a decision in three days' time. If she left the Fricks' employ, she'd never see Miss Helen's art history library come to fruition, which to her surprise made her feel slightly mournful. Lillian had found a deep satisfaction helping Miss Helen sift through images of the world's most beautiful artwork, figuring out how best to categorize various landscapes and portraits, bronzes and busts. The work combined her love for order, which she'd discovered after she'd begun taking her job as private secretary seriously, with her love for art, from her previous career.

The repercussions of her decision weighed heavily on her.

Mr. Frick looked up and followed her gaze. "When I first started collecting art, I never imagined I'd end up in a house surrounded by masters."

"You must be very proud."

"Proud? It's not like I painted them." He sat back. "It all feels so ordinary now."

Ordinary. Not the word she would have chosen. He fell into a coughing fit again, and for the first time she saw him as a vulnerable old man, his forehead creased and wide eyes fearful. Over his lifetime, he'd conquered everything he'd set out to, only to be reminded by his failing lungs that he was a mere mortal.

"What a legacy, to leave all this for the people of New York," she said, hoping to boost his spirits.

"But will they appreciate it, seventy, eighty years from now? Who will care about the house of a dead rich man, filled with old art?" He paused. "I'll be gone soon, you know."

She didn't meet his eye, not wanting to engage in such morbid talk. "The doctor is quite positive."

"He's lying."

Lillian murmured a quiet dissent.

"I almost died once before, did you know that?" He moved one of his pieces to the far side of the board, and she dutifully crowned it.

She remembered Bertha's recounting of his attempted murder, something involving a Russian anarchist. "How very scary that must have been."

"There I was, sitting in my office in Pittsburgh, having a meeting, and I looked up to see a man with a gun. I was shot twice in the neck, stabbed multiple times in the legs and chest. I refused to be put under during the four hours it took the surgeon to remove the bullets. The doctors saved me, but you know who truly saved me?"

"Who?"

"My first daughter. When the madman pointed his gun at me, there was a flash of light, and I am certain it was Martha. She blinded him so that he misfired. Martha saved me." He held out his right hand, the one with the tiny bite marks. "Of all my scars, this is the one that haunts me most. My daughter suffered for four years. In comparison, my wounds were nothing." He took the last of Lillian's checkers pieces with a satisfied flourish. "Did you throw the game on purpose, to cheer up an old man?"

"Never."

They both smiled.

"Will you promise me you'll take care of my daughter after I'm gone? She'll need guidance. You have a good head on your shoulders, you understand the way the world works, I can tell. Will you watch over her?"

Before she could answer, the door flew open and Miss Helen entered, carrying a tray.

"Papsie, I've brought you a hot toddy. That will set you right. Isn't that what you always told me when I was ill, that a hot toddy was the cure?"

"I don't want it. For God's sake, stop fussing over me. Send it back."

Miss Helen's face fell. She banged the tray down on the sideboard and sat at the end of the sofa. Her father refused to move his feet to make room, so she perched uncomfortably, half on and half off. "How was the game? I see you've bested Miss Lilly. She's terrible at games."

"Not because she's terrible, but because she lets her opponent win," Mr. Frick answered. "Miss Lilly is a smart one, you ought to listen to her."

"What have you been talking about?" Miss Helen eyed Lillian suspiciously.

"Miss Lilly has been my confessor," he said. "Exactly what I needed. I feel much better now."

Lillian could have choked him if he hadn't already had breathing difficulties. Pitting people against each other was as natural to him as breathing. Perhaps it worked in the business world, but his family, already frayed, was falling apart.

"Who knows what will happen once I'm married?" said Miss Helen. "Mr. Danforth and I may very well decide to revisit our staffing requirements." She pointed to a chair in the far corner. "Miss Lilly, please take the *New York Times* and sit over there. Mark which articles you think my father would like to hear me read out loud."

Again with the commands, not to mention Miss Helen's not-so-subtle threat to fire her. But Lillian obeyed, planting herself in the most uncomfortable chair in the room. Mr. Frick was ill, she reminded herself. The family was under a great deal of stress, wondering how their world would go on after his death, wondering if they'd be able to manage without him at the helm.

"Papsie, while she does that," Miss Helen said, "I will read to you from *The World*. Would you like that?"

"I would. Very much." He settled back down, content at having put Miss Helen and Lillian at odds.

What *if* Lillian ran off with Mr. Danforth?

Richard. She'd have to get used to calling him by his Christian name if she were to elope with him. There were times, like today, when she was sure Miss Helen didn't deserve him; Richard was far too kind and good for the likes of her. They'd be miserable within a month, and no doubt Mr. Frick would torture him in what little time he had left, as he did the others. If she accepted Richard's proposal, Lillian would be free from the entanglement of cruelty in this house, and she'd have a decent life, as the wife of a good man. She had earned that, hadn't she? But even as she considered her options, she knew it wasn't right to accept a man's hand in marriage out of spite. She had to drill down further, figure out if she was willing to take such a leap of faith. And she only had until Monday to do so.

As Miss Helen read out loud to her father, Lillian leafed through the *Times.* Mr. Frick preferred the business items, but she scanned the arts section first. God only knew how long Miss Helen would take, just to keep Lillian squirming in the corner.

Exclusive interview with Alan Broderick, silent film producer.

Lillian's heart jumped at the headline, and she quickly skimmed through the article. He was in town, scouting locations for a new movie that wasn't yet cast. The interview had been conducted at the Plaza Hotel, where Mr. Broderick was staying until the middle of next week, before returning to California.

He was here.

She remained in the corner until Mr. Frick dozed off, and then asked Miss Helen if she could attend to the books. Miss Helen dismissed her, but instead of going to Miss Helen's sitting room, Lillian went to her own chamber, where she put on a bright slash of lipstick and ran a comb through her hair before dashing down the front stairs.

At the hotel, she pulled her veil low and approached the clerk, asking to send a note up to Mr. Broderick. Told that he was still in his suite, she stated that she'd wait for a reply, and gave the man a tip for his trouble.

She took a seat at the base of a large jardiniere, watching the guests come and go through the lobby. The rococo interior, with walls of rose-and-green brocade, gave her a slight headache after the relative austerity of the Frick house. Right now, Miss Helen was probably stamping her feet, asking Bertha to find Lillian, angry at her sudden disappearance. She was taking a terrible risk.

After ten interminable minutes, the clerk approached her with a note. "From Mr. Broderick," he said with a bow.

She tore it open, praying for good news. It stated that Mr. Broderick would be pleased to meet with her early next week.

Monday at eleven.

Right when she was supposed to meet Richard.

The weekend crawled by, with Miss Helen becoming more and more frantic as her father grew sicker, his body swelling with fluid, the doctor administering morphine to keep him comfortable. Mr. Childs and his family had visited his bedside on Sunday, the children wide-eyed and solemn before being delivered quickly out to their nursemaid. Mr. Childs and his wife remained by Mr. Frick's bedside for an hour before shuttling back home to Long Island.

Miss Helen, not liking the prognosis the doctor had given the family, fired him and brought in another. She hadn't slept in twenty-four hours at that point, and Mrs. Frick finally demanded that she rest, an unusual surge of motherly sentiment. At nine in the morning on Monday, Lillian sat in her room, two notes in her hand. One to Mr. Broderick, declining his invitation to meet. The other to Richard, expressing her regret. Which to send?

Kitty had bitterly cursed Lillian's father for leaving them with nothing. As far as Lillian was concerned, men were not to be trusted easily.

Not her father, nor Mr. Watkins, and definitely not Mr. Frick, who played with his family like they were puppets on a string. Richard, while he seemed kind, didn't know who she really was, and would certainly never allow her to work as an actress. That wasn't ladylike, not in the circles in which he traveled. In the end, he saw only a fantasy of her, as a prim private secretary, which in many ways was no different from the fantasy of Angelica.

The anonymity of being a working girl had been fine, for a time, but Lillian's power had always lain in her beauty, her appearance. If she didn't take this chance to be an actress now, she might wonder for the rest of her life what might have been. Looming over her still was the January trial of Mr. Watkins. Even if she accepted Richard's offer and was a respectable married woman by then, there were no guarantees that she would remain free from the scandal. No, the only way forward was to put herself at Mr. Broderick's mercy and leave the East Coast for good.

She tore up the note to Mr. Broderick and tossed it in the wastebasket, and handed the one addressed to Richard to the footman on the way out, with instructions to deliver it right away.

At the Plaza Hotel, a little before eleven, she knocked on a door on the fifth floor. A young man with a pronounced overbite but an eager smile showed her into a luxurious sitting room done in a soft yellow, with two windows looking out to Central Park through embroidered organdy curtains. "We're excited to meet you," the assistant said as he welcomed her inside.

Mr. Broderick rose from the sofa and held out his hands to her. He was younger than she'd expected, probably in his late thirties, and sported a tan that made his green eyes sparkle. The very picture of health, especially when compared with the wheezing, sickly pallor of Mr. Frick. "Very nice to meet you. Tell me your name, please."

She looked over at the assistant and back to Mr. Broderick, confused. "Angelica."

Mr. Broderick gave her a sly look. "Right. Early on, we heard from a number of women claiming they were Angelica. All pretty with long, dark hair. But not a one since the scandal broke. You have quite a bit of courage coming forward, whoever you are."

Whoever she was? But he knew who she was. "You were so kind in your letters, I figured I could trust you."

"Letters?" He waved a hand in the air. "Oh, right. I don't handle the correspondence. That's up to my assistant."

She looked over at the toothy kid. *That* was who she'd been exchanging letters with? Who she'd confided in with great detail about her life as Angelica, as a way to prove her identity?

And who'd replied with such an enthusiastic response?

Mr. Broderick had neither written nor read any of it.

"I think she's the real deal, Mr. Broderick," said the assistant. "I think this is her." He gave Lillian an encouraging and slightly apologetic smile.

"You don't say?" Mr. Broderick looked her up and down.

Well, Lillian was certainly getting her just rewards, having forged many a note herself these past few months. But she wouldn't let this hitch stop her; she'd made it this far. "I am her. Angelica, I mean."

Mr. Broderick sent away the assistant and offered her a seat on the sofa. "In that case, how are you doing, my dear Angelica?"

Such a simple question, yet she found herself tongue-tied. So much was at stake on the answer. Mr. Broderick was looking at her so deeply, with such compassion, that, much to her own surprise, she burst into tears.

He reached into his jacket pocket and took out a monogrammed handkerchief. She pressed it to her eyes, careful not to smudge the kohl liner. The makeup she'd applied that morning felt like a thick mask on her skin after months of sporting a clean face. "I'm sorry," she said.

"There, there." He took her hand in his. His touch was as soft as a kid leather glove. "You've been through so much lately, I'm sure. Tell me all about it, my dear girl."

Dare she? He could call the police at any moment. She had to earn his sympathy, make him see her value and agree to take her back to Hollywood with him. "I've been lying low, after all the articles in the press. Again, thank you for seeing me."

"I feel like I see you whenever I'm in New York. You're outside my hotel, above a fountain, up on a pedestal near the park, embedded in the library's facade. You're everywhere, Angelica."

"Lately, I've wished that wasn't so. That terrible murder, I didn't have anything to do with it. The man was my landlord, but that was all."

"Of course. Where have you been all this time?"

"I found a job working for a family and stayed out of sight. My plan was to come to you in California, but then I read in the newspaper that you were in the city, and here I am."

Mr. Broderick leaned in closer. "What a time you've had of it, my girl. Trust me, I know these reporters, and they don't care what the real story is. Nor do the police. You were right to stay out of sight and then seek me out. I will take care of you. Don't you worry about a thing."

"You will?" Opening up to him had been the right decision. "I'd be happy to audition for any role, no matter how small."

He stood and began to pace. "I can already see it in my mind's eye, which is always a good sign. This is how I work, I wait until the story comes to me. One can't rush the creative process."

A ripple of courage zinged through her. "You remind me of the artists I posed for," she said. "The best ones often circled me in the studio for an hour before they even began. They'd mumble to themselves, make sketches, that sort of thing. Once they started work, it became a partnership, in many ways. I'd often offer up suggestions that came to mind as I posed."

"You were a muse to them and you'll be a muse to me, I can see that. Do you have anything that's keeping you here in New York?"

She thought of Miss Helen and Richard. It was better for her to leave so they could figure out whatever arrangement would work best without her muddying things up. "No. I have no one."

"I meant, this investigation. Do the police have a warrant out for your arrest?"

"I believe I may be wanted for questioning, or at least that's the way it's been written about in the press."

"Fine. Then you can leave with me tomorrow, and we'll put you up somewhere quiet near the studio while we figure out the best story for the press. We'll say that you fled the big, bad city for the sunshine of Los Angeles, and that you've been reborn."

"Reborn?"

"I'd prefer to give you a screen test in the studio, with the proper sets and costumes, but I'm willing to make do with what we have here. Stand there." He pointed to the center of the room.

She did so and waited. He backed away, holding out his hands in two L shapes, and knelt low. "That's right, bring your chin up, look above me, over me."

For a fleeting moment, her nerves kicked in again, but she reminded herself she'd been studied closely before, that this was no different from the hundreds of other times she'd been inspected, scrutinized. She hoped the bags under her eyes from the weekend of sleep deprivation didn't show.

"My God, you look good from every angle," he said. "I'm going to talk, and I'd like you to react to what I'm saying in whatever way feels natural. Are you ready?"

She nodded.

"Go to the doorway."

She walked to where she'd first entered.

"Here's what I envision. I want to tell your story."

"My story?"

"Yes. This will be a collaboration. *Angelica, the Artists' Muse.*"

A collaboration. Her name in the movie's title.

He continued. "We must capitalize on what you've done before, show that you're an emblem, embedded in the culture of New York City. That you've been persecuted and called vile names, but that your essence is still pure."

Vile names? She didn't want to draw attention to the scandal with her landlord. The whole point of going to California and acting was to get beyond all that, move forward. She was about to volunteer that she'd be happy to act in a movie that had already been written, but she couldn't get a word in. He was backing up, talking quickly.

"Let's pretend it's the first time that you've come to an artist's studio and been asked to pose. Go ahead, action."

"Action?"

He stood and blew out a breath. "Yes. Enter the room as if it was a studio. Can you do that?"

"My mother was always with me."

"No mother. We need to raise the stakes, heighten the narrative. You're all alone, and this is the first time you've done this. Can you remember that?"

She could, and shivered a little at the memory.

"Yes! Exactly what I'm looking for. What you did there. Keep on going."

She'd impress him with her acting skills, even if this was not what she had expected. Lillian entered the room and stood, looking about with wide eyes, as if she were surrounded by finished statues and works in progress.

"Wonderful! Now here comes the artist. He's circling you."

She stiffened, watching the imaginary man as he passed by.

"Terrific. Now, we'll have to re-create what happened to you in the studio. You sense that he wants more than just a model, and it frightens you. Show me that."

She broke out of character, confused. "But that never happened. All the sculptors I worked with were working artists, not seducers. My mother made quite sure of that."

"Again with the mother. There is no mother, all right?"

"But if it's going to be my story, then shouldn't we be true to it? I'm not ashamed of what I did, posing as a model. There was nothing untoward about it."

Mr. Broderick plunked down in a chair, knees wide, elbows on his knees, chin in his hands. He spoke evenly, like a disappointed parent patiently explaining the rules to a young child. "You're not some farm girl from Omaha who no one has heard of before. If you are the true Angelica, we have to embrace your recent notoriety."

"I'd like to get beyond my notoriety, if I can."

"It's too late for that. But if you can make the audience fall in love with you, feel like they understand your plight and empathize with you, then you'll have all the power in the world. Power will get you out of a pickle, and that's what you're in, at the moment."

She crossed her arms, uncertain.

"The studio wouldn't allow me to film anything that's the least bit distasteful or gauche," Mr. Broderick offered. "You'll be safe with me. But you have to trust me, can you do that?"

She eyed him warily. "I guess."

"I'm going to demand a lot from you, Angelica. You'll need to expose yourself, and I want to know now, right now, if you're going to be able to do that."

"What do you mean?"

"Well, for one thing, I'll need you to offer up raw, undiluted emotion.

Really dig deep. And there should be at least one shot of your legendary dimples." The last sentence was said almost to himself, as if she weren't even in the room.

Her heart sank, but maybe she could put him off. "Like this?" She smiled.

"No, not those dimples." His voice hardened. "Yes or no, Angelica? You decide. If you are in fact the real Angelica, why would that be a problem? *Are* you the real Angelica?"

Mr. Broderick wasn't interested in working together to create something wonderful. He wanted to take her story and turn it into something sordid. To portray her as a victim, a childlike creature with no power, instead of a muse to the best artists in the world who had, in fact, done quite well for herself. For a while.

"I lied."

"What?" he asked.

"I lied. I'm not Angelica. I'm sorry I wasted your time."

He swore under his breath. "Stupid girl. I knew it the whole time. Your nose is far too big. You'd never last one day in an artist's studio, never mind a film lot."

As she left, she heard him bellowing for the assistant to send in the next girl.

Chapter Fourteen

1966

Inside the Frick mansion, a grandfather clock chimed, the sound echoing around the dark house, reaching deep into rooms filled with thickly painted canvases and silk settees. The sound bounced around the spacious cavern of the art gallery, where Veronica reunited with Joshua, the pink diamond tucked deep inside her pocket. She should tell him what she'd found. But then she thought of Polly, and couldn't quite find the right words.

Armed with a new gas lamp, Joshua offered Veronica a tour of the building now that they'd finished the clues. "A tour that's reserved for special patrons of the Frick."

"Inmates with no means of escape, you mean?" she asked.

"Exactly."

She agreed, figuring that maybe at some point there would be a moment to admit what she'd found. It still wasn't too late. But Joshua was off to the races, proudly pointing out the new additions since Frick's day:

a fountain-and-plant-filled garden courtyard that used to be a drive-way, and a reception area and entrance hall where a porte-cochère once stood. "Did you happen to see the figure above the doorway when you walked in?"

She'd been in a hurry, but she vaguely recalled a naked woman carved in stone, sporting long braids on either side of her head. It had seemed oddly out of place, considering the architecture of the building was so square and stolid. "I did."

"That was once above the porte-cochère, and was moved to become the new front door of the museum. The model for it was a woman named Angelica, whose likeness can be found in statues all over Manhattan, and she was celebrated in her day for her classic beauty. But then she became embroiled in some kind of murderous love triangle and disappeared."

Veronica had witnessed firsthand the plight of models who were lauded for their beauty before losing everything, from drug or alcohol abuse, from not eating enough or eating too much. How sad for this Angelica, to have left behind a grand legacy of beauty but not be able to enjoy it. "She disappeared? I wonder what happened to her."

"I tried to dig into that over the fall, but it appears no one knows."

They took the stairs all the way up to the top floor, where Joshua pointed out the old fur vault that was now storage, and a linen room where the massive drawers slid out without a creak. "The mechanisms were built using Frick's steel," he said.

His unbridled excitement at sharing that detail made her smile.

"What?" he asked.

"Nothing. Continue, please."

One floor below, he opened the door to the director's office, where a portrait of the magnate hung above a grand piano. "That's our man, Mr. Henry Clay Frick. He's got eyes that could bore a hole through you."

"The Frick Collection is lucky to have you. You've been working here for how long?" She wandered farther into the room, running her finger lightly along the piano's lid.

"Since September."

"I hope they appreciate you. You could probably give more detailed tours than any of the docents."

"The staff here are top-notch. I've been learning a lot." He shrugged. "Although sometimes it bothers me what stories aren't being told."

"Like what?"

"Like the story behind all this wealth." He gestured around the room. "Visitors are in awe of the place, but they rarely question how the man behind it amassed all his money. He did it on the backs of the working-man, by busting up strikes, violently. Men were gunned down because they were protesting for better pay, better conditions. All this gilded love-liness hides a dark past. I thought about writing about that for my final project, even raised the idea with my advisor, but he discouraged it. He said maybe by the time I've earned my PhD it would be all right, but not as an undergraduate."

"Because it would be considered causing trouble?"

Joshua nodded. "I'm automatically considered an outsider, a threat to the status quo, so writing anything even vaguely controversial would not be well received. It's hard enough to be a Black man in these spaces, to go on a tour at the Met and have the docent ignore your raised hand while everyone else stares uncomfortably at the floor."

"I imagine that must be infuriating, especially since you're one of the nerdiest arty people I've ever met."

"I will take that as a compliment."

"As you should." She considered her clash with Barnaby the day before. Now that the initial shock had worn off, she was no longer mor-tified. In fact, she was kind of proud of what she'd done by standing up for herself. "Maybe you should go ahead and do what interests you any-way. Why put up with their nonsense?"

"If I'm going to move the art world in a new direction, I'm going to have to understand the old. Like, fully understand it, in my bones. Just because I disagree with Mr. Frick's methods of accumulating his fortune doesn't mean I don't appreciate his taste. I mean, the man had taste."

"He certainly did. Old meanie." She yawned.

"Sorry, I've been going on and on. You must be exhausted, and starving."

Together, they scavenged a dinner in the kitchen and then warmed up before the fireplace.

"Tonight, if you like," said Joshua, "you can sleep in Mrs. Frick's bedroom, although I'm not sure how comfortable a fifty-year-old mattress will be."

"It'll be better than this sofa, for certain. Especially if I pile on the blankets. What about you?"

He looked at the couch. "I'll crash here. But let me light your way up there before I do."

Up in Mrs. Frick's bedroom, he pointed at her suitcases. "Good thing you have your toothbrush with you."

"I'm sorry I don't have a spare. But if you need a waist cinch or a coral lipstick, do let me know."

"I sure will."

Outside, the wind howled. The storm was only getting worse. Joshua setting up camp a floor below her didn't appeal at all, not after they'd tramped around together for the past however many hours. "Hey, you can crash on that chaise longue, if you want." She tossed out the suggestion lightly, trying to make it sound like it was no big deal, either way. "No need to go all the way downstairs."

"You scared?" He shot her a mischievous grin.

"No. Yes. This house is eerie. I mean, people died in it, right?"

"Mr. Frick certainly did, but not in this room, if that helps. Anyway, that's just the way things were done, back then."

"Still. I'd prefer not to be alone, to be perfectly honest."

"Then I'll keep guard." He went to the chaise and took off his shoes. She sat on the edge of the bed and watched as he undid the double knots on the black leather lace-ups, first one, then the other, and gently eased them off, placing them neatly side by side. He valued those shoes, she could tell, as she had valued her silk high heels. The thought of him shining his shoes before coming to work each day made her heart skip, for some odd reason.

She settled on the bed and distracted herself from its slightly musty odor by studying the painted ceiling, which was decorated with florals and swirls. "Earlier today you mentioned that there was another Frick daughter, besides Helen. What happened to her?"

"Martha?"

"Right, Martha."

"Are you sure you want to know? It might give you bad dreams."

She said she'd be fine, and he went on to explain, with a gentleness that she appreciated in that cold, dark room, about a swallowed pin, years of pain and misdiagnoses, and the girl's lingering death. It made Veronica unbearably sad for the poor child, as well as for the family who witnessed her suffering. Mr. Frick suddenly loomed less like a capitalist monster and more like a flawed human being. "How did you find this out?"

"From reading the Fricks' letters," said Joshua. "They didn't realize what was wrong with her until it was too late. The child was too little to communicate."

"My sister can't communicate."

Veronica had no idea why she'd just said that. Lying in the dark with Joshua, where neither of them could really make out each other's faces, felt safe, like she was back in the room she'd shared with Polly in Notting Hill. They'd pasted glow-in-the-dark stars on the ceiling, and every night Polly would laugh in amazement as they emerged after the lights were out. "Something happened when she was born and she's never been able to talk. My mum and I can understand what she's saying, but no one else does."

"Like a secret language?"

"I know what she wants by her sounds. And her laugh. She has a wicked sense of humor, and gets the joke. She always, always gets the joke. When our mum came home from shopping one day and didn't know she'd left a lone pink foam roller hanging off the back of her head, Polly practically fell off her chair. As did I, we were laughing so hard."

"I've always wished I had a brother or sister, to be able to share inside jokes like that," said Joshua. "Is Polly older or younger than you?"

"We're twins." They were silent for a moment, but it was an encouraging type of silence, like he was giving her room to formulate her thoughts, decide what to share. "Polly doesn't make eye contact, but she sees everything that's going on. Unfortunately, most people avoid her completely. She scares them. She lived with us until a few months ago, when my mum insisted that she move to a home so we both could work. I hate to think of her there, surrounded by people who don't understand her."

"What about your dad?"

"He used to drive the night shift, as a cabbie, and one morning I came out and found him asleep in his cab, which wasn't unusual. He hated to come in late and wake us all up. But he wasn't asleep. He'd had a heart attack."

"I'm so sorry. That's a terrible thing to have to go through."

She pushed the image of him sitting behind the wheel, chin to chest, out of her mind. "I suppose the good news is I'll be seeing Polly sooner than expected."

"Why is that?"

"The photo shoot was supposed to last a week. The next stop was the Breakers, in Newport, but I made a mess of things."

"How do you mean?"

"The photographer was yelling at one of the girls, being really rude. I told him to stop."

"Sounds heroic."

"Certainly, the other models didn't seem to think so. Then they all left without me. Probably thought that I'd quit and walked out. I should've."

"Then we wouldn't have found the clues or the secret compartments."

"That was kind of fun."

"I agree."

"I suppose that's your job, really," she said. "Nosing about. Discovering lost secrets."

They lay in silence for a moment. Veronica thought that Joshua might have fallen asleep, but then he spoke again. "Maybe Polly will enjoy it once she's settled in."

She sat up on one elbow. Her eyes had gotten used to the dark, and she could just make out his features. "How could you say that? She's miserable."

"So was my grandmother when she had to move into a nursing home. She was falling, it was dangerous, and my father hated to do it. But now she's happy as can be, made lots of friends. I swear, her social calendar is so full she's too busy to see us."

"My mother said the same thing, and she's wrong. You're wrong. This isn't like that."

"Okay, sorry."

She heard him settle back down. She hadn't meant to snap at him, but he had no idea what her family situation was like. Polly shouldn't be in an institution—Veronica was certain of that.

And now she had the means to change everything sitting right there in her pocket. A thin river of hope had spread through her ever since she'd first held the diamond up to the light. It'd been missing for so long, no one was actively looking for it anymore; no one would miss it. Mr. Frick probably would have done the same, she told herself, stealing whatever he could get his hands on to crawl his way up in the world. Much better that the diamond go to someone who needed it rather than an institution that already dripped with riches.

She felt bad for her knee-jerk reaction, though. "How old are you, Joshua?" she asked.

"Twenty-one." he said. "How about you?"

"Eighteen. Have you always known what you wanted to do, career-wise?" Something about the dark and the quiet made her unafraid to pry. His life was so different from her own, in a myriad of ways.

"My parents took me to museums and galleries ever since I was a kid. But I don't think working in a place like this is in my future. I have other ideas."

"Like what?"

"My dream would be to mount a show of *art brut*."

"What does that mean?"

"It's French for 'rough art' or 'raw art.' It refers to artists without formal training, who aren't part of the mainstream art world, like Joshua Johnson. Or Bill Traylor, who was born into slavery and died in the late forties. I bet if I go to the South and travel around, I'll find even more artists who are undiscovered."

"That sounds incredible. Maybe I'll come with you."

As soon as she said the words, she regretted them. First, because they assumed an intimacy that she didn't mean to imply. And second, because even though she wasn't from the States, she knew a Black man and a white woman wouldn't get far in the South before running into trouble.

"I think we both know that's not possible," said Joshua quietly.

"I'm sorry, you're right." Back in London, her father's mates would gather on weekends to watch West Ham United on the telly, and make all sorts of nasty comments about John Charles, the football team's first Black player. While her father hadn't added to the racist vitriol, he hadn't put a stop to it, either. "But maybe one day it will be."

"That day is a long way away. In any event, I appreciate the offer."

She'd been wanting to say something to him since they'd first found each other, and now there was finally an opening. She took a breath. "I'm sorry about the way Barnaby treated you, when you first appeared."

"You mean mistaking me for the janitor? Not the first time it's happened. The first day of my Intro to Art History class, the professor asked if I was in the wrong room. As if a Black person studying art wouldn't even cross his mind."

"That's awful."

"I agree. And one day I will mount a show of Black artists that will make them reconsider everything, I can promise you that." His confidence in his abilities impressed Veronica to no end. Here was a man who was unafraid of asking for what he wanted out of life.

"Now can I ask you a question?" he said.

"Sure."

"Two questions, actually. Did you always want to be a model? And what's with your hair?"

She let out a laugh. "My hair was a terrible mistake that launched a fiery but brief modeling career."

"I like the way it swings."

"Thanks. And to answer your other question, no, I didn't plan on modeling at all."

A gust of wind rattled the window. With a loud bang, it swung open, the snow and wind penetrating the room in a flood of cold. They both ran to it, but Joshua got there first and secured the latch.

"Do you think that set off the alarm?" she asked, shivering in the remaining draft.

"It's only for the ground floor. Too bad we don't have a ladder." He placed an index finger on the pane of glass. *"He heard the snow falling faintly through the universe and faintly falling, like the descent of their last end."*

"Upon all the living and the dead," she answered.

He looked at her in surprise. "You know James Joyce?"

"Sure, like I've told you, models can read."

"So you're not just a pretty face."

The way he stared, as if she were some exotic species of bird or something, made her blush. She'd had a couple of boyfriends in London, but no one serious, just boys who took her to dances or to the pub for a drink. She still lived with her parents, as did all of the boys she still knew from school—the few who had left to go to university rarely came back. "I suppose not. My guess is we're both often underestimated."

"Probably right."

"What do you think you'll do after you graduate?" she asked.

"I'd like to go to Columbia for my master's degree, but since my father works at Brooklyn College, that makes better economic sense. Also, he'll be able to keep an eye on me, make sure I'm living up to my potential."

She thought of the diamond. How that might solve both of their problems. "Is Columbia expensive?"

"Very."

She was tempted to pull out the diamond again, show him, but before she could do so, he changed the subject.

"What will you do, once we're freed?" he asked.

"Head to the airport and fly home. Ignore my agent's calls berating me for my bad behavior."

"What if money was no object?" asked Joshua. "What then?"

It was almost as if he knew what she'd done. "I don't know," she said airily. "Never really thought about it."

"Would you go to college?"

"In England, there's one track for those who go to university and another for those who have to go out and get jobs. After my father's death, I was placed on the latter track."

"The fact that you use words like *latter* makes me think you should have remained on the first track. To be honest, I'm jealous. Sometimes, the pressure from my parents to make them proud makes me want to do what you did at the photo shoot. Stand up to authority and blow it all up."

"What kind of pressure?"

"I have to be fluent in two cultures: the world that my highly educated parents live in, where we are tolerated by the white majority, and the world inhabited by most young Black people, which is burning up."

"I'm sorry, Joshua."

"Me too, V, me too."

They settled into the quiet—Veronica smiling to herself, chuffed that he'd given her a nickname.

The next thing Veronica heard was the clock chiming six times. She'd fallen asleep, and her shoulder ached from the stiff mattress. Outside, a snowplow drove by, the harsh scrape of metal on tarmac the first indication of impending freedom. The blizzard was over.

From across the room, Joshua stirred.

"You up?" she asked.

"I am."

"Did you sleep at all?"

"Some."

"What time does the building open up on a normal day?"

"The security guard comes in at eight," said Joshua.

Two more hours. "I wonder what Mr. Frick would say about the two of us lounging about in his bedrooms, gallivanting around his home in the dark."

Joshua gave a strangled chuckle. "He's probably rolling over in his grave."

She enjoyed making him laugh. When she'd first seen him, standing in the doorway of the room with the beautiful panels, he'd radiated a mixture of concern and authority that most guys his age doing a part-time job might not have managed. He'd been brought up to cherish art and was personally invested in the care of these beautiful objects.

She fingered the hard stone that lay in her pocket. It would not only help her with Polly's care; it might help Joshua with the tuition for grad school at Columbia. She slowly started to draw it out.

"Joshua, there's something I have to tell you."

"What's that?"

Her response was stopped by a loud slam downstairs.

"Was that the wind?" She sat up and began to put on her shoes, as did Joshua.

"The wind's died down." Large flakes made leisurely loop-de-loops on the other side of the windows. Joshua extricated an iron from the fireplace tool set. "Someone else is inside. Stay here and lock the door behind me."

"I don't think that's a good idea. We should hide, not go down there and confront them."

"What if someone is stealing something?"

"Or what if it's the police, checking on things?" she said hopefully, before remembering their earlier discussion of how it would look if the police showed up. "Maybe I should go down."

"Definitely not."

"Then we go together."

They took the front stairs, creeping as quietly as they could.

Another noise, another bang. "It's in the direction of the garden court," said Joshua.

He'd shown her the enclosed courtyard, which consisted mainly of plants arrayed around a fountain, during her tour. It had been added later, after the Fricks had moved out, as a serene spot for visitors to rest and gather their thoughts.

They ventured in, Joshua first. The first dabs of morning light peeked in through the arched skylights in uneven patches, wherever the snow had become too heavy and slid off. To the left was a line of French doors that ran along the main-floor hallway.

A strange muttering floated across the room, but Veronica couldn't figure out where it came from. A cackle followed, like a witch might make. Veronica's heart rose to her throat. "What was that?" she whispered.

Joshua stepped forward. She grabbed at his shirt to pull him back, but the fabric slipped through her fingers.

Slowly, she stepped out as well.

There was nothing there. Only the plants and the quiet gurgle of the fountain.

Maybe it was just the sound of the snow falling off the roof. She looked at Joshua, and was about to tell him that, when a shadowy apparition appeared on the steps at the opposite end from them.

In the dim light, Veronica could make out a woman, dressed in black. Her mouth was clenched in fury, her hands like claws. They weren't alone, possibly hadn't been this entire time.

And now she was barreling toward them, screaming.

Chapter Fifteen

1919

Lillian replayed the meeting with Mr. Broderick in her mind as she hurried up Fifth Avenue. How stupid to think that a film producer could solve all of her problems, save her from ruin. The hours she'd spent in the sculptors' studios had been for the sake of art; this was something else entirely. What Mr. Broderick had in mind for Angelica the actress was far from the comedic genius of former model Mabel Normand or the spunky sweetness of Mary Pickford. He wanted her to debase herself for a chance at stardom.

Back at the Frick mansion, Lillian tucked herself into the ladies' dressing room just off the foyer to collect herself. It was tiny, a place for female visitors to shed their coats and hats and check their reflection in the mirror before being received by the hosts. The family had hardly seen any guests since Mr. Frick had fallen ill, so the room was a forgotten hideaway for Lillian to recover her composure. She needed time to think before having to transform from failed starlet into Miss Helen's private secretary.

She took the pins out of her hat and stared at her reflection in the mirror. Her makeup looked garish in the afternoon light, and she pulled a handkerchief out of her handbag and wiped it off, cleaning herself up as best she could.

Lillian had no one but herself to blame. She'd burned both bridges, with Mr. Danforth—no longer "Richard," not after he'd received her note of rejection—and with Mr. Broderick. Which only left her job as private secretary, and the threat of exposure if anyone recognized her. An avalanche of tears threatened, but she swallowed hard. There was no time to mourn her lost dream.

She walked out of the room to find Mr. Graham setting up at the organ.

"Good day, Miss Lilly." She hoped he would turn back to his music, but instead, he paused and studied her. "Is everything all right?"

To her horror, her face crumpled.

"Please, sit down, take a moment." He gestured to the organ bench.

It was imperative she collect herself, fast.

Lillian slid onto the bench, grateful to not have to make eye contact. She placed her hands gently on the lower keyboard and let her breathing settle down. How soothing it must be, to run one's fingers over the keys and become the conduit of beautiful music.

"Is it Mr. Frick?" Mr. Graham asked.

She shook her head. In the span of one hour, she'd turned down a marriage offer as well as a chance to be in the motion pictures. Now it was back to placating Miss Helen. The ludicrousness of her morning made her laugh out loud, the sound echoing under the arched niche, and she didn't care that she came across like a madwoman.

"Do you love your job, Mr. Graham?" she asked. "Playing music all day?"

"There are aspects I love, yes. Some not so much. But it's a privilege to live a life that's full of music. I try to remember that when things get difficult."

"I live a life of menial tasks performed to please others."

"I suppose that must be difficult, even in a home that's brimming with beautiful art around every corner."

She thought of the Vermeer hanging not twenty feet away in the hall, the one of the laughing girl that she loved so much. "That does help. And I admit not all of my work is menial."

"What is it you like about it?"

"When Miss Helen allows me to help out with her library research, I'm in my element."

Mr. Graham's eyes lit up. "A library?"

"An art reference library," she said. "The Frick Art Reference Library." Miss Helen had settled on that name just a few days ago.

"Now, that's a surprise." Mr. Graham tapped his chin. "Miss Helen, never to be underestimated, that one. What a splendid idea."

A tiny barb of jealousy rose up in Lillian. "It was my idea, actually."

"A brilliant one, Miss Lilly. Nothing like that exists in the States, as far as I know. A library for art."

"You think so?"

"Sure. Say, my cousin works at the art and architecture division at the New York Public Library, and this would be right up her alley. When Miss Helen starts looking for head librarians, do let me know."

Head librarian. A distinguished title. What did one have to do to become a head librarian? Or any sort of librarian? If Lillian was going to be stuck working for the Fricks, she might as well aim for a more professional role than head toilet-paper-orderer. Before she could ask Mr. Graham more about his cousin's job, Miss Winnie's voice rang out, calling her name.

Lillian slid off the organ bench and looked up to find her leaning over the banister.

"Where on earth have you been? Miss Helen needs you at once. She's with Mr. Frick in his bedroom."

"On my way."

Upstairs in the hallway, she gently knocked on Mr. Frick's door before entering.

Mr. Frick was asleep in his bed, snoring slightly. Miss Helen sat beside him, a folder in her lap.

"How is he?" asked Lillian, quietly.

"He's finally sleeping. I'm thinking of finding another doctor to see him. I don't like the new one."

Lillian doubted a third doctor would be able to give them a more hopeful prognosis, but she knew better than to say so. "Would you like me to call for one?"

"Yes. No. I'm not sure."

Lillian waited. "Can I take those papers for you?" she asked.

Miss Helen looked down at the folder, as if she didn't recognize it. "These are some old debts my father wanted taken care of. He thinks it's the end. I told him he's a silly goose, that he's perfectly fine. I mean, he's not yet seventy. It's simply indigestion, right?"

"I'm sure that's all it is." Lillian laid a hand on Miss Helen's shoulder. At that, Miss Helen burst into tears, much in the way that Lillian almost had with Mr. Graham. Neither of them was used to kindness, to gentleness. Which meant when someone reached out, softly and with care, it was enough to bring the walls of defiance and defensiveness crashing down.

She stood there, rubbing Miss Helen's bony shoulder for a couple of minutes until she had composed herself.

"Thank you, Miss Lilly." Miss Helen took a handkerchief from her sleeve and wiped her nose. "I can count on you, like no one else."

If she only knew. A knock sounded on the door, and Miss Winnie stuck her head in. "Mr. Danforth is here to see you, Miss Helen."

"Goodness, no. I can't see him at the moment." She looked up at Lillian. "Will you go down and explain, tell him about Papsie? I can't leave his side."

"Perhaps it's better if I stay with you," countered Lillian. "Miss Winnie can relay the message."

"No. Better it come from you. Go on. Tell him I shall reach out when I'm ready to receive visitors."

As Lillian descended the stairs, Mr. Graham was in the midst of a dangerous-sounding fugue. Mr. Danforth had his hat in his hands and looked up at her. His face was pale.

"Miss Helen can't see you right now." Lillian found herself speaking too loudly, both to compensate for the music and as a warning to Mr. Danforth to be careful what he said. "Her father is ill. She'll send word when she's receiving visitors again."

He moved closer to her. "What happened?" He wasn't referring to Miss Helen.

"Not here."

Lillian led the way outside, where a slight rain fell. They stood in a corner of the porte-cochère farthest from the front door, out of sight of anyone lurking in the foyer.

"Why did you send that note, breaking it off?" he said.

"I couldn't do that to Miss Helen. She doesn't deserve to be mistreated in that way."

"I went to the castle hoping you'd changed your mind and would come anyway."

"It wouldn't have been fair to elope with you, and I'm sorry for misleading you earlier. I'm not who you think I am."

He shook his head. "I know we may not come from the same social circles, but times are different. It doesn't matter to me one whit that you're not New York high society. Heck, *I'm* not New York high society anymore."

"That's not it. You don't know me."

"Whoever it is you are, or you think you are, I want that. Nothing can dissuade me, and I promise to take care of you. From what I can see,

Miss Helen treats you unkindly, is changeable and irritating. I guess I don't understand why you want to protect her."

"She is all of that, but right now it would be hurting her when she's most vulnerable."

"She treats her dogs better than you."

The remark was cutting, but at the same time, partly true. Only last week, Miss Helen had plucked Lillian's sandwich from the lunch tray that had been brought up to them in the sitting room and fed it to Wrigley.

In spite of the fraught tension with Mr. Danforth, she let out a rueful laugh. "You've got a point."

A footman came out of the doorway, and Lillian and Mr. Danforth stepped apart, waiting until he'd passed by and turned onto the street. Mr. Danforth's face softened. "I know the way we came together is unorthodox, to say the least. I think we both deserve a fresh start."

"What do you mean?"

"I came here to tell Miss Helen that I will not be proposing. I want to start a life with you cleanly, honorably. I'll accept the place offered me at Harvard Medical School in Boston. I'll sell my parents' brownstone, and we'll find rooms up there while I study, far away from the Fricks. Imagine, picnics on the Common, strolling along the Charles River. I'll come home after seeing patients all day and walk straight into your arms."

No matter what tempting tableaus he conjured, there was always Angelica, lurking in the background. The trial in January would only mean an increase in newspaper articles, an increase in press coverage, which could easily reach Boston. She tried again. "You don't know everything about me."

"I know that you see everything that's going on around you, that you're able to sit still and observe in a way that few others do. I know that you miss your mother dearly, as I do my mother and father. I know that you're able to mold yourself to please other people, like Miss Helen, but that isn't the entirety of you. I know you like your coffee with milk but no sugar, and I'd be proud to have you by my side as my wife. I won't stop until you say 'yes.'"

What was missing in his romantic narrative was that she wasn't truly herself with him. She'd molded herself to fit his perception of her, just as she had for Miss Helen. "That's not the half of it."

"Where's the other half? Please, Lillian, you are the sweetest, purest woman I know. If you like, I will break the news to Miss Helen about us today, so you can be free. I will go down on one knee right here, right now. Say you'll marry me."

He couldn't do that. Someone would see. "Please, Mr. Danforth. That's enough."

"My dear Miss Lilly. Lillian." He began to kneel, holding both hands over his heart. "Please marry me."

This simply would not do. It was time he knew the truth. How he reacted would prove whether he truly loved her, or only loved the *idea* of her. She grabbed one arm and pulled him up to his feet. "Come with me."

She brought him halfway down the driveway and turned back around, pointing up at the reclining figure carved in stone at the top of the porte-cochère. "Do you see that?" she asked him.

"Yes."

"That's me."

She was taking a risk—he might go right to the police and turn her in. But she didn't think it was in his nature.

He looked at the carving, then back at Lillian, and laughed. "Right."

"Before I worked for Miss Helen, I was a model for artists. A successful one. For this particular piece, I was hired to pose as Truth for the sculptor Sherry Fry. Not my favorite, I'll confess. That statue of Pomona you admired in front of the Plaza? Me as well. You were correct when you noticed the similar profile."

"What? Why?" He seemed bewildered.

"Because I had to make money so my mother and I could afford to eat and pay rent."

He looked up at the figure, back at her, studying her differently, objectively. Comparing the noses, the chins. "You were a model?"

"Yes. That was me. I was Angelica. I am Angelica."

His face went slack with shock.

"Miss Lilly?"

Mr. Graham had appeared under the archway. He hadn't been there a second ago. Had he been hiding in the shadows, listening in?

"Yes?" Panic rose like bile in her throat.

"Miss Helen is calling for you. Quite loudly, I might add. I'm sorry for interrupting."

He had been listening; she was sure of it. He'd been there when Mrs. Whitney identified her, and now this. But she had more pressing matters to deal with.

She answered sharply. "I'll be there in a moment. Thank you."

After he disappeared, she turned to Mr. Danforth, who had been staring up at her stone image the entire time. "I'm sorry if you're shocked, but I'm not sorry for having done it. Posing, I mean. I was a muse, you see."

Mr. Danforth had turned bright red. "You would take off your clothes so men could paint you?"

"I worked mainly for sculptors. Not painters."

"Your mother made you do it?" He was struggling for an excuse, a way to accommodate the new information. She almost felt sorry for him.

"Not really. We did it together. It was a successful business, you might say."

"You did it, and you liked it." A statement, not a question. A test.

"I made good money, and was the inspiration for great art. So yes, I liked it. I'm not ashamed."

With that, he stepped back, clumsily. "I must go."

As she'd feared, his interest in her had evaporated. If Mr. Danforth truly loved her, he wouldn't judge her so harshly. He liked to think he wasn't part of the New York elite, but deep down, he was. That would never change. He could never stoop to marrying a woman like Lillian.

Her first kiss, her first fleeting experience with love, had been crushed by the truth.

Lillian gave a tiny sigh as she let herself into Miss Helen's sitting room. Although Mr. Danforth had pushed her into it, she'd done the right thing by telling him about her past, as it made it clear exactly where she stood with him. There would be no running away to Boston, no long walks along the Charles River. She'd forgotten all of Kitty's words of warning when it came to men and been carried away with visions of love. Lillian's naïveté when it came to courtship was about equal to Miss Helen's, if she was being honest.

"Are you listening to me at all?" Miss Helen sat at her desk, the folder she'd been clutching in her father's bedroom open to reveal several bright white envelopes, sealed with red wax. "I've been going through my father's things, since he's been indisposed."

"Sorry, what can I help you with? And how is your father feeling?"

"Much better. Even the doctor says he's improved."

That was good news.

Miss Helen shifted in the chair, her eyes narrowing. "Did you talk to Mr. Danforth?"

"Yes. He knows your father is ill." Lillian doubted he'd ever be back, but Miss Helen didn't have to know that right now.

A shard of worry cut into her. Maybe she'd made a mistake. What if Mr. Danforth told the Fricks the truth? No. He wouldn't. Rumors of the engagement had already shown up in the gossip columns, and his association with the family was a matter of public record. Anything he did to bring them down would tar his reputation as well. The information she'd unexpectedly divulged was hopefully enough to put him off, but not take them all down.

"I know what you did."

Only now did she notice that Miss Helen's fists were clenched. A vein in her forehead throbbed.

Lillian glanced at the window. Could Miss Helen have seen the argument, Mr. Danforth trying to kneel before her private secretary, and recognized it as a lovers' quarrel? Lillian was sure they'd been hidden from view. But perhaps the sound had traveled up. The window was closed, but if she'd opened it—

"Don't lie to me. I know everything."

Lillian tried to stay calm, focus on Miss Helen. "What is this 'everything'?"

"You have a horse in this race. One that you didn't let on about."

"Please, Miss Helen, I really don't understand."

Miss Helen snatched one of the envelopes off the desk. Unlike the others, the seal on it was broken. "Papsie said that he wanted to take care of his debts, and the correspondence that I was to distribute included his art dealer, his tailor, his barber." She held the envelope at its very corner with her index finger and thumb, as if it were infectious. "This one had your name on it, which made no sense. I pay you from the household accounts, not his professional one. Why was he settling a debt with you?"

Lillian knew better than to answer.

"I opened it and read the note. It appears you and Papsie had some kind of arrangement to do with me and Mr. Danforth." She pulled out the note and unfolded it. "He wrote that he was certain you'd be able to see the marriage through even if he wasn't around to be there himself, and so he was enclosing a check for the one thousand dollars he'd promised, as he wanted to be remembered as a man of his word."

Lillian raced to come up with an excuse. At least Miss Helen didn't know about Mr. Danforth's interest in her. There was that to be thankful for. Still, this note struck at the very core of Miss Helen's vulnerability: That her father would control her every move, even beyond the grave. That she was always to be a daddy's girl with no independence, even after he was gone. No wonder she was angry. Lillian didn't blame her. "It wasn't like that."

"You both thought that I couldn't handle it on my own? How could you?"

"Please, let me explain."

Lillian took a seat in one of the chairs near the fireplace, an attempt to de-escalate the tension in the room. For a moment, it seemed that Miss Helen wouldn't budge, but then she finally relented and joined her, avoiding Lillian's eyes, instead glaring up at the stern portrait of Mr. Frick on the far wall, as if he were present in the room as well.

"When I first started working here," Lillian began, "your father mentioned his desire that you and Mr. Danforth get married. He asked that I facilitate the arrangement."

"Facilitate?"

"It was nothing more than what I was already doing. Remember the letters? How I helped you write them when you asked?"

"But he promised you money. A thousand dollars. That's an enormous sum."

"Your father is a generous man. I didn't want to do it, but he insisted. I couldn't say no without offending him."

Her voice pitched up into a little girl's whine. "But I made Mr. Danforth fall in love with me, didn't I?"

Lillian didn't know how to answer that. "You did all the right things."

Miss Helen reached into the envelope and pulled out the check. "Here you go, then. Take it."

"I don't want it."

Miss Helen waved it at Lillian, the image of Martha dancing in the air. "He wants you to have it. Your matchmaking fee." She tossed it in Lillian's lap.

Lillian studied it. One thousand dollars. The signature was shaky, weak. She didn't need the extra money anymore. She would never be a starlet. She would never need a wardrobe of fancy clothes, or acting lessons, or an automobile to drive around Los Angeles in.

Before she could say a word, Miss Helen grabbed the check back and ripped it in half. Lillian let out a soft cry at her ferocity.

"I changed my mind. You can't have it," said Miss Helen with a wicked smile.

"I don't want it. I told you, it was before I knew you well. Just as you were worried about success in love, I was worried about the same with my duties, that I couldn't do the job well, that I'd be a failure. To you, not to your father. I'm sorry you learned about it at this awful time, but you must know that I want what's best for you."

"Which is what?" Miss Helen asked.

"You want the truth?"

"Yes. You owe me that."

Mr. Danforth was never going to propose. Not after the way Lillian had mucked it all up. The least she could do was to let Miss Helen think that it was all her idea. "Maybe Mr. Danforth isn't the best match for you. You are from similar circles, but you have your library and your dogs, you've constructed a wonderful life for yourself around your interests, and I worry that by marrying you'd have to give some of those things up."

"What do you mean? You've seen his letters. We share exactly the same interests, in art, in hounds. He's said nice things about the library."

How to explain? "What one writes during courtship isn't necessarily what one truly believes."

Miss Helen considered that for a moment, then gave a slight shake of her head. "Perhaps you don't think I'm the marrying kind."

"No." She paused. "Even if that's what your father wanted, I don't think you are."

Miss Helen lifted Wrigley up into her lap and scratched his head. It was a moment before she spoke. "You may be right. I might have been the marrying kind before the war. But for now, I prefer uncomplicated relationships, like those with my furry beasts. What about you? Are you the marrying kind?"

Lillian considered her answer carefully. "No, I don't think I am, either. I want to make my own way in the world."

"So we'll be doddering spinsters together?" There was a whiff of excitement in Miss Helen's question. Her connection to Mr. Danforth had been tenuous at best, and deep down, she knew that. "We shall be companions until the end of days?"

Mr. Graham's enthusiastic response to the library idea drifted back to Lillian. If they could get the Frick Art Reference Library launched, it would be the first of its kind in America, and that was something of an achievement, wasn't it? The work would be fulfilling, demanding. Miss Helen didn't have the temperament to interact with architects and scholars without coming off as bossy and brusque. Lillian could help smooth the way, as she had with Mr. Danforth. As she had with Mr. Frick. She could make a decent wage, maybe even become head librarian. It wasn't the life Lillian had intended for herself, but perhaps it would do.

"If that's what you need," she finally answered.

Very early the next morning, Lillian was woken by a pounding on the door to her room. She sat up, confused, thinking she was back in the apartment with her mother and had overslept, that she was late for a session and about to be scolded. The sun hadn't yet risen.

But no, she was in her room at the top of the Frick mansion. Surrounded by all the food she could eat, and walls filled with the finest works of art for her to pass by and appreciate every day. She was safe.

The pounding grew louder.

"What is it?" she called out, swinging her legs off the side of the bed.

"Miss Lilly?" The voice was Miss Winnie's.

Lillian opened the door. Down the hallway, Bertha was just coming out of the bathroom, looking confused and sleepy. "What's going on?" Bertha asked.

Miss Winnie was panting from the stair climb. "Never you mind, go back to bed. I came for Miss Lilly."

"What's wrong?" asked Lillian, grabbing her dressing gown from the hook where it hung on the back of the door.

"Miss Helen needs you, in her father's bedroom. Now."

Chapter Sixteen

I n the dim light, Lillian noticed dark circles under her employer's eyes. Miss Helen must have been up all night with her father, who lay facing the wall, heaving with each breath, his eyelids shut.

Mr. Frick's bedroom was paneled in dark wood from floor to ceiling, and Lillian's gaze was drawn to a painting on the near wall of a girl wearing a tiny blue stone on a gold chain around her narrow neck, so lifelike it was as if Lillian could reach up and pluck it right off.

"That painting is by Sir Thomas Lawrence," said Miss Helen from Mr. Frick's bedside. "I never liked it."

"Why is that?" Lillian pulled up a chair. The situation didn't appear to be as dire as Miss Winnie had portended, and in fact Miss Helen appeared more quiet and thoughtful than frantic.

"He scrunched all of her features together in the middle of her face. The effect is as if she's smirking at the viewer, not inviting us in."

Lillian didn't point out all the similarities to Martha. The reddish curls, the pink cheeks. Mr. Frick was never far from his lost daughter, even when he slept.

"Where's your mother?" Lillian asked.

"She stopped in last night. Said she needed to rest, that her head was bothering her again."

Which left Miss Helen alone for the vigil. If only she and Mr. Childs had a better relationship and could share the burden.

"What can I do to help?"

With a groan, Mr. Frick turned over and stared at the two women, wide-eyed, his face shiny with sweat. "Who are you?"

Miss Helen tucked in his covers. "It's me, your Rosebud."

He heaved himself to a sitting position. "How on earth can I sleep if you're yammering on the entire time? I was doing fine until now." The lost expression of a second ago had been replaced with his usual businesslike mien. "Waiting for me to drop, are you? Get me something for this pain, for God's sake."

Miss Helen's face crumpled. "Of course, Papsie."

Lillian followed her out into the small hallway that connected the bedroom to the sitting room. The nurse—who Miss Helen had hired a few days ago—rose from a sofa as soon as they entered.

"Why aren't you helping?" demanded Miss Helen. "He's in pain again. There's no point in us paying you to lounge around all night." Lillian had witnessed a similar ripple effect many times now: Mr. Frick would needle or insult his daughter, sending her off on the warpath at anyone who had the bad fortune of appearing next in her periphery, whether a chambermaid dusting the bookcase or, more often, Lillian.

The nurse crossed her arms in front of her. "I'm right here." She followed them into the bedroom, where Mr. Frick's breathing had turned to moans. Lillian and Miss Helen stood back as the nurse examined him. He moaned again.

"You have to do something!" said Miss Helen.

The nurse turned to her, a sullen look on her face. "We did six applications of turpentine stoops at midnight, and he was given a sleeping draft soon after. For now, we must wait for Dr. Partridge's visit, which is set for nine o'clock."

"Nine o'clock! That's four hours away. I refuse to let him suffer for that long. His color is off and he's perspiring a great deal. There must be something we can do. Go and call for the doctor."

"Miss Helen, there's nothing that can be done."

Lillian had to agree. The man needed rest, quiet.

But that wasn't good enough for Miss Helen. "Go downstairs and have them call for the doctor. Now."

As the nurse left, Mr. Frick put a hand to his chest. Miss Helen ran to his side and placed her hand over his. "What do you need, Papsie?"

"Water. Get me water."

"Get him water!" Helen called out to Lillian. "Hurry."

Lillian went to the bathroom, where a glass of water sat on the edge of the porcelain sink. She picked it up and caught her reflection in the mirror. In the faded morning light, all of her exuberance and youth had been drained away. Her hair, pulled back in a bun, the way Miss Helen preferred it, made her nose appear beakish, not aquiline, and her mouth too small. *Haggard*, that's what Kitty would have said. *You look haggard.*

"What are you waiting for?"

Miss Helen appeared behind her in the mirror, wearing a nasty frown. "My father is ill and you're admiring yourself in his mirror?"

She grabbed the glass out of Lillian's hand and retreated into the bedroom. Lillian took one last look and let out a sigh.

Back in the bedroom, Miss Helen had lifted her father's head. "Drink this, you'll feel much better. Dr. Partridge is on his way and then you'll feel good as gold again."

"Thank you, my girl."

Lillian watched from the doorway as the father and daughter shared a quiet laugh. She'd overheard the doctor talking to the nurse a few days ago, saying that his heart was giving out. It couldn't pump enough blood to keep his lungs going, and they were filling with fluid. It wouldn't be long, the doctor said. One or two weeks, at most.

Poor Miss Helen. She was going to need Lillian more than ever very soon, and Lillian refused to let the woman's bad behavior bother her. Now was the time for compassion. When Lillian had been in mourning, Mr. Watkins had tried to take advantage, but Lillian would be there to protect Miss Helen in her grief, protect her from people who wanted something from her. And they would crawl out of the woodwork, for sure, with the inheritance she'd be left with.

Maybe, with Mr. Frick gone, Miss Helen would be free to figure out where she stood in the world without a parent scrutinizing her at every turn, comparing her unfairly to a long-dead sibling. It might be exciting, thrilling, to watch Miss Helen come into her own. She had every advantage—intelligence, social standing, a passion for her library, money—and maybe that would be enough to eradicate her pettiness and quell her temper so that she would become a softer version of herself. A kinder version.

"Papsie?"

Mr. Frick's head thumped back on the pillow, his eyes closed.

Miss Helen looked over at Lillian, confused, then back at her father. "What's happened?"

Lillian joined her at the bedside. She stared at the figure under the comforter, waiting for movement. Nothing.

"Papsie?" Miss Helen patted his cheek, leaned in close, and kept calling to him.

The nurse reappeared and wrapped her fingers around Mr. Frick's thick wrist. Lillian could tell by the heavy weight of it that there would be no pulse, and the nurse soon confirmed it. "I'm sorry, Miss Helen."

Miss Helen looked vacantly over at the nurse. "You were too late. He's gone. Useless woman." She rose. "We should go tell Mother."

The disconnect between what had just happened and Miss Helen's muted reaction was most likely due to shock, Lillian knew. She put her arm around Miss Helen's shoulders as they walked to the door. "I'm very sorry," she said.

She looked back at the nurse and shot her a look of what she hoped was apology for her employer's behavior, though no doubt she had seen worse.

But the nurse wasn't looking at her. She had lifted the empty glass on the bedside table and was sniffing it strangely.

Lillian turned her attention back to Miss Helen and guided her into the empty hall, in the house that Mr. Frick had spent his entire life imagining, and enjoyed for only five short years.

Lillian spent the morning and early afternoon frantically organizing a viewing that same day for Mr. Frick. The internment was to take place at the family's cemetery plot, outside of Pittsburgh, but they wanted an opportunity for an intimate group of his New York friends and business acquaintances to pay their respects at the Frick mansion before then.

Mrs. Frick had hidden away on the second floor, leaving Miss Helen and Lillian to manage the details. Or, to be honest, Lillian to do so, as Miss Helen tended to burst into tears every ten minutes or so and run out of her sitting room. Lillian raced through the to-do list she'd drafted up soon after Mr. Frick took a turn for the worse a couple of weeks ago. An artist was brought in to make deathbed studies; then the body was sent off to the funeral home. In the afternoon, the undertaker would deliver the coffin with Mr. Frick's remains, which would be taken to the art gallery and covered in roses, lilies of the valley, and tulips. At precisely five thirty, the guests would gather in the living hall, where they would listen to a reading of the Sermon on the Mount before being invited to partake in the viewing, during which time Mr. Graham would play the organ. The invitations had been sent out first thing, and Mr. Danforth's butler had returned word that his employer was out of town but sent his condolences. Lillian wasn't sure if Mr. Danforth was lying about his whereabouts, but was relieved to strike him off the list.

The entire family would then leave by train, along with Mr. Frick's coffin, later that evening, for Pennsylvania.

Lillian was in the front hall, handing various correspondence to the driver to deliver, when Miss Helen called out her name from the second floor.

Lillian took off at a trot up the stairs toward her. "What is it?"

"I want my father's bed moved into my bedroom."

"You want what?"

"You heard me."

"Right now the servants have their hands full preparing for the service." The chambermaids had been brought downstairs to help rearrange furniture for the viewing, and the parlor maids were stationed in the kitchen assisting the cooking staff. "Can it wait until tomorrow? Remember, you'll be gone for almost a week in Pittsburgh."

"No. It must be done right now."

Lillian stifled a sigh of impatience, but she understood the strange impulse. The day after Kitty had died, she'd lain down in her mother's bed and breathed in what was left of her essence, a mix of menthol and Pears soap, of sickness and health. Her mother's body had been taken away and disposed of quickly—it had been the height of the second wave of influenza, and every doctor, hospital, and undertaker was overwhelmed with the dead and dying. She hadn't even been able to put a rose on her grave.

"Very well. I'll have the chore man see to it." She asked Kearns to send the chore man upstairs with a few of the footmen, and watched with Miss Helen as they disassembled both Mr. Frick's and Miss Helen's beds, then brought Miss Helen's down to a storeroom in the basement before reassembling Mr. Frick's in Miss Helen's room. The whole time, Miss Helen fretted about, warning them not to scratch the wood.

After they left, Lillian half expected Miss Helen to throw herself on the bed in a fit of hysterics, but instead, she went to her dressing table and sat staring out the window, the bed switch-around entirely forgotten.

"Have my father's remains come back from the undertaker yet?" she asked.

Lillian checked the clock on the mantel. "Very soon."

Miss Helen opened a drawer. "I want this to be buried with him." She held Martha's cameo in her hand.

Lillian considered all the things that diamond hidden inside could buy: clothes, food, rent money. The thought of it being buried underground, lost forever, seemed indecent. "Are you sure? What if you buried the cameo, but sold the diamond and donated the money to one of Mr. Frick's causes instead?"

"No. He loved Martha best. This will be like he's being laid to rest with a small piece of her."

A valuable piece of her.

Lillian was concerned that Miss Helen would toss it away so cavalierly. She could never get it back, and Miss Helen was never one for having much foresight. What if she regretted it? "What if you had it made into a ring for your mother?"

"No. Papsie would want this, I'm sure of it. Come with me."

They walked together down the back staircase. "When I get back from Pennsylvania," said Miss Helen, "I'm going to insist that Mr. Danforth and I marry as soon as the mourning period is over."

Lillian's stomach dropped. "But what of our talk yesterday, about remaining independent?"

"My father wanted me wed. He very strongly wanted me wed, as we can see from his arrangement with you. So, wed I will be."

Which meant Lillian would soon be caught in the middle once again. Would Mr. Danforth reconsider, now that Lillian had removed herself from the running, and choose Miss Helen after all? Her first reaction was no, he would not, but the more she considered his histrionics in the driveway—threatening to go down on one knee—the more she realized how little she knew him. His presence in the house would make her own untenable.

Bertha was exiting the art gallery as they approached.

"Are the flowers here yet, Bertha?" asked Lillian.

"No, miss. Not yet."

"Have them brought in as soon as they arrive. We don't have much time."

The casket had been set up at the far end, near the enamels room, just below a melancholy Rembrandt self-portrait.

"How he would love this," said Miss Helen. "It's perfect, isn't it?"

Lillian had to admit that this was the ideal send-off for Mr. Frick. Surrounded by the works he loved most, and his family, in the palace he created with his wealth and eye for beauty. "It is."

"Thank you, Miss Lilly, for taking such good care of him. And of me."

Lillian shifted uncomfortably. She'd put everything she had into the preparations for Mr. Frick's viewing, ensuring that they were executed precisely to her specifications, mainly because she hadn't been able to do so with Kitty. On that cold February day, the undertakers had clumsily maneuvered the stretcher carrying her mother's body down the stairs of their apartment building, slid her into the back of a dirty truck caked with mud, slammed the doors shut, and driven off. Miss Helen's father would receive a very different send-off; Lillian would make sure of that.

Miss Helen took the cameo out of her pocket. Inside the coffin, Mr. Frick appeared serene and pale yet still strangely present, as if he'd just closed his eyes to remember something important and would open them at any moment.

Miss Helen placed the cameo in his palm and closed his thick fingers around it. The same hand with the scar from Martha's pain now held Martha's pink diamond. A fitting pairing. Maybe Miss Helen had been right, and this would be a way to lay to rest the ghost of the lost daughter and her father at the same time, to let them both go.

Bertha popped back in to say that the florists had arrived, and Lillian oversaw the placement of the arrangements while Miss Helen went up to dress. Then it was down to the kitchen to check in with the cook and back up to the gallery to go through the final checklist.

As the notes of the organ floated down the hall, Lillian stood next to Miss Winnie and watched as the family gathered around the coffin in a quiet moment before the other guests arrived. Mr. Childs stood next to his wife, Dixie, at the foot of the casket. Mrs. Frick blew loudly into a handkerchief as she and Miss Helen approached and took up a position on the side.

But Miss Helen immediately jumped back, as if pushed by an invisible force.

"It's gone!" She turned to look at Lillian. "Where is it?"

"Where's what?" Mrs. Frick blew her nose again.

"Martha's cameo, with the diamond!"

Now she had the family's attention. "What diamond?" asked Mrs. Dixie.

"What on earth did you do with it?" demanded Mrs. Frick.

"I put it in Papsie's hand, to take with him," said Miss Helen. "But it's not there." She pointed into the coffin. Miss Winnie and Lillian drew close. It was true: Mr. Frick's lifeless fingers were outstretched, not curled around the cameo the way Miss Helen had left them. Miss Helen reached in and lifted the hand, but there was nothing underneath.

Someone had taken the cameo.

The week the family was away for the burial, the whole house felt dark and muted, as if it were draped in velvet. Lillian went about her duties, assembling the towering stack of condolence cards for Miss Helen to respond to, watching as the flowers in the art gallery faded away, selecting which ones ought to be tossed out.

Before they'd left, Miss Helen had instructed the head housekeeper to search every servant's room, but the cameo remained missing. Someone had taken it right out of Mr. Frick's hand, a gruesome thought. How did whoever took it know what they were looking for? Only Lillian knew that Miss Helen had placed it there. She prayed it would turn up soon.

Lillian spent the afternoon before they were to return working among the archives in the bowling alley. She'd done everything she possibly could with regards to her regular household duties, and knew that Miss Helen had been planning on examining the contents of several crates filled with archival documents before her father had taken ill. She figured she'd get a jump on it and please Miss Helen with her initiative, get her enthused about creating a library instead of rushing into an ill-advised marriage. The quiet of the room, deep underground, soothed Lillian, as did the act of arranging the many invoices for art purchases by date. Degas, El Greco, Manet—the total value for the bronzes and paintings had to be in the tens of millions.

Yet Miss Helen valued that cameo with the diamond most of all. If they didn't find it, she didn't know what would happen.

"Miss Lilly?"

A man's voice called out from the stairway, and Mr. Graham came into view. Even though he was silhouetted by the lamps in the stairway, his thick shock of hair gave him away immediately.

"Mr. Graham. What are you doing down here?"

"Kearns mentioned I might find you. I came to pick up my paycheck."

She'd completely forgotten, which wasn't like her. But the week had been a strange one. "I do apologize for that. I'm a little topsy-turvy, and I'm afraid I forgot to ask Miss Helen to sign the check before she left."

"That's all right. I can pick it up next week. You look like you're well in the weeds down here."

"Yes, just going through some old records."

She waited for him to excuse himself and leave, but he hesitated, hovering over her.

"Is all this for the new library?" he asked.

"Hopefully. To be honest, I don't know if Miss Helen will be interested in continuing the project now that her father's gone."

"That would be a shame."

"Is there something else I can help you with?" she asked.

He cleared his throat. His usual boyish charm was gone, replaced with something darker. "I was wondering, do you think the Fricks will still want me to play for them during the dinner hours? I know it was Mr. Frick's idea in the first place, but I'm hoping you might convince them to keep me on."

She considered it. The music might only serve to remind the family of their loss. Still, Mr. Graham had been part of the staff for some time now, and deserved at least some notice. "I will speak with Miss Helen and her mother."

"Also, I wanted to say—this is difficult and I don't want to alarm you—" He paused. "But just be careful."

"I'm sorry?" She couldn't read the expression on his face. Was he threatening her? Or trying to help her? "What are you talking about?"

"Not long ago, I overheard a conversation that bothered me. One that might cause you trouble."

He had to be referring to her fraught conversation with Mr. Danforth, when she turned him away by acknowledging her past.

Was Mr. Graham hinting that he knew what had gone on? Would he tell the family if she didn't convince them to keep him on the payroll? Lillian had come so far, and wasn't about to be blackmailed by the family's entertainer. "I have no idea what you're referring to, Mr. Graham."

He recoiled slightly at her aggressive tone. "No, what I'm trying to say—"

She cut him off. "If you don't mind, I really ought to get back to work. I'll leave your paycheck with Kearns on Monday."

"But, Miss Lilly—"

"Enough. I said, enough."

She stared down at the papers on the table, frozen, until she heard his steps disappear up the stairwell.

There was only so much she could handle. As soon as Miss Helen returned, Lillian had to convince her that it was in her best interest to cut all ties with Mr. Danforth and fire Mr. Graham. If not, both men would have leverage on Lillian, and could come forth with the truth about her identity at any time. The walls of the basement suddenly felt like they were closing in. A wave of desperation threatened to crash down on her, but instead, Lillian threw herself back into her work researching the provenance of the Fricks' assemblage of Gainsborough portraits. Anything not to think of the present.

The reading of the will was scheduled for the day the family returned. Lillian got the Fricks' lawyer settled in the library with coffee, then, once the entourage arrived, rushed with Miss Helen up to her rooms.

"Have they caught the diamond thief?" Miss Helen asked as soon as the door was closed. Her eyes were red-rimmed, her freckles flaming.

"I'm sorry, not yet."

"There was hardly any time from when I placed it in his hand to when it went missing."

That was true. It was as if one of the figures in the paintings had stepped down from the wall and snuck it away. "I hope it will turn up soon."

"I don't trust Childs, so I want you to come to the reading of the will and take notes," said Miss Helen. "Bring something to write on."

Lillian did as she was told. In the room, a palpable tension hung in the air between Miss Helen and her brother, who didn't say a word to each other. He and Mrs. Dixie settled into the armchairs, while Miss Helen remained standing behind the wingback chair where her mother sat with a straight spine and her chin held high, as if on a throne. Earlier, Lillian had spoken briefly with Miss Winnie in the upstairs hallway, and asked how the week had gone. Miss Winnie had put her hand to her ear, and Lillian had asked again, louder than she would have liked.

"They want to kill each other," Miss Winnie had shouted back.

Exactly as Mr. Frick would have desired, really. He was always one for riling them up, and even after his death he held all the power. Never mind that there was probably enough money in the estate for everyone. While the mansion and the art collection were to be left to the city, the remainder was a large sum, to be sure.

The lawyer sat behind a Chippendale table with Mr. Frick's last will and testament laid out before him, wearing spectacles that slid partway down his nose. Lillian retreated to a chair by a window, where she could take in whatever unfolded discreetly. Everyone was still and silent, other than Mrs. Dixie, who swayed ever so slightly and hummed under her breath. Nerves, or perhaps Bertha's gossip that she liked to regularly dip into the sherry was true.

"Shall we begin?" intoned the attorney.

"Please do. We know he wanted all this"—Mr. Childs gave an expansive wave in the air around him, as if he were conjuring spirits—"to be left to the City of New York." He gestured for him to go ahead, a smug smile on his face.

"That is true. Now, if we are all assembled, I will read aloud the last will and testament of Mr. Henry Clay Frick, dated June 24, 1915."

"What?" Mr. Childs leaned forward. "Nineteen fifteen? He told me that he was going to draft a new one." He stared wildly at his mother. "You remember, don't you? You were there, Mother. Remember?"

Mrs. Frick looked up at her daughter, then over at her son. "I do remember, but he's been so ill . . ." She trailed off and turned to the lawyer. "What does this one say?"

"*This* one," he answered, "is the only one. Let me make that perfectly clear." He began reading in a monotone, perhaps hoping to offset the volatile effect the document might produce.

Mr. Childs interrupted after only one page. "Summarize it, please. Get to the point."

Mr. Smith cleared his throat. "Very well. According to the will, Mrs. Frick receives life tenancy of One East Seventieth Street and the Eagle Rock residence, as well as one million dollars outright and five million dollars in trust."

"That's ridiculous," said Mr. Childs. "A paltry sum."

Mr. Smith didn't answer, just waited for Mr. Childs to settle. Mrs. Frick stayed mute, although her hands clenched and unclenched in her lap.

"Mr. Childs will receive one million outright and two million in trust."

"No! What?" Mr. Childs cried out, and his wife went pale.

Miss Helen bit her lip as she tended to do when she was excited. "What else?"

"For you, Miss Helen, there will be five million outright, title to Eagle Rock and its contents upon your mother's death, title to the Pittsburgh mansion, and, um, several million in securities."

Mr. Childs pulled his lips back, baring his teeth. "Good God. How much, total, does my sister get?"

"Thirty-eight million dollars."

Even Lillian was shocked at that. The unevenness of the distribution was cruel. Mr. Frick's wife and son were being punished, it appeared. Yet for most of her life, Miss Helen had acted as her father's confidante, more than her mother, and certainly more than her brother. So perhaps this was her reward.

Mr. Childs rose. "Mr. Smith, I demand to see his revised will. Not this one. This one is invalid."

Mr. Smith tapped an index finger on the document. "This is it, I'm afraid. He did reach out to me in late November, and I assumed it was to go over his final requests. But then he fell ill, and asked to postpone it."

"That's not right! What will people say when they see that the younger sister, who doesn't even have an heir, who is worthless, gets everything?"

"Worthless?" Miss Helen looked down her nose at Mr. Childs. "They will say Father knew what he was doing, and that he knew that I would carry on his legacy as he wished, not waste his money on fossils and rocks."

Mr. Childs glanced over at his wife, who gave a tiny shake of her head.

"Don't," she said quietly. "Not now. We don't know for sure yet."

"What's that?" asked Miss Helen. "You can contest the will if you like, but Mr. Smith says Papsie didn't draw up another one."

"Because you made sure he couldn't." Mr. Childs rose and began pacing the room, his words punctuated with a finger that he jabbed in

Miss Helen's direction. "I was hoping I wouldn't have to bring this up, but circumstances have forced me to."

"Bring up what, my dear?" said Mrs. Frick.

"The nurse approached me the morning he died. She said she noticed a faint film of residue, much like when a sleeping draft is added to water, in the bottom of his drinking glass. The one that Helen gave him right before he stopped breathing."

Miss Helen laughed. "That's ridiculous. I gave him water. I knew he'd been given a draft already several hours earlier."

"The nurse came to me, concerned that you'd administered another."

Miss Helen looked over at Lillian, as if for confirmation. "It was a glass of water. I remember seeing it by the sink. You gave it to me."

All eyes turned to Lillian.

"Yes. I remember." She pictured the glass, three-quarters full, perched on the edge of the sink. A simple glass of water. "I picked it up from the edge of the sink and gave it to you."

Lillian remembered the way Mr. Frick had gone limp not long after drinking from the glass. Miss Helen was probably replaying the moment in her own mind as well.

"If there was a sleeping draft in it, then the nurse made a mistake," Miss Helen insisted, her face flushing with anger. "A deadly one. I'll have her license revoked if that's so, I'll have her tossed in jail."

"The nurse said she didn't leave any draft out for him," answered Mr. Childs. "Which was why she was so worried when she noticed the residue. She told me he passed away soon after he'd taken it."

"How dare you!" Miss Helen shuddered. "I would never do such a thing. I thought it was water. Besides—" She turned to Lillian.

"It was Miss Lilly who went into the bathroom before me."

Chapter Seventeen

1966

W hat the hell are you doing in my house?"

The screeching woman came to a sudden halt ten feet away from Veronica and Joshua, just as a chunk of snow slid off the skylight with a crash. In the morning light, Veronica could see that she was dressed like a Sicilian widow, in a black blazer, a long black skirt, and chunky black oxfords on her feet. The only touch of color was a green silk scarf tied in a knot at the base of her throat. She stood unsteadily, a dark figure against the white marble of their surroundings. Her hair was piled in a bun at the back of her head, several frizzy tendrils escaping behind her ears. The skin on her face was mottled with age, the eyelids layered with folds, the lips thin and straight. And eyes as blue as robins' eggs.

"Who are you?" she demanded, shifting her weight from foot to foot, like an elderly lightweight boxer.

This wasn't a prowler, a ghost, or the police. Only a barmy old lady.

Joshua stepped closer and Veronica moved with him. But the woman misread their approach as an attack and burst forward again, screaming, hands held out in front of her, palms flat. Before they could move out of the way, she was on them.

Joshua barely registered her touch, but Veronica, wearing the damned kitten heels, was unable to brace herself. She stepped back to stop from falling, but something banged into the backs of her knees, and before she knew it, she'd landed right on her bottom.

In the fountain.

It was only filled a couple of inches with water, but the shock of cold and wet, along with the humiliation of the unladylike position she was in, her feet hanging over the lip of the fountain, knees wide, was more than she could take. Who was this screaming banshee, and how dare she? "Get me out!"

Joshua grabbed her by her arms and helped her back to her feet. The water had soaked through her jeans and was now dripping onto the marble floor.

"That was absolutely unnecessary," Veronica sputtered.

The old lady didn't seem bothered in the slightest. "What the hell are you doing in my house?"

"I was trying to answer you," said Joshua, "when you came at us. I'm an intern here, Joshua Lawrence. This is Veronica. She's a model who worked at a photo shoot here two days ago."

The woman sniffed at them. "Right. I heard the board approved that. Wouldn't have happened if I were still involved, I can tell you that. Is it still going on? You think this is some kind of nightclub, don't you?"

"No. We both got locked in. We're waiting for Sam to arrive and let us out."

The mention of the security guard's name calmed her slightly.

"Are you locked in as well, Miss Helen?" asked Joshua.

So this was the infamously difficult Miss Helen. It was hard to imagine this woman planting clues for a lover around the house, or writing those coy lines of verse. Maybe they had it all wrong.

"Good God, no, I didn't lock myself in," Miss Helen said. "Why would I be so stupid as to do that? I stayed over next door in the library; only an idiot would try to drive in this snow. Last night I noticed lights flickering in here and figured it was the night watchman. Then, just now, I remembered that we haven't had a night watchman since 1931, which meant something nefarious was going on. I came down to investigate."

"I assure you, that's not true." He paused. "Wait. You were in the library? How did you get in here without setting off the alarm?"

"The library and the house are connected. Not information I like to share, as it allows me to come and go as I please."

To think they could have gotten out this entire time. Although Veronica had to admit it had been a few days she wouldn't soon forget, and it wasn't as if they could have gone anywhere with the city closed down. "Excuse me, but I need to dry off. If you don't mind." She started to head toward the back stairway, but the woman stopped her with a surprisingly strong grip on her arm.

"No. I'm not letting either of you out of my sight. For all I know, you're a couple of teenagers who broke in here for a tryst."

"I assure you that's not the case," said Veronica. She was about to add that she didn't appreciate being manhandled when she noticed Joshua's pleading look. This internship was important to him, Veronica remembered. She would feel terrible if she got him fired. She softened her tone. "I have a change of clothes upstairs, and you're free to accompany me if you don't believe me."

"No, that won't do. I have an employee list in my office, and I plan to check it, so both of you come with me." She made a move to go, but Veronica remained where she was.

Miss Helen hesitated, looking her up and down. "You *are* rather wet, aren't you? I'll give you something else to wear."

As she walked past them, Veronica and Joshua exchanged looks. She could tell he was eager to see the secret door, as well as avoid further ruffling Miss Helen's feathers.

"Are you coming or not?" called Miss Helen, impatient.

Veronica nodded. "Yes. We're coming."

They exited out the door at the northeast corner of the garden court, into a round room lined with chairs. "The music room," sniffed Miss Helen. "Yet another ungainly addition. My father would not be pleased."

At the far wall, Miss Helen pushed on what Veronica thought was just a panel, until it slid open. This house was full of tricks, it appeared.

Just behind the doorway was a small foyer with a coatroom, a half circle of a desk, and an elevator, all of exquisitely carved oak. "Where are we?" Veronica asked, confounded.

"We're just off Seventy-First Street, in the Frick Art Reference Library," said Joshua. "I had no idea there was a secret door that connected the two."

Miss Helen opened the half door to the coat check and disappeared inside, returning with a couple of hangers draped with long black skirts—similar to what Miss Helen wore. "One of these should do." She pushed the elevator button, and they all crowded in. "Would you like a tour of my masterpiece?"

Veronica just wanted to get out of her wet clothes, but Joshua nodded fiercely. A private tour by Miss Helen Frick was probably not a typical intern's perk.

They took a sharp right when the elevator opened, into a room with four long tables, each with eight wooden chairs. A gold-leafed fresco hung on one wall and a portrait of Henry Clay Frick on another. With its red-tiled floor and thick wooden beams that traversed the ceiling, the room felt more like an Italian chapel, albeit one that gave off the slightly musty scent of old books.

"The Reading Room," announced Miss Helen. "We had it designed like the sixteenth-century reading rooms found in Italy, although *they* don't have walls specially designed to absorb sound."

"It's stunning," said Joshua. "To think, this all began in a bowling alley. That's mainly where I've been working."

"Poor you, why do they have you down there?" Miss Helen asked.

Joshua opened his mouth, then closed it. During their locked-in tour of the mansion, he'd alluded to Miss Helen's rather fraught relationship with the board of the Frick Collection, which had culminated in her resigning in a huff five years ago. Veronica knew he couldn't answer truthfully: that he was nosing through Miss Helen's private correspondence.

But Miss Helen had already moved on. "I founded my library in 1920, and it opened in 1924. In 1933, the building was expanded, and we now welcome six thousand visitors annually. The only time we've closed down was during the Second World War, when we helped the War Department draft maps of important cultural sites in Europe. In doing so, we saved thousands of treasures from destruction by the bombers."

"Incredible."

Joshua was in heaven, but Veronica still had a wet backside. "Can I change, please?"

Back inside the elevator, Miss Helen hit the button for the penthouse. "You can try these clothes on upstairs. I need a cup of coffee after the shock you gave me earlier, and you may partake as well, if you like."

How generous. The woman was quite a pill.

Miss Helen led them into an office that reminded Veronica of the rooms at the Frick: large windows, tastefully restrained furnishings, the requisite portrait of Martha above the fireplace. Miss Helen seemed to read Veronica's mind. "When I designed this, it was to keep the memory of my family very much alive. All of the hardware—hinges, doorknobs, light-switch plates, window levers—are from my father's old bedroom."

An odd choice, but Veronica stayed mum.

"Go try these on in my bathroom." Miss Helen pointed to a door.

Inside, Veronica took a moment to collect herself. In all the chaos she'd completely forgotten about the pink diamond sitting in the pocket of her jeans. It felt hot to her fingers as she extracted it, even though she knew that couldn't be possible. Her conscience was getting the better of her.

She pulled on the only skirt with pockets, which hung low on her hips, and placed the diamond carefully inside.

Back in the office, Miss Helen gave a nod of approval from the far corner where she was fiddling with a French press. "That does nicely. I don't understand the appeal of the miniskirts so popular these days. There's no need to show so much leg."

"May I ask, why do you have multiple skirts hanging in the coat check?" Veronica asked. She'd heard of ties for underdressed diners at fancy restaurants, but skirts?

Miss Helen shot her a sharp look. "Because visitors to my library must conform to my dress code. No slacks, no short skirts, no spike heels on the women, and the men must wear jackets." She nodded in Joshua's direction. "If it were business hours, you would be in a jacket, young man."

Veronica sat next to Joshua on the sofa.

"I have standards," said Miss Helen. She set a tray holding coffee cups down on the low table in front of them. "What's your last name?" The question was directed at Joshua.

"Lawrence."

She went to her desk and pulled out a file. "Let's see here." She ran her finger down a sheet of paper. "*Joshua Lawrence, intern, Brooklyn College.*"

"That's me," he answered.

"*Lawrence*, anglicized from the French *Laurent*. A good, solid name. Ever since the Great War, I have washed my hands of all things Teutonic, and I would advise you young people to do the same. I live on a farm north of here, and believe me when I say no German visitor has stepped foot on my property. When I had the power, I refused German visitors entry to view the Frick Collection, and same with my library. I have softened in that aspect since. Reluctantly." She settled her gaze on Veronica. "What's your surname?"

Oh, no.

She could lie and make up a fake one, but her father had always been proud of their family ancestry. "Weber."

Miss Helen recoiled as if she'd just been given an electric shock. "That won't do. That won't do at all."

"You can't be serious," said Veronica to Miss Helen. "You'd dismiss an entire country of people?"

"I was proven correct in World War II, wasn't I? Yet no one would listen to me. No one."

"My parents are English," Veronica said, as calmly as she could. "We've lived there for generations. I'm British, not German." The fact that she had to defend herself against this insanity rankled her. "Not that it matters. All that was decades ago."

"I saw firsthand what those heathens did." She pointed to Joshua. "He can stay. But you, take off that skirt and get out of here. For all I know, you were here ransacking my father's home, my father's pride. Typical German."

Veronica rose, her heart pounding. She *had* been ransacking the house. It was best if she gathered her things and got out of here as quickly as possible.

"Wait!" said Joshua, getting to his feet. "Miss Helen, we have something to show you. Something that we think is from your past."

Joshua spoke calmly and evenly, as if approaching an excitable foal. He explained that they'd found clues to a scavenger hunt that appeared to have taken place decades ago, before the Frick residence became the Frick Collection.

Veronica expected Miss Helen to get even angrier at their discovery, but instead, she withdrew into herself as Joshua talked, becoming smaller in stature, weaker.

"Can I see them, the clues?" she said hoarsely.

"Veronica, show her," said Joshua.

Veronica reached into her sweater pocket and pulled them out.

"What are you, a kangaroo?" said Miss Helen. But her hands began to shake as she read through each note. A couple drifted to the floor, but Joshua quickly retrieved them.

"The past two days, when we were locked inside, we followed them," Joshua said. "It was a unique way to view the art, from an insider's perspective. It occurred to me that maybe we could incorporate these into the tours. Have visitors try their hand."

Miss Helen stiffened. "That's a stupid idea. This was some trifling game done for a gentleman caller, from another age."

"Richard J. Danforth," offered Joshua.

Miss Helen lifted her chin. "I haven't heard the name Richard Danforth since 1919. How did you know?"

"Veronica saw it on a guest list for a dinner party, dated around the same time, and we compared it to the monogram on the watch fob we found."

"Good Lord. I'd forgotten all about that. You made it to the end of the scavenger hunt? Mr. Danforth certainly did not. Perhaps I should marry you."

"I, uh, we did make it to the very end," Joshua stammered. "If you like, we can show you."

"Lead the way, Mr. Lawrence. Lead the way."

Veronica followed Joshua and Miss Helen through the secret door to the Frick mansion and back into the art gallery. As they neared the enamels room, her legs began to shake. She'd been so stupid to hide the diamond.

Joshua approached the first secret compartment and opened it with his pen, taking out the fob, which he handed to Miss Helen.

She rubbed her thumb along the silk. "I ordered it myself, especially for the hunt, but my intended didn't make it this far. Funny how no one wears these anymore." She lifted it up, holding it with her forefinger and thumb, and handed it to Joshua. "You can keep it. It means nothing to me."

She stepped back and looked around. "When we first moved in, this was my father's office. He used to keep a stash of peppermints inside that compartment. He thought I didn't know, but I'd sneak in and steal a few regularly." One hand went to her jaw. "No wonder my teeth are so bad now."

Her voice was soft, musical, lost in her past. For a moment, Veronica could see the ghost of the younger woman she once had been. A woman with good posture and untamable hair. Not a classical beauty, more of a handsome one.

"What happened, with your beau?" asked Veronica.

Miss Helen flashed her an angry look. "I was betrayed by one of my own employees. She stole him, along with something even more valuable to me."

"There was something else we found," Joshua said. He opened up the second compartment and Veronica braced herself as he reached inside. He turned to Miss Helen and opened his palm to reveal the cameo.

She grabbed it out of his hand and held it up for closer scrutiny. "It can't be. No, I don't believe it. It's been in there all this time?"

"I don't know for sure," said Joshua. "Is this what you thought your employee stole?"

"My private secretary. Yes. But that doesn't make sense. She wouldn't have known about the panels. She wasn't here when they were in use."

"What happened to her?"

Outside, the sun beamed for the first time in three days, but Miss Helen looked as pale as the snowdrifts. "I don't want to think about that. It was a terrible time." She stood staring into the distance, clutching the cameo with both hands like it was a rosary.

"Can we get you some water?" asked Veronica. She didn't want to be in this room right now; everything was closing in.

"No. No. I'm fine. There's one thing, though." She began to laugh, a note of hysteria in her pitch. "There's a secret compartment inside the cameo, which was discovered inside a secret compartment. Isn't that a peach of a thing? Now, *that* would make a good clue for a scavenger hunt. Frick's Folly, indeed."

Her words tumbled out like she was losing her grasp on reality.

Veronica waited, hoping Miss Helen would stop talking, show them out, and thank them for their help. But her hopes faded as Miss Helen turned the cameo over. Her finger found the tiny button, and with a soft click, the back of the brooch opened.

Veronica was done for.

Chapter Eighteen

1919

In the library, a slew of faces stared at Lillian: Mr. Childs, Mrs. Dixie, Miss Helen, Mrs. Frick, and the attorney. She shrank into her seat, aghast at what was being implied: that she had doctored the drink that caused Mr. Frick to overdose and die.

"I didn't add anything to the glass of water," Lillian blurted out. "I simply handed it to Miss Helen, I assure you." In the early-morning hours, she'd been tired and confused, but certainly not enough to accidentally add something to the glass. Someone else had done that, and left it waiting for an unsuspecting person to administer.

"Maybe the nurse made a mistake and left a second dose out," said Miss Helen.

"Then why would she come to me?" answered Mr. Childs. "She wouldn't have to say anything and we would be none the wiser. No. She suspected someone did so intentionally. And because of that, I've asked a private detective to join us." He rose and went to the door, calling down the hall for Kearns. "Tell Mr. DeWitt we are ready for him."

"How dare you, Childs?" said Miss Helen. "You went with us to bury Papsie, knowing all the time that you would challenge the will with this false accusation. What if the bulk of the money had come to you, would you have simply sent this detective person away?"

"I'm simply trying to get to the bottom of what happened the night Father died."

"It's terrible enough, Childs," said his mother, a handkerchief clenched to her mouth, muffling the words. "How could you?"

The private detective—a slight man with a pink turned-up nose—entered, and Mr. Childs addressed the family's attorney with a dismissive wave of his hand, as if he were a mere chimney sweep. "We are done with your services for now, Mr. Smith." As the attorney scurried out clutching his stack of papers, the private detective surveyed the room's interior. Lillian imagined him calculating the total cost of the artwork, furniture, and drapes, estimating how much he could make off the Frick family's squabbles.

Her first impulse was to run. She hadn't done anything wrong, but how easy would it be for Mr. Childs to say that she'd been in cahoots with Miss Helen?

She tried to shake off the shock at this strange turn of events, to think clearly. Anyone in the family might have wanted to kill Mr. Frick. As ludicrous as it sounded, even Miss Helen—if she'd known that her father was planning on changing his will—had motive. But if he had no intention of updating his will, Mr. Childs had every reason to see his father dead in a suspicious manner, one that would clear the way for Mr. Childs to contest the will or, even better, have Miss Helen blamed for the death and stripped of her inheritance. To be perfectly honest, even Mrs. Frick, who had endured years of teasing and disaffection from her husband, might have wanted to free herself of his torment. But while the family was certainly not the happiest of clans, would one of them really be capable of such a deadly act?

Mr. DeWitt spoke. "I understand that there is some discrepancy regarding the death of Mr. Frick. I've already interviewed the nurse who was on duty that night, per Mr. Childs's instructions. She has informed me that it appears that Mr. Frick was given a second, deadly dose of sleeping medicine. I've also been told that there is another possible crime surrounding his death. That a cameo containing a valuable gem was stolen from his coffin a week prior. Is that right?"

Miss Helen nodded. "Yes. I placed it in his hand myself, and then it was gone." Her gaze turned to Lillian. The one person, other than Miss Helen, who had been present on both occasions.

Would Miss Helen have it in her to set Lillian up to take the fall for her father's murder?

Lillian stared back at her, terrified.

"I understand you and your private secretary"—Mr. DeWitt consulted a small leather-bound notebook—"a Miss Lillian Carter, were present in both instances."

"Yes, we were," Miss Helen said uneasily, as if she didn't quite believe it.

"And you"—he turned to Lillian—"are the private secretary?"

"I am."

He addressed the wider group. "Is there any reason Miss Lillian would want to see Mr. Frick dead?"

A chill settled over the room. Miss Helen's lips moved, but no sound came out at first. Lillian could practically see Miss Helen's mind spinning to find an explanation, wanting to deflect blame. And Lillian made the perfect target.

She finally broke the silence with a low murmur that only Lillian understood. "The payment."

"I'm sorry, what?" said Mr. DeWitt.

"My father had a secret arrangement with Miss Lilly, that she would get a sum of money upon my engagement. When I found out about it, I tore up the check."

Lillian rose. Better not to deny what was true. "Mr. Frick offered to pay me a thousand dollars, yes." Mr. DeWitt's eyebrows rose, and the entire Frick family, other than Miss Helen, gasped. "But I never planned on taking it, I didn't think it was right. I mean, at first, I thought about it, but once I got to know Miss Helen, I decided against it." She was talking herself right off a cliff. Better to be blunt. "I was relieved when she tore up the check."

Mrs. Dixie cried out. "Perhaps that's why Miss Lilly stole the cameo with the Magnolia diamond, to make up for the lost money."

This was getting out of hand, and the private detective didn't appear to be interested in doing anything to stop the false accusations from flying around the room. In fact, he looked quite pleased with himself.

Miss Helen gave a hard shake of her head, as if she couldn't quite believe what she'd started. "No. I can't believe Miss Lilly would do such a thing. Something else is going on here, but I don't understand it."

"It's not your job to understand, Miss Helen," said Mr. DeWitt. "It's mine. For now, I'd like everyone to go to their rooms. I'll interview the servants first, and then each of you."

"Very well." Mr. Childs appeared quite satisfied with the outcome. "Dixie and I will go to Father's study and wait. You will find us in there. If we have a scoundrel in our midst, the private detective will find him— or her—out. Mr. DeWitt, keep in mind the last thing we want is a scandal. We'd like to keep this within the family, if possible."

"I'll do what I can, Mr. Childs."

Lillian went upstairs to the third floor, stopping first in the women's bathroom, where she splashed cold water on her face in an effort to compose herself. If she had time to think, she could figure a way out of this mess. Someone had set her up; she just had to determine who. She dried her face with a towel and took some deep breaths before heading back to her room.

"Are you all right, my dear?" Miss Winnie was coming from the other direction. She pulled Lillian close. "These accusations are baseless, they'll come to understand that. You are not a scoundrel, I know that, and they do as well. It's their grief getting the best of them."

What a relief to have one person who believed her. "Will you say something to Mrs. Frick on my behalf? Please, anything you can do."

"I will. I'm sure this mess will be sorted out soon."

But Lillian wasn't so certain.

She retreated to her room and paced the floor, going from the door to the window, back and forth. She was already suspected in one murder, and now this? What if Mr. DeWitt figured out who she was? Her life might as well be over.

She went to the window and opened it, letting the cool air rush over her. How could she convince them that she hadn't done anything wrong? Mr. Childs was out for blood—that was obvious. Lillian's head swam with the accusations, with the double-crossing that might be going on. Mr. Childs had never had much of an affinity with his father, to say the least. Could he have masterminded the whole thing, then called in a private detective—who was probably in his pocket—to finish it off?

A tap sounded at the door. Lillian braced herself, but it wasn't Mr. DeWitt on the other side of the door. It was Miss Helen.

She rushed in, closing the door softly behind her. "Everything is spinning out of control."

Lillian had one chance to ensure Miss Helen believed her. She couldn't waste it. "I promise you, I walked into the bathroom and saw the glass, and then a moment later you came in and took it from me. There would have been no time for me to add something to it, nor did I have any kind of access to a sleeping powder. I swear, I had nothing to do with either the cameo or the draft."

Miss Helen nodded. "I believe you. That private detective and Childs, they're in cahoots. They're trying to break me." She walked over to the window, arms crossed, her shoulders caving in. "For all we know, Childs paid off the nurse to make the accusation so he could contest the will and get at Papsie's money. Even at the funeral, I could tell that Childs was furious. He was no better than the rest of the so-called mourners, saying kind things but simmering with jealousy at our family's success. I knew what they were really thinking."

"What were they thinking?" Lillian could feel the muscles and nerves in her body releasing, ever so slightly, as she and Miss Helen joined forces.

"That my father made his money on the backs of common workers. That he was single-minded and at times vicious in his business endeavors. Oh, the envy in their eyes! For goodness' sake, one of the local Pennsylvania newspapers wrote an entire article rehashing that awful flood, which happened years ago. The inquiry determined that Papsie wasn't to blame. Can they not let the man rest in peace?" She looked at Lillian straight on. "I keep thinking of the night he died, and wondering what I should have done differently. Miss Lilly, do you think I could have accidentally killed him? The way it happened, right after I handed him the glass, makes me think the liquid inside couldn't have been only water. But if someone did add a sleeping draft to his water, who could it be?"

"I don't know."

"Well, we're in this together." Miss Helen surveyed the small quarters, as if just remembering where she was. "This is where we put you?"

Lillian viewed it through Miss Helen's eyes. The furnishings were simple, austere. Miss Helen wouldn't know what to do with herself in a room like this. She'd go mad in a matter of hours at the lack of luxury: the cotton quilt on the bed, which Lillian was glad she'd made that morning; the hooked rug; the dresser where her brush and comb sat.

And on the nightstand, a stack of letters.

Lillian's heart stopped.

She'd taken Mr. Danforth's passionate letters out of the top drawer the night before and reread them, as a reminder that she had been loved once, ever so briefly. His rejection, even if it had been of her own making, still stung. He'd been willing to throw away the Frick fortune for her until she'd scandalized him with her past.

She moved toward the door, hoping to encourage Miss Helen to do the same, but Miss Helen was frozen, staring in the direction of the nightstand.

"Is that Mr. Danforth's handwriting?" Miss Helen asked, stepping closer.

Lillian scooped the letters up and tucked them into the pocket of her skirt. "I was going to add them to your files today. I'll take care of it later."

Miss Helen held out her hand. "No. I ought to go back to my rooms and await that ridiculous private detective. I'll bring them with me and leave them on the desk."

Lillian slowly pulled them out of her pocket and handed them over, the blank side up.

But Miss Helen turned them over and squinted at the handwriting. "Why is your name on the envelope?"

There was nothing to say, no way to stop her. Miss Helen opened the first one and read it, staring up at Lillian for a moment afterward. Then she sat down on the chair and made her way through each one, her face ashen, the only movement that of her eyes as she read the wretched words of love written on them. Love for Lillian.

Miss Helen finished the last one and then stood, letting them all drop to the floor in a cascade of white.

"It was a mistake, Miss Helen, I'm sorry. I said no."

"So all this time I thought Mr. Danforth was pursuing me, he was pursuing you?"

"He's not deserving of you. How could he be? I'm terribly sorry, I tried to put him off."

"I'm too plain. Is that it? He found me too plain?"

That Miss Helen would turn on herself instead of turn on Lillian at a time like this broke Lillian's heart. The poor woman had always been found unworthy, her father constantly reminding her that she was not good enough. "Please don't blame yourself."

"Who should I blame?" She stepped closer, staring hard at Lillian.

"Him. Mr. Danforth."

When Miss Helen finally spoke, all of the uncertainty was gone, replaced by a steely voice belonging to the richest unmarried woman in America. "You fooled me, didn't you? You took advantage of everything I gave you and then you took everything I had. I will take you down, Miss Lilly, for this. How dare you make me look like a laughingstock? I know what you are, now. A treacherous liar."

She was so close that Lillian could see the thin red veins in her eyes.

"And not only that. You're a murderer."

The detective came to Lillian's room a few hours later and questioned her about the particulars of Mr. Frick's death and her relationship with Miss Helen, whether she harbored resentment toward the family, what kinds of interactions she'd witnessed between Mr. Childs and Miss Helen. She answered as honestly as she could, relieved that the love letters were never brought up. Miss Helen probably didn't want the fact that her suitor had been stolen by her private secretary brought out into the light. It would be a private grievance, not a public one.

And she had every right to grieve, thought Lillian, as she watched the sun set over Central Park from her window. The sky put on a show for what she figured would be her last night in the Frick household, a riot of purples and oranges. Tomorrow, she'd be taken to jail and her life would no longer be her own. She'd aimed too high and now it was all crashing down.

Around two in the morning, still unable to sleep, Lillian padded out of her room, down the back stairway, and then along the main corridor on the first floor. In the moonlight, the portraits on the wall seemed to glare down at her in disappointment. She wasn't sure where she was going, but when she got to the front entry, a movement startled her. One of the footmen—one of the larger footmen—was sitting in the chair to the left of the door and rose as she approached.

He didn't step toward her but instead moved directly in front of the door, as if he was expecting her to make a run for it.

Which maybe she had been, or at least checking out the possibility.

"Miss Lilly?" he said. "I'm afraid I must ask you to return to your quarters. The Fricks have asked me to not permit anyone to leave."

"I see." Lillian pulled her wrap close around her. "We're trapped, is that it?"

"I don't know, miss. I'm simply doing what I'm told."

"Of course. I'm sorry."

It certainly wasn't his fault. Back up on the third floor, a door flew open right next to her, making Lillian jump and cry out in alarm. But it was only Bertha, rubbing her eyes.

"Miss Lilly, is everything all right?" she asked. "I thought I heard footsteps."

"Oh, dear, you gave me a fright!"

"Everyone's on tenterhooks." She spoke in a whisper. "I can't believe they think someone killed Mr. Frick. It can't be true, can it?"

Lillian thought of what Miss Helen said right before she spied the letters, about how her father had amassed many jealous enemies. About the long-ago flood that had killed thousands of innocent people. Which meant that more than Mr. Frick's immediate family had reason to want him dead.

No, Lillian was grasping at straws; shock and lack of sleep had rendered her incapable of clear thinking. The house was impenetrable; no one would've been able to sneak in.

"I have some whiskey, would you like it to help you sleep?" asked Bertha, stifling a yawn.

She shouldn't keep everyone else up; that wasn't fair. "No, I'm fine," she said.

They parted, and soon after, Bertha's snores droned through their shared wall. Lillian couldn't sleep anyway. She had to figure out who had placed that draft if she wanted to clear her name. No one else was going to stand up for her.

The answer was there, in some behavior or word, she was certain. Something was off, but she couldn't put her finger on it. Something had happened the day before that didn't make sense. But what was it?

She spent the rest of the early hours running through what the family had said at the will reading, how they had reacted, trying to put her finger on what was bothering her, with no luck.

At eight o'clock that morning, overtired to the point of exhaustion, she answered a knock at her door. A chambermaid stood before her. "Miss Helen has asked that you join her in the Fragonard Room in an hour, Miss Lilly."

"Very well. Thank you."

She cleaned herself up as best she could, the dark circles under her eyes like smudges of fireplace ash, and entered the room at the appointed hour. How fitting that she be fired, or sent off to jail, or whatever they were planning on doing to her, in the very room where she had first fooled Miss Helen into offering her the job. There, amid the panels where nymphs pranced and lovers blushed, solemnly sat Mrs. Frick, Miss Winnie, Miss Helen, Mrs. Dixie, and the private detective, while Mr. Childs leaned on a wall near one of the windows, an ugly grimace on his face.

Mr. DeWitt rose to his feet, took out his notebook, and addressed Lillian. "I've recently learned of a deception perpetrated by you upon the Frick family."

So Miss Helen had told them after all. Lillian answered before he could go on. "I apologized to Miss Helen earlier, and I apologize to the family now. It was not my intention to attract the attentions of Mr. Danforth, I assure you."

The last thing she wanted to do was further humiliate Miss Helen, but she had to try to explain. "He pursued me, and for a time I was briefly entranced, but then told him in no uncertain terms that I was not interested. I'm sorry for having hurt Miss Helen so, after all she's done for me."

"For God's sake, you can't even do that right." But Mr. Childs's angry words weren't directed at Lillian. They were directed at his sister. He let out an ugly snort. "Danforth pursued a penniless working girl over you, an heiress? How Father would be laughing at this entire situation. At you."

Miss Helen cried out. "You are too cruel, Childs. Mother, make him stop."

Mr. DeWitt hadn't been referring to the letters. In her panic, Lillian had opened up the wound she'd most wanted to avoid.

Miss Winnie and Mrs. Frick exchanged a glance, as if they weren't surprised by the news. Poor Miss Helen, always the disappointment.

"That is not the deception I was referring to," said Mr. DeWitt.

The family turned and stared at him. "What else?" asked Mrs. Frick.

"Miss Lilly," asked Mr. DeWitt, "do you go by any other aliases?"

"I'm not sure what you mean."

"We've been informed that you are not who you appear to be. That you are also known as"—he glanced down—"Miss Angelica Carter. Or better known, simply, as Angelica."

Lillian could tell by the way he was eyeing her that he knew exactly who Angelica was, had seen the suggestive illustrations in the press. Mrs. Frick and Miss Winnie simply looked confused, but Miss Helen sat frozen, mouth open. "The model?" she said.

"Yes," answered Mr. DeWitt. "The artists' model."

All of her secrets were now out in the open, and for a brief moment she felt a flash of abandon, of being able to be exactly who she was and stop hiding. But that was quickly replaced by panic. A sliver of hope lay with Miss Helen, whose familiarity with the art world might make her more understanding of the role that models played in the creative process, less scandalized by her prior career. But deep in her heart she knew that only a few art collectors—Mrs. Whitney among them, as she was also an artist—entertained such liberal views. It would be one more reason to distrust her, not that she needed more reasons after seeing Mr. Danforth's letters. Still, Lillian addressed Miss Helen, not the private detective. "I was a model, yes."

Mr. Childs threw back his head and laughed. "All this time we've had the infamous Angelica under our roof? Wait a minute, didn't Father say she was the model for the woman above the carriageway? Now standing right before us, in the flesh. That's delicious."

"Childs!" protested Mrs. Dixie.

"This is not a laughing matter," said Mrs. Frick. "What on earth have you done, Helen?"

Miss Helen studied Lillian as if she were one of the portraits on the wall, taking in her shoulders, her waist, her hair, her feet. "You posed? For money?"

"I was an artists' muse in the past. But I've done nothing wrong."

"Is it true that you murdered your landlord's wife?" Mr. Childs was fully enjoying himself now, secure in his position in the family once again, having brought his sister to her knees.

"What on earth?" It was Miss Winnie's turn to go pale.

This was all happening too quickly. Lillian couldn't explain fast enough, not with so many people in the room staring at her. There was so much ground to cover: her mother's death, Mr. Watkins's proposition, Mrs. Watkins's lifeless hand, the blood on the rug. The words wouldn't come.

Mr. DeWitt grew weary of waiting for her response. "After I was informed of Miss Lillian's true identity, I followed up with the investigation into the death of a Mrs. Watkins of West Sixty-Seventh Street. It does appear that Miss Lillian, or Angelica, is wanted for questioning in that case."

Who had informed him? Most likely not Mr. Danforth, as she couldn't imagine Mr. Childs confiding in him about the family's current turmoil. He was an outsider, after all. It had to have been someone in the household. The only one who could possibly know about her was Mr. Graham. She remembered how he'd come to her in the basement with a warning. Could he have turned her in? With his job in jeopardy, would he have offered up what he knew in return for some kind of reward?

But that was the least of her worries. "I'm innocent, I swear."

But the list of coincidences, all connected to Lillian, was impossible to surmount. She could tell by the looks on everyone's faces, ranging from dismay to horror, betrayal to mockery. She was done for.

"What happens now?" asked Miss Helen.

"I'll take her to the police station, and they'll start an investigation," said Mr. DeWitt.

"No!"

Mrs. Frick's voice, usually birdlike, resonated loudly across the room. "We cannot have that kind of scandal associated with the Frick name.

My husband spent his entire life creating this bastion of art and culture, and now, a week after his death, you plan to trot this woman out in public and shame us all? My daughter's stupidity notwithstanding, I cannot allow that."

Mr. DeWitt blinked a couple of times and looked over at Mr. Childs for direction.

Mr. Childs nodded. "She has a point. We don't want our name besmirched. Can it be handled quietly?"

"I don't see how, sir," said Mr. DeWitt. "Angelica's been missing for almost three months now. It will make news, no matter what you do."

"Then give us a day," said Mrs. Frick. "We'll leave town, go up to Eagle Rock for the rest of the month, until it all calms down."

"What do you want me to do with her in the meantime?" said Mr. DeWitt.

Lillian hated that she was being talked about as if she were a load of laundry. "Please, I didn't do anything."

"You lied about your identity," said Mr. Childs. "You obtained a position on our staff fraudulently. You interfered with the affairs of my sister. You extorted money from our father. There's a chance you poisoned him and, afterward, stole a cameo brooch and jewel that belonged to our dear, dead sister. Need I go on?"

Lillian dropped her head, staring down at the complicated parquetry floor, a series of interlocking diamonds. "I didn't do it," she repeated softly.

But no one was paying attention to her anymore. Her fate had been decided.

"We'll keep her in her room until tomorrow," said Mr. Childs. "After we leave, Mr. DeWitt can come and take her to the police station. There will be no mention that you discovered Angelica here. Can you promise me that, Mr. DeWitt?"

"I will do my best to keep the Frick name out of the police report."

"You will be well compensated for that, as well as for so expeditiously getting to the bottom of our troubles."

"I didn't do it!" protested Lillian, louder this time. "For goodness' sake, everyone in this room had a motive to kill the man."

The collective outcry threatened to suck all of the air out of the room.

"How dare you!" Mrs. Frick said as Miss Winnie fanned her mistress's face with her chubby hand. Miss Helen stepped up to Lillian, paused, and then slapped her hard across the face.

Lillian didn't flinch. She deserved that, from Miss Helen.

Miss Helen turned to the others in the room. "I'll take her upstairs."

"Are you sure?" said Mr. DeWitt.

"There are footmen stationed at every door," said Mr. Childs. "No one is going anywhere. Not until I give the order."

Mr. Childs called for the housekeeper, and she and Lillian waited, without speaking, in the main hallway until the master key to the house was delivered into Miss Helen's hand. They took the elevator up to the third floor, and Lillian took advantage of their forced proximity to plead her case again.

"I didn't come here on purpose. I was on the street outside and Miss Winnie assumed I was an applicant. I was so thirsty, and she offered tea, so I went along with it. It wasn't done to trick you."

Miss Helen stayed silent. The elevator doors opened, and they walked down the long hallway toward Lillian's room, which would soon be her temporary jail cell.

"I was a model, and a very successful one. But it wasn't sordid in any way. My mother was with me whenever I modeled. I became more and more popular, and then my landlord became infatuated with me, after my mother died, and tried to take advantage. He killed his wife and suddenly my name was linked with his."

"Much like you linked yourself with Mr. Danforth."

There was no more to be said. Lillian had been a fool in many ways, but especially to think that she could have had a long-term position by Miss Helen's side, that they could work together to build a spectacular library of art. That this could be her profession, her life's work.

Miss Helen opened the door to Lillian's room and motioned for her to enter. Lillian did; then Miss Helen slammed the door shut and locked it from the outside.

Chapter Nineteen

"M iss Helen would like to see you."

The chambermaid who unlocked Lillian's door carried a tray with a bowl of tomato soup and a cup of tea. Lillian was hungry, but she took it from the girl and laid it on her dresser, then followed her downstairs. They would grow cold, but that was the least of her worries.

A flurry of activity greeted her inside Miss Helen's bedroom. The woman was tossing clothes in the air, Bertha trailing behind to pick them up, barely missing getting hit by a brocade shoe.

"Where is it?" said Miss Helen. "I know it was here, and now it's gone. I must find it!"

"Where is what?" asked Lillian, not moving from the doorway.

Miss Helen straightened, her mouth set in a tense line. "I sent for you because I'm hoping you know."

Lillian inhaled. "Know what?"

"The file of letters from Sir Robert Witt. The ones where he laid out his system of classification for his London art library. I must take it with me to Eagle Rock, and I can't find it."

"You asked me to place it in the bowling alley, in the bookshelves reserved for correspondence."

"I did?" Miss Helen stared just above Lillian's head, as if the truth could be found in the crevices of the crown moldings.

"You did. May I go now and eat my rations?"

"Oh, now, don't be so dramatic."

That Miss Helen could say something so blithely, as if Lillian weren't about to be hauled off to jail, infuriated her. Lillian gestured around at the riot of fabrics and books that covered the gray carpet. "I am not the one being dramatic. Bertha will now have to clean all of this up, when the file wasn't even here in the first place."

"Right. She will." Miss Helen glanced over at Bertha. "She doesn't mind, though."

A fleeting, hateful look passed over Bertha's face, but Miss Helen had already turned away. Nothing pierced her bubble of insularity. She motioned to Miss Lillian. "Come with me so I don't waste another minute."

In the basement, they headed to the work space. It seemed so long ago that they'd bowled together. A lifetime ago.

Lillian easily located the overstuffed file on the bottom shelf. "Here. It's filed under *C* for *Correspondence.*"

Miss Helen looked at it as if she wasn't sure why she wanted it in the first place, and sighed. "It's awfully large. Maybe I'll leave it here anyway."

It was all Lillian could do not to give the woman a good shove.

"Is that all?" Lillian asked.

"Oh, don't be like that." Helen paused. "I have something to tell you. I mean, it's not why I brought you down here, but while we're alone . . ."

Lillian waited.

"The family has spoken with Mr. DeWitt, and we've decided that if you tell us the location of the cameo, we will set you free. It does us no good to have the Frick name dragged through the mud, which it would certainly be, if you get taken to the police station and charged."

Always thinking of themselves. "I don't know where it is. I didn't take it."

"I know you say that, but be reasonable. You will be free; we'll all be better off if you tell us."

"I don't know."

Miss Helen considered Lillian. "I still can't believe you took off your clothes and posed for men."

"It was how I kept myself and my mother fed and housed."

"Still. I can't imagine doing such a thing. When you told me before the dinner party to pretend that everyone was undressed, was that what you would do?"

"Sometimes. Once you're used to being in the altogether, it feels quite natural. Think of all of the nudes painted by the greatest artists. Titian, Botticelli. Someone had to pose for them."

Miss Helen cocked her head. "Funny. I had all but forgotten that there were actual people involved."

"You approach it from a different vantage point, as an artwork to be catalogued, the value noted."

"I can't believe how many of you are out there, around the city." She spoke with awe, not repulsion. "You're everywhere."

"They aren't me. They're idealized, exaggerated versions of what a man thinks a woman should be. In any event, I think it's swell that they're out in the world, no admission fee necessary. If the common man can look upon a statue and be moved, I find nothing offensive about that."

"I suppose you have a point."

"Look, more than anyone, I would like to figure out who stole the cameo. And who left the draft on the sink. Maybe, if we work together, we can figure it out."

Miss Helen hugged the file to her chest. "But you were the only person I told about Martha's cameo and diamond."

"What if someone overheard us talking? What if someone was in the enamels room when you placed it with Mr. Frick, and we didn't know it?"

Miss Helen paused. "If someone was in there, they would have heard everything. But that's really quite a stretch."

"What if your mother or your brother heard us coming, and hid in there?"

Miss Helen let out a harsh laugh. "Why would my mother or brother want to take the cameo?"

Lillian struggled for an answer, anything to keep this conversation going, keep Miss Helen considering other options. "Your mother might have wanted it as a remembrance of Martha, not wanted to see it be buried with your father."

"My mother would have told me such a thing, and not allowed an innocent woman to be accused. You might as well be accusing Miss Winnie."

"What about her? Might she have taken it?"

"To what end? She adores the entire family, has been with us for decades. What's she going to do, steal the cameo and run off with the butler? Also, don't forget that she's quite deaf. She couldn't have overheard us talking."

That was true. And regardless, no one in the family would take the blame for this, even if they had done it. "Well then, as I said, I didn't do it, so I can't tell you where it is."

"So you'd go to jail when you could be free?"

"I have no choice in the matter. Who told Mr. DeWitt that I was Angelica?"

"I can't say."

Not that it mattered.

"Well, I'm sorry it has to end like this," said Miss Helen. "I valued your assistance."

She was dismissing Lillian, as if she were moving on to take another job, not being sent to jail.

"You are cruel." The words flew out of Lillian's mouth.

"And you are stubborn. I'll call for one of the footmen to take you back to your room." She walked to the far wall of the billiard room and gave a yank on the embroidered bellpull.

Lillian's instinct told her to run. To hide. She had only a minute or so before she'd be locked in her room again.

The basement was full of corners and hideaways. How tempting it would be to find one and tuck herself away. Or make her way up to the third floor and crawl into an empty trunk in the storage room, or one of the massive drawers in the linen closet. Then, in the dead of night, she'd figure out how to escape. After all, she'd done it before, from the apartment. But the Fricks' servants knew the house better than she did. She'd eventually be caught.

"I will show myself to my room, I don't need an escort."

Lillian strode to the stairs, wondering if Miss Helen would try to stop her.

She did not.

Instead of continuing up to the third floor, Lillian walked out onto the main hallway on the first floor. A parlor maid let out a soft "Oh" as Lillian walked by, but otherwise didn't call out. If the front door was clear, Lillian would continue, with only the clothes on her back. She had nothing to lose.

But the same beefy footman was outside, standing under the porte-cochère.

Over at the organ niche, she spied Mr. Graham's leather case resting next to the bench. A quick glance up the stairway showed an open door to the organ chamber, where she and Mr. Danforth had shared that lethal kiss.

She tiptoed up the marble stairs and slipped inside.

Mr. Graham was inspecting one of the pipes near the window. He turned around and wiped his hands on his trousers. "Ah, Miss Lilly. I was just doing a final visit. Mrs. Frick said the sound of organ music reminds her too much of her husband. I'm to play today, but then that's the end of it. On to bigger and better things."

How he could blithely make small talk when Lillian's life had been ripped to shreds infuriated her. "Or maybe they want to get rid of you, after you brought my scandal to their attention?"

"I'm sorry?"

"They know everything, now. If I wasn't already in trouble, you doubled it."

"How?" He pushed his glasses farther up on the bridge of his nose.

"You told the private detective who I was, and now they're about to cart me off to jail."

"Whatever you're accusing me of, I didn't do it." His cadence was even, not the overemphatic denial of a liar. But maybe he was a good one.

"You overheard Mrs. Whitney call me Angelica. And later, you listened as I admitted the same to Mr. Danforth, in the driveway."

"Yes, I was there on both counts. And yes, I did suspect who you were. But I would never have told anyone else."

"I'm guessing you were recompensed generously for the information. I should have known after you came to me in the basement and threatened me."

"I was trying to warn you." The words tumbled out. "You see, the niche where the organ is located captures the utterances of anyone in range, like a whispering gallery. Before the family left to bury Mr. Frick in Pennsylvania, I overheard Mrs. Dixie and Mr. Childs talking about the missing cameo, mentioning your name in connection with it. I was trying to tell you to be careful."

She revisited their conversation. Had she jumped to conclusions, having already been on the defensive, and missed his whole point? She remembered the harsh way that she'd dismissed him. "I didn't realize . . ." She trailed off, unsure.

"In any case, I don't find it the least bit scandalous that you are Angelica. The Fricks have quite a double standard, surrounded by hundreds of bronzed nudes yet mortified at the thought of a naked woman in the flesh."

There was no salaciousness behind his statement. He was simply stating a fact, and his eyes didn't wander over her body as he spoke, as Mr. Childs's and the private detective's had. After all this time, someone besides herself understood the bitter irony of the situation.

She believed him, and all her bluster fell away.

She walked to the small window and leaned on the sill. Too bad it was too small for her to crawl through. "I have to get out of here. I'm in terrible trouble."

"What can I do to help?"

She turned to him. "I'm at a loss. I've tried everything. The family doesn't care what the truth is. And I don't *know* what the truth is, which leaves me vulnerable to their terrible accusations."

"Defend yourself."

"I have and they don't care. No one cares who actually did the things that I'm accused of: killing Mr. Frick, stealing the cameo and diamond that belonged to Martha. I'm simply an easy target."

"Then you can explain it to the police, and maybe they can investigate."

"The private detective was hired by Mr. Childs. I don't stand a chance, especially now they know I'm Angelica."

"You got here in the first place, that says something. I admit I was quite impressed when I realized who you were, and that you'd been able to wrangle the position of private secretary to the Fricks."

"That's the thing, I didn't mean to pull anything off. I just stumbled into this house hoping for a cup of tea." Still, she *had* accomplished the impossible, moving upward in both class and circumstance, adjusting to the whims of Miss Helen, learning how to do things that three months ago she would never have dreamed of. It hadn't just been luck; she'd used her head, relied on her own wits.

Just then, someone called out her name, followed by heavy steps. The footman was coming for her.

The sky above the park was gray, the trees stripped bare. Lillian stared out of her window and thought of all of the statues of her likeness around the city. If only she could magically trade places with one. She'd remain motionless on top of whatever pedestal she found herself on, staring silently down at the people below, and once day turned to evening, she'd crawl down in the darkness to the street, disappear into the vast anonymity of New York. The police would arrive at her room on the top floor of the Frick mansion to take her away and find only a marble figure standing by the window, as if she'd turned to stone.

"To think what that woman did before she came here."

Mrs. Dixie's jagged alto rose up from the garden. Lillian leaned precariously over the sill and spied the tops of the heads of Mrs. Dixie and Mr. Childs. They were standing just below her, on the steps outside that led down to the lawn.

She pulled back a little so that if they looked up, they wouldn't see her. Their words floated up easily.

"It's abominable," answered Mr. Childs.

"Do you think our children were affected?"

"She was barely around them. It's not like she was their governess."

"Still. Helen should have known. Should have checked her references. Stupid girl. It's a good thing Mr. Danforth reached out to you to say he wasn't going to propose to Helen. Otherwise we'd still be completely in the dark."

A sharp buzzing rang in Lillian's ears. Mr. Danforth, the rat, had leaked the truth. All this time she'd thought it *couldn't* have been him, and yet the more she considered it, the less she was surprised. This was exactly what Kitty had warned her of, whirlwind courtships that turned ruinous. Lillian had been too naive to realize it, swept up in the possibility that someone might love her.

"I could tell something else was eating away at the old bloke when he showed up to return Father's check, beyond the fact that he didn't think he and Helen would make a good match," intoned Mr. Childs.

"You've always been so intuitive, my dear. How on earth did he bring it up?"

"He mentioned that he'd come upon some damaging information and couldn't bear to see our family's good name tarnished, then suggested we get rid of Miss Lilly sooner rather than later."

She'd repelled Mr. Danforth's advances and, in turn, he'd set out to ruin her. For all of her mother's training, the caprices of the upper classes were as foreign as some European country where Lillian didn't speak the language or understand the customs. If she had, maybe she would have realized that Mr. Danforth's proclamations of love were like the surface of a scummy pond, brilliantly hued but slimy to the touch.

"Good thing Mr. Danforth told you," Mrs. Dixie sniffed. "Otherwise she might have killed us all off, one by one."

"That's what's odd. Helen told me she has doubts about Miss Lilly's involvement. Or Angelica's. Whatever you call her. She doesn't think the woman did it. Said that there wasn't enough time between when she told her to fetch the water and when she came after her to get it herself." Mr. Childs let out a long, audible breath. "It's also strange that she didn't confess when offered her freedom."

"Maybe she didn't believe we'd be true to our word."

"She'd be right about that."

So it had been a setup after all. Lillian doubted that Miss Helen knew about that part of the deal. Yet the way Mr. Childs and Mrs. Dixie were talking, it certainly didn't appear as if they had planted the draft or stolen the cameo. The conversation ruled them out as suspects, unless Mr. Childs hadn't included his wife in his plans.

Lillian's head hurt from all the second thoughts and double crosses.

"Who else had access?" asked Mrs. Dixie, after a moment. "Your mother's room is connected to Helen's, which is connected to your father's."

"You think my mother killed my father?"

"She'd put up with enough nonsense from him over the years, after all."

"Enough, Dixie. Stop with this. My entire family was seduced by this stranger with a nefarious background, and our children's reputations are on the line. Someone needs to be held accountable."

"Fine."

"By the time the police have arrived, we'll be gone, and they can take her away and do whatever they like with her . . ."

Mr. Childs's voice trailed off as they moved indoors, but Lillian kept thinking about what Mrs. Dixie had said. If the pair of them were innocent, as well as Helen—her grief had been deep and real, and Lillian just couldn't imagine she had instigated her father's demise—could it have been Mrs. Frick? She was the only one left. Along with any of the servants, supposedly.

She thought back to both incidents, when Mr. Frick had died and when the cameo had been stolen. Something connected both events.

Some*one*.

Next door, she heard Bertha return to her room, humming under her breath.

Bertha.

Bertha was awake and in the hallway when Miss Winnie rushed to fetch Lillian that fateful early morning of Mr. Frick's death.

Bertha had been coming out of the art gallery when Miss Helen and Lillian went in to place the cameo in Mr. Frick's hand.

Lillian remembered the hateful look Bertha had given Miss Helen earlier today, as Miss Helen ransacked her own bedroom searching for Sir Robert Witt's correspondence file. It had flashed across the maid's face quickly, but Lillian hadn't missed it.

Early on in their friendship, Bertha had mentioned where she was from.

Pennsylvania. Where Mr. Frick had garnered many enemies, and possibly been responsible for the death of thousands.

She could hear Bertha in the room next door, opening and closing a drawer. She was so close. How to reach her?

The window was dotted with ice; it had begun sleeting. Lillian lifted it open. Below her, a very narrow ledge and balustrade ran along the exterior of the house. She carefully stepped out, holding tight to the windowsill, and then executed a sideways shuffle step to work her way over to Bertha's window. A couple of times her foot slipped, but she clung to the side of the house as if it were a lifeboat and waited until her heart stopped pounding to continue.

She finally made it. Bertha was lying on her bed, reading a magazine, but jumped up fast when she heard Lillian's tap on the glass.

"Let me in!" Lillian mouthed.

Bertha didn't hesitate, opening the window and holding out a hand so that Lillian could ease her way into the room.

"You're crazy! You could have fallen to your death, what were you thinking?"

"I have to ask you something, Bertha." Lillian brushed the sleet off her hair and dress.

"Do you want me to help you escape?" Bertha answered. "I would if I could, it's terrible what's happening. But they have someone stationed at every door."

"Bertha, where are you from in Pennsylvania?"

She looked away. "Let me make sure the window is secure. It can get drafty in here otherwise."

"You're from the same town as where the flood was, aren't you?"

Bertha gave her a blank look. "What flood?"

"A dam burst and wiped out an entire town. Mr. Frick was considered negligent but never accused, never brought to trial. You're from Pennsylvania, aren't you? You were there." She waited, watching as the flatness in Bertha's eyes was replaced by fear. "It must have been terrifying."

Bertha's normally rosy cheeks were white, and her lower lip trembled.

"You can tell me," urged Lillian.

"There's nothing to tell."

Lillian waited a beat. "You were in the gallery as well, right before Miss Helen placed the diamond in Mr. Frick's hand. You could have been listening in at the door, returned, and stolen it."

"What? No!"

"If you don't talk to me, I will share my suspicions with Miss Helen in the morning."

Bertha winced, as if protecting her body from a physical blow. She sat on the bed, her hands twisting. Finally, something in her surrendered. "They say the wave was seventy-five feet high, as tall as the treetops. I'd been with my aunt in the hills, hunting mushrooms. We watched as it wiped out a wire factory, where the furnaces exploded and rolls of barbed wire became caught up in the wave. I could see my parents and two sisters emerge from our house, drawn by the sound of explosions. It was Memorial Day, everyone was at home. I screamed at the top of my lungs, but we were too far away and the sound of the destruction was deafening. I always wonder, did they die from drowning, unable to breathe? Or did they bleed to death, after being strafed by barbed wire? Or some dreadful combination of the two?"

The effort of the confession left Bertha trembling. "So yes, it's no coincidence that I ended up working for the Fricks. I wanted to make them pay somehow. But once I got here, my courage flagged. They were real people, not monsters. I hated myself for my weakness, but I kept on, figuring one day I'd find the strength to act."

Lillian folded her arms. "So you finally found your courage."

"No. I didn't kill him. I almost did, but I couldn't."

"What do you mean? You were awake that night, the night of his death. I saw you."

"I had been asked to stay up in case Mr. Frick or Miss Helen needed anything. I went into his bathroom and I saw the bottle of Veronal sitting there. My father used to take it for his insomnia and I took that as a sign that this was my chance, finally. For four years, I had bided my time."

Bertha's mouth contorted, as if she were about to cry. "I filled a glass with water, and then I picked up the Veronal and opened the stopper. But my hands were shaking so; I simply couldn't go through with it. I thought of Roddy, and how we plan to be married in the spring, of our promise to each other. I realized that killing Mr. Frick wouldn't bring my family back, but it could destroy the chance I have at making my own. So I placed the bottle back down on the side of the sink, put back the stopper, and fled. I didn't go through with it, I swear."

Lillian studied her. "But the bottle wasn't next to the glass when I went into the bathroom." She could picture it perfectly, the lone glass sitting there on the side of the sink, no Veronal in sight.

"That was how I left it."

Which meant someone else had come in and finished off the job before spiriting away the evidence.

"I'm sorry for what I've done," cried Bertha. "For what I almost did. I'll confess, tell them everything."

Bertha's story broke Lillian's heart. She couldn't blame her, even if Lillian had gotten swept up in the aftermath. And she hadn't done anything wrong. "No. You have Roddy. Go get married and get away from here, all right? Promise me that."

"I promise." Her eyes were red. "You know, I wasn't the only person in the art gallery the day the diamond was stolen."

"No? Miss Helen and I were in there for some time, and we didn't see anyone else."

"Then they were hiding."

"Who? Where?" She paused, waiting for an answer. "Bertha?"

Bertha swallowed. And began to speak.

Lillian carefully climbed back into her own room after her talk with Bertha, still shaking from what she'd heard. She waited, standing right next to the door, until she heard footsteps, and then called out weakly. "Who's there? Is someone out there?"

The person drew closer.

"Yes, Miss Lilly?" She recognized the voice as the head housekeeper. Perfect.

"I have to go to the women's room. I'm not feeling well. Would you mind letting me out?"

"We were told not to."

"I'm quite ill. I'm going to be sick. You can stand watch, if you like." After a moment, the key sounded in the lock and the door swung open. The housekeeper tilted her head down the hall. "Off you go. Make it quick."

Lillian went into the women's bathroom and locked herself in the far stall. After a few minutes, the housekeeper ventured in. "What's going on in here? Are you finished?"

Lillian groaned. "I can't go anywhere. Can you call for a doctor? I think it's serious."

"Are you sure?"

Lillian made a retching noise that surprised even her with its indelicateness.

"Oh, for goodness' sake."

As soon as the woman left, Lillian let herself out and down the front stairs to the second floor, treading as lightly as she could. She heard a couple of servants on the main stairway, but was able to duck into the small foyer off the landing to avoid them. From there, it was easy to slip through the breakfast room and service pantry, and finally into Mrs. Frick's boudoir.

"What on earth!"

Mrs. Frick sat behind a small desk, writing in a leather-bound book, while Miss Winnie was perched on a chaise longue along the far wall.

Lillian held out her hands. "I'm here to apologize for my untruths. I thought you should hear them from me."

"Untruths?" sputtered Mrs. Frick. "Lies is more like it." She gestured to Miss Winnie. "Call for Kearns at once."

Miss Winnie rose and lumbered over to the long, tasseled cord that summoned the butler. Lillian didn't have long. "I was fond of Mr. Frick, I would never hurt him. Please believe me."

"I thought you were good for my daughter, but now we all know better, don't we?" said Mrs. Frick.

Just as Miss Winnie reached for the cord, Lillian let out a low, angry growl.

Both women startled, and Mrs. Frick laid one hand on her heart. "What on earth? Are you quite mad?"

She'd gotten her answer. "No. I am not."

But what to do now? No one would believe her accusation.

So she ran.

Back out into the smaller hallway, and then onto the landing. Mr. Graham was sliding out from the organ bench and looked up as she peered over the railing. She froze, waiting to see if he'd call out. If so, it would only be a moment before the footman at the door came after her. No doubt word was spreading fast that she'd escaped.

He didn't speak, just glanced at the door to the organ chamber. She slid along the wall, out of sight, inching toward it, then dashed inside.

After a minute, the door opened and he joined her. "What are you doing?"

"I know who killed Mr. Frick. And who probably stole the cameo as well."

"Who—"

"There's no time. But I won't take the fall for something I didn't do. I need to get out of here."

He paused, as if deciding something, then nodded. "I'll do what I can to help you. But there's someone at every door."

She had to escape, and there was only one way that might work. "I have an idea."

Lillian waited alone inside the organ chamber, listening to the footmen's grunts and shouts as they lugged the family's trunks out to the idling automobiles. After what felt like hours but was only a few minutes, Mr. Graham reappeared and gestured to her that it was safe. They took off fast, staying close to the walls. The police would be along to scoop up Lillian any moment.

She followed Mr. Graham along the hallway, past the Fricks' bed-chambers to the entrance to Mr. Frick's sitting room. Once inside, she headed straight for the window to the left of the fireplace. She'd noticed the window's proximity to the roof of the loggia when she'd climbed out onto the ledge to get into Bertha's room. She would make her way to the roof's northeast corner and crouch against the edge of the art gallery's skylights, like a gargoyle, until she could make her escape. The sleet had stopped, and she hoped the drop would be slightly less dangerous.

Mr. Graham pulled a cashmere throw blanket from the sofa and handed it to her. "To keep you warm. I'll run to Seventy-First Street as fast as I can."

"I can't thank you enough." If this didn't work, she would end up in jail with a broken leg, or possibly dead. That Mr. Graham was willing to put himself in harm's way moved her greatly. Reckless with fear, she threw her arms around him and kissed him. This was nothing like the kiss she'd had with Mr. Danforth, or the one she'd watched in the silent film in Times Square. This was something else entirely, brimming with mystery yet strangely familiar and safe.

When they finally pulled apart, they were both breathing hard.

"Be careful, Miss Lilly," said Mr. Graham, his cheeks burning red.

A noise sounded within the house, nearby. "You should go," she said. "If they find you, they'll want to know why you're in this part of the house."

After he'd left, Lillian gave a last glance at the portrait of Mr. Frick over the piano.

She'd never see this house again, if she was lucky.

She opened the window.

And jumped.

1966

M iss Helen let out a soft cry. The sound evaporated like a mist into
the upper reaches of the enamels room, where Veronica and Joshua
stood on either side of her.

"The diamond is missing," she said.

Joshua guided her over to one of the hard-backed chairs against the
wall, where she sat with a thud and held out the cameo. "Here, you see,
there is a secret catch. Inside was a diamond that was meant for my
sister."

"Wait a minute, are you talking about the Magnolia diamond?"
asked Joshua.

"Yes." Miss Helen stared at him wide-eyed for a moment, as her neck
turned a splotchy red. "My father gave it to her when she was born; the
dear man's generosity knew no bounds. I placed Martha's cameo, with
the diamond inside it, in my father's hand the day he died, knowing that
he missed Martha most of all. But it was stolen soon after, taken right
out of his coffin. And placed in here, apparently."

Veronica stood dumbly by. She should hand the gem over right now, apologize profusely. But if she did that, they might call the police on her. Miss Helen would *definitely* call the police on her, with a last name like Weber—there was no question about that.

"It happened just before the viewing began." Miss Helen pulled a handkerchief out of her sleeve and dabbed at her eyes. "When my sister, Martha, died, it was a bitter relief to us all, to see her out of her pain. But can you imagine what that did to my father? To be one of the richest men in America but be of no use at all to your tiny girl? I thought it might bring him some peace, to leave Martha's diamond with him." Miss Helen's face was red, her nose running. "But after it was stolen, we had no choice but to bury him without it. Very few people knew of the cameo or the diamond in the first place, or that I'd wanted to bury it with my father. Only Miss Lilly."

"Miss Lilly?" asked Veronica.

"My private secretary."

Joshua nodded. "The one who stole your boyfriend. I'm so sorry this has caused you distress."

Miss Helen's mood changed like quicksilver. "It certainly has, you both nosing about in my home, reminding me of the worst day of my life. How dare you?" she demanded.

Joshua would lose everything if Miss Helen reported what they'd done. He'd be fired, and never get into graduate school.

Veronica's decision to take the diamond had been a terrible one, she realized now. The Frick family had gone through a torturous time, and taking the diamond to help solve her own domestic travails was not the right way to go about things. In spite of Miss Helen's wealth, this jewel meant more to her than all of the paintings and sculptures put together, and Veronica had no right to it. None at all.

But how to make things right?

She nonchalantly slid it out from her pocket, hiding it in her closed fist. "Hold on a moment, let me take another look."

Veronica walked over to the second secret compartment, blocking their view with her back, and made a show of running her hand around the bottom of it.

"Wait a minute." Slowly, she pulled out the diamond, as if she'd only now come upon it. Her sleight of hand was clumsy, even to herself. "Look, is this it?"

Miss Helen gasped. "Did you find it?"

"It must've fallen out of the cameo at some point." Veronica carefully placed the stone in Miss Helen's palm. Joshua cast a strange look at Veronica. He knew it hadn't been inside the secret compartment earlier. He had to know that she'd pretended to find it. She was ashamed of herself. There was no excuse, and she hated that she'd let him down.

Suddenly, the electricity burst on with a glaring efficiency. The blackout and the snowstorm were over.

Veronica glanced up at the blazing light bulbs in the brass chandelier, then over at Miss Helen. "So you think your secretary stole the cameo?" she asked, desperate to divert attention from herself.

"At the time. But now I don't think she could've done it."

"Why is that?"

"She didn't know about this compartment. It's not something that you can see from just looking around the room; you have to know that it's there."

"But it was part of the scavenger hunt," said Joshua.

"Mr. Danforth never made it to his fob, and I wrote all of the clues myself, without Miss Lilly's help. It was a very difficult time for my family, and when everything fell apart, Miss Lilly was accused of two crimes: stealing the cameo and also poisoning my father. It was believed that she added a sleeping draft to his water, which killed him. When questioned, she always denied it, swore she was innocent, and then escaped before the police arrived to take her away. And now we'll never know the truth. My brother and his wife are gone; my father, my mother, all dead. No one is left except me."

But that wasn't necessarily the case. "What if we found this Miss Lilly?" said Veronica.

Miss Helen shook her head. "After all this time? Who knows where she is. Probably far from here. She did reach out to me once, when my mother died. Sent a condolence note, said that she had something important to tell me."

So she hadn't completely disappeared.

"What was her full name?" Veronica asked.

"Lilly. Lillian Carter. Or Angelica." She practically spat out the last word.

"I'm sorry?" said Joshua, confused.

"She went by Angelica back when she was a model."

"You mean *the* Angelica? The Gilded Age muse?"

"You've heard of her?" said Miss Helen, surprised.

"I have. Wait a minute—so your private secretary was Angelica, who was the model for the relief at the entrance?" said Joshua.

Veronica remembered him mentioning the model during her tour, saying that she'd disappeared. The model and the secretary were one and the same. It was comforting to hear that the woman hadn't met with a tragic end, as Veronica had imagined.

"Believe me, I had no idea who she really was," said Miss Helen.

"How did she become your private secretary?" Veronica asked.

"A mistake. I'm still not sure how that happened. But we were good together, for a while." Miss Helen swayed a little, lost in some distant time.

"When she wrote to you, was there a return address on the envelope?" asked Veronica. "We could track her down, see if she's still alive." She was desperate to keep Miss Helen talking, not let Joshua ask any questions about her miraculous discovery of the diamond.

"Good Lord, how would I remember that? It was 1931. I tossed it in the trash, where it belonged." But then she froze, as if trying to conjure up the memory. "Upstate somewhere."

"Do you remember the postmark, anything like that?" asked Joshua. Miss Helen paused. "It was a tree. Pine something."

"Maybe we can figure it out, help you find her," suggested Veronica.

"It's a lost cause. Don't know why you'd bother." But Miss Helen didn't wholeheartedly object, either.

"We need a map of the state," Veronica said. "Do you have anything like that?"

"I run a library. Of course I do."

Back in her office in the library building, Miss Helen rummaged through the drawers of a small desk that sat in the corner. "Had to fire my current secretary last week, as she didn't understand my filing system, no matter how many times I explained it. Here."

She pulled out a map of New York State and handed it to Veronica, who laid it out on the coffee table in front of the sofa. She ran her finger down the index of town names. "Pine Knolls. Could that be it?"

Miss Helen smiled, impressed with herself. "Yes, of course. Pine Knolls. I've always had a keen eye for detail and a good memory. That's what my father always told me."

The man had been gone for almost fifty years, yet Miss Helen mentioned him repeatedly, as if he were still busy collecting art in the mansion next door. Veronica remembered how proudly Miss Helen had announced that all of the fixtures and doorknobs in her office came straight from his bedroom. Mr. Henry Clay Frick had a powerful hold on his daughter.

"Do you mind if I use your phone?" Joshua asked. "If it's working, I can call the operator for her information."

Miss Helen nodded.

Joshua avoided Veronica's eye as he walked to the desk. He had to be horrified at the fact that she'd had the diamond in her possession these past many hours. Hopefully he wasn't calling the police, turning her in for her blatant deception. It struck Veronica that she was utterly alone here in America, with no one to come to her rescue, and in a rush of panic she wanted desperately to hear her mother's voice. She'd promised to call her collect after the photo shoot, and Trish was probably worrying that she'd been swallowed up by the Big Apple by now. "I need to make a call as well, do you mind if I step out?"

Neither Joshua nor Miss Helen responded, so she ducked out and took the elevator down to the bank of telephone booths she'd spied earlier in the library's lobby. Inside one, she waited for the operator to connect her.

"Veronica, how are you?" her mother said, the words tinny and hollow.

"I'm fine, Mum. Sorry I didn't get back to you before. There was a snowstorm and everything shut down."

"How unfortunate. Are you off to Newport today, then?"

All that—Barnaby, the photo shoot—seemed like a distant life. A less-than-desirable life. Even if on the off chance Sabrina asked her to continue, Veronica wouldn't do it. She didn't want to have to put up with inflated male egos and skinny mean girls. The past couple of days in the Frick house had opened her eyes to the possibilities. If Joshua could infiltrate the art scene, follow his passion, then she could, too. Not that she knew what exactly that passion was.

She swallowed hard, thinking of Polly. There was no easy answer.

"No, I won't be going to Newport. In fact, I think I'll be coming home soon. How's Polly?"

"Oh, my dear."

Veronica's heart sank. "What's wrong, what's happened?"

"She's refusing to eat. They've tried all her favorite foods, I even brought over a trifle, but she simply won't do it."

Poor Polly. She must be miserable to not eat even one bite of trifle. Who knew what was going on in that place? Tears pricked Veronica's eyes. "She has to come home, Mum."

"You know I can't do that. The nursing staff says that it's typical, that she just needs more time to settle in. She'll be fine in no time."

The cheery offhandedness in her mother's delivery only increased Veronica's anxiety. Her mum was desperate to believe what the staff said was true; she wanted so badly for both of her daughters to be happy.

"I'll be on the next flight out."

"Don't rush anything. I'll keep an eye on her, I promise."

After Veronica hung up, she called the airline, but flights were backed up after the storm and she wasn't able to get a seat until tomorrow afternoon. She switched her reservation and headed back to Miss Helen's office. The past night felt like a dream, one that had dissipated in the morning light, and now the real world was pressing in on Veronica on all sides. For a brief moment, she considered collecting her suitcases and disappearing into the snow-covered city with her proverbial tail between her legs, but she couldn't do that to Joshua. Not after the three days they'd spent together.

"I can't remember his name for the life of me," Miss Helen was saying to Joshua when Veronica returned. "How angry Papsie would be. He loved the man."

"Who's that?" Veronica asked.

"The organist who used to play for us at dinner."

Joshua explained. "We can't find a Lillian Carter in Pine Knolls, and Miss Helen said the family believed she ran off with the organist who used to play here."

"He left our employ right as Miss Lilly went on the lam, and we always wondered if there was a link," said Miss Helen. "But then the family started fighting amongst ourselves, over inheritances and the like, and it never came up again. But I simply can't remember his name."

The answer came to Veronica out of the blue. "Archer Graham," she said. In her head, she could see it clearly on the page, written in fountain pen.

"What?" said Joshua.

"Archer Graham," she repeated. "I'm pretty sure that's who it was."

"Brilliant!" Miss Helen snapped her fingers. "That's it. You're right."

"How do you know that?" Joshua asked Veronica, dumbfounded.

"He wrote a letter to Mr. Frick, confirming that he'd be playing for him for another season. It was one of the documents downstairs."

"Well done, girly," said Miss Helen. "You remind me of Miss Lilly. The woman had an uncanny ability to remember details like that, to know exactly where items were that I'd lost. Too bad she was a brazen hussy of a woman." She shook a bony finger at Joshua. "Yes, Archer Graham. That was it. Call again and ask for that name."

Joshua dialed the operator. "I'm looking for a phone number and address for an Archer Graham in Pine Knolls, please."

There was a pause. He scribbled wildly on a notepad, then hung up the phone. "We've found him."

"So they did run off together," said Miss Helen. "My hunch was right, yet again."

"Do you want to call her?" Joshua turned the notepad so it was facing Miss Helen.

She shook her head. "No. That's not the way to do it. I want to see that woman's face when I question her. How far away is Pine Knolls?"

Joshua studied the map. "About two hours."

"My car is outside," said Miss Helen. "The roads are probably being cleared by now." She looked at each of them, her usual glare of disdain replaced by a waggish gleam. "Do you want to join me? It's always nice to have company on a jaunt into the countryside."

"I'm guessing my classes are canceled today," said Joshua. "I'd love to. Veronica, are you in?"

The question wasn't delivered warmly.

The alternative to joining them was to spend the time waiting in what was probably an already-crowded airport. This would keep Veronica's mind off of Polly's plight, and give her the chance to apologize to Joshua for her selfish decision to steal the diamond. Also, she had to admit, she found herself eager to find out more, to meet the supermodel of the 1910s.

"Yes. I'm in."

Veronica sat in the back of Miss Helen's Lincoln Continental trying to focus on the horizon, which her father had always said helped prevent motion sickness. Maybe on the open seas, but it sure didn't work on the winding roads north of the city. First of all, there was no horizon, only tree after tree whizzing by the window at a dizzying rate. Secondly, Miss Helen didn't bother to obey the speed limit or proper driving etiquette. She tended to come up fast behind some unsuspecting driver, then stamp the brake repeatedly, coming perilously close to the back bumper of the car ahead of them. Joshua reached for the dashboard a few of times to brace himself, but after the fourth time, Miss Helen gave him a dirty look and uttered something under her breath about "lily-livers" and he'd been sitting on his hands ever since.

The temperature had risen above freezing, turning last night's snow piles shiny and wet. Water sluiced from underneath the drifts that lined either side of the roads, and Veronica thanked her stars it wasn't icy. Otherwise they'd certainly end up in a ditch before making it to Pine Knolls. The only thing that kept Veronica's heart rate from sky-rocketing was the fact that she was utterly exhausted. She hadn't gotten much sleep the past two nights, as the rattling of the windows had kept her from sleeping soundly. A foggy fatigue weighed down her every thought.

Other than seeing Polly, she didn't have much of a reason to return home, and the thought of what was ahead depressed her terribly. Explaining to her mother that she was all washed up. Dealing with Sabrina's wrath and disappointment at her misbehavior. Going back to work for Uncle Donny.

A couple of hours later, they reached the main street of Pine Knolls, where the storefronts looked tired and shabby against the white gleam of new snow. They crossed over a set of railroad tracks and, with Joshua's assistance on the map—Veronica didn't envy him that task one bit; at one point he'd turned quite green—they eventually pulled up to a small farmhouse with gray shutters, set off from the road by a rock wall. An enormous oak soared over the front yard, the branches like splayed fingers.

Miss Helen pulled into the driveway and jammed the gear into park. For the drive, she'd put on a ridiculous hat with a wide brim and a ribbon, as well as leather driving gloves, as if she were handling a horse-drawn carriage, not a modern car. The woman was not of this time.

"Shall we go in?" asked Joshua.

"Maybe it's not the right house." Miss Helen had only peeled off one glove, like she was having second thoughts at the entire venture.

"I'm pretty sure it is," answered Joshua.

Veronica tried to allay her fears, lower her expectations. "She may no longer live here, or might have passed away," she offered.

"Dead? No. That woman had nerves of steel. She'll definitely outlive me." The second glove came off with a flourish. "Time to give her a piece of my mind. How dare she run away like she did!"

A narrow path to the front door had been cleared, and Joshua let Miss Helen go first. Veronica moved to follow, but Joshua did so at the same time, and they bumped into each other.

"Sorry," she said. "Go ahead."

"No. You go."

Miss Helen by now had reached the porch. "Come on, you two."

Veronica touched the arm of his coat and spoke softly. "I'm sorry, Joshua, about the diamond."

"So you *did* take it," he whispered.

"I did, and I'm sorry about that. I'd like to explain."

But she didn't get the chance. "Come on, I don't have all day!" yelled Miss Helen.

They gathered at the front door, where a cornflower blue bench sat between two porch lamps. Miss Helen gave a firm knock.

An older man with a thick head of silver hair and round spectacles answered the door. He surveyed them with a baffled look on his face. "Can I help you?"

Miss Helen swallowed before answering, the only sign of nerves that Veronica could see. Her face remained a cold mask. "Archer. What on earth are you doing in this godawful town? I'm guessing you're playing every Sunday in some two-bit church, teaching a choir of tone-deaf vagrants. My father would be very upset that you threw away your talent. What a waste."

The man's eyes widened. "Miss Helen?"

"That is correct. Let us in."

He did, stepping back into a small foyer as Miss Helen waltzed through the doorway. Joshua motioned for Veronica to enter next, then hesitated a split second, waiting until the owner of the house had specifically beckoned him inside as well. It occurred to Veronica how blithely she walked through the world, as she and Miss Helen didn't think twice about the invitation, while Joshua could never assume he was welcome.

"What are you doing here, Miss Helen?" asked Archer Graham. From another room came the sound of someone washing dishes.

"I'm seeking answers. Where's Miss Lilly? I'm fairly certain she's on the premises."

"Lillian!" the man called out.

They'd found her.

The running water stopped. "Yes, darling?"

The trio followed him into the kitchen, where a woman in her late sixties stood at the sink, drying a glass. She saw Miss Helen and froze for a second, before carefully placing the glass on the counter.

Joshua had said the woman had been the top model of her time, and Veronica could see why. She had perfectly classical features, including a regal nose and dewy brown eyes. While her skin was delicately wrinkled, the bone structure underneath was undeniably handsome, with a strong chin and high cheekbones. Veronica, fifty years younger, felt like a wallflower in comparison, with her mop of hair and gangly limbs. Fashions and styles had changed, but Miss Lilly, as Miss Helen called her, would always be a beauty.

"Would you like some coffee or tea?" asked Miss Lilly, as if they were neighbors who'd popped in to say hello.

"Tea for all of us," demanded Miss Helen, equally determined to remain unflappable.

They all accepted Mr. Graham's invitation to take a seat at the kitchen table. The dark wood was etched with scratches like ancient hieroglyphics, mottled with water stains, a far cry from the glossy mahogany tables at the Frick. Veronica had noticed a mantel full of photos as they'd passed through the living room, of the older couple with a young woman who held a baby in her arms. This was a table where children and grandchildren sat and made a mess and it didn't matter.

"I am here with my colleagues," announced Miss Helen. She waved in Joshua and Veronica's general direction. "Go on, introduce yourselves."

Joshua gave a slight wave. "Joshua Lawrence, I work part-time at the Frick."

"Nice to meet you, Joshua," answered Miss Lilly. "I'm Lillian, and this is my husband, Archer."

Veronica's turn, but she wasn't sure how she fit in to the puzzle. "Veronica Weber. I'm rather new on the scene."

Miss Helen cringed briefly at the sound of her last name, but then nodded her approval, as if they were children who'd finally behaved properly.

"I received your note, Miss Lilly, after Mother's death," Miss Helen said.

Lillian poured hot water into a teapot and placed it on the table, where Archer had laid out cups and saucers, a small pitcher of milk, and a sugar bowl. "Your mother was a kind person, in her own way. I was sorry to hear of her passing."

"Well, that was long ago. I won't waste time. I'm here because of that letter. You implied that you had something to tell me, about the circumstances of November 1919."

"It's 1966, Helen. What took you so long?"

Miss Helen gulped at the insouciance. Clearly, she'd never been called "Helen" by a servant, current or former. "Well, as you know, *Miss* Lilly, I had a library to run, as well as having to deal with the transformation of the mansion into the Frick Collection. It was a busy time."

"Of course."

"Go ahead, then. You may apologize."

Lillian cocked her head, her eyes flinty and sharp. "For what?"

"For the trauma you put my family through. I assume that's why you wrote to me."

"Well, you'd be wrong. I should think you ought to apologize to me, after what you put *me* through."

Miss Helen leaned forward in her chair, itching for a fight. "Two words, dear girl: *Richard Danforth*."

At that, Lillian deflated slightly. "That's true. I am sorry about that. I was young."

"I thought we were friends. Friends wouldn't do such a thing to each other."

"Friends? I worked for you. You were my employer."

"Fine, I won't quibble with you. I'm here now because I found something. This."

She took the cameo out of her purse and placed it on the table.

Lillian let out a small breath. "The cameo." She reached out and gingerly touched it, but didn't pick it up. "Where was it?"

"In the enamels room, in a secret compartment in the wall."

"Of all places? How did you find it?"

Miss Helen waved her hand. "These two came upon it while they were sneaking around the mansion after hours."

"And the Magnolia diamond?"

"We found that as well." She opened the cameo to reveal the diamond, which seemed even bigger and more translucent in the bright light of day, before snapping it back shut.

Veronica felt Joshua's eyes rest on her for a split second before he turned away.

"Who would put the cameo in the enamels room?" asked Lillian.

"I don't know. I'm assuming you didn't?"

"Of course I didn't. I didn't even know about any hidden spot in the enamels room. You know that."

"I do," admitted Miss Helen.

"So someone took it and tucked it away," said Lillian. "But didn't steal it."

"Which is odd."

"They wanted to punish you, maybe?"

"That could have been one of many people, as I've never been well-liked," said Miss Helen. "Something I'm rather proud of."

Lillian and Archer exchanged a long look. Veronica couldn't tell what they were signaling to each other, but after they broke it off, Lillian seemed to brace herself before speaking. "What about your mother's private secretary?"

"Miss Winnie? No. There's no reason she'd ever go in there, even when it was Father's study."

"Really? Never?"

"Well, I don't remember. Perhaps once or twice. But she was devoted to the family and would have no reason to betray me in that way. Nor Martha, whom she loved dearly."

"Are you sure?"

"Of course. Is this what you wanted to tell me in your note? That you thought Miss Winnie was some kind of sick criminal? She never abandoned us, even when things were terrible. When Martha was ill, she was by her side day in and day out. Mother said they'd never had a better nursemaid, and that if only they'd taken her with them on that awful European trip, Martha would never have been allowed to swallow the pin in the first place."

"Hold on," said Lillian. "Nursemaid? She was your mother's secretary."

"She was originally hired as Martha's nursemaid. Only after Martha's death did my mother bring her on as her secretary. She couldn't bear to lose her, after what they'd gone through together." She paused.

"Not that she was much help. The woman became deaf as a doornail. But my mother needed a companion in her grief, and even more so later, as her depression took hold. Miss Winnie is a saint." She looked over at Joshua. "Well, that was a waste of a trip."

The story was getting more and more interesting, in Veronica's opinion. "*Is* a saint?" she repeated. "Miss Winnie is alive?"

"She is. I visit her every couple of weeks. They take good care of her there, although I still have to remind the staff to look at her while they're speaking."

"I don't think so," Lillian countered.

"What do you mean?"

"That's what I was trying to tell you when I wrote the letter. That Miss Winnie can hear better than she lets on. At least she could back then. She wasn't partially deaf at all."

"Of course she was. Why would you say such a thing?"

Lillian took one more look at her husband, who nodded. Whatever she was about to divulge had already been discussed at length between them. "One day, near the end, when things were in an uproar, Miss Winnie came to me with reassurance that all would be all right. She said that the accusations were baseless, and that I wasn't a scoundrel, no matter what Mr. Childs said. I appreciated her thoughtfulness, of course, but only later I realized she was repeating what had been discussed in the library in front of the private detective, with the doors closed. A room where she wasn't present."

"What if someone had mentioned to her what was said?"

"I wondered about that as well. So I did a test. I growled."

"You did what?"

"When your mother and Miss Winnie weren't looking at me. I made a strange noise."

"And I'm sure they thought you insane."

"They both turned around."

Miss Helen touched her own throat with a trembling hand. "Both?"

"Both."

She looked down at the cameo, as if seeing it for the first time. "Well then. Off we go."

"Where to, Miss Helen?" asked Joshua.

"To speak with Miss Winnie. To find out the truth, for once and for all."

Chapter Twenty-One

Lillian had always wondered what had become of her former employer. Sometimes there were small items in the newspapers about Helen Frick's art reference library or the Collection in general, but little else. Her own frenzied three months in the Frick mansion were like a fever dream, hazy and remote. But one summer she and Archer had splurged on a trip to Paris, and the walls of the Louvre had brought back a vivid recollection of painters and paintings. The bucolic serenity of a Constable, the cottony softness of a Fragonard—to think at one time she'd lived among them, passed by them several times a day.

Helen hadn't lost any of her imperiousness, even after almost five decades. She blasted classical music on the radio during the forty-five-minute drive to the nursing home, making any chitchat among Lillian, Veronica, and Joshua impossible, a fact that Lillian relished as the Lincoln charged down the highway, sliding from lane to lane. Once they'd arrived at the nursing home—a beautifully landscaped Victorian mansion—Miss Helen strode up to the reception desk, banging her flat palm on the counter to call for attention. Some things never changed. But then again, she'd been protected from most perils of life by her piles of money, by her library, by creating a domain where she could rule with little pushback.

Lillian, on the other hand, had experienced the normal trials and tribulations. Her life with Archer hadn't been easy, but they'd laughed their way through most of it. A surprise, really, considering how little she'd known him before her escape. Not long after her frightening leap from Mr. Frick's sitting room to the roof of the loggia, Archer's voice had risen up from the street below. With the help of some crates precariously stacked on top of each other, he'd guided her down to the safety of the sidewalk, and been by her side ever since. First in an uptown hotel, where he'd slept on the floor, then here in Pine Knolls, where he had a cousin who let them find their bearings. During that time, she'd fallen in love with Archer and been able to forge a new life for herself, far away from the Fricks' calamitous influence. He'd seen her as a whole person, and hadn't judged her by her past, nor been offended by it.

They'd scraped by with the money he brought in from playing at services and weddings at the local church, the organ a rangy, difficult beast compared to the Fricks' thoroughbred of an instrument. But he'd never complained, not when he returned from teaching private lessons to children who had little talent or inclination, or directing the church's shrill choir, top-heavy with sopranos. They'd made a tranquil life together, growing vegetables and fixing up the house, taking long walks in forests that used to be farmland, following rock walls that no longer fenced in livestock or delineated crops but had survived centuries.

No one here knew who she used to be, and neither would they care, Lillian surmised. Interest in Angelica's whereabouts had faded with the conviction of Mr. Watkins for murder, the newspapers speculating that she'd fled to Europe. Most of the local townspeople rarely, if ever, ventured into the big city. Her likeness was only to be found in the mirror, and she'd watched with a removed curiosity as her skin drooped and became dotted with sunspots—how her mother would have cried to see her daughter's ivory skin darken—and her hair became streaked with gray, growing finer, more likely to tangle. Archer still viewed her as a beauty, that was all that mattered, and when she looked at him, she still envisioned the handsome young gentleman with the shock of thick hair, never mind that it was silver now.

They'd had one daughter, Anna, who lived close by with her husband and her own baby girl. Lillian was eternally grateful that she and Archer had created a happy family with few disagreements. Maybe it was her hands-off approach, so different from Kitty's overbearing style or Mr. Frick's incessant meddling, that had done the trick. Or maybe it was simply luck.

So quickly, it seemed, she'd become a mother and then a grand-mother, and had found genuine delight in the sound of a toddler's gig-gles erupting like bubbles of joy. She'd reconnected with Bertha, and twice a year they met in the city and proudly shared family photos (Ber-tha had six grandchildren now). Although they rarely spoke of that final night at the mansion, they knew their secrets were safe with each other, that it was a bond that would never be broken.

When Lillian ventured into New York, she did her best to avoid pass-ing any of her statues, as each stone-cold likeness stood as a reminder of how young and innocent she'd been, and how easily forgotten. While the sculptors' names were etched into history, hers was lost forever.

As Helen harangued the receptionist at the front desk of the nursing home, Lillian studied the two young people in tow. They looked tired and confused, and she still wasn't sure how they fit in to all this. The girl, Veronica, was an exquisite creature with the oddest haircut, and she kept looking at the man—Joshua was his name—as if she needed something from him.

"Miss Winnie's in the solarium," announced Helen. "Follow me."

At the back of the building, they went through a door to a sunny room filled with ferns and orchids. The intense humidity inside brought back hot summer days when the thick air dripped with moisture. Helen stopped and pointed.

Miss Winnie looked almost exactly the same, stout and wrinkled, even though she had to be in her early nineties by now. Her hair was thinning, the scalp underneath a smooth and shiny pale pink. She was dozing in her wheelchair, her chin dropped forward, her hands clasped atop a plaid blanket.

"Wait." Lillian stopped Helen with a hand on her arm. "I should go."

"Why you?"

"The element of surprise. Didn't you say you visit her regularly?"

"I come once a month." Helen hesitated only for a moment. "I guess you're right. We'll go around to the back, where she can't see us but we can hear."

Lillian nodded. "I'll wait until you're in position."

"I'd like to come with you as well, Lillian, if it's okay?" said Veronica. She shifted from one foot to the other. "Maybe I can help in some way, if you get stuck." She peered up at her from beneath thick bangs, reminding Lillian of a dog who'd misbehaved. Something was going on between this odd trio who'd shown up on her doorstep this morning, but she couldn't suss out exactly what it was.

Lillian checked with Helen, who shrugged.

Miss Winnie was waking up just as Lillian and Veronica approached. Lillian drew up a chair while Veronica remained standing, a little off to the side.

"Miss Winnie. Do you remember me?" Lillian asked.

"No." She coughed several times, her breathing wet and heavy. "Who are you?"

"I was Miss Helen's private secretary, around the time that Mr. Frick passed away. Do you remember?"

Miss Winnie nodded but didn't smile. Her eyes flicked back and forth between Lillian and Veronica, then settled on Lillian. "You were the pretty one. I remember."

"It turns out I don't live far from here. Some coincidence, right?"

"Well, that's nice. Why are you here? Who is this, your daughter?"

Veronica held out her hand to Miss Winnie. "I'm a friend, my name's Veronica. We came to visit someone we know who lives here, and then Lillian realized she knew you."

Miss Winnie studied Lillian's features, like she was analyzing an artist's canvas. "You're not as pretty anymore."

"Neither are you."

Miss Winnie laughed. "Never was. But now you're pretty in a different way."

"Thank you."

A nurse wandered through, and Lillian remained silent after she'd passed. Miss Winnie spoke first. "That was a terrible time."

Lillian nodded but didn't answer, hoping her silence would draw Miss Winnie out.

Her strategy worked. After a moment or two, Miss Winnie let out a thick sigh. "The rich think they're protected, that they have magical powers, when in fact they're only mere mortals, like the rest of us. Bodies break down, betray you. People you love die. Children die."

Earlier, when Helen revealed that Miss Winnie had been Martha's nursemaid, Lillian had vaguely remembered being told that her first day at the house, as Miss Helen gave her an orientation. At the time, it hadn't seemed important, not when Lillian was still in shock at having landed the job of private secretary. "You must have seen a lot during your time working for the family, including Martha's decline."

Miss Winnie threw out a suspicious glance. "They don't like me talking about that."

"Mr. and Mrs. Frick are gone now."

"True. Long gone. Can't believe I'm still kicking."

"Why didn't they want you to talk about it?"

"Because I knew the truth."

"What truth?"

Miss Winnie clamped her lips shut and looked away.

"The death of Martha was painful for the entire family, I'm sure," said Lillian. "No parent should have to go through that. How awful for them."

"Bah!" A darkness spread over the woman's features. "You weren't there when Mr. Frick was forcing the poor child to ride a bike, to be like a normal girl. Urging her on, even though she was obviously in pain. It used to make my blood boil. If they'd taken me to Europe with them instead of hiring some foreign girl to watch over her, it would have never happened in the first place. And later, if they'd listened to me when I insisted that something was wrong, we might have saved her."

"Why did you stay on, then, after Martha's death?"

"Someone had to take care of Mrs. Frick, poor woman. She wasn't strong. She had no one to lean on." Her face grew pinched. "I don't want to talk about this. I don't want to talk to you anymore. Nurse!"

Suddenly, Veronica, who had shifted off to the side, spoke so quietly that even Lillian had to strain to hear her. "We found the missing cameo. After all these years."

Miss Winnie's neck snapped to the left, and she began to rotate in her chair, then just as quickly caught herself, facing forward again. At first, Lillian was annoyed at Veronica for injecting herself into the conversation, but then she realized what the girl had done. From where Veronica stood, Miss Winnie couldn't have heard her or read her lips. Yet the effect was like a bomb going off.

Smart girl, that Veronica. She'd picked up on what Lillian had said earlier, about how she'd tested Miss Winnie in a similar manner right before she'd fled.

"What was that?" said Miss Winnie, craning her neck around in an exaggerated attempt to hide her initial response.

Lillian held up the cameo, and then placed it in Miss Winnie's hand. "You remember this, don't you?"

Miss Winnie examined it, turning it over. She didn't open the back, but gave it a little shake. The diamond inside offered up a light rattle. "Martha's cameo. Yes. I remember it. Why are you showing it to me? Give it to Miss Helen, she'll be quite happy."

She hadn't asked where it was found, the most obvious question. That, along with her sharp sense of hearing, confirmed that Lillian's suspicions were correct. After all this time.

"Do you want to know where it was discovered?" she asked Miss Winnie.

"Fine. Sure. Where was it discovered?"

"I think you know already since you're the one who put it there."

Miss Winnie let out a breath, then glared at Lillian. "How dare that man be laid to rest with Martha's cameo."

"So you *were* there."

"Yes, I was. I was in the gallery with one of the maids, helping to get everything ready to receive the mourners. I'd stepped into the enamels room to check that it was tidy, and heard you and Miss Helen approach, overheard everything you said. After you left, I snatched that thing right out of his cold, dead hand. I didn't want it for myself, I just didn't want him to have it."

"But why didn't you take it with you?"

"I was unsure what to do with it, how to dispose of it, when I remembered the compartments behind the panels. That was where Mr. Frick kept the lock of Martha's hair, before his study was moved to make room for the enamels."

"The lock of hair that you and he drank to on the anniversary of her death?" asked Lillian.

"I told you about that, did I? Yes. They'd unscrewed the knobs, but I used a hairpin to pry one of the doors open and tossed the cameo inside."

"But then you let me take the blame for it," said Lillian.

Miss Winnie didn't meet her eye. "I didn't mean for that to happen. I didn't know the Magnolia diamond was inside until I heard Miss Helen getting upset."

"You're not deaf," said Veronica. A statement, not a question.

"No, not even at my age, now. I can hear perfectly fine." Miss Winnie puffed with pride. "Everything else is shot, but my ears are good."

"So why did you pretend?" asked Lillian.

"It made it easier to sit for hours with Mrs. Frick. How she would go on and on, about her ailments, about the terrible injustices against her. I sympathized to a point, but she knew nothing of how hard life could be in the real world. I'd come from true poverty, was put to work at the age of thirteen, and spent most of my time fetching tonics and administering salves for a woman who ate too much marzipan and then complained of indigestion, who found sunny days a personal affront. I began to notice that my false infirmity made people more willing to speak freely around me. I would hear things I shouldn't. Oh, people dismissed me as a batty idiot, but I was always listening, always."

She regarded Lillian. "I felt guilty at what happened to you, shouldering the blame, but you were an interloper, coming in, getting in everyone's good graces. I never trusted you. And then that business with Helen's suitor. I knew you were a bad apple. So pretty, had to lord it over Miss Helen, who never had a chance. I did what was best for her, for the family."

The sharp sting of guilt over Lillian's dalliance with Mr. Danforth hadn't lessened over the years. But she kept on. "Like leaving a water glass out for Mr. Frick after putting a sleeping draft in it?"

A small, triumphant smile appeared on Miss Winnie's lips. "That wasn't my idea. A good idea, but not mine."

"What do you mean?"

"I walked by Mr. Frick's bathroom, and there she was, that same maid—what was her name, Bertha, yes, that was it—hovering over the sink, a bottle of Veronal in her hot little hand. She didn't see me, but I watched her as she began to tip it into a glass, then stopped. She looked at herself in the mirror, set the bottle down next to the glass, and ran off. Coward."

"So you poisoned him instead."

"I figured I'd finish what she started. I poured the powder into the glass, hid the bottle in my pocket, and then filled the glass with water and left it on the edge of the sink. I didn't kill him in the end, you see. It wasn't my idea, even."

"But then Helen went and gave it to him," said Lillian. "You put her in a terrible position."

"I hadn't meant for anyone to get in trouble, that meddling nurse . . ." She didn't finish the thought. "I freed Miss Helen from the restraints of being her father's daughter. She was better off without him."

"If anything, it made it harder for her to let him go, to move on with her life."

"I did them all a favor, and served Martha's memory. They are grateful to me for my service to the family. It's because of their largesse that I'm here." Miss Winnie gestured around the solarium. "Everyone ended up just fine."

The woman had twisted reality around to suit her own purposes.

"Except Mr. Frick," said Lillian.

Miss Winnie leaned forward, furious. "Don't you judge me. You were one of the pretty ones. Miss Helen never had a chance, with that horsey face. Not with her father, not with that suitor. A girl like that, she needed my protection."

"That's audacious, coming from you," answered Lillian. "You say you were taking revenge on Mr. Frick, but you were exactly like him.

Judging people by your own harsh standards, making assumptions. Manipulating those around you who trusted you."

"I certainly did not."

"You certainly did." Helen emerged from where she'd been hiding, Joshua right behind her.

Miss Winnie's head jerked around, her rheumy eyes wide with shock. "Miss Helen!"

Helen drew close, her fists clenched. "I have lived with the guilt all these years when it was your fault. I blamed Miss Lilly wrongly for the theft, which, again, you committed."

Miss Winnie leaned forward in her wheelchair, hands braced on the armrests. "Look at everything you've accomplished after his death. You'd been his sycophant prior to that, bending to his will in every way. As did your mother, year after year. But you turned around and made something of yourself. I'm proud of you, Miss Helen."

As Helen sputtered, unable to reply to the contorted compliment, Lillian spoke up. "You made yourself the judge and jury."

"I certainly did. And if I had to do it all over again, I would do the same thing." Miss Winnie sat back again, satisfied with herself. "Actually, no. If I had to do it all over again, I'd steal Martha away from that household when she was still a baby, and save her from a short life filled with pain."

Helen recoiled. "You might want to remember who you're talking to. I pay for all this out of my *largesse*, as you put it. At the end of this month, I can have them wheel you out and lock the door behind you."

All the color drained from Miss Winnie's face. "You wouldn't."

"Try me."

Helen wouldn't hesitate to bulldoze anyone in her path. But turning a weak old lady out in the streets was coldhearted, even for her. Veronica looked like she was about to cry.

Lillian had to stop Helen from following in the heartless footsteps of her father. "Helen," she said, "I am in no way defending Miss Winnie for what she did, but you have to imagine what it would have been like for her back then. All of us, including you, were at the receiving end of your father's bullying ways; I remember so many instances when he made you feel small or inadequate. I'm not saying he didn't love you, perhaps that was his way of showing it. But imagine being a sickly child and having that same fierce energy directed at you. Imagine being the one in charge of that child, and helpless to step in and stop it." She thought of Bertha's bottled-up fury, all of the people of that Pennsylvania town who'd been wiped from the earth. "You have a chance to end the generations of pain."

"Through bankrolling his murderer?"

"Through forgiveness. Toward Miss Winnie, your father, me." She paused. "And most of all, yourself."

The foursome were silent on the drive back to Lillian's house. Helen drove as if she were imagining Miss Winnie lying prone in the road in front of her, gunning the engine after every turn. On one sharp corner, the two kids in the back seat bumped into each other, and Lillian turned around in time to see Joshua gently tap Veronica's leg.

"Whoa, there, missy," he'd said.

Lillian wondered if they were a couple, what the story was, but this was no time to ask.

After Lillian's plea, Helen had let out a guffaw and begun walking away. But she'd only made it a few steps when she hesitated, turned, and walked back to Miss Winnie. She lifted her hand and placed it on Miss Winnie's cheek. Everyone froze, wondering what was to come next, and Miss Winnie began to cry. Helen wiped her tears with her thumb before straightening up and saying goodbye. It was a sign, Lillian hoped, that her words might have had an effect.

Once they were back at the farmhouse, Lillian invited them inside. Archer gave her an inquisitive look when they first walked in, but knew better than to pepper her with questions after taking in their somber faces.

Helen rubbed her eyes. "I hate that my family died still wondering if I'd accidentally killed Papsie. My mother, on her deathbed, told me she forgave me. I wish I could go back in time and prove to her that she was wrong, that I hadn't done it."

Lillian leaned over and rubbed Helen's arm. "Everyone did as best they could with the knowledge that they had. Your mother always loved you, you know that. As did your father, in his own way."

"It's been almost fifty years that I've been tormented by the thought that I'd killed my father. It helps to know the truth, finally. I have all of you to thank for that. And I do thank you. Even if it came at such a cost. While I may never forgive Miss Winnie, we will always share a love for Martha."

"So you won't turn her out of the nursing home?" asked Veronica.

"I will not."

Helen drew the cameo out of her pocket and placed it on the table. They all studied it as if it were some animal to be dissected in a science lab.

"They loved Martha best," said Helen. "And that's all right. She deserved all the love she could get, in her brief life."

"What will you do with the cameo now?" asked Joshua.

"I don't know. It's been tucked away all these years. I have half a mind to put it back where it came from." She gave him a sharp look, but there was a twinkle in her eye. "Unless you busybodies go fussing about in my house again."

"I know what you should do," said Veronica. She picked it up and turned to Helen. "Wear it." Without asking, she pinned it onto the lapel of Miss Helen's coat. "You'll be carrying Martha's memory with you all the time. I bet she'd like that."

Helen ran her finger over it and smiled. "Perhaps she would. Funny, but I can't picture her anymore. In my head, I see the portrait, not the actual girl. It was so many years ago, and I was so young."

"You've made her proud, and your father proud," said Lillian. "An unconventional life is what you're leading, as your father did."

"I never let anyone push me around. Not easy, for a woman in my time. Even a rich one. I made my dreams come true. The library, my farm. You'll have to visit me some time, Miss Lilly."

"That's kind of you. Perhaps we will," answered Lillian. "Those months at the Frick mansion changed my life, I will admit. By the time I left, I knew that I could manage in the world without having to rely on my beauty. Better to have learned that early on rather than try to fight the inevitable decline of age."

"You're welcome," said Helen, and everyone laughed. "I rather enjoy being an eccentric old lady. The power that comes with not caring what others think is invigorating."

Lillian took Helen's hand in hers. "I am sorry, Helen, for getting swept up by Mr. Danforth's advances. That was cruel of me."

"Well, while we're being honest, you helped me dodge a disastrous union. My father, as much as he said he wanted it, would have hated to have to share me, had he lived. On top of that, I was never the wifely sort; it would have ended in a terrible scandal, certainly. But I do appreciate you saying so."

Helen took a sip of tea and shared a kind look with Lillian, who patted her hand some more.

Chapter Twenty-Two

Veronica watched the exchange between Miss Helen and Lillian, relieved that they'd reached an understanding. She looked over at Joshua, who offered up a quick smile. She hoped what she'd done, helping to expose Miss Winnie's deception, had softened him toward her. But they still needed to talk.

"What about the diamond?" Veronica directed the question to Miss Helen.

Miss Helen touched the cameo on her lapel, then gave it a little shake. The diamond rattled in response. "I think I'll sell it and donate the proceeds to the library."

Veronica took a deep breath. "How about setting up a scholarship for students who want to pursue a career in the fine arts?"

Miss Helen stared at her for a long moment, which in normal circumstances would have unnerved Veronica. She'd never really gotten used to being looked at and studied by photographers and fashion editors, or random people on the bus who reacted to her crazy haircut. But unlike those stares, Miss Helen's was different. She wasn't observing Veronica's outside; she was trying to understand her inside. It wasn't about being looked at; it was about being seen. "A scholarship?" she finally said.

"Sure. For people like Joshua, for example."

Joshua blinked in surprise. "Um, Veronica. Can I talk to you?"

Veronica followed him, heart pounding, out onto the front porch. "Did I say something wrong?"

"Well, you're obviously trying to make up for something. Like having tried to steal the diamond in the first place."

She looked down at her feet, then back at him. Like Miss Helen, Joshua had really *seen* her over the past forty-eight hours, citywide blackout notwithstanding. "Since today seems to be the day of apologies, I'm sorry about that. It flew out of the cameo when you were off getting the other lamp, and for a moment, I didn't know what to do. I was overwhelmed about being fired from the photo shoot, ruining my career, taking care of my sister, and snatched it up."

He exhaled slowly. "I thought you would have made a smarter decision under those circumstances."

"I know," she conceded. "It was only a split second and I immediately regretted it, but by then you were back and it was burning a hole in my pocket."

Joshua didn't respond, but the look of disappointment on his face hurt more than any words.

"My mum told me this morning that Polly's stopped eating. I don't want to lose her like I lost my father." She choked back tears; this was not a time for histrionics. "But it was a terrible lapse of judgment, to do what I did. I planned to tell you a number of times when we were locked inside. I thought maybe we could split the proceeds so that you could get your degree at Columbia and I could bring Polly home."

"That doesn't help. I would never have accepted it."

Of course he wouldn't have. Fatigue mixed with self-loathing, and all she wanted to do was curl up in a ball and disappear into sleep. To drift off, drift away from it all.

But instead of wallowing in her own misfortune, she straightened up. "I'm sorry, and I'll do what I can to make it right. If you want me to tell Miss Helen what I did, I will. I accept full responsibility."

Her heart caught in her throat as she waited for his reply. "I won't ask you to do that," he finally said.

Joshua had been a true friend the past couple of days, had taken care of her and protected her, guided her through the scavenger hunt to its surprising end. And in return, she'd tried to steal the Magnolia diamond, a vital part of the house and its history. Joshua respected and loved the Collection for its breadth and historical significance, and by taking the diamond she'd betrayed that love.

Her heart broke for having shattered the fragile trust they'd forged over the past two days.

There was nothing more to be said, but as she reached for the door-knob to go back inside, he placed his hand over hers.

"Hold on a moment. I'm sorry about Polly, V. Even if I don't have a sister, I understand what drove you to consider taking the diamond. And you made things right, in the end. I appreciate that."

They stood facing each other again. "You do?"

"I do. And you know, there's another way for you to make a ton of money."

"What's that?"

She knew he was pulling her leg before he even spoke, by the way one side of his mouth lifted.

"Professional bowler."

She swatted him with her hand, as relief flooded through her.

When they reentered the kitchen, Miss Helen nodded in their direction. "We've been discussing the idea of a scholarship," she said. "Not a bad one." She addressed Joshua. "From what I've observed, after a rather rocky introduction, it appears that you are an asset to the Frick Collection, Mr. Lawrence. And is it true you want attend graduate school?"

"That's my plan."

"I imagine it's not easy for you. Perhaps I can make it just a slight bit easier."

He stammered a thank-you and Veronica couldn't help but smile.

"And as for you"—Miss Helen's voice dropped an octave as she turned her icy-blue eyes on Veronica—"I like the way you think. You're a smart lady. You helped solve a mystery that had long stymied my family."

Lillian spoke up. "That was brilliant, at the nursing home, how you made Miss Winnie admit to her lack of lack of hearing." Her husband chuckled at the wordplay, and Lillian threw him a silly grin in response. They were obviously fond of each other, still in love after all these years.

All of this praise weighed heavily on Veronica, knowing that Joshua was listening and judging every word. "I took the cue from what you'd told us about your own experiment."

"What is it you do again, my girl?" asked Miss Helen.

Veronica cast about, unsure of how to answer. "At the moment, I'm unemployed. I worked in a pawnshop, and then was a model, for a time."

"A model. I've had experiences with your sort." Miss Helen looked over at Lillian and smiled. "In fact, I'm in the market for a private secretary. I know that's not the proper term these days, one should say 'assistant,' but I don't care to update my vocabulary."

"Your private secretary?" Veronica repeated, dumbly. "You want me to be your private secretary?"

Miss Helen waved her hands dramatically in the air. "They never last long under my employ, God knows why."

Everyone laughed, including Miss Helen.

Joshua cleared his throat to speak, and Veronica held her breath at what was coming next. "Veronica made a number of connections that helped solve the puzzle, after only barely scanning through the archives. Her memory and observational skills are quite exceptional."

His praise, given when she least deserved it, choked Veronica up.

However, the offer, while appreciated, wouldn't work for two reasons. First of all, Polly. Veronica would never leave her to take a job in America, under any circumstances.

Miss Helen sensed her hesitation. "What is it, girl?"

"I do appreciate your kind offer, Miss Helen. But I'm afraid I have family back in London that I can't leave. I have a sister, you see, who's in an institution, and I'm trying to get her out of there and back home with me and my mum, but it's been frustrating . . ." She trailed off, aware that she'd gotten into far more detail than she'd meant to.

"I'm sorry to hear that." Miss Helen pressed her fingertips to her throat. "I would have done anything for my sister, anything. I adored her and hated that she suffered so." She flicked a handkerchief from her sleeve and dabbed delicately at the corners of each eye.

"So you understand," said Veronica. Although they'd started out on the wrong foot, she had to admit she was coming to admire Miss Helen. They had more in common than she could have imagined.

Miss Helen suddenly slammed her hand on the table, making the spoons rattle in the saucers. "I know, we'll bring her over here," she said, as if it were the most obvious answer in the world. "There are all kinds of arrangements that can be made. Your mother, too, if she likes. It will be my way of making right what I couldn't do for Martha."

Veronica sat for a moment, stunned. She could bring Polly here. They could all start a new life together. Of all things. "That would be . . . remarkable." She spoke slowly, thoughtfully. "Um, there's one thing, though. I really loved going through the old letters and documents with Joshua, figuring out how they relate to the past, and to what's going on today. Do you think, down the road, I could apply for a job as an archivist? If I need additional school or training, I'd be willing to do that. Whatever it takes."

She glanced over at Joshua, who gave her a subtle nod of approval. Over the past two days, he'd taught her a lot about taking risks and charting one's own path, even if the world of art and history she was stepping into seemed daunting—and, in his case, uninviting—at first.

"You're a tough one, I can see that. Archivist? At the Frick?" Miss Helen raised her chin imperiously. For a moment, Veronica couldn't tell if she was irritated or impressed. "Well, I might have a few connections there, as it happens."

"So I've heard," Veronica volleyed back.

"That haircut, though, is unfortunate. You ought to wear it like I do." Miss Helen patted her pompadour. "It's functional and stays out of one's eyes. I haven't changed my style since 1903, and I'm quite proud of that fact."

Lillian let out a most unladylike snort as Veronica looked around the room, at these people who she'd just met, who'd very possibly changed the course of her life. "It's a classic, for certain, Miss Helen. Just like you."

Chapter Twenty-Three

Lillian and Archer ventured into New York City to visit the Frick Collection at Helen's behest—or, more aptly, at her command—just as spring was beginning to unfold. The setting sun lent a vibrant pink blush to the limestone mansion, one that almost rivaled that of the expansive magnolia trees that flanked the steps to the living hall.

Around the corner, at the front entrance, Lillian stopped and looked up, just as she had years ago at the dawn of the Jazz Age, and studied the reclining figure above the doorway.

"You look quite languid up there, my girl," remarked Archer. "But why is the fat baby on the right holding a Ping-Pong paddle?"

"It's a cherub holding a mirror, you dolt."

"Could've sworn it was a Ping-Pong paddle."

She was about to give him a good swat with her purse when Helen appeared at the entrance. "There you are. Come on then, you're late."

They followed her through the new reception hall and back out into a garden, where a rectangular lily pond reflected the color of the sky. In the middle of the small lawn stood Veronica and Joshua, holding hands. Lillian smiled at the match. That snowy winter's day up in Pine Knolls, she'd sensed an electric connection between them, something deeper than an alliance forged to manage Helen's moods and machinations. She and Archer approached, and all shook hands.

"Congratulations on the new job, Veronica," said Lillian.

"Thank you, yes, Miss Helen got me a position as an assistant archivist. I'm currently helping out with a new exhibit highlighting the role of the household staff, back when it was a residence."

"That sounds lovely," said Lillian.

"In fact, I was hoping I could interview you sometime," Veronica added.

"Of course. I promise to tell all."

Helen harrumphed but kept a smile on her face.

"And what about your sister?" asked Lillian. "Helen mentioned that she's here in New York with you. How is she doing?"

Veronica's face lit up into a bright smile. "Polly's great, she has a caretaker she adores while my mum and I are at work. My mum works as a secretary at the library, in fact. All thanks to Miss Helen, of course. And Joshua here will be attending Columbia in the fall, on the very first Frick Scholarship."

"What wonderful news." Lillian looked about, unsure of why they were all standing around in the garden. "Shall we head to dinner now? Helen, you said something about all of us going to an Italian place nearby. I'm afraid Archer here is starving."

"We have something to show you first," said Helen.

Joshua stepped aside, revealing a figure covered with a white sheet just behind him.

As Veronica slowly slid off the sheet, Lillian found herself face-to-face with Angelica. She remembered posing for the statue—it was one of her first jobs—and the memories flooded back in a curious wave:

her mother nestled in an armchair in a West Side studio, the artist working away, silent and methodical, and Lillian staring up into the distance, her arms slightly lifted, one foot stepping forward as if she were about to levitate into the mist. She'd been at her prime, her body smooth and strong, her neckline long and sharp. The statue was in remarkably good shape after so many decades, the marble an alabaster white.

"That's me," was all she was able to say; her throat had suddenly constricted. It was Lillian when she'd been heralded and acclaimed as a young beauty, when she'd had a mother to take care of her. Before she'd realized that the world was not as welcoming as she'd been led to believe, and that floundering through confusion and misfortune was the only way to figure out who she was and what she wanted out of life.

Archer spoke up, sensing that she was speechless. "Where did you find this?"

"At my direction, Veronica has been on a hunt for any of Angelica's statuary that came up for auction, and this appeared a few weeks ago," said Helen. "The minute I saw it, I knew we had to add it to the Collection. The board of directors agreed, and snapped it right up."

Lillian shook her head in amazement and held on to Archer for support.

"This will be included in the Frick tours going forward," added Helen. "Docents will be instructed to mention not only the artist, but also the model who inspired him. Angelica, otherwise known as Lillian Carter Graham."

After years of having her anonymous image scattered about Manhattan and the world at large, Lillian would finally be named. Be recognized. And not in a salacious way, associated with a scandal or as a pretty puppet for some Hollywood producer, but for her serious contributions to the art world. With respect. It was everything she had been quietly hoping for all of these years.

She stepped forward and embraced Helen, holding her close. Since the encounter upstairs, they'd continued to meet regularly, going for long walks on Helen's farm or chatting over coffee in her office at the library. Lillian's presence helped to soften Helen's mercurial tendencies, while Helen brought a joyful love of art and history back into Lillian's life. Once they got started, they could talk for hours.

The two women had survived decades of heady changes when the world had tilted on its edge. Wars punctured by an uneasy peace, horse-drawn carts replaced by finned automobiles, hemlines that brushed the ankles and then rose to unimaginable heights. The Frick mansion, which had once housed a living, breathing family and their staff, was now a relic from another era, a place of ancient aspirations. Yet day after day, modern visitors eagerly ventured inside and filled each room with wonder.

Lillian and Helen stood there, holding each other quietly and firmly, as the statue regarded them with a serene, all-knowing grace.

On a cold winter's day in late 2019, after taking a marvelous tour of the Frick Collection, I stared up at the front entrance and wondered what might have happened if the woman who posed for the figure in the pediment above the door—considered the "supermodel" of the 1910s—encountered Helen Clay Frick, the headstrong adult daughter of Henry Clay Frick. The storyline for this book bloomed from there, although there is no evidence the two women ever crossed paths. In all of my books, I like to layer a fictional story over the scaffolding of historical facts, and then parse out the inspiration for the plot and characters in the Author's Note, as well as provide ideas for further reading.

The character of Lillian is lightly based on the real-life artists' model whose figure graces the pediment above the front door of the Frick Collection. Her name was Audrey Munson, and she was the darling of the artistic set in New York City in the early 1900s, posing for all of the famous statues mentioned in *The Magnolia Palace* and over a hundred more. In 1919, Audrey's landlord brutally murdered his wife, and Audrey became ensnared in the investigation on scant evidence. The ensuing scandal ruined her budding film career, and Audrey and her mother retreated to upstate New York. Unfortunately, Audrey's real-life ending is quite different from Lillian's. In 1922, Audrey tried to die by suicide by swallowing mercury, and nine years later, as her mental state deteriorated, was admitted to an asylum, where she remained for sixty-five years. She died in 1996 at the age of 104, and was buried in an unmarked grave. Years later, her relatives added a headstone. For further reading, I highly recommend *The Curse of Beauty: The Scandalous & Tragic Life of Audrey Munson, America's First Supermodel*, by James Bone.

In writing about the Fricks, I was inspired by two volumes by Martha Frick Symington Sanger, great-granddaughter of Henry Clay Frick: *Helen Clay Frick: Bittersweet Heiress* and *Henry Clay Frick: An Intimate Portrait*. Both dive deeply into the history of the Frick family as well as the provenance and significance of the art found in the Frick Collection. The following plot points of *The Magnolia Palace* echo events in the family history: Martha, the firstborn daughter of Henry Clay and Adelaide Frick, passed away at the age of five from the tragedy described in my book. The Fricks also had a young son who died in infancy, and one can only imagine the pain those losses must have caused them. I decided to exclude mentioning the son so as to keep the focus on Martha and Helen. While Henry Clay Frick was known for lavishing expensive gemstones and jewelry on his wife and daughter, the Magnolia diamond is my own invention. Helen Clay Frick was almost engaged, but never married, and then in 1917 sailed to France to assist the Red Cross during World War I. Helen's brother Childs and his wife, Dixie, were quite unhappy regarding the terms of Henry Clay Frick's will and accused Helen of poisoning her father, although there was never a formal investigation. Helen founded the Frick Art Reference Library in 1920 and worked tirelessly to carry on her father's legacy after his death.

Helen Clay Frick accomplished far more in her life than my novel could possibly encompass. In 1909, she founded the Iron Rail Vacation Home for Working Girls in Wenham, Massachusetts, where young women who toiled in factory work could rest and recuperate. After she returned from the Great War in 1918, she organized a Red Cross thrift store in Manhattan that raised over $50,000 for veterans, and then later financed the Frick Fine Arts Building at the University of Pittsburgh. Helen never married nor had children, and died in 1984 at the age of ninety-six at her home in Pittsburgh.

All of the artwork and sculptures mentioned in the novel are based on actual creations, except the bust mentioned in the scene where Lillian and Helen first meet, which I invented. Also, Isidore Konti's *Three Graces* in the Hotel Astor was actually completed in 1909—I pushed the date forward in the novel to fit the plot's timeline. Books that were helpful for my research include *Millionaires and Grub Street: Comrades and Contacts in the Last Half Century*, by James Howard Bridge and Don C. Seitz; *The Frick Collection: Handbook of Paintings*, edited by Elaine Koss; *The Sleeve Should Be Illegal*, edited by Michaelyn Mitchell; *Building the Frick Collection: An Introduction to the House and Its Collections*, by Colin B. Bailey; *Mirror to America: The Autobiography of John Hope Franklin*, by John Hope Franklin; *Young, Gifted and Black: A New Generation of Artists*, edited by Antwaun Sargent; *Model: The Ugly Business of Beautiful Women*, by Michael Gross; and *Wonderful Tonight*, by Pattie Boyd with Penny Junor.

The Frick's website (frick.org) includes a terrific virtual tour and dozens of online programs that provide a behind-the-scenes look at the Collection. The Frick Collection is an innovator when it comes to developing initiatives aimed at diversity and inclusion, including arts internships, career readiness programs, and the Frick Film Project, a unique collaboration with the Bronx-based Ghetto Film School, which provides on-site education. I highly recommend catching the Frick's "Cocktails with a Curator" series online, which features brilliant curators like Aimee Ng and Xavier F. Salomon discussing selected works, and I urge you to learn more about the building, its treasures, and its outreach.

Thank you for reading *The Magnolia Palace*. I'm thrilled and honored to be able to share this New York City gem—the Frick Collection—with you.

Acknowledgments

Thank you to Stefanie Lieberman for believing in me six books ago and guiding me with your wisdom and wit every step of the way. Also, thanks to Molly Steinblatt and Adam Hobbins for providing brilliant insights and suggestions on the manuscript.

Stephanie Kelly, you have been a dream editor; I can't thank you enough for the ingenious ways you helped turn a manuscript into a novel. These past six years together have been an absolute joy, and I'm excited for what's ahead for you. To the entire team at Dutton—Madeline McIntosh, Allison Dobson, Ivan Held, Christine Ball, John Parsley, Amanda Walker, Lindsey Rose, Alice Dalrymple, Becky Odell, Stephanie Cooper, Natalie Church, Lexy Cassola, Katie Taylor, and Christopher Lin—thank you for your enthusiasm and steadfastness, and for making the process of bringing a book out into the world such fun. A huge shout-out to Kathleen Carter, who's been by my side since the very beginning.

I'm deeply indebted to the current and former staff at the Frick Collection, including Heidi Rosenau, Colin B. Bailey, Ian Wardropper, Sally Brazil, and Julie Ludwig. Major thanks to Jennifer Quinlan, Nikki Slota-Terry, William Johnson, Tammi Lawson, LeRonn P. Brooks, Thelma Golden, Yael Peres, Meredith Bergmann, Margeaux Weston,

Mary Morgan, Linda Powell, Coco Arnesen, Andrew Alpern, Dilys Davis, and *The Bowery Boys* podcast.

I'm so grateful to the wide community of booksellers, librarians, book bloggers, and authors. The list is long, but I'll start by thanking Amy Poeppel, Susie Orman Schnall, Nicola Harrison, Lynda Cohen Loigman, Jamie Brenner, Suzanne Leopold, Kristin Harmel, Wendy Walker, Georgia Clark, Brenda Janowitz, Lauren Willig, Christina Baker Kline, and Kerri Maher. I'm indebted to so many people who help spread the word, including Andrea Peskind Katz, Pamela Klinger-Horn, Zibby Owens, the fab five at Friends and Fiction, Robin Kall Homonoff, Cindy Burnett, Jamie Rosenblit, Kristy Barrett, Christie Hinrichs, and Susan McBeth. There are far too many to list here, but I thank you all for connecting readers and authors.

Thank you to my family: Brian, Dilys, Martin, Mace, Caitlin, Erin, and Lauren. And finally, thanks to Greg Wands for your generous spirit and your love.

The

Magnolia
Palace

FIONA DAVIS

Reading Group Guide

An Excerpt from
The Spectacular

DUTTON

Reading Group Guide

1. If you could meet any of these characters and have a conversation with them, who would it be? What would your conversation be about?

2. When Miss Helen meets Lillian, she says, "I like to make things difficult for other people. You should know that right off: I'm known to be difficult." How does their relationship evolve over the course of the book?

3. While trying to convince Lillian to pose for his statues, Mr. Konti says that if the people of New York "walk by one of my statues and look up and see something beautiful, an idea or person who inspires them, then I have done my job. I do this not for me. It's for humanity." What do you think of this statement? Does it resonate with you and the role public art plays in your life? Why or why not?

4. Miss Helen seems disconnected from reality and is frequently oblivious to the feelings and motives of those around her. Why do you think that is? How do you think her wealth and position have altered her worldview? How did it affect the way she treated people like Lillian, or the way her father regarded people like Bertha?

5. How do Joshua's experiences as a Black man in the art world affect the way he views the art at the Frick? Does his experience alter your views of art history in any way?

6. How do Lillian and Veronica's experiences working as models in two different decades compare? In what ways does the novel explore the difference between being *looked at* versus being *seen*?

7. The tenuous friendship Joshua and Veronica build during their stay in the Frick Collection is almost destroyed when Veronica betrays his trust. What are the stakes for each of them in that moment? What makes Veronica's actions dangerous for both, and how do their situations differ? What would you have encouraged Veronica to do with her find?

8. Did the ending surprise you? How do you think the truth of what really happened to Henry Clay Frick and the Magnolia diamond affected the different characters at the end?

9. If you could go back in time to one of the eras Fiona Davis writes about in *The Magnolia Palace*, would you? Which would you choose?

Turn the page for an excerpt from Fiona Davis's

THE SPECTACULAR,

Coming Soon from Dutton.

Chapter One

I still dance in my dreams.

But not in my life. In my life, I shuffle around this too-large house, tossing whatever is within reach into the nearest cardboard box, not bothering to wrap anything in newspaper or to make sure the box labeled LIVING ROOM actually contains items from the living room.

The movers are far more worried about my belongings than I am. When you get to the age of seventy-five, the stuff that surrounds you every day loses its charm. Like the clock over the fireplace that hasn't worked in a decade. Or the cast-iron Le Creuset pot that sits in a drawer doing absolutely nothing. I haven't given a dinner party in ages, and I'm not about to start now. Some people end up hoarding their possessions, unable to get rid of the plastic bags that the groceries came in, but that's not me. To be honest, I'm getting a kick out of seeing box after box go out the door, like a snake shedding its skin. Out the door and into the big truck, to be dropped off at the Salvation Army. The few pieces that are left, including my antique bed and my favorite rocker, will be delivered to a sunny studio with high ceilings in Sutton Gardens, an independent living community. Never mind that most of its residents have been living independently for the past fifty years. I said so during my tour, but the young lady just gave me a vague look and opened the door to the crafts room, where several silver-haired ladies were painting with watercolors.

You would think that after independent living comes dependent living, but instead it's "assisted," which brings to mind someone delicately holding your elbow as you cross the street in the best of circumstances, or offering extra leverage as you rise from the commode in the worst. Having been the assistant myself for many years, I know full well what's involved. Finally, there's the memory care floor, which is a laugh because for most folks behind those locked doors, there aren't that many memories left to be careful about.

That's not me, though. Not by a long shot. I have all my memories intact. There are days when I wouldn't mind blocking out the more painful ones, but I have nothing to complain about, not yet. At least at Sutton Gardens someone will be there to pick me up when I tumble. Which seems to happen a lot these days.

My new lodgings are just down the road from this house, so it's not as if I'm venturing very far. Even though Bronxville is only eighteen miles from Midtown Manhattan, it's an oasis of green, renowned for its "stockbroker Tudor" houses, the term coined after the newly rich who snapped them up in the 1920s and '30s. People like my father, who was looking for a home that was close to the city but not too close, a place that showed he had good taste and a good job. My father never got tired of pointing out the slate roof and leaded glass windows to visitors. He may not have been a stockbroker, but he was a company man and proud of it.

I look about my living room, almost expecting to see him drinking a scotch in his favorite armchair, and my throat tightens with sorrow.

"Let me help you with that."

One of the movers, a skinny kid with freckles whom the others have teased all afternoon, puts the box he was carrying on the coffee table and comes toward me, eyes wide. He gently takes the clock from my hands.

"It doesn't work," I say, wiping the dust from my palms. "You can have it, if you like. Maybe it can be fixed."

"We're not allowed to take anything," he says. "But thanks."

He looks like he's barely sixteen and is more tentative in his actions than his cohorts, who move about the house like they own it. "You're new at this," I say.

"It's my first job."

"That's why they're making you do all the hard work, like climbing up into the attic. You better not take that kind of guff from them. They'll never stop."

"I don't mind." He pauses. "I found something in the attic that I thought you might want to see. It seems like the kind of thing you might not want to give away without a last look."

I wave my hand. "No one's been up there in decades—whatever it is, I don't need it. Not for the tiny cell I'm heading to." I know I'm being dramatic but I can't help myself sometimes.

"You're going to jail?" asks the boy with a sly smile.

"Might as well be. Space the size of a closet."

He turns to the large box sitting on the coffee table and opens it. "The bottom of this one broke when I was upstairs." He lifts out a pair of pointe shoes from when I took ballet class as a teenager, the ribbons fluttering loose like silk ringlets. "You were a dancer?"

I wish I had taken a moment, just one moment, back when I was dancing, to stop and appreciate what it feels like to lift your leg effortlessly high, what it's like when your limbs and mind are rich with music and your body snaps into place. When your arms and legs do exactly what you tell them to do. In my dreams, I stretch like a rubber band and my body is nineteen again. And then I wake up stiff and sore and realize it's only getting worse.

He places the shoes carefully on the coffee table, as if they were made of glass. Reaching back into the box, he pulls out a program for the Radio City Music Hall Christmas Spectacular of 1956. Then a pair of worn Capezio character shoes. I remember exactly what it felt like to buckle them up and dash out of the dressing room, how they eventually molded to my feet after hours dancing onstage. When I see those shoes, the voices of the other dancers fill my ears, along with the strains of the orchestra warming up.

But some memories are not as welcome. Screams of fear, the smell of smoke. Blood stains on my dance tights, a lone red ribbon.

A combination of terror and regret wraps around me like a straitjacket.

The boy is about to dig deeper, but I stop him. "Enough."

The doorbell rings and I leave him so I can answer it. He can decide what to do with that box. I don't want it.

A young girl with raindrops in her hair stands on my porch.

"Yes?" I ask.

"Ms. Brooks? It's Piper Cole. I'm here to pick you up."

"For what?"

She blinks. "Um. The anniversary? It starts at seven P.M. Sorry I'm early, I didn't want us to run into rush-hour traffic." Behind her, a black sedan with a driver sits idling at the curb.

I don't remember ever saying that I'd attend. The Rockette alumni group is always sending me newsletters with chipper reports of grand-children and moves to Florida. I usually give it a quick scan for any familiar names and then toss it in the bin.

"Do you mind if I come in?" Piper asks. The wind has picked up and the rain is getting both of us wet now.

I let her in, and she follows me to the kitchen. There, on the refrigerator, is the invitation, held in place with a small magnet. *Radio City Music Hall invites you to the 80th Anniversary of the Rockettes.* Right, of course. A couple of weeks ago a woman had called to confirm I was coming. Ann Burris was her name. I'd said I couldn't because I don't drive or take the train anymore. She'd told me she'd take care of that, and apparently Piper was the result.

"Are you a Rockette?" I ask.

"Gosh, no." She says it with a rush of air, as if I'd asked if she was the Queen of England. "I'm an assistant to the events coordinator, Ms. Burris. I was told that you were precious cargo and to make sure you made it to the theater in one piece."

"Precious cargo." What a strange phrase. "I'm sorry to make you come all this way, but it's not a good day. I'm moving, you see."

"Oh." Her face is crestfallen. "Ms. Burris will be very upset. She'll think I did something wrong or said something wrong. Won't you reconsider?"

She looks like she might cry.

"Why? I'm sure you'll have a bevy of current and former dancers in attendance. Why do I have to go?"

"It's because of the book. I hope you won't think me insensitive—I mean, I still can't believe what you went through—but the book is the reason they want you there. Everyone is so eager to know more about what happened when you were a Rockette."

Right. A recent nonfiction account of the events of 1956, published a couple of months ago, has stirred up interest in a time I'd rather not dwell on. Since it came out, I've had all kinds of former friends and foes resurface, not to mention reporters who looked up my address and stopped by unannounced, hoping for an interview. I prefer not to talk about that time. It was when I was at my best as a dancer, yet the worst happened.

I haven't been in that theater, that beautiful, majestic space, since.

"That was long ago. I don't wish to talk about it. Or think about it."

"Oh. Okay." Her eyes flit to the windowsill, where several family photos sit in silver frames. "Of course." She pulls out a cell phone. "I just need to call and let Ms. Burris know."

As she murmurs into the phone, I go back into the living room, where the young mover has left another box on the coffee table, this one marked with my mother's handwriting. Inside are her treasures, objects that she touched and worried over, pages she leafed through and scribbled on in pencil. But as far as I'm concerned, the programs and diaries might as well be dusted with cyanide.

Piper comes into the room, tucking her phone into her coat pocket. "Ms. Burris is so disappointed. And I'm sorry to have wasted your time. I'll excuse myself now and head back."

Just then, the young mover bounds down the stairs carrying a dress on a hanger across his arms as if it were a sleeping maiden.

"Oh my gosh!" Piper takes the dress from him. She holds the hanger high so it doesn't drag on the floor. It's one of my favorite frocks, sapphire blue with a high neck and long sleeves. I haven't seen it in years, but I know it would still fit.

I wore it one of the last times I saw my first love.

"This is beautiful," Piper says.

"Do you want to keep this, Ms. Brooks?" asks the boy. "Or donate?"

He's only doing his job, but I don't want to engage with these questions—or these objects—anymore. The slow drip-drip of memories feels lethal, or at least dangerous enough to drive me from the house. I've got to get out; it doesn't matter where. I could stay here and have my heart torn open or I could go into the city and lose myself in the bright lights and the constant swirl of people. I could mix in with the crowd and disappear for a while, and when I return, all this detritus will be gone for good. I'll sleep in my house for the last time, and tomorrow, I'll start fresh at Sutton Gardens.

I take the hanger from Piper and swoop up the fabric with my free hand so it doesn't touch the floor.

"I've changed my mind," I reply. "I'm going after all."

FIONA DAVIS

"The master of the unputdownable novel."

—*Redbook*

For a complete list of titles,
please visit prh.com/FionaDavis